I0691972

Jenna's Creek Series—Book 5

LEGACY OF FAITH

A Novel

BY

TERESA SLACK

Copyright © 2018 by Teresa D. Slack.

Published by GraceArbor Press
Library of Congress Control Number: 2018912695

All rights reserved. No portion of this publication may be reproduced or distributed in any form or by any means, or stored in a database or retrieval system, without the prior written permission of the Publisher.

This book is a work of fiction. Though it is based on research and shared stories of the Great Blizzard of 1978, names, characters, incidents, and dialog are products of the author's imagination and are not to be construed as real. Any resemblance to actual persons, living or dead, is purely coincidental.

Scripture quotations herein are from the King James Bible.

Also by Teresa Slack

The Jenna's Creek Series

Streams of Mercy
Redemption's Song
Evidence of Grace
A Jenna's Creek Wedding
(A Christmas Novella)
Legacy of Faith

The Tender Blessings Series

Love Begins
A Little Goodbye

Joy Redefined
Runaway Heart
The Ultimate Guide to Darcy Carter

What Readers are Saying

"*Legacy of Faith* by Teresa Slack will grab your interest on page one, and won't let go. Some authors create interesting plots, characters, and settings. Teresa's inspiring books do all that and more because they are written with the highest degree of excellence, turning readers into silent witnesses to all that is going on in the story. I live in a hot climate, and never experienced the freezing cold of a blizzard. But through Teresa's writing, now I have."
–Molly Noble Bull, award-winning Christian fiction author

"You'll never doubt you're neck deep in the lives of real people in this highly compelling book. Slack takes us right into the heart and soul of her characters so that you end up seeing your own. That's a rare gift."
- Linore Rose Burkard, award winning author of *Before the Season Ends*

"…Slack creates a compelling plot in her debut novel. *(Streams of Mercy)* Jamie has a strong, consistent and realistic voice throughout the novel…This book would be a good addition to any mystery lover's library." –Christian Library Journal

"A finely crafted mystery with a strong story line and unforgettable characters. A hard-to-put-down novel. The reader is mystified…until the last few pages." —Margaret Johnson, Author of 18, No Time to Waste.

"*Streams of Mercy* is a mystery which takes hold of you at the outset and won't let go until the end…By the time I finished reading the book I felt I knew her characters personally, people out of my own experience. I would recommend it to anyone who enjoys a good mystery." —Ottie Reno

"…*Redemption's Song* balances the misery caused by selfish behavior with the potential for atonement through God's love. A heartfelt novel reflecting the author's deeply held faith. Also recommended is the first book in the Jenna's Creek series, *Streams of Mercy*" — Midwest Book Review

"Teresa Slack has another winner on her hands. *Joy Redefined* is a great read…I was hooked by the end of the first chapter. I felt sorry for the heroine in the beginning, but I could see her evolve throughout the story. This is another one of Teresa's books that is a keeper. I give it 5 stars." —Reader review

"…*The Ultimate Guide to Darcy Carter*, a romantic contemporary novel, feels like going on a vacation complete with funny misunderstandings and wrong turns. Slack's characters come complete with flaws and face faith issues common to most believers. This light hearted novel ends too soon, just like a vacation." –Christian Library Journal

"…Slack is pretty funny, and the girl-guide idea…(will) keep readers turning the pages." –Booklist

"This book *(Runaway Heart)* is all about its characters, including its setting. I would say this isn't a book any author could be successful at, but Teresa Slack clearly has the gift. This was a refreshing and heart warming read I can happily recommend. This was my first taste of Teresa Slack's writing and I look forward to reading more." —Reader review

"YES! A funny, clean romance. Believable and loveable characters keep the reader engaged while the plot plays out many hilarious scenes." —Reader review

"Teresa creates a perfect blend of humor and humanity as she reveals the story of a young woman's struggle with in herself. She also addresses the feelings of men and their relationship with a woman who is already established in a career, something often not covered in the Christian writing world. Thank you, Teresa, for creating delightful characters in a relaxing setting. Great read!" —Reader review

"…Infused with humor and practical insights, *(Tender Blessings)* and its characters will capture the hearts of readers who love children, understand their challenges, and appreciate the many definitions of family." –Aspiring Retail Magazine

"I have given very few 5-star reviews in the almost three years I have had my Kindle. But this one deserves it…" — Reader review

"This series is wonderful…Slack puts into perspective real life troubles that we see in our world and sometimes our own lives. If you have children or irresponsible siblings, you can connect with this story for sure." —Reader review

Dedicated to my sister Gail Hooley Jackson who survived the Great Blizzard of '78 with me.

Acknowledgments: Not long after the release of Streams of Mercy, my first Jenna's Creek novel, a reader reminded me you can't set a series of books in 1970's Ohio and not include the Great Blizzard of 1978. I had a wonderful time researching that fateful winter. This is a fictional account. While I did my best to stay true to actual events, this is fiction, and I'm not really that smart. All inaccuracies and inconsistencies are purely my fault.

Thanks to everyone who offered memories and stories about that terrible storm in which 51 Ohioans lost their lives. Congratulations goes to Liz Reid of Hillsboro, Ohio who submitted the winning entry in my BLIZZARD of '78 Contest. Her story of tiles freezing and popping off her bathroom wall was a fun addition to this book. I hope you enjoy it.

As always, a special thanks goes to my family, especially my husband Ralph who continues to support and encourage me every day. You are my knight in shining armor, my prince charming. Every morning I fall in love with you all over again.

I Corinthians 13:2 And though I have the gift of prophesy, and understand all mysteries and all knowledge, and though I have all faith, so that I could remove mountains, but have not love, I am nothing.

CHAPTER ONE

Thursday, January 26th, 1978
4:00 a.m.

The crash shook the beams of the old house and rattled the glass in the wooden panes.

Warner Beckwith's eyes snapped open. He lay in the darkness, poised for the next sound. Beside him, Clarice inhaled sharply but did not awaken. In the old days she was always the one jerked awake by the slightest noise, especially if one of the children hadn't made it home when she and Warner turned in for the night. She would shake him awake and insist he get out of bed and go downstairs to make sure all was well. With the medication coursing through her body these days, she usually slept through his rising. Only the smell of coffee wafting upstairs and the morning sun's rays breaking through the window roused her from sleep.

Warner waited until his wife's breathing leveled off again before he rolled over to face the window. Light from a starless sky cast a gray pallor across the room. The sound came again, muffled this time and not as close, but still unmistakable. Thunder in January. If that didn't beat all.

Late last night the National Weather Service had issued blizzard warnings for the entire state. Around midnight Warner drifted off to sleep to the sound of rain tattooing on the roof over his head. He figured the overpaid meteorologists in Wilmington had once again missed the forecast by a mile. Sometime during the night the rain turned to snow as the predicted blizzard arrived.

Three massive snowstorms had already dumped nearly three feet of snow on the region since the first of the year. The National Guard had been called last week to clear roads when the governor declared much of Ohio a disaster area. Warner had hoped yesterday's rain and warmer temperatures would melt some of the snow on the ground. Instead, it looked like more would be added to the problem by sunrise.

Another rumble of thunder rattled the window. Warner couldn't remember the last time he'd heard thunder during a blizzard, though at his age it took more than a freak snowstorm to shake him. He fumbled on the nightstand for his glasses. His gnarled hand bumped the alarm clock and knocked it to the floor. It banged against the wall before it jerked to a halt at the end of the electrical cord.

He froze and hissed at his carelessness. Clarice stirred. The mattress shifted as she rolled onto her side away from him.

He lay motionless, his liver-spotted arm outstretched from under the covers until her breathing deepened again. She didn't awaken. He wasn't surprised.

If the doctors were right, she wouldn't last the winter. The diagnosis had come two summers ago. Clarice had lymphoma. She had already survived a year longer than expected, but the last few months had reminded all of them the end was near. The light in her once-hazel eyes faded more with each passing month. She didn't smile as warmly or as often as she used to, and Warner couldn't remember the last time she'd laughed out loud. At the first of the year she had opted to stop radiation treatments. She was tired of fighting. Truth be told, Warner was tired of watching what the treatments did to her.

His fingers closed around his glasses in the dark. He adjusted them on his nose, and the room rushed into focus. He fumbled to find the clock on the floor and return it to the nightstand.

The clock was as dark as the rest of the room. He followed the cord to the outlet in the wall with his fingers. It hadn't come unplugged when he dropped it. That meant the electricity was out. Naturally. The power went out all too often during heavy winds or severe weather. Some speed demon might've hit a pole while trying to beat the blizzard home. More likely, a transformer was down and power would be out at least a day or two. The power company seldom explained the outage and never apologized or gave Warner a break on his bill for the inconvenience.

He might as well go downstairs and stoke the furnace. He sat up and reached for his heavy robe at the end of the bed. As he slipped it on, careful not to move around too much and wake Clarice, an eerie light flashed across the room, followed quickly by a crash of thunder directly over his head. Warner flinched at the rumble as he toed the old rug for his slippers. He threw the slice of blanket over the warm spot where he had lain and moved to the window.

He pulled back the curtains and gaped at the scene outside. Snow sliced horizontally past the window. Wind screeched past the pane. Beneath his feet, the old house strained against the force. The barn and outbuildings were gray outlines on the landscape, barely discernible through the white onslaught.

Directly below the window was the cellar door. Warner peered through the white but couldn't make it out.

The bizarre light must have been lightning. Thunder during a blizzard was one thing, but lightning? This must have been what Dad meant those long ago winter evenings when he regaled Warner and little Ivan with stories in front of the fireplace while the wind wailed and shrieked outside their door. *Thunder snow*, Dad called it. Warner never believed half the yarns the old man liked to spin, but Ivan bought every word. Looked like Ivan had been the wiser one with at least this story.

Before Clarice's diagnosis, Warner would've awakened her so she could see the phenomenon for herself. If not, the next morning she would accuse him of exaggerating and not believe a word of it. This time he wouldn't bother. She needed her rest. He thought of waking his sons and grandson asleep down the hall. In the old days, he wouldn't hesitate to hurry into the children's rooms and rouse them from bed. Allen would offer a scientific explanation while Lowell and Jay would marvel and imagine little green men landing in the front yard.

Things were different now. He barely knew Carson, Lowell's son, who had moved in last summer. He didn't think the young man would be impressed by a blizzard, even one that surpassed any in Warner's eighty-plus-year memory.

Jay, his and Clarice's middle son, was quiet and morose these days and no longer interested in little green men. Clarice said he was depressed from having been laid off two years ago as the recession tightened its grip on the Midwest. Warner suspected Jay's depression stemmed from the prospect of getting off his backside and looking for a job.

Last night as Warner put away the last of the dinner dishes, Lowell had shown up with a buddy and a cockamamie story about a tree falling over power lines and shutting off the electricity on his end of the trailer park where he lived on the edge of Jenna's Creek. Warner figured it was more likely he hadn't paid his rent in a few months and the landlord had booted him out. Again.

The last thing Warner needed was another freeloading son under his roof. But he couldn't very well turn Lowell out with Clarice beaming up at her baby boy and hanging on every deceitful word out of his mouth.

Anytime Lowell showed up on the farm, Warner tightened his grip on his wallet. With his buddy Lenny Brown in tow, Warner anticipated the worst. Lenny was a thug and known drug pusher. The cops could never get enough evidence on him to make a conviction, but he'd spent his share of weekends in county lockup. Warner always wondered if local law enforcement intentionally looked the other way where Lenny was concerned. Theirs wouldn't be the first corrupt county in the state. But since he had nothing solid to back up his suspicions, he kept them to himself. For the most part.

Both his younger sons knew how he felt about Lenny Brown. He had told them more than once the man wasn't welcome in his home. His wishes were usually respected—at least in this matter—though Lenny dropped by the house several times a week to talk to Jay. He stayed in the car, and Jay always went out to meet him. Such meetings caused Warner great concern. Every time Clarice saw the tightening of his lips, she reminded him the men were only doing what he asked by keeping Lenny outside. Warner saw the meetings as suspect. What type of man showed up at another man's house at all hours of the day and night, and only stayed a few minutes at a time? Despite his suspicions, he didn't bother Clarice with the truth of what he figured was going on.

Last night Lenny only hung around long enough to drop Lowell off. Warner stood at the window and watched as Jay hurried outside and hunched his shoulders against the rain as he leaned inside Lenny's car. Warner couldn't tell from his vantage point at the window, but he thought he saw a packet changes hands through the car window. For Clarice's sake, he wouldn't go to the authorities. Not yet. But he was a Christian, a believer in respecting the laws of the land. He wouldn't keep looking the other way.

The creases on his forehead didn't relax last night until Lenny's brake lights came on, and he eased the car onto the road. Warner watched until the car rounded the curve between two plowed, four-foot high snow banks. At least one lowlife was out of his hair. Now he only had to contend with his own flesh and blood.

Warner turned his face westward, though he couldn't make out the fencerow through the driving snow, let alone the house beyond it where his youngest daughter lived with her family. He pictured his twenty-five-year old granddaughter Melody at the window, her bathrobe cinched around her tiny frame, wondering if he was watching the storm too.

Kindred spirits. That's what she called them. He didn't know about that; he just knew she loved and understood him better than anyone else ever had. Even Clarice. Warner Beckwith had never been good at dealing with people, even after he met the Lord. Most folks were put off by his gruff manner and propensity for speaking his mind whether his opinions were not welcome or not. But the instant that six-pound, strawberry-blond cherub fought and argued her way into the world, he knew he'd met his match.

He left the window and moved stealthily across the room to the dresser. He slipped his watch into the pocket of his robe and headed downstairs. He moved slowly, relying on the banister for support. He was mindful to place each foot on the stair in front of him before shifting his weight to take the next step. Looking at the wrong side of eighty, every move he made was methodical and precise. He couldn't afford to be careless. In the old days, he would've bounced down the stairs, buttoning his shirt as he went, his hand never touching the banister. Back then if he slipped or got one foot ahead of the other, he would right himself, laugh at his clumsiness, and keep going with barely a pause. Not anymore. Now he was old—trapped inside a body that no longer obeyed his brain's commands.

Every now and then he thought of moving the bedroom downstairs to the small room off the kitchen. It had been used as a pantry when the children were young, then converted into a sewing room even though Clarice seldom finished a project. Now it was a catchall for household overflow that never made it to the attic or one of the outbuildings. Maybe in the spring he would clean it out and move the bed and dressers downstairs. Avoiding the trip up and down the stairs would be easier on Clarice—if she lasted that long.

He moved through the small farmhouse in semi-darkness. The snow outside the window bathed the house's interior in an ethereal light, not that he needed light to find his way around. He could make the trip blindfolded. Every morning he made it to the kitchen without relying on electricity. Warner didn't need the President to remind him to conserve energy.

"Use it up, wear it out. Make it do or do without," his mother always said.

The Beckwiths had conserved everything out of necessity, long before actors and politicians brought it into vogue.

Warner took a large flashlight off the shelf above the window and hit the button with his thumb. No response. He slapped the flashlight with the heel of his hand until a weak beam cast across the room. He opened a cabinet drawer and took out a tablet barely as wide as his hand. He stirred through the drawer's contents until his fist closed around a pen. He trained the flashlight's beam first onto the watch he drew from his pocket, then on a blank page in the tablet. He scribbled in the margin until ink began to flow from the ballpoint. At the top of the page he scrawled the date in his pinched, tight script, followed by *4:16 a.m.* He followed the time with a notation: *Lightning strikes during blizzard. Electricity out.*

The family still teased him about his compulsion to write things down. He paid them as little mind as he had his chums at school when he was a boy and they egged him about the same thing. Some psychologist somewhere could probably read all sorts of psycho mumbo jumbo into his need to record every occurrence in his day, but he didn't care. Nor did he give it much thought or worry. After eighty-two years, he was barely conscious of doing it.

He dropped the pen and tablet back in the drawer and moved to the basement door. He needed to revive the fire in the furnace before the batteries in the flashlight died completely. He wouldn't waste fresh batteries this early in a storm. Better to save them in case the power stayed out for a while. In a storm like this, the family could be stuck on the hill for weeks before the county got around to rectifying the problem.

Warner took an old pair of rubber boots from the broom closet and slipped them on over his slippers. The basement leaked, and the floor was always cold, even in summer. Too cold for his aging feet.

When he opened the basement door, an icy blast shot up the stairs and wrapped around his legs. The flashlight beam reached halfway down the flight of stairs. In the gloom, he could make out the dark hulk of the furnace below with its red, glowing eye staring up at him from the center of the door. The glow wasn't as bright as it had been six hours ago when he last stoked the fire.

He put his hand on the railing and stepped carefully off the landing, the beam of light trained at his feet. The cold from the wooden stairs seeping through his boots and slippers urged him to hurry, but he moved cautiously. The stairs were icy from condensation. Even a young man could fall in these conditions.

He was nearly at the bottom when he saw water on the basement floor. He panned the weak beam around the small room. Moisture clung to the stone walls. He shivered and released his grip on the handrail to tighten the robe around his neck and gather his nerve before stepping into the icy water. Every year it took longer to warm up after the cold settled into his bones.

Warner extended one foot toward the basement floor and reached for the handrail. His back foot lost traction on the icy stair. He let go of the flashlight and scrambled with both hands for the railing as he started to fall. He brushed it with his fingertips as the floor rushed up to meet him. His tailbone cracked on the bottom step. His head snapped back and hit a step behind him. He bounced off the bottom step and came to rest in the frigid water on the floor.

He raised a hand to the back of his head. A knot was already rising through what remained of his hair. He laid his head back on his cupped hand. Things were blurry and vague. He could only rest a moment. He thought of Clarice asleep upstairs depending on him to light the furnace so the house would be warm and toasty by the time she woke up. Cold weather had always been hard on her. More so now that the cancer had robbed her strength.

A sound caught Warner's attention. Or maybe it was his imagination. He leaned back to look over the top of his head to the landing. The unnatural position sent daggers of pain from the back of his head out through his eyeballs.

"Is anyone there?"

He meant to shout, but his voice came out as little more than a croak.

He waited but heard nothing over the wind buffeting the house. He took a deep breath in an effort to relax. He needed to regain his strength if he was ever going to get out of the water. A wave of dizziness washed over him. He wanted nothing more than to close his eyes and rest.

His eyes snapped open. *Don't go to sleep,* he ordered.

Warner expected immediate and unquestioning obedience whenever he spoke, even from himself. It was probably why he didn't have much of a relationship with his children or most of his grandchildren. His oldest daughter, Linda, had left home when she was seventeen to marry a man Warner didn't approve of. He told her if she left, not to plan on coming back. She didn't. That was forty years ago. Her children had children now, and he couldn't even remember their names.

The back of his head throbbed. The cold water sucked heat from his body. He felt blackness overtaking him. He wouldn't stay awake much longer. With great effort, he drew his knees to his chest. If he could push up onto the bottom step, he would at least be out of the water. Once there he could gather his strength before getting to his feet. He put his hands on the stairs behind him and pushed with all his might. His legs and arms were as heavy as lead. He couldn't even raise his backside off the floor.

He turned his head toward the window, the only light source now that the flashlight had gone out when it crashed against the floor and rolled somewhere into the dark recesses of the basement. Wind rattled the pane. All was dark. He couldn't see the swirling snow anymore. An eerie flash of light illuminated the darkness, followed by a rumble of thunder.

He saw it clearly this time. Green lightning. Dad hadn't been pulling his leg after all.

He rested his weary head on the step behind him. He opened his mouth to cry for help, but no sound came out. He thought of Jay, Lowell, and Carson asleep upstairs. If only one of them would wake up and come looking for him. But no one was coming. He was alone.

Poor Clarice. What would she do without him? Who would take her to the doctor? Who would light the furnace? Who would keep the boys from taking advantage of her?

His mind turned again to Linda, his red-haired girl with the laughing green eyes. If only he could talk to her one more time. There was so much he needed to say. So much to put right. She probably wouldn't recognize his voice after all these years. He wondered if he would recognize hers.

Why had he been so foolish? He could see now why she left. If he had been a younger man, he would've been tempted to go, too, while he had the chance.

He thought of his other children. Allen would step in and take care of Clarice. Warner prayed he would protect her best interests. Jay and Lowell would bleed her dry within a few months if left unheeded. Dear Clarice. She meant well, but she couldn't tell anyone no, especially her boys.

Warner knew he could entrust Judy, the baby of the family, to fix all the things his passing would leave undone. She had always been his favorite, even before she gave him Melody, his greatest gift.

Melody. His little golden nugget. His heart ached to think he would never see her face again, never hear the sound of her laugh, never throw a fishing line into the old pond with her sitting on the bank beside him. Never see her walk down the aisle on her daddy's arm.

Tears slid out from between his closed eyelids. So many regrets. So many things left unsaid, undone.

"I'm sorry, Clarice," Warner said, though he couldn't be sure if the words were coming out of his mouth or just in his head. "I'm sorry I didn't listen to you about Linda. She's a good girl. I'm sorry I made you miss so much of her life. I'm sorry I didn't try to understand the boys better. I'm sorry I didn't pay closer attention coming down the stairs. Now you'll have to pay for my foolishness the way you've always done."

A sense of peace filled his spirit. In the last few years he had begun to think about dying, the way all old men did, he supposed. He wasn't macabre or fearful, just curious. Would there be pain? Would he see it coming? What about the bright light people spoke of on operating tables?

A few questions were answered as he lay on the floor and stared at the cobwebs hanging from the ceiling. He was intensely aware of life seeping from his body. The only pain he experienced, beyond the regrets of things left undone, emanated from the lump on his head. There was no bright light. He didn't see further flashes of green lightning.

"Well, God, I guess I'm coming a little sooner than expected," he said aloud, his voice a hoarse whisper. "Take care of Clarice for me. Tell Melody not to worry or hold anybody responsible. You know how she is, Lord. More like me than any one person deserves to be. I guess you sent her down here to keep me in line."

He wanted to say more. He wanted to pray for his sons. He wanted to bless them the way Jacob had blessed his twelve sons in the Old Testament, but it became increasingly difficult to hold onto a thought. All he wanted to do was sleep.

Warner Beckwith closed his eyes, unable to withstand the darkness that pulled him into sweet oblivion.

CHAPTER TWO

Friday, January 27th
7:00 a.m.

Melody Knauff awoke with a start. She held her breath and listened. The fire in the grate popped and cracked. The old fashioned clock on the mantle ticked reassuringly. From the other side of the room came her mother's gentle breathing. Everything else was quiet and still.

After more than twenty-four hours of wind buffeting the house and rattling the windows, the silence was eerie. All day yesterday the screeching wind had made her imagine someone outside screaming. She had known, of course, that was impossible. No one could've survived outside for long. Still, she stood at the window and stared into the blinding snow and rubbed the gooseflesh rising on her arms. She couldn't decide which was worse—the endless keening of the wind or the realization she was trapped inside the four walls with no way of reaching her grandparents, a mere four hundred yards away.

Melody stuffed her arms inside her robe before throwing back the covers. The fireplace was mostly cosmetic and not designed to heat the large house. When the power went out yesterday morning around four a.m., her parents decided to close off the second story and most of the smaller rooms downstairs. The severity of the blizzard was something even they had never seen before, and they had no idea how long the situation would last.

Melody hadn't slept in the same room with her parents in twenty-four years. She might've enjoyed the slumber party atmosphere if not for the wind rattling the panes so hard she feared the glass would burst in on them. Not to mention, the real and constant threat of running out of toilet paper. The house, still relatively young in house years, had groaned and shook against the onslaught. Mom, who never worried about anything, gazed anxiously at the ceiling and wondered aloud if the roof would lift off and carry them away to the Land of Oz.

More than the wind and the fifty-degrees below zero wind chill factor and the risk to the farm animals corralled for the time being in the barns, Melody couldn't stop worrying about her grandparents at the top of the hill. She had not gone two days her entire life without seeing them. Even while attending Marshall University in Huntington, West Virginia, and later, during the brief period she lived in her own apartment in Jenna's Creek, she maintained daily contact. Since Grandma's cancer diagnosis, Melody had become even more diligent about checking in on them.

The phone lines were out from the storm as well. According to reports on Pete's battery powered radio, even the Interstate highways were impassable. It could be weeks before a snowplow made it up the township road to the top of the hill. Her grandparents' house was barely a quarter of a mile away. Yesterday, she couldn't see their farmhouse through the blowing snow. The silence this morning assured her the worst was over. She would bundle up, slip into her coveralls, climb over a few snowdrifts, and walk the short distance to the farmhouse the way she'd been doing since she was three.

She secured her robe around her waist and found her slippers with her feet. She tiptoed across the room to the window that faced her grandparents' farm and pulled back a corner of the drape. She shrieked in alarm.

"Melody?"

She dropped the curtain. "Mom, you aren't going to believe this."

Judy was already fastening her own robe and climbing out of the foldout sofa she had shared with Pete last night. "What's wrong?"

"We can't get out."

"What?"

"We're buried."

"It can't be that bad."

Judy joined Melody at the window and threw back the drapes with a flourish. A wall of white reached all the way past the sash. Melody's eyes bulged in astonishment. She wasn't claustrophobic, but the room suddenly felt a whole lot smaller.

Judy opened the curtains over the sofa where Melody had been sleeping. The south wall was sheltered by the porch roof. The storm's northeasterly winds had blown snow under the roof, but it had only piled halfway up the windowsill. Beyond the front of the porch, the road was indistinguishable in the sea of white.

Melody dropped to her knees on the sofa beside Mom and gazed out the window. "Grandma must be scared to death. The top of the hill always gets the brunt of the wind."

"Your grandmother has seen plenty of blizzards. She has Pop. Jay and Carson are there too."

Melody snorted. "A lot of use they are."

"Melody, don't start. Just because you and Pop think they're freeloaders doesn't mean Mom doesn't like having them around."

"I've never called them freeloaders."

"Not to their faces."

"I just think a fifty-something-year-old man is a little old to be living with his parents. And Carson's almost thirty. How long is he planning on hanging around?"

Judy backed off the couch. "Isn't that the pot calling the kettle black? I'm sure some people wonder the same thing about you."

"I go to work every day. It's more than I can say for those two. And I moved home to help out after Dad's heart attack."

"You came home because you were homesick and worried about your father."

Melody flopped down on the couch. "Is this your way of pushing me out of the nest?"

"No, darling. I just wish you wouldn't hold such severe opinions when you don't know the whole situation. You're like Pop. None of us know what's going on with Jay and Carson. It's unfair to judge them when we don't know the whole story."

Melody resisted a sigh and eye roll. Pointing out that she did know what they were going through wouldn't advance the argument. Uncle Jay was a bum, plain and simple. He moved back to the farm two years ago after his shipping job at a furniture company relocated to North Carolina. Last summer, Uncle Lowell's son Carson, who no one had seen in at least twelve years, showed up from Texas with even less of an excuse than Jay had. Neither man appeared to be beating the bushes in search of work, though Jay strangely was never strapped for cash.

Melody wasn't a detective, but she was pretty sure the increased flow of traffic to the farmhouse and Jay's frequent trips out of town indicated illegal activity. She had pointed this out before, but Mom was always defensive of her deadbeat brother.

She stood up and began to fold a blanket. "Even if Grandma is having the time of her life, I'll feel a lot better when I get up there and see how they're weathering the storm."

Judy added another log to the fire. "You're not leaving this house, young lady. In case you missed the news all day yesterday, we're in the middle of the worst blizzard in Ohio history."

Melody snapped another blanket to remove any wrinkles. "Only toddlers and the old and infirm get lost in the snow. I've been climbing that hill for two decades. I can handle it."

"Did you not notice the east side of the house is blocked by snowdrifts? You can't just take off walking. You'll be buried to your shoulders with the first step."

"Mom, you're so dramatic," Melody said, though doubts began to crowd into her head. Visibility was zero all day yesterday. The blizzard had been dubbed the Storm of the Century across the Midwest, New England, and Mid-Atlantic states. Last night the governor declared a state of emergency across the entire state. Government offices in Ohio were closed statewide until Monday, though no one expected business to resume that quickly. For the first time in history, the Ohio turnpike in northern Ohio was closed to traffic. National Guard troops were deployed to many northern counties where the storm had hit hardest to rescue stranded motorists and deliver food and medicine.

Just because the wind no longer threatened to lift the house from its foundation didn't mean getting up the hill would be an easy feat.

Yesterday morning, about the same time the power went out, Melody had been awakened by a crash of thunder. A sense of dread more powerful than anything she ever experienced catapulted her out of bed and to the window that faced her grandparents' farm. She wasn't superstitious. She was a Christian, and the two weren't compatible. However, as she listened to the wind tear at the shingles on the side of the house, she knew something terrible had happened on top of the hill. She wouldn't rest until she got up there to see what it was.

Footfalls sounded at the back door. The door opened and closed. Without a glance in her mother's direction. Melody threw down the half-folded blanket and hurried into the kitchen. "Dad, how'd you get out there? We're buried."

Pete Knauff pushed back the hood of his coat and removed his woolen cap. Auburn hair, much like Melody's, but thinned with time and streaked with gray, lay damp against his scalp. "Good morning to you, too, daughter."

Melody pushed an unruly strand from his forehead. She kissed his unshaven cheek. "I'm sorry, Dad. You should've woke me up to help with the chores."

"There's not a whole lot that can be done. Since we corralled the animals yesterday, the milking and feeding went quickly. Daphne isn't giving much milk and the chickens aren't laying."

"How did Graciela fare through the night?"

"That old sow is as tough as she is mean. Looks like she won't farrow for another week or so after all. I hope the snow is gone by then."

"That's good. I prayed for her last night."

Pete smiled and chucked her under the chin. "So did I. I prayed for all the animals. A lot of farmers have stock missing in the fields. They might not find them until spring. By then, it'll be too late. I hope Warner got all his in before the blizzard hit."

Melody's stomach clenched at the mention of her grandfather. She hoped keeping his livestock safe in the barn was his only concern this wintry morning.

Judy came into the kitchen. "What's this I hear about no eggs this morning."

Pete climbed out of his coveralls and hung them on a peg on the wall. "I'm sure the chickens'll be back on schedule by tomorrow or Sunday. A little more warning from the weather service would've been nice. Wednesday night they predicted a mild rainy evening. It wasn't until after most of us were in bed they updated the forecast. Caught us farmers completely unprepared."

Melody nodded sympathetically. Dad's complaints were simply his way of dealing with his frustrations at being helpless to the weather. Dad had been a gentleman farmer since marrying Mom, and had only begun to take it seriously after a heart attack forced him into early retirement. After a scary year recovering and rebuilding his strength, he discovered he loved working both farms full time with Grandpa.

"How long do you think it'll be before we can get up the hill to check on the rest of the family?"

Pete gave her a long look. "How about we fix breakfast first? There's plenty of eggs in the fridge even if the chickens take a few days off. If we run out of milk, I'll send you over to the Sheltons' in a few days to beg a few gallons. In the meantime, we need to shovel some snow off the roof. If we don't lighten the weight, we'll have the ceiling in on our heads."

Melody jerked her gaze toward the ceiling. Was he kidding? Surely the roof wouldn't crash in on them. "How will we get up there? The ladders are buried in the outbuildings."

"We'll walk out the upstairs windows. Two sides of the house are buried past the first floor Remind me to take the camera and snap some pictures. This is going to be a winter to remember."

Melody cast a nervous glance at the kitchen window, claustrophobia pressing in again. At least she'd have something to take her mind off her grandparents at the top of the hill. Physical labor always helped relieve tension when she was worried. Her job at Auburn County's children's services department kept her stuck behind a desk more often than not. Working with families in distress was a ministry for her. Time on the farm gave her an outlet for the tension that often threatened to overwhelm her.

She lit the gas burner under the teakettle for coffee. "I'll get dressed. It feels good to finally have something constructive to do."

Pete smiled. "No kidding. Your mom told me if I didn't come up with something to stop your pacing I was sleeping in the barn with Graciela tonight."

❦❦❦

With a sweater layered over a heavy blouse and an open door on the gas range the only heat source in the room, Harriet Shelton poured a cup of coffee and set it in front of her son. Tim wrapped his raw hands around the hot cup and brought it to his mouth for a cautious sip.

"Thanks, Mom," he muttered, too exhausted for conversation. He had spent the last two hours shoveling his way to the barn where the cows were stowed against the storm, and back again. With the blizzard and stressful conditions, the cows weren't producing much milk. Within a day or two, there might not be any milk at all. It was just as well since the milk truck couldn't make it up the hill in the snow.

Harriet went back to the stove and turned a few strips of thick bacon in the skillet. "You shouldn't go out again. They said on the radio wind gusts were clocked at a hundred miles an hour yesterday. A hundred miles an hour. I never heard the like."

"It's not that bad in the barn. The drifts have filled in the cracks and the cows are heating it up. Besides the winds' have died down."

"To what? Fifty miles an hour? The wind chill factor is still well below zero. You and your father need to stay inside.

He's an old man. You're not exactly a spring chicken yourself," she added, nudging him with her elbow.

"Thanks, Mom, you really know how to make a guy feel good. But seriously, we don't have much choice. After I get warmed up, I'm taking some milk to the neighbors. I don't want to pour it out like we did yesterday when they might need it. The whole lot of us will probably be stuck on this hill for quite some time.""

"They know we have milk. Let them come and get it."

"Mom," Tim reasoned, "if I didn't have a snow blade on the tractor, I wouldn't be able to get out. The milk will freeze if we leave it too long and then it won't do anyone any good."

"Just get back as quickly as you can. You'll get frostbite."

"I'm fifty years old. I think I know how to avoid frostbite."

"That's what I'm saying. It wouldn't take long for a person your age to die of exposure in this weather."

Tim laughed. "Thanks for reminding me what a geezer I am. You're full of compliments this morning."

She refilled his cup. "Just be sure to double your coveralls and wear an extra pair of socks in case you get stuck and have to walk."

Tim smiled over the rim of his cup. It had been a long time since anyone had fussed over him.

When his divorce was finalized last spring, he'd had nowhere else to turn. He spent the first twenty years of his life trying to get away from the dairy farm where he was raised and the next thirty pretending he'd come from more auspicious beginnings. Yet when his life fell apart, there was nowhere else he wanted to be. For all his efforts to put as much distance between him and his simple upbringing as possible, restoring his relationship with his parents was the one good thing that came from the termination of his marriage.

He was sure his wife and children were faring much better than he was in the big house in Jenna's Creek, bought from the proceeds of his lucrative real estate career at Blake Realty. His daughter Leslie had an apartment in town. Tim was sure she was enjoying a few days off work. He wished Leslie wasn't as ambitious and driven as she was. He feared she would become like her mother and never learn to relax and enjoy life. Tim wanted her to find love and get married, but he worried there wasn't a man alive who could tolerate her.

His oldest son, Kenny, was currently driving a semi truck through the southwest, practically the only region of the country experiencing no ill effects from the blizzard. At least one son was warm and dry. Two more were in college in northern Ohio. The phones were out so Tim couldn't call to check on them, but he had no doubts they were safe on campus with plenty to eat, the only thing either seemed to care about at this point in their lives. Butch, the family's youngest son, was probably at home with Joyce, Tim's ex-wife. Out of his five children, Butch received the lion's share of Tim's sympathy.

After a hardy country breakfast, courtesy of a doting mother happy to have her baby chick back in the nest, Tim bundled against the subzero temperatires and headed back out into the snow. Under normal circumstances it took him all of two minutes to reach the barn from the back door. By the time he shoveled through the drifts that obliterated the path he had cleared an hour earlier and stepped into the shelter of the barn, twenty minutes had elapsed and his legs trembled with fatigue inside his double layer of coveralls. The old John Deere startled the cattle as it rumbled to life. Tim hated adding to their already considerable stress, but some things couldn't be avoided.

It took another half hour astride the tractor to clear a path from the barn to the road. He hoped the wind wouldn't undo his work by the time he returned. Though it felt like a summer breeze compared to yesterday's gale force winds, he still had to reach up and secure his hat to his head every time the wind threatened to snatch it away.

Four other families lived on top of the hill. This wasn't the first time a storm had marooned them all together. Spring rains often washed out portions of the road below, not to mention the countless blizzards that left them at the mercy of nature and one another's generosity.

Mike and Erlene Kennedy had bought the property west of the Shelton farm five years ago. Two children had since been added to the family, bringing the number of Kennedys occupying the brick four-square house to six. Tim could barely believe his eyes when the old John Deere lumbered past a stand of trees, and the house came into view. The entire first floor was encased in a massive snowdrift, shrinking the size of the house by half. The porch roof seemed to sit on top of the snow.

Though it seemed like an exercise in futility and a waste of fuel, Tim made several passes with the tractor in front of the house in case Mike needed to get his truck out. Even if the wind cooperated and kept the drifts from blowing higher, it wasn't likely any of them were leaving the hill in the near future.

He didn't hear someone shout his name over the wind or the tractor's engine until he noticed movement out of the corner of his eye.

He shut off the motor. "Hello, neighbor," he called to Mike. "How're you faring?"

Two boys about ten and eight-years-old—mirror images of their father with dark hair and brown eyes peering out from beneath the brims of woolen caps pulled down to their lashes—stood clear until Tim dropped to the ground beside the tractor. They immediately ran forward to investigate the snow blade.

"We're getting by," Mike said after yelling a warning to the boys. Marooned only a day by the blizzard, Tim could see they were already bored. Tunnels and half-constructed fort walls crisscrossed the side yard that had been somewhat sheltered from the drifts. Tim remembered doing the same thing with his brother and sister when he was a kid. The tunnels looked sturdy enough not to cave in, but he hoped Mike kept an eye on the boys nonetheless. It didn't take long for kids that age to find mischief.

"I measured the fresh snowfall as best I could a little while ago," Mike said. "As far as I can tell, we got another fifteen inches."

"It's not the snowfall so much as the blasted wind."

Mike nodded. "And the three feet already on the ground. We're not as bad off as folks up north. You got electricity? Ours went out along with phone lines yesterday morning."

"Ours too. We've got plenty of firewood. Don't hesitate to bring Erlene and the kids over if you need to. There's plenty to eat. We'll muddle through together."

"Can we, Dad? Please," the boys chorused.

Tim almost wished he could take back the invitation. School would be out of session for weeks. He sent a quick prayer of thanks heavenward that he wasn't stuck in a house full of kids.

He heaved an inward sigh of relief when Mike turned him down. "Thanks, but Erlene won't want to go anywhere with the baby if she doesn't have to. We'll stay put."

"That's part of the reason I stopped. Can you use some milk? We don't have any way to get it to market until they clear the roads. If you don't take it off our hands, we'll have to pour it out."

"Sure. We go through milk in this house."

Tim followed Mike and the boys around the side of the house, each of them lugging jugs of milk that had already frozen solid. Though it was obvious Mike had recently shoveled a path to the back door, it was nearly filled in with fresh drifts. Tim turned down the offer of coffee. The house was warm and cozy but not welcoming enough to make up for the noise level.

The baby cried incessantly, and the boys pestered their sister, keeping her in tears as well. Tim promised them if they behaved he'd come back in a few days and give them a ride on the tractor. He directed sympathetic smiles to Mike and Erlene before practically running for the door. He didn't remember his own boys causing such chaos though he was sure they had. He must've blocked out their childhood the way soldiers often did after escaping the battlefield.

He brushed snow off the tractor seat and continued west to the next house. The Storers were retired and turned down his offer of milk. Again, coffee was offered along with homemade bread and honey from the Storers' honeycombs. Since Tim was cold and bone weary and no children resided inside the house, he accepted. He'd been gone for two hours already, and it was getting close to lunchtime. Every radio station in the area had preempted regular broadcasts to keep residents up to date on the blizzard. Tim sat in the Storers' kitchen and listened to the radio while he ate. The snow was supposed to end by nightfall with no more in the forecast for a few days, however the damage had been done.

He had to double back past his family's property in order to reach the last two neighbors. The only indication anyone was home at the Knauffs' in the solid two-story Warner Beckwith had built in an effort to keep his youngest daughter close to home was a thick curl of smoke hanging over the chimney. Darkened windows half obscured by drifts gazed down on Tim in disapproval. Like he had done for the Kennedys and the Storers, he made a few passes with the tractor between the house and the road. As long as the wind did not reach yesterday's ferocity, his efforts might last the night.

Someone had already cleared a path from the back door to the barns. Tim killed the tractor's engine and climbed down. He groaned aloud as his boots hit the packed snow. His back had stiffened during the ride between the Storers' house and the

Knauffs'. Maybe his mother was right. He was too old to spend this much time on the tractor seat in the cold. His cheeks were raw inside his ski mask, and his thighs chafed against his coveralls.

His boots crunched through the snow as he tramped across the back porch. Before he could lift his hand to knock, the door flung inward. Melody Knauff stared out at him. She zipped her coat with a loud tearing sound and jammed her hands into a pair of bulky ski gloves. A knitted cap was pulled low over her face and a matching scarf wound around her neck and up to her nose. She pulled the scarf down with a gloved hand to expose her mouth. "I was just coming out to meet you."

Her hazel eyes glittered from beneath the brim of the hat. Her cheeks were pink, probably from the exertion of layering clothes inside a warm house. That healthy pink would chap within minutes of venturing outside.

Tim held aloft two plastic jugs of milk his mother had carefully strained. It wasn't as sanitary or appealing as the homogenized, pasteurized version from the grocery store, but it would go a long way if the blizzard kept the families snowbound for long. "I brought milk."

She barely glanced at his offering. "You haven't been to the farm yet, have you?"

Tim knew she meant Warner and Clarice Beckwith's place. Even though everyone on the hill farmed to some capacity, they all referred to the Beckwith place as 'the farm'. Every property on the hill had once been part of the original farm.

"That was my next stop."

She stepped into the threshold forcing Tim to backpedal onto the porch and into the wind. "Good. I'm going with you. Our shed is drifted shut and Dad can't get the tractor out to take me."

"Melody," a woman called from inside the house, "have you lost all your good sense? Ask the man inside. He must be frozen solid."

Tim watched Melody's inner struggle. She was apparently anxious to get to her grandparents' house, but she knew Tim needed to warm up before he set off again. After all, she needed him. He would be of no use to her if he froze to death halfway up the hill.

He was pretty sure she was the same age as his daughter. He thought they had gone to school together. Like Leslie, Melody was petite with porcelain skin and gentle features. Her auburn hair and direct gaze gave her a more mature appearance than Leslie, though he doubted Melody possessed Leslie's shrewd ambition. At least he hoped not. For now, the only emotion on Melody's face was concern for her grandparents.

Reluctantly, she backed into the house and closed the door behind them.

Judy Knauff stood at the sink up to her elbows in soapy water. "Tim Shelton, what are you thinking, coming out in this weather?"

"I was as restless as the Kennedy boys cooped up in the house," he explained with a smile.

Judy dried her hands on a towel. "You sound like Pete. He shoveled the porches and driveway three times yesterday before he admitted defeat and let the wind have its way. Now he's listening to the radio."

Tim set the frozen jugs of milk on the table and peeled off his gloves. An oil lamp glowed in the center of the table. Candles were scattered around the room. "Have you been without power since the storm hit?" He moved to the open oven door and stuck his hands toward the blue gas flame. They immediately turned red. He took a step back so they wouldn't warm too quickly.

"I think that's what woke Pete up yesterday morning. What about you?"

He nodded. "Ours went out at the first crash of thunder. Do you need anything? Fresh batteries? Firewood?"

"Thanks for asking, but we're in good shape. You know how we country people are; hope for the best, prepare for the worst."

"Can we go now?" Melody still waited by the door, bundled against the weather. Her cheeks had gone from pink to bright red. She had to be sweltering inside her heavy clothes. She'd freeze before Tim got the tractor turned around in the driveway.

"Give Tim a chance to warm up," Judy scolded. "There's no need to rush up there anyway. A few minutes one way of the other won't make a difference."

Melody whipped off her hat and unwound the scarf from around her neck. "I'm sure we're not the only ones without power. Grandma and Grandpa could be freezing."

Judy shook her head in response to Melody's frustration. "They're probably the warmest ones on the hill. They were living here before electricity ever came this far. Don't forget they have a wood furnace. I'm sure Pop is having a great time roughing it and reliving the old days with Jay and Carson."

Tim didn't miss the scowl that darkened Melody's hazel eyes.

"I seriously doubt that," she said. "I've got a bad feeling, Mom. Something's wrong."

The playfulness slipped from Judy's features. She went to her daughter and pulled a handful of tangled auburn hair out of the back of her coat. "You've been saying that since yesterday. Someone would've come down to let us know if anything happened."

"How? They're stranded the same as we are. Something's not right. I can feel it."

Judy turned to Tim. "Do you mind if she rides along on the tractor when you go? It's taken all my strength to keep her from taking off this morning and walking up there. I'm scared to death she'll get lost without as much as a fencerow to follow. I don't know how much longer I can keep her here, even though nothing's wrong and she's worried for nothing," she added pointedly in Melody's direction.

Tim would've liked nothing more than to spend another fifteen or twenty minutes hovering over the oven door. Instead, he turned away from the gas stove and donned his gloves. "Of course I don't mind. I'd be worried, too, if I didn't know for myself my parents were all right."

Melody exhaled, relief evident on her face. She pulled her hat back down over her head without bothering to straighten her hair. Ginger-colored tufts stuck out in all directions making her look even younger than her twenty-something years.

"You should wait in here while I turn the tractor around," Tim told her.

"No thanks, I'm fine." With that, she pushed out the door ahead of him.

He turned back to Judy. "We'll be back as soon as her curiosity is satisfied."

Judy shook her head. "Don't bother. I'm sure she'll want to stay the night. She doesn't trust my brother or nephew to take care of Mom. Pete can figure out a way to get her home in a day or two."

"I'll stop back on the way home and let you know everything's all right."

"Thanks, Tim. I appreciate it."

He nodded in reply and headed out the door where an anxious Melody waited on the porch.

CHAPTER THREE

Christy Blackwood spun the pillowcase in her hand and tied a knot in the twisted length of fabric. She hefted it carefully over her shoulder so not to smash the bread against the eggs, and began her ascent over the mound of snow left by the snowplows. Thanks to the city's snow clearing efforts on the streets, sidewalks were buried under five to six feet of densely packed snow. Foot traffic was done down the center of the street, provided one could get to the street. Cars were hardly moving at all. Christy could count the ones she saw on her way to and from the market on one hand.

She leaned into the snow bank and kicked two toeholds before starting up. It was a difficult climb. She was thankful Mom had suggested taking a pillowcase to the store for carrying the groceries home. The store's brown paper bags wouldn't have survived the handling of her wet gloves or the three times she slipped and fell. As it was, she doubted she would make it into the house without a couple cracked eggs and dented loaf of bread.

She paused at the crest of the snow bank to catch her breath. It was hard to imagine she was standing several feet above the wrought iron fence that separated her yard from the sidewalk. Everything about this blizzard and the havoc it created was hard to believe.

She looked around to make sure no one was watching and then dropped to her bottom and slid down the bank to the driveway. She sank to her calves into the snow. She threw the pillowcase over her shoulder and high-stepped as fast as she could across the yard. By the time she reached the porch, her boots were full of snow. Her gloves were soaked through, and she had lost her scarf somewhere between the grocery store and home.

"This is insane," she hissed aloud. At least the porch was still clear of snow from the last time she shoveled it off.

Her wet glove slipped a few times on the doorknob before it finally turned in her hand. For once she was relieved Mom hadn't locked the door behind her. She doubted her frozen fingers could have rung the bell or found the house key buried inside her coat pocket. She hoped it was still in her pocket anyway. She couldn't be certain after the trip she'd just endured.

She had long since given up telling her mother to lock the front door when she was home alone. It went in one ear and out the other.

"Oh, Christy, who would rob us? We know everyone in this neighborhood—in this town, for that matter."

"That's not the point, Mom. Everyone knows we're two women living alone. They could come in and do whatever they wanted."

"Who? Who would come in? Mr. Earley next door? He's the only one home in the middle of the day and he uses a walker. By the time he got here, you'd be home from work to save me."

"This isn't a laughing matter," Christy had insisted. "Just because we're in Jenna's Creek and not a big city doesn't mean crime can't happen. I heard on the radio the other day…"

Mom always waved away her concerns before she could launch into another news story from some far off crime-ridden city. The crime and despair running rampant everywhere else in the world wouldn't affect her as long as she refused to think about it. Christy couldn't do much to make her mother see the cold hard facts of life, but when she was home, she locked the doors. So far, no one had tried to break in. No one even came up the front walk.

Maybe Mom was right. Even criminals knew Jenna's Creek, Ohio wasn't worth the hassle.

Christy pushed the door open and slumped across the threshold. She peeled her gloves off her fingers with her teeth and dropped them in little puddles of slush on the floor. Wearily, she leaned over and chipped away at the ice on her laces so she could untie her boots. She should've gone around back to avoid making a mess in the hallway, but the back porch was still buried under snow, not to mention she hadn't the strength to take one more step. She shook the snow off her coat and hung it on the hall tree. She was tempted to run upstairs in her wet socks and change into something warm and flannel, but she needed to get a mop and tend to the widening pool of melting snow before Mom came out of the kitchen. The Storm of the Century wouldn't stop her from fretting over her hardwood floors.

She peeled off her double layers of wet socks and tossed them on top of her boots. A shiver shook her body when her bare feet touched the wood floor. They had been warmer inside her wet boots. It was almost as cold inside the house as out. The power had gone out a few hours into the storm and hadn't come back on yet. Lines all over the county had snapped in the high winds or from the weight of the snow. She and Mom blocked off the upstairs and were living in the dining room and kitchen. They managed to keep a fire going in the fireplace, though it didn't put off much heat. The meager flames barely warmed the two rooms enough to keep the pipes—and the women—from freezing.

Christy scooped up her socks, gloves, and boots in one arm and the wet pillowcase in the other and padded quickly to the dining room. She laid her socks and gloves on the hearth to dry and set her wet boots nearby. She added a few logs to the small fire and prodded the coals in hopes of inspiring the fire to relinquish a little more warmth. She and Mom were probably wasting their time keeping the fire going when most of the heat was simply going up the chimney and into the frigid January sky. It sure wasn't like this when Dad was alive. He could coax a roaring, cozy fire from embers and a stick of wet firewood.

She leaned away from the hearth and extended one foot toward the flames and then the other, alternating feet until she regained the feeling in her toes. She dug a pair of wooly socks out of the basket of clothes she'd brought down from her bedroom and pulled them on. She gave the fire another prod before grabbing the pillowcase and heading for the kitchen.

"Smells good in here." She deposited the pillowcase on the floor and began setting groceries on the Formica table. As expected, everything was wet. The brown paper bags had come apart and clung in shreds to the canned goods.

Abby turned away from the stove. "Goodness gracious. What happened to you? Where are your boots?"

"Drying out in front of the fireplace. I fell down a couple of times so everything's a mess."

"Oh, honey, I'm sorry. I never should've sent you out. Get upstairs and into some dry clothes. You'll catch your death."

"My death? I'm twenty-six. It'll take more than a four-block walk to the market to do me in."

"Maybe so, but I feel terrible. If it hadn't been an emergency, I wouldn't have asked." Abby peered at the empty pillowcase on the floor and the meager stack of groceries. "Where's the rest of the eggs? I asked you to get two dozen."

"That's all they let me have. They're rationing staples until the delivery trucks get through. I thought about getting in line again with a different checker."

"Oh, no. That wouldn't be fair to everyone else."

"I wasn't really going to. It would be like taking food out of little kids' mouths. Some people are saying the National Guard is bringing bread and milk to the rural areas." Christy opened the carton and lifted it triumphantly into the air. "Only one broken. It's a miracle."

Abby sighed. "I was hoping to bake a cake before it got too dark in here to work." She gasped. "Where's the toilet paper?"

Christy hissed through her teeth. "Not a roll to be had in the whole town."

Abby's head dropped back, and she gazed at the ceiling. "This could turn into quite a predicament."

"Surely we're not in bad shape already."

Abby laughed. "We might be if things continue like this much longer. I hope we don't have to rely on the Sears catalog."

"The Sears catalog? For what?"

Abby raised her eyebrows. "What do you think?"

Horrified realization creased Christy's face. "You've got to be kidding. That's… impossible."

"Nothing's impossible when you're desperate. Old timers used to stock their outhouses with newspapers and whatever paper products were available. The Sears catalog was the sign of a well-dressed facility."

"That's disgusting."

"Disgusting, yes, but serviceable in an emergency."

"Let's pray it doesn't come to that," Christy said with a shudder.

"I already am. I've never seen conditions like this in my life. Rationing eggs. I never heard of such a thing. Even during the war it wasn't like this."

"At least during the war they gave soldiers bathroom supplies."

"We're spoiled, that's all."

Christy began putting the perishable groceries in the box they kept on the back porch since there was no electricity to operate the refrigerator. Inside, the food would spoil. Outside, it was in danger of freezing, so they had fashioned a wall of firewood to shelter the groceries from the wind. "They were plowing the Myles-Munroe intersection again when I walked past," she said. "The turn lanes are blocked with a wall of snow at least twenty feet high. The curbs are almost as bad. Sort of makes you claustrophobic walking down the middle of the street."

"I heard we're supposed to get more snow next week. At least we don't have a houseful of kids to appease. Can you imagine what poor Karen is going through?"

Christy shuddered at the thought of her sister snowbound with three energetic youngsters. "I'm glad we're on this side of town."

Abby sighed wistfully and turned back to the pot roast. "I remember snow days when you kids were little. The first morning was fun. You would all bundle up and go outside to play and then come in for hot chocolate. It only took about ten minutes, though, for the novelty to wear off and you'd be snapping at each other. One winter, you didn't go to school for a solid week. I about went out of my mind. From the looks of things, it'll be a lot longer before school's back in session this time around."

Claustrophobia was what had sent Christy to the market this morning, and she'd only been stuck in the house a day and a half. She couldn't imagine what it would be like for a child, or worse, a parent stuck in the same house with children.

"Christy, did you hear me?"

She looked up to see Mom staring at her, ladle in hand. "Hmm?"

"I said you need to get into some dry clothes. I'll hang your wet things over the chairs in front of the fireplace."

"Let me get warmed up first. I bet it's not thirty degrees upstairs." She waited for Abby to put the roast back into the oven and then wrapped her arms around herself and hunched over the stove. It was the warmest spot in the house. "You ever notice how snow is beautiful and romantic until a bunch of people tramp over it and snowplows run through it a hundred times? You're right, it doesn't take long for the novelty to wear off."

Abby gazed warily at her for a moment before going back to the table. Christy knew what she was thinking. This was one of the first halfway comfortable conversations they'd had since Christy moved back home a year and a half ago. If the blizzard lasted much longer, their relationship might very well repair itself out of sheer desperation for human contact. She didn't know if she was ready for that to happen. Mom had lied to the family for over twenty years about the paternity of her youngest child. Everyone else may have forgiven her, but Christy wasn't the forgive-and-forget type.

Abby sat down at the table and took up the child's dress she was mending. Her six-year-old granddaughter liked to dress like a princess but played with the intensity of warriors invading Troy. She was always ripping sleeves and tearing hems. "Thanks again for going to the store. We should have plenty of everything as long as we're careful."

Christy turned around to warm her backside. She entertained the notion of crawling inside the oven with the pot roast. "Don't worry, I'm going to conserve like I've never conserved before. You scared me with that Sears catalog story. This house is freezing. I wonder if we might have a back draft or something in the fireplace that's keeping the fire from burning any hotter."

"I'll ask Arnold to check it out the next time he brings firewood."

"Let's hope the power comes back on and we don't need more firewood. It probably isn't such a great idea burning a fire when neither of us knows what we're doing. We could burn the house down or die from carbon monoxide poisoning."

"Don't say that even as a joke."

"It wasn't a joke."

A loud bang sounded upstairs. Both women's heads snapped upward in the direction of the ceiling. "What the—"

Another bang cut off Christy's words. The sound was followed by a crash and the sound of something breaking. Abby jumped out of her chair. Christy raced ahead of her toward the staircase at the front of the house, pushing aside blankets they had hung to keep as much heat as possible in the dining room and kitchen. She bounded up the stairs. Another bang and a crash sounded as she reached the landing. She paused to wait for Abby to catch up and to give her eyes time to adjust to the gloom. More blankets had been hung over the windows upstairs to keep out drafts. With no lights overhead, the hallway was as dark as pitch.

"What is it?" Abby whispered from behind her.

"I have no idea. I think it's coming from the bathroom," she whispered back.

"Well, what are we waiting for?" Abby said at a normal volume. She pushed past Christy.

Christy reached out in the darkness. "Mom, wait. It could be..."

"It could be what?"

"I don't know. You left the front door unlocked while I was gone. Maybe someone came in to get out of the cold."

"If they came into this house to get out of the cold, the joke's on them. They should've taken pity and killed us already."

"Mom, I'm serious."

"So am I. It's freezing up here and I need to get back to my roast." Another crash came from the end of the hallway. It was definitely coming from the bathroom. This time the noise sounded vaguely familiar.

"Whoever's in there is going to be in big trouble if they're tearing up my bathroom," Abby yelled as she marched down the hallway. She snatched a blanket from a curtain rod on her way past. Late morning light dazzled Christy's eyes. Sunlight reflected off the icicles hanging from the dormers, creating brilliant prisms that would've been awe-inspiring had she not been so afraid she and her mother were about to be murdered.

She grabbed hold of Abby's belt and tiptoed after her. The bedrooms had been carpeted a few years ago, but the hallway floor was still bare. Her feet ached from the cold through her thick socks. She almost welcomed an intruder as long as he let her put on a pair of slippers before doing whatever it was he came to do.

Outside the bathroom door, they heard another bang though it wasn't as loud as the previous ones. After the bang, something thudded against the wall and fell to the floor.

Abby looked around the doorframe and let out a shriek. "Duck!" She dropped to the hallway floor. Christy didn't react quickly enough. An object whizzed past her right shoulder and slammed into the wall behind her.

She crouched behind Abby and turned to see what almost hit her. A four-inch square wall tile had left a knick in the plaster before falling to the floor. She flinched as another tile popped loose from the wall. This time she was ready when it flew across the bathroom and thumped into the opposite wall.

"What's going on?" she asked Abby.

"Moisture must've gotten behind the tiles. It's freezing and expanding and busting them right off the walls."

"What are we going to do?"

"Well, we can't just sit here and wait for spring. They're ruining my walls."

"All we can do is close the door so they won't damage anything else."

Another tile popped loose and flew into the hallway, narrowly missing Abby's ear. "If we go in there, one of those missiles will take our heads off."

Christy assumed a stance she'd seen in the movies. "Cover me. I'm going in." She dropped to her knees and rolled into the bathroom doorway. She grabbed the bottom corner of the door and pulled it toward her. Two more tiles came loose and crashed against the door. Abby shrieked as Christy rolled into the hallway, pulling the door shut behind her. She lay on the floor, staring up at her mother. Then she started laughing. Abby stared at her for a split second before joining in. She stood up and offered Christy her hand. Christy got to her feet and sagged against the closed door, relief and laughter making her knees weak. Another crash sounded behind her, and she jumped away from the door.

"There's your intruder, Christy," Abby said. "I was beginning to think you might be right about locking the doors when I was home alone."

Christy looked at her mother. An unfamiliar longing stirred inside her. For the briefest of moments she couldn't even remember why she'd been mad the last two years. Staying angry with this woman for past mistakes was getting harder and harder to do, especially since Christy had made plenty of her own. How long did she plan to punish Mom for the pain and heartache she caused the family? Why couldn't Christy forgive and move on like her brother and sisters seemed to have done? Even if she couldn't do it for Mom, she needed to do it for herself. Playing the martyr was a heavy load to carry.

Sadly, it wasn't that simple. Mom had cheated on Dad and given birth to another man's baby. It was the most grievous sin a wife could commit against her husband. If Christy forgave her, there would be no one left to remember the betrayal. It would be as if Dad's pain meant nothing.

She couldn't do it. Not to the only decent man she'd ever known.

"Now that I know no one's waiting in the bathroom to kill us, I'm going change my clothes," she said. "My teeth are chattering."

She moved down the hallway to her room, leaving Abby standing outside the bathroom looking after her.

CHAPTER FOUR

Melody Knauff didn't care what anyone thought of her behavior. Something was wrong at the farm. She knew it as well as she knew she was freezing to death next to Tim Shelton on the tractor fender. Yesterday morning when she was startled awake by the overwhelming and foreboding sensation, she attributed it to the wind and strange thunder. But the more she thought about it, the more convinced she became something more sinister had stirred her from sleep.

As she lay in bed and listened to the wind tear at the shingles on the side of the house, she wondered if God was telling her something. Whenever someone at church said God told them to apply for a new job or move to the city, she figured it was their own common sense prodding them to action rather than divine providence. She had nothing against seeking the Lord before making a decision. Usually, if one sought him in prayer or studied the Word, the right move became clear. But she was hesitant to believe the Almighty came down from the throne room of heaven to tell people where to live or what kind of car to drive.

Then again, she'd been wrong about other things.

She and Dad had nearly finished shoveling snow off the roof when they heard the rumble of a tractor's engine. Someone was coming. Melody would make it up the hill to check on her grandparents and satisfy the nagging apprehension in her chest.

Squeezed in next to Tim, Melody kept her head down and as close to him as she dared, letting his body shield her from the brunt of the wind. She didn't know Tim very well. He had returned to his parents' dairy farm last year after his wife kicked him out of their house. Dad and Mom wouldn't speculate on the demise of the Shelton marriage, but anyone not living under a rock for the last year and a half knew the divorce had something to do with Tim testifying on behalf of an old girlfriend charged with murdering another old girlfriend.

That could never bode well for a marriage.

Melody had never met Tim before he moved home with his parents, though she remembered some of the Shelton kids from school. She had graduated the same year as his daughter. They hadn't been friends. Leslie had considered herself above the farm kids of Auburn County, which always struck Melody as odd since half of Leslie's parents had grown up on the farm next to Melody

Petite and blonde with fair skin and a smattering of well-placed freckles, Leslie was undisputedly the prettiest girl in school from the first day of kindergarten. Brimming with poise and confidence, the boys teased her ruthlessly because they didn't know what else to do with her. The girls learned to hate her soon enough. She tattled on them when they got their dresses dirty at recess, if they threw too hard during dodge ball, or for passing notes in class. Everything about her was perfect, from her grades to her hair to her pert little nose. She was the only girl in school whose mother took her to the city to shop for clothes and to get her hair done. She regarded girls like Melody with disdain and a little pity.

If it was true the apple didn't fall far from the tree, Melody didn't have much use for Tim Shelton either. Until today.

She hunched her shoulders against the wind and crouched even closer while he shifted and re-shifted the old tractor's gears. Backing up and bucking forward a few feet at a time, his plow chomped away at the snow with mind numbing slowness. For every blade of snow pushed aside, it seemed two feet more accumulated on top of it. Several times Melody feared the tractor would bog down, and she and Tim would be forced to walk back to the house in defeat. Fortunately he managed to keep the machine moving forward. She hoped there was enough gas in the tank to make it to the farmhouse. He could fill up for the return trip from the gas tank Grandpa kept next to the garage as long as it wasn't hopelessly buried like everything else.

As the tractor inched forward, Melody gazed in awe at the winter wonderland around them. The road and fencerows had disappeared under snowdrifts at least ten feet high. Across the pasture, outbuildings' peeked roofs looked like a child's toys forgotten in the snow. Only a few dried branches of Mom's twenty-year-old lilac bushes sprouted through the crusted snow. On the other side of the pond—a barely discernible dip in the landscape—a copse of evergreens resembled hedgerows. She had seen plenty of blizzards on the farm but none that engulfed entire buildings and trees.

The Beckwith farm sat on the hill's highest point. Trees had been planted over a century ago to protect it from the elements, but it still bore the brunt of every storm. Six wooden steps rose from the ground to the front porch. Now those steps were buried under snow, making the structure look like a fat bug squatted on the ground. The west side of the barn was obscured by snow nearly up to the rafters. The other side had apparently been sheltered by wind gusts that had nearly cleared the front porch of snow.

After thirty frigid, nearly unbearable minutes atop the tractor, the machine rumbled to a stop between the house and a row of bare trees. From her perch, Melody could almost climb from the tractor onto the porch roof. She jumped to the ground instead and sank to her thighs in drifts.

She burrowed out and stumbled as quickly as she could to the back door, the only entrance that showed signs an attempt had been made to free the family from its crystal prison.

She climbed over a mound of snow and onto the porch. It had been swept clean to allow access to the supply of wood neatly stacked around the perimeter. The door opened just as she felt the solid porch floor beneath her feet. Her cousin Carson gazed grimly out at her.

Carson was the son of her mother's brother Lowell. Like Lowell, Carson had long legs and narrow shoulders and didn't look like he possessed the necessary strength for survival on a working farm. His saving grace was the strong Beckwith nose and a head full of wavy dark hair he must've inherited from his mother.

Lowell had met his wife Amy in Texas during a brief stint in the Air Force. Amy's family had a little money—presumably from oil though no one knew for sure—which explained Lowell's ardor. How Lowell ever landed someone like Amy remained a mystery to Melody. She couldn't help but wonder if the woman was a sucker for a man in uniform, a slave to the bottle, or—the most likely scenario in Melody's opinion—not very bright.

It came as no surprise to anyone but Grandma when Amy divorced Lowell and moved little Carson to the Houston suburb where she grew up. Melody only saw her cousin a few times while they were growing up when Amy would send him to Ohio to connect with his father. Carson spent most of those summers on the farm since Lowell wasn't too into parenting. Melody remembered Carson's visits as the longest summers of her life.

The gaze he leveled at her now chilled her more than the raw January cold that had soaked through her garments. With stiff fingers, she grabbed the broom Grandma kept leaning against the door lintel and knocked the worst of the snow from her clothing. She handed the broom to Tim, who had joined her on the porch, and pushed past Carson into the house.

She peeled the two layers of gloves from her icy fingers and scanned the empty kitchen. Even during a power outage Grandpa always found an indoor task to occupy his time. The ticking of the clock on the wall amplified the eerie silence.

"Where is everybody?" she asked Carson as she chipped ice off her bootlaces.

"The power's out," he explained unnecessarily. "So's the phone. We couldn't get hold of anyone."

Melody straightened and kicked off her boots, then stepped out of the coveralls. "Everyone on the hill is without power." She hung the coveralls on a row of hooks by the door that was already crowded with outerwear of every shape and size.

Tim came in behind her and set two frozen jugs of milk on the table. He began to shed his coveralls. Their outer clothes were soaked through and would need to dry before they could put them on again. Otherwise, they would freeze solid within minutes of going back outside. Not that Melody had any intention of going anywhere.

Regardless of her impatience to get on with her purpose at the farm, courtesy demanded she make introductions. "Carson, have you met our neighbor? Tim's been working to dig everyone out of the snow. Tim, this is my cousin Carson."

The two men met in the middle of the room and shook hands. "Thanks, Tim."

"I don't know how much use I've been," Tim said. "At least the plowing will make it easier to tend to chores."

"We appreciate your efforts." Carson wrung his hands and glanced toward the door leading to the rest of the house before bringing his gaze back to Melody. Icy dread worked its way down her spine, making her forget the cold from the blizzard outside.

"We would've called if we could," he repeated. He looked at Tim as if hoping he would help explain.

Melody's heart seemed to stand still. "What do you mean?"

"Don't get mad, Mel. If we could've done anything, we would have."

She lunged forward and grabbed the front of his shirt. "What are you talking about? Where's Grandma?"

Carson stepped back to reclaim his personal space. "Grandma's fine. She…"

Lowell Beckwith strode into the kitchen. He looked past Melody to Tim. "I thought I heard someone. You got any smokes."

Tim shook his head. "I don't smoke anymore."

"Lucky bum. I can't quit 'em."

Melody let go of Carson and turned to Lowell. "How did you get here? There's nothing moving in this storm."

"Nice to see you, too, Melody. Lenny Brown dropped me off night before last, before the blizzard started. Why the third degree?"

Melody made an effort to calm her anxiety. She had no right to interrogate Uncle Lowell. He was always showing up unannounced and uninvited. He'd hang around a few days, ham it up with everyone, sweet talk Grandma out of a few dollars, and be on his way.

Now that she thought about it, she did remember seeing headlights going up the hill Wednesday night, but she hadn't noticed anyone leave later. At the time she thought it was Jay or Carson coming home with cigarettes or something. She told Lowell as much.

He directed a belabored sigh at Tim. "I wish they had. You know how it is. Stuck on this hill, low on smokes with everything else going on. I don't know how much more I can take."

Carson shot a furtive glance at Melody.

Her heart slammed in her chest. "What do you mean by everything going on?"

Lowell turned an angry gaze on Carson. "I thought you told her."

Melody took a step toward him. "Told me what? Has something happened to Grandma?"

"She's fine. She's in the living room in front of the fire."

At that moment Clarice Beckwith's voice sounded from the front of the house. "Melody, honey, is that you?"

Melody's knees weakened with relief. "It's me, Grandma." She looked from Lowell to where Carson was cowering at the sink. "You better tell me what's going on before I go in there," she hissed.

Tim stepped forward. "Where's Warner?" he asked warily.

Carson's eyes flitted to Lowell. Lowell dropped his gaze to the floor.

"He's in the front room," Carson said.

Before Melody could exhale in relief, he continued.

"He fell down the basement stairs yesterday morning when he went to light the furnace. By the time we found him it was too late."

Melody looked helplessly from one man to the other. "Too late for what?" Her skin tingled, and her breath caught in her throat.

"Too late for what?" she repeated around her clenched jaw as the three men exchanged glances.

A pair of strong hands guided her to a chair. She was barely aware of the sound of running water before someone pressed a glass into her hands. Tim gazed down at her in concern. Carson remained rooted at the sink. Lowell still stood in the middle of the room. She fought the urge to jump up and slap him as hard as she could.

She gulped down the water and willed herself not to lose control. Lashing out at Lowell or anyone else would only hurt Grandma.

Grandma.

She set the glass on the table and jumped out of the chair. She pushed past Lowell and went down the short hall to the living room. At the sight of Grandma in her usual spot in the rocker in front of the fireplace with a worn afghan across her lap, she lost the battle of her emotions.

"Grandma," she wailed and rushed across the old rug in three strides. She dropped to the floor in front of the rocking chair and buried her head in Grandma's lap. She knew she should be strong for her grandmother's sake, but it wasn't in her. Not now.

She cried for several minutes while Grandma rocked the chair forward and back. Grandma made shushing noises and combed her fingers through Melody's tangled hair.

After a while Melody's tears succumbed to hiccupping gasps for air. She dried her face on the afghan and rose onto her knees to embrace her grandmother. She rested her chin on the sharp angle of Grandma's shoulder and marveled at how her grandmother was disappearing before her eyes. She had always been petite like most of the women in the family. She carried an extra thirty pounds she blamed on a lackadaisical metabolism and not her hearty appetite for sweets and white flour. Since her cancer diagnosis, she had lost two inches of height and the extra padding Melody associated with all grandmothers.

Melody searched for words, but nothing would come. Grandma had always been fragile. Pampered and petted by her parents and then her husband, Melody wondered how she would survive without Grandpa. Fresh tears sprang to her eyes as realization settled in.

Clarice traced the trail of a tear down her cheek with her thumb. "You should take comfort in knowing your grandpa loved you very much. You brought so much joy to his life."

Melody wasn't comforted. Fresh tears threatened to erupt, but she fought them back. Now wasn't the time. She wanted answers. There had to be a mistake. Warner Beckwith wouldn't die at the bottom of a flight of stairs like a…a helpless old man. She half expected him to come through the door, his shirt wrinkled and dusty from a job he'd just completed. He would smile and ask her what all the fuss was about.

"You know me better than that, Nugget," he'd say. "It'll take more than a tumble down the stairs to do me in."

She swallowed her tears. "What happened? Grandpa's been going down those stairs his whole life."

"The steps were covered with ice and the electricity was out. Jay said he probably couldn't see very well in the dark. He must've slipped and wasn't able to get up. I guess it was God's plan. I just don't understand why he took Warner first. I was the one ready to go."

Melody sat back on her haunches. "It was an accident, Grandma, not God. An accident."

She looked around the room at the men who had followed her in. Tim was still in the doorway, looking like he wished he'd never dug his tractor out of the barn this morning. Jay sat on the sagging sofa, his eyes fixed on a spot on the floor. Carson stood next to the fireplace, his face devoid of emotion. Lowell was in the center of the room, digging under a thumbnail with his opposite finger and thumb.

Clarice nodded and sniffed back tears. "I suppose you're right. None of us are guaranteed a tomorrow. It's just such a blow. What would've happened if I'd been here alone? What would I have done if I'd woken up and found Warner at the bottom of those stairs? At least God saw fit to have my boys here with me." She reached for Lowell. He took her hand. "I don't know what I would've done without them."

"Of course," Melody mumbled when all she wanted to do was scream in frustration. Jay and Lowell were of little use under the best of circumstances. Carson wasn't much better. Grandma was right about one thing. If the men hadn't been there, Warner would still be lying at the bottom of the stairs waiting for someone to carry him upstairs.

She looked across the hall and past the stairs to the closed door that led to the front room he used as an office. She shuddered.

Clarice followed her gaze and looked knowingly back at Melody. "We put him in there to keep him comfortable. Jay thought of everything. He closed off the room to keep it cold."

Jay looked pleased at his ingenuity. "Who knows how long it will take an ambulance to get up the hill in this snow."

Melody shuddered again. She couldn't bear the thought of Grandpa in the next room all alone while the family went about their business as if he were taking a nap. There were few alternatives under the circumstances, but it seemed so callous. This wasn't the Dark Ages.

Tim stepped out of the doorframe and approached the rocking chair. "Mrs. Beckwith, if there's anything my family or I can do, please don't hesitate to ask."

She let go of Lowell's hand and grasped Tim's. "You've already done more than you know, young man. You brought my baby girl to me." She smiled at Melody through eyes glistening with tears.

Tim turned to Jay. "You're right to assume it'll be a while before anyone can get up the hill. I've been plowing all day and haven't made any headway in clearing the road. According to the radio, the rural areas are going to have to hunker down and tough it out."

"You sound like Warner," Clarice said with a sad smile.

"I brought some milk from the farm. The chickens haven't been laying, but that will probably change in a few days."

Clarice patted his hand once more before letting go. "Don't worry about us. We have plenty to make it through for a while. Warner always makes sure…"

A tear spilled down her cheek. "Oh, dear."

Melody leaned into her again. They cried softly together for a few minutes. After a while the tears subsided, and Melody became aware of the stiffness in her knees. She dried her face again and stood up. The living room had cleared except for Jay who was leafing through a magazine. She wanted to roll it up and smack him across the nose like a disobedient dog. Instead, she excused herself and went back into the kitchen.

Carson stood at the sink, his arms crossed over his chest. Tim sat at the table with his hands wrapped around a cup of coffee. They had been talking but stopped when Melody came in. Lowell was nowhere to be seen. The emotional scene in the living room had probably been too much for him. He was probably upstairs taking a nap and dreaming of a cigarette.

Melody went to Tim. "Could you stop at my house on your way past and tell my mother what happened? I hate to ask, but I can't leave—"

"You don't need to stay," Carson said from the sink.

She spun around to face him. "Excuse me. My grandfather just died. My place is with Grandma."

"He was my grandfather, too, in case you forgot. Go home to your mother, Mel. Dad, Jay, and I have everything under control."

"Apparently not. If you had, Grandpa never would've fallen down those stairs. What was he doing lighting the furnace anyway? He's an old man."

"He was the first one awake every morning."

"You could've set an alarm and did it for him."

"Have you ever tried to keep him from doing anything?"

He had a point, though she'd never admit it out loud.

Tim cleared his throat to remind them he was in the room. "Melody, I'll take care of things with your mother."

"Thank you. She'll want to come as soon as she hears. Tell her it isn't necessary until Dad can dig our tractor out. We'll be fine for a day or two. There's nothing anyone can do anyway."

"That's right, there isn't," Carson agreed. "You might as well go home, too. Judy will feel better if you're with her. Having you here will only upset Grandma further."

Melody could no longer hold her anger in check. "Don't tell me what'll upset her. I've been the one here for twenty-five years while you couldn't take a moment out of your life to call her on her birthday. What could possibly upset her more than knowing her husband is lying dead in the next room?"

Her rebuff seemed to roll off Carson's back. "She doesn't need someone holding her hand and feeling sorry for her. She needs to be strong. She does that by taking care of us and living life as normally as possible."

"Certainly you don't expect her to wait on you hand and foot."

"That's not what I said. I just meant sometimes the more attention a person gets, the worse they react to things."

Melody planted her hands on her hips, even though she couldn't deny his words held a measure of truth. Grandma had always possessed a delicate nature. She loved nothing more than to be stroked and fawned over.

"And my mother will be comforted in knowing I've stayed to help out however I can." She turned to the cabinets. "I'll make a pot of coffee. Tim has been out all day. His clothes need time to dry." She hoped he wouldn't tell Carson how she had been the one to force him back out in the cold less than an hour ago when he stopped at her house to warm up.

Tim took the jugs of milk from the table and set them in the sink to thaw. Melody frowned at the lunch dishes on the counter. Grandma had never been much of a housekeeper. Even before old age forced Grandpa to cut back on his farming duties, he was the one who kept the house in order. One thing he couldn't abide was dirty dishes in the sink.

Melody took a large pot from the cabinet and set it in the empty half of the sink with an angry bang. She turned on the tap and filled the pot with water to heat for the dishes. If the men couldn't keep the dishes done, how could she expect them to take care of Grandma? Without Grandpa around, the place would fall apart inside of a week.

After she set the pot of water over a gas flame, she filled the coffeepot. Everyone would have to settle for instant coffee as long as the power was out. She glanced toward the front of the house. She wouldn't believe Grandpa was truly gone until she saw him for herself. But she wasn't ready for that. Instead, she crossed the kitchen to the basement door. Tim and Carson sat at the table talking about the blizzard and the economic repercussions it would have on the region as if they had already forgotten Warner Beckwith was stored in the front room like a side of beef.

Melody opened the basement door and peered down the narrow staircase. Light from the window and the glass panel on the old stove illuminated the interior enough so she didn't need a flashlight. The basement was warm and cozy with the furnace blazing away. It seemed odd this innocuous place was where Grandpa met his end. Her hand instinctively tightened around the railing as she started down. At what spot had he lost his footing? How long had he lain at the bottom of the stairs waiting for someone to help him up? Had he hit his head so he didn't know what was happening, or had the cold water seeped into his bones and slowly robbed his aged body of its last ounce of strength?

Anger welled up again as she imagined Jay, Lowell, and Carson tucked upstairs fast asleep while Grandpa waited for sweet death to end his suffering. If one of them had awoken and come downstairs to check on the furnace instead of waiting for him to do it, they would've seen him at the bottom of the stairs. His death was so senseless, so unnecessary.

She turned and gazed at the open door at the top of the landing. The wooden stairs were worn with use. They were treacherous, even when dry. No one had ever bothered to tack down rubber tread guards to make the descent less hazardous. Even if they had, it might not have made a difference to an eighty-two-year-old man.

She took a deep breath and swiped tears from her eyes. She couldn't blame Grandpa's fall on anyone. Carson was right; he was as stubborn as the day was long. He would've insisted Jay or Carson didn't know how to stoke the furnace the way he liked and gone behind them to redo the job. Nor was he as steady on his feet as he used to be. His body had begun to succumb to the natural deterioration of old age. While still strong and straight-backed, he didn't move as easily as he once had.

Melody sat down on the bottom step and stared at the floor. "I'm sorry you died alone, Grandpa," she murmured through her tears. "I hope you weren't afraid or in pain."

She choked out a sob even as a smile curled her lips. She dried her face on her shirtsleeve. Her grandpa was a devout man of faith who often talked about heaven. How many times had she heard him say to be absent from the body was to be present with the Lord? He told her a fear of death was for those who were uncertain of what lay ahead. He knew and anticipated it.

"You're dancing on streets of gold now with no chance of falling," she said.

She looked toward the ceiling. "Thank you, Lord, for the grandpa you gave me. I couldn't have asked for a better one."

She took a ragged breath. "I'd be lying if I said I didn't want him with me a little longer though. Grandma needs him. We all do."

She stood up and dried her face with her hands. The heat from the furnace blasted her tear-stained cheeks, but her hands and feet were still numb from the tractor ride.

She surveyed the room and thought of the last time she'd been down here. She and Grandpa had been gathering canning jars. It was July, and the garden was bursting with green beans, ready for picking first thing the next morning. Grandma was anxious to put up her first batch. More accurately, she was anxious to sit in the kitchen and oversee things while Melody and Mom did the work.

Carson had arrived from Texas the week before.

"Why do you suppose he's here?" Melody had asked softly, knowing sound carried easily to the kitchen through the heating vents. "We haven't seen him in years."

"I imagine he came to make sure he gets his share of the inheritance," Grandpa stated. "He probably heard how bad off your grandma is and wants to get on my good side before it's too late. He knows his daddy and uncle well enough to know they're up to the same thing. He doesn't want to give them the chance to squander everything."

"Won't they be surprised to hear you aren't going anywhere?"

Grandpa had turned pensive. "A man is accounted a certain number of years on this earth, Nugget. I've already outlived mine." He picked up a box of jars and motioned for her to go up the stairs ahead of him. "Watch the stairs, missy. They're more rickety than I am. It wouldn't take much of a nudge to send either one of us to the bottom."

Melody thought of the sense of dread that had yanked her out of sleep yesterday morning. Had Grandpa's words last summer proven prophetic? Had he willed her awake in the waning moments of his life? Had he been trying to summon her for help? Or had he needed to tell her something?

She didn't believe in psychic hocus pocus, but the situation was too eerie, too weird, to disregard.

Even if she'd had a vision of Grandpa at the bottom of the stairs, she never would've made it up the hill before he succumbed to hypothermia. Was there another message to be gleaned from her sudden wakening? Gooseflesh rose on her arms inside her heavy knit sweater despite the heat from the furnace. She didn't want to consider it, but she couldn't help thinking there was more to the accident than an old man slipping on the icy stairs.

CHAPTER FIVE

Jan 31st

Tuesday morning Melody awoke to the blessed hum of the furnace blowing warm air through the vents on the living room floor. Judy woke up at nearly the same instant and sat up on the mattress on the floor and raised her hands toward the ceiling. "Thank you, Jesus," she squealed as she threw off the covers and clambered up off the floor.

Pete opened one eye. "What's all the hubbub?"

Melody jumped off the couch and met her mother in the middle of the room. "We've got power." The women danced in a circle while Pete laughed and then joked he got the first shower.

As he headed to the downstairs bathroom, Melody lunged across the rug and snagged the phone off the cradle, her mind already going through the list of people she needed to call. Her boss at work. Aunt Linda. The funeral director...

Most of the family had been notified about Grandpa's death thanks to Tim Shelton's hike over the hill yesterday, but no one had details. She also wanted to check on them to see how they were taking the news.

A deafening silence greeted her ears. She shook her head at her mother's questioning look. Judy exhaled in disappointment. "Oh, well, at least we have lights."

After breakfast and showers and as many chores as were possible with snowdrifts higher than the rafters, Mom and Melody set out to make the quarter-mile trek to the farm. Under ordinary conditions, it took Melody all of five minutes to climb the hill to her grandparents' house if she wasn't in a hurry while the return downhill trip could be measured in moments.

When she arrived home alone yesterday afternoon, Mom had burst into tears at the sight of her. She accused Melody of intentionally worrying her. "How would I cope if I lost you to this blizzard, too?" she had demanded, all the while crying and holding Melody against her.

"How could you lose me?" Melody asked gently. "You can see the farmhouse from our living room window."

Mom hadn't answered. She only pulled her tighter. Melody knew Mom was mourning Grandpa instead of worrying about her, but mothers had a hard time separating the two.

Today she had planned to walk back to the farmhouse by herself, but she knew better than to suggest it. Her parents' fears that she would lose track of the road or fall into a drift and perish before anyone realized she was missing weren't completely unfounded. The drifts were packed pretty solid. She didn't think she would fall all the way to the bottom of one, but even she didn't want to take the chance. Dad had offered to take them up the hill on the tractor as soon as he finished tending the livestock, but neither woman felt like waiting. A rigorous hike through the snow would work off the tension that had been mounting the last five days.

"What's he doing here anyway?" Melody grumbled inside her ski mask and hooded pink parka when she and Mom were close enough to the farmhouse to make out a figure on the porch.

"Did you say something?" Mom asked breathlessly, weighted down under her own winter gear.

Melody pointed to the house and the lone figure sweeping drifted snow away from the front door. "Uncle Lowell. He only comes to visit when he wants something."

"Slow down, Melody. He isn't going anywhere."

Melody stopped to allow her mother to catch up. It was all she could do not to tap her foot impatiently in the snow.

Judy goose-stepped her way into the tractor tracks. When she got alongside Melody, she grabbed her arm through her bulky coat. "Your grandma's been through enough already. I'm sure Lowell has her best interests in mind."

Melody rolled her eyes behind her sunglasses where her mother couldn't see. Of course Mom wouldn't admit her brother might be here to take advantage of Grandma. "I asked an innocent question."

"Your questions are never innocent." Judy squeezed her arm for emphasis. "I don't want you saying or doing anything to upset your grandmother."

Melody resisted the urge to jerk away. "Don't worry, I'll behave myself. Regardless of what I'm thinking, I'll keep my mouth shut."

She resumed walking. She thought she heard Mom say, "That'll be the day," but she didn't bother to turn around to check.

Even if Lowell's motives were as pure as the snow around them, he had aroused Melody's suspicions by sweeping the porch. He never pitched in to help with a chore if he could avoid it. Grandpa always said he was too lazy to work as a taster in a peanut butter factory.

By the time she and Judy climbed onto the porch, he had finished sweeping and disappeared inside the house. The women paused long enough to knock the snow off their clothes with the broom he left leaning against the doorframe.

Inside the house Melody's eyes took in the small, cramped living room at a glance. The framed department store prints over the sun-faded, sagging couch and matching loveseat reminded her of the thousands of times she had passed through the door to find Grandma in her rocker and Grandpa at his desk in the front room across the hall. A fire crackled in the stone fireplace Dad had helped him install fifteen years ago. A heavy beam from a cherry tree the two men felled that same winter served as a mantle. Melody was ten at the time, and she still remembered the smile on Grandpa's face when he and Dad dragged the tree into the yard and announced their plans for it. Grandma had been doubtful the twisted tree could be converted into a suitable mantle. Melody was confident in Grandpa's abilities. If he told her he was bringing home the moon, she would've cleared off a spot on the bookcase for it.

Like always, Clarice dozed in the rocker with a familiar frayed afghan across her lap. The only indication something was amiss inside the house was the front room's closed door. Someone had tied a ribbon of black cloth into a bow and hung it on the door. Tears pooled in Melody's eyes at the sight of it. It brought a measure of comfort to know she wasn't the only one mourning his passing.

She pushed her grief aside and advanced into the living room to the rocking chair. Grandma's cheeks were pink from the heat of the fire in the grate, but underneath, her skin bore a sickly gray pallor.

Melody knelt in front of her and gently touched her hand. "Grandma?"

Clarice opened her eyes and smiled dreamily. "Hello, dear. Have you been here long?"

"Mom and I just got here. How are you?"

Her smile widened. "Much better since my boys are here with me."

Melody stood up and brushed lint and firewood splinters from the knees of her pants. It had only been five days since the accident, and the house had already taken on an untidy appearance.

"Is Uncle Allen here too?"

She knew Allen couldn't have possibly made the trip from town, but she couldn't resist reminding Grandma that one of her 'boys'—the only responsible one of the lot—was still absent.

"Of course not." Clarice looked unfazed. "He has Bonnie and those beautiful grandchildren to look after. I don't expect him to come out here in this blizzard."

Judy sent Melody a warning glance as she pushed between her and Clarice. "Hello, Mom. I just can't believe this happened." She leaned forward to kiss Clarice's cheek.

Clarice caught hold of her hands. "None of us can, darling. I wasn't ready for your daddy to go before me." Tears filled her eyes. "I don't suppose anyone ever is."

Judy pulled her mother's hands to her lips and kissed them. She cleared her throat. "I'm so thankful Tim Shelton was able to get word to Allen about Pop?"

Clarice nodded. "Me too. That young man is a godsend." Anyone under the age of sixty was young as far as she was concerned. "He walked all the way over to Jacob Evers' place yesterday. The phones are still working on that side of the hill. He called my doctor for me too."

Judy shook off her layers of clothing. She already knew but smiled down at her mother anyway. "That was thoughtful."

Clarice opened her mouth to say something else, but closed it and smiled warmly over Melody's shoulder. Melody knew without looking that Lowell had entered the room. She also knew he wouldn't be here unless he was after something. Anytime Jay or Lowell needed money they went to Grandma, and always behind Grandpa's back.

Her mind took a sinister turn. Since she heard about the fall down the basement stairs, she'd been trying to piece together the events of the morning the blizzard struck. She couldn't accept that he merely slipped. Could his death have something to do with Lowell's unexpected appearance? What if Grandpa had died earlier in the day and the rest of the family assumed he fell going down the stairs? Was it possible he had been lying there longer than Grandma realized?

She shook her head to get her thoughts back on track. Lowell was harmless. More than harmless, he was lazy. Didn't a killer need gumption? Ambition? Killing his father was an extreme step to take in order to bum a few dollars off his mother for beer and cigarettes when he could easily ask when Grandpa went outside to feed the animals.

She thought of the headlights reflected in her bedroom window Wednesday night. What about Lenny Brown, the man who dropped Lowell off? Could he have done Lowell's dirty work for him? If Lenny had been involved, maybe Lowell didn't know. But Lenny had no motivation. He knew Lowell couldn't get his hands on more than a few dollars at a time. The Beckwiths' chief assets were farmland and livestock. Their money was kept at the bank. Every item in the house combined was probably only worth a few thousand dollars.

None of it made sense. A burglar, or even an impatient family member, would know killing Grandpa wouldn't reap many immediate rewards.

"Warner would be so proud of us," Clarice said. "Pulling together in a crisis. It's all he ever wanted."

Melody didn't think they'd pulled together as much as were thrown together. She pushed all thoughts of foul play out of her head. There was nothing more to Grandpa's death than what they all thought.

Still…

Judy sat down on the corner of the sofa, facing Clarice, their knees nearly touching. "It seems odd sitting around like this, waiting, not doing anything. Usually after a death, we're cooking and preparing the house for an influx of visitors. With all this snow, we can't even talk to family, let alone prepare for their arrival."

Clarice sighed. "The worst part is it gives us too much time to think. Poor Warner." She turned her head and studied the black bow hanging on the front room door. All eyes in the room followed her gaze. "I don't know what I'll do without him."

"Mom..." Judy said gently.

Melody's eyes clouded over for the hundredth time since learning of his death.

Clarice dabbed her eyes with the corner of a handkerchief. "Don't worry. I'm fine. I think I'm all cried out. There's nothing we can do until the county gets around to clearing the roads so there's no point fretting over preparing for a funeral."

Judy clapped her hands together and got to her feet. "There's plenty we can do right now. Can I get you anything? Do you need another blanket? Have you been eating? You know what the doctor said about your appetite."

Clarice waved away her words. "Jay brought me toast and coffee in bed this morning."

"That was hours ago. I'll fix you a decent lunch. Something the guys can heat up for supper."

"Don't go to any trouble, darling. Jay is taking care of it."

Melody was relieved someone was doing something.

"In that case, Melody and I will take advantage of being snowbound from work and do a little housekeeping. We'll start in the dining room. I doubt anyone's been in there since Christmas. I imagine all the downstairs floors could use a good scrubbing."

"There's no need to get started right away. Sit here and keep me company."

"I must say, Mom, you certainly are holding up better than any of us expected."

"It's from having my boys here."

Lowell rested his hand on her shoulder and gazed adoringly down at her.

Melody cringed. She wondered if he'd be so attentive after the will was read.

As if sensing the tender moment, Jay materialized from the direction of the kitchen. At one time he had been quite handsome. He was a star athlete in school. According to Judy, the phone in the kitchen rang off the hook with giggling girls on the other end wanting to talk to him. Warner threatened to have the number changed every other month. Clarice laughed and said he should be thankful his son could have his pick of any girl in the county.

Had Clarice known the damage caused by her son's reckless behavior, she might not have been so happy to hear the phone ring. More than one girl's heart and reputation were shattered by his callous treatment. He moved from one one-night stand to the next, unconcerned about the repercussions of his actions. At school, Judy overheard whispered conversations about suspected pregnancies. One girl told her Warner had given money to a friend to make one of Jay's errors in judgment go away.

"That happened long before Pop met Jesus," Judy had assured Melody when Melody asked her about it. "That is, if it ever happened. He would never do such a thing today."

Jay quit high school before graduation, claiming he was ready to join the workforce. It seemed a grown up and exciting move at the time. The girls at school pursued him all the more. The fact that he couldn't hold onto a job or commit to one girl did little to tarnish his appeal. He talked of joining the military but never went through with it. They were sending boys to Korea in those days, and Jay had no desire to huddle in a foxhole while someone lobbed grenades at him.

He moved to Cincinnati for a few years. When he returned, he had a wife and a little one on the way. The marriage lasted a year. Judy never heard what became of the baby. She couldn't get a straight answer out of her mother. Clarice was fond of reminding anyone who would listen they couldn't be certain the baby belonged to Jay, insinuating the young woman's character was less than honorable, and Jay had been duped into marrying her.

A lifetime of drinking and hard living had not been kind. The barrel chest that once filled out a football uniform had long since turned to fat. A pot belly hung over cotton trousers that constantly slipped down his narrow hips. The thick brown hair he had been so proud of had long since disappeared down the drain. His face sagged, and he was always in need of a shave.

Melody wondered if he ever looked at his reflection in the mirror and wished he'd made better choices.

Jay glared at Lowell's hand resting on Clarice's shoulder. Lowell smirked and tightened his grip. Jay went to Clarice and straightened the afghan around her knees. He apparently had no intention of relinquishing the role of caretaker to Lowell. "Are you doing all right, Mom? Can I fix you a cup of tea?"

"I'll do it," Lowell said quickly. "I looked in the cabinets but couldn't find any Earl Gray you like so much."

Clarice beamed at the attention. "You're so thoughtful, Lowell. I wish I'd had Warner pick some up at the store the last time he—"

She covered her mouth with her hand.

Jay patted her knee. "I'll make some from what we have and put a dollop of honey in it the way you like." His eyes shot daggers at Lowell over Clarice's head.

"Isn't there a matter we should discuss first?" Lowell said.

Jay's jaw clenched. "It can wait until later."

Melody had been thoroughly enjoying the dance between the men for Grandma's affections. She sat forward on the couch, her curiosity piqued.

Clarice cleared her throat and dabbed again at her eyes. "What is it, darling?"

Jay stole a look at Melody and Judy. "We don't need to go into it now."

Melody tensed, all the more anxious to hear what was coming.

"Any matters in this house can be discussed in front of all of us," Clarice said firmly. "This family doesn't keep secrets."

Since when? Melody barely refrained from asking aloud.

"It's about...Pop."

Her breath caught in her throat. "Grandpa?"

"Carson and I were talking this morning about... Then Lowell came in and, well, we—"

"Tell them, Jay," Lowell urged. "Like you said earlier, it's an urgent matter."

Jay clenched and unclenched his jaw. "I didn't exactly use that term. I said it was something that needed dealt with." He gazed at Clarice. "I'm afraid you'll find it ...distasteful."

"For heaven's sake, Jay, spit it out," Judy cut in as his hesitation lengthened.

"Carson and I think we should move Pop to the summer kitchen. It's hard keeping the temperature in the front room low enough to..." His voice trailed off as he scanned the horrified faces staring back at him.

The tiny stone building off the back porch had been built at the request of Clarice's mother, Grandma Salinski before the turn of the last century when the family had a host of farmhands to feed. Many families built separate quarters for preparing meals when the summer sun made it too hot to cook inside. The summer kitchen hadn't been used for cooking since Aunt Linda married Hart Bowden and moved to Indianapolis. Without her to do most of the carrying back and forth, Clarice decided it was easier to deal with the heat than the inconvenience of cooking in the little house in the back yard.

"You can't be serious," Melody shrieked before she could check her voice.

"It could be weeks before they open the roads," Jay explained. He looked helplessly from Judy to Clarice.

Clarice's flushed cheeks turned white. She sat back in the chair and fanned herself with the corner of the afghan.

Judy's eyes widened in concern. "Maybe we should talk about this later."

"No, no, Jay's right. It needs to be...taken care of."

"It's the only solution," Lowell said, swaying to Jay's side when he saw how well Clarice took the news. "Things used to be done this way all the time."

Melody couldn't wrap her mind around what they were planning. "But the summer kitchen? It's so..." She stopped herself just before she could say cold. "...cruel." She didn't want anyone to accuse her of giving in to hysteria by suggesting Grandpa would freeze outside, though that was exactly what she was thinking.

Grandpa no longer dwelt in the physical body that had been his home during his earthly tenure. He was blissfully unaware he had died during the worst blizzard in Ohio history and couldn't have a decent burial because there was no way to get him off the hill. Even after his delivery to the funeral home, it would be some time before anyone could burrow beneath ten feet of snow to dig a hole in the frozen ground. While her logical mind accepted those facts, Melody wasn't ready to banish him to the summer kitchen like a Christmas ham.

"How do we know it's safe?" she asked instead. "What if something…gets in there with him?"

"Nothing's moving in this weather," Jay assured her. "The building's practically snowed under. It'll take us a day to plow through to the door as it is. We'll keep an eye on it and make sure it's secure."

She jumped to her feet, unable to bear the warmth of the room one more minute. "I'm going upstairs to gather some cleaning supplies. I need to get started on those floors."

She barely made it to the top of the stairs before bursting into tears. She buried her face in her hands, hoping the others wouldn't hear her sobs. Grandpa had been gone five days. She had never gone this long without talking to him. He was her best friend and confidante. Yes, he was demanding and opinionated. Sometimes too demanding but only because he wanted his children to be strong and self-sufficient. To think his life had been reduced to waiting in the summer kitchen for an undertaker to pick him up was more than she could bear. The notion was barbaric—she didn't care if it was how it had been done since the dawn of time. This was the twentieth century, for crying out loud. Doctors once practiced bloodletting and didn't wash their hands before surgery. She didn't want to go back to those days either.

She sniffed back the rest of her tears and dried her face with the tail of her shirt. She patted her pants pockets in search of a tissue. Coming up empty, she headed to her grandparents' room. The door was slightly ajar. Light spilled out into the hallway. Grandma must've left it on this morning.

Melody pushed open the door. Carson stood in the narrow space between the bed and the dresser. He whirled around. He clutched Grandma's purse to his chest, his hand buried inside.

Anger bubbled inside Melody. "What are you doing with that?"

"I…uh…was looking for…" He set the purse on the dresser and backed away.

"You have no business looking for anything in Grandma's purse. You shouldn't be in this room at all."

"You're right. I'm sorry." He took another step away from the dresser. "Listen, Mel, you don't need to say anything about this. It wasn't like I was stealing. I'm going stir crazy in this house. You can't imagine what it's like here with Uncle Jay and Grandma. Now Dad's here, too, riding my case like he owns the place. I needed a cigarette. Grandma confiscated a couple packs from Jay a few days ago. She caught him smoking in the house. He told her he was trying to quit and asked her to keep them for him in case he got desperate. I think he was really hiding them from Dad."

He lowered his voice conspiratorially. "Between you and me, he's smoking like a stovepipe, but he'll say anything to placate Grandma."

Like some others I know, Melody thought. She didn't believe for a minute Carson was looking for cigarettes. If Grandma had indeed taken them from Jay, she would've hidden them in her bureau or possibly the closet, not her purse. It wouldn't do any good, though, to contradict him. Nor could she report what she'd seen. Grandma would believe whatever lame excuse he came up with and accuse Melody of tattling. She snatched the purse off the dresser and shoved it into the top drawer. She turned around and leaned against the dresser as if to barricade him from going after it again. "Since you didn't find any cigarettes…"

He held up his hands in surrender. "Yeah, yeah. I'll go downstairs so Dad can hassle me about something else."

Melody crossed her arms over her chest and scowled at him. It was bad enough they were preparing to put Grandpa's body in the summer kitchen. Now Carson was up here going through Grandma's purse, no doubt looking for money or something he could sell as soon as the snow melted enough to get off the hill.

Carson gave her one last measuring glance and headed for the door. Melody took a few tissues from a crocheted dispenser on the dresser and blew her nose, her grief replaced by anger.

⸎

Carson sauntered down the stairs, fully aware of Melody watching him from the landing. He smiled to himself. As long as she thought he was after a few dollars from the old woman's purse she'd never figure out what he'd really been looking for.

He had thought Warner's demise would alleviate the Gestapo atmosphere in the house. Instead, Melody had assumed the role of gatekeeper. As if being snowbound on this God-forsaken hill wasn't bad enough, now he had an amateur Columbo tracking his every move.

He was pretty sure she wouldn't say anything about finding his hand in Clarice's purse. Not this time. She was too worried about their grandmother's fragile health. Carson shook his head. No one gave the old woman credit. She wasn't as helpless and unaware as she pretended to be.

Within weeks of his arrival last summer he had realized the farm wasn't valuable enough to parcel out to ten or twelve heirs. Even if a few family members were left out of the equation, there were still too many forks left in the pie. With Warner gone and everything in Clarice's hands, he stood a better chance of inheriting something. But a tiny share of the farm wasn't enough to satisfy his hunger. He had something else in mind—something to last the rest of his life.

"Work smart, Carson, not hard," his stepfather Milt Jameson was fond of saying. When Milt spoke, Carson listened. Milt had made more money by doing less than anyone on this hill ever dreamed of.

Carson had made mistakes, chiefly mistakes involving money and less than reputable business partners who took it out on him when deals went south. After a sucker bet and too many hands out wanting a piece of him, he made an important discovery about himself. He wasn't smart enough to earn money the easy way and was too lazy to break his back on an honest living. Maybe he was more like Lowell Beckwith than he cared to admit.

Instead of languishing in his shortcomings the way Dad had always done, Carson came up with a plan that would spare him from doing either. It was why he came to the farm, why he was pandering to his manipulative grandmother and avoiding his self-righteous cousin. Before long he wouldn't have to work hard or smart, and it would pay off big time.

He touched the weight of the ruby ring in his pocket. He was confident it wouldn't be missed from the jewelry armoire for a long time, if ever. The only jewelry Clarice wore these days were the pearl necklace her mother gave her and a gold cross from Warner.

If anyone noticed the missing ring, it would be Melody. Carson would renew his efforts to steer clear of her. He couldn't risk alienating Clarice at this point in the game. He had been going above and beyond the call to prove himself indispensable to her and the farm. He couldn't have Melody messing that up. He had already burned his bridges in Texas; this was all he had left.

CHAPTER SIX

Mountains of grimy snow lined both sides of Jenna's Creek's main thoroughfares, bottle-necking traffic into two narrow lanes and making street parking impossible. Those who did manage to find a parking spot on the street between snow banks were forced to walk to the nearest alley or intersection to get from the street to the sidewalk. A few brave—or perhaps reckless—souls climbed over the mountains of snow and slid down the other side to the sidewalk, receiving catcalls and honks of admiration for their efforts.

Friday was the first day back in operation for most of the county offices as well as the Janelle C. Wyatt Memorial Library. Mrs. Gardner, the library's director and Christy Blackwood's boss, had called last night to warn her city parking lots had become depositories for excess snow, including the one behind the library. If she wanted a place to park she better get to work early. Christy arrived twenty minutes before the library opened and considered herself lucky to snag one of the last remaining spots. Surprisingly, considering the headache of navigating the streets, library business was brisk. She supposed Jenna's Creek's residents were as sick with cabin fever as she was.

She didn't get a chance to take her lunch break until one o'clock. Instead of staying inside the warm library and listening to patrons hair-raising tales of how they survived the first week of the Great Blizzard of '78, she pulled on her coat and gloves and turned up her collar to prepare for the two-block walk to the courthouse. The last thing she wanted to do on a blustery February afternoon was run an errand, especially when she had to walk due to the unlikelihood her parking space would be there when she got back, and the even greater unlikelihood she'd find a spot on Main Street.

Outside Christy leaned into the bitter wind and picked her way down the street and across the icy intersection to the courthouse. The stone sidewalk and steps had been liberally salted, but she exercised caution nonetheless. According to library policy, female employees wore skirts, regardless of weather. Besides risk of bodily harm she didn't to fall and display the cut-off thermal underwear she wore under her wool skirt to half the town.

The first floor hallway of the county courthouse was packed. Missing five business days had put every office woefully behind schedule. Nearly every resident in the county seemed to have business of some sort at the courthouse. Christy maneuvered through the throng who had apparently used their lunch hours for the same purpose as she. Tax bills went out to every property owner in the county the same week. Abby had given Christy her check for the first half of the annual tax bill with instructions to pay it today no matter what. She wouldn't risk the check arriving a day late if mail was backed up and seeing her name in the local paper for a negligent tax bill. Christy was pretty sure even small town newspapers had more worthy topics of interest to print, but Abby wasn't taking any chances.

The narrow space inside the treasurer's office allowed one customer per clerk at the counter that ran the length of the room.

Nearly ten minutes elapsed before Christy made it into the room and parted company with her mother's check. Just as the clerk stamped her half of the receipt and slid it back to her, a pot-bellied farmer in overalls and a flannel cap pushed between her and the counter.

Christy sidestepped the man as best she could. She was nearly double her normal size inside her heavy winter coat. At the door, she bumped into another woman battling the same encumbrances. She had never looked so forward to spring in her life.

Another man who didn't look like he'd gone hungry during the blizzard stood in the doorway waiting his turn. There was no way she could get out of the office as long as he stood there. Certainly he realized the same thing, though he made no effort to move out of her way. It wasn't entirely his fault. People in the hallway had crowded near the door, anxious to pay what they owed the county and be on their way.

The woman behind her finished her transaction and was now waiting for Christy to exit the office.

"I can help you here," a clerk said to the man in the doorway.

Christy squeezed against the doorjamb as the big man pushed past her. He grunted an apology and inhaled as though it would help. She tried to avoid brushing her shoulder against his protruding stomach as she squeezed through the door. Aware of the woman on her heels, she stepped to the side and out of the way as soon as she cleared the threshold. Unfortunately, she didn't see the gray haired man in a polyester suit until she tripped over his foot.

The woman behind her whipped past Christy and toward the exit as Christy stumbled headlong into the arms of another man in a tan trench coat, brown trousers, and wing-tipped shoes.

So much for her dignity. She only hoped no one saw her thermal underwear.

Her purse flew out of her hands. She hadn't zipped it shut after stuffing the tax receipt and checkbook inside, and its contents clattered to the floor around the feet of the man she had practically accosted.

Aware of an abrupt hush in conversation and the flaming heat that undoubtedly painted her face a bright crimson, she dropped to her knees to gather her things with as much decorum as the situation allowed. She took a mental inventory as she worked feverishly to return everything to the depths of her purse. Per the current style, her bag was large enough to stow a small child so she carried too much stuff everywhere she went. She could only hope nothing more embarrassing than a compact or nearly empty wallet had flown out and was on display on the polished courthouse floor.

The brown shoes turned toward her, and the tail of the tan trench brushed the floor as the wearer knelt beside her.

Just keep walking, Wingtips, she silently begged. The last thing she wanted was a pretentious prosecuting attorney or county auditor looking down his elected nose at her clumsiness.

"Everyone's in a hurry today," a male voice that sounded vaguely familiar said in her ear. She could tell he was smiling. Laughing at her, no doubt.

"Thanks, but I've got it." She reached for a crumpled tissue she prayed was clean and brushed the back of his hand with her knuckles. As soon as she made contact, a spark of electricity passed from her hand to his. "Oh," she cried and jerked her hand away.

Laughter rumbled in the man's throat.

"I am so sorry." Christy's gaze traveled up the man's wrist to his arm, his shoulder, and finally his face. Her nose was mere inches from his. A relatively nice nose as noses went, perfectly suited for the owner's angular face and square jaw. An easy smile exposed a set of gleaming teeth, and lively brown eyes regarded her from under a thatch of dark brown hair.

Though he bore no physical resemblance, Christy immediately thought of Sean.

She had met Sean Hatcher when she literally plowed into him on her way out of a deli near her law office in Columbus. Like today, she had been in a hurry and wasn't watching where she was going when she collided into the best looking creature she'd seen in a long time. She hadn't known at the time Sean orchestrated the whole event as a way to meet her. It would've been flattering had he not only been interested in using her to break into her company's file room.

The man in front of her now grinned as recognition registered on his face. At the same instant, she recognized him. He handed her two ink pens, a paper clip, and an old envelope she'd used to jot down the directions to a coworker's house after she was invited to a Christmas party. She really needed to clean out her purse. The envelope had been in there for weeks, and she hadn't even gone to the party. She stuffed the items into her purse, zipped it shut, and sat back on her heels.

"Believe it or not, this does not happen to me every time I go out in public."

He laughed again. Christy couldn't help but notice how good he looked when he did so. "Nor do I lurk around corners waiting for unsuspecting women to step in front of me so I can knock them to the ground, even though it must look that way."

"I was beginning to wonder."

Jarrod Bruckner stood up and held out his hand. Christy hesitated only a moment, feeling every eye in the hallway on them, before she took it. "Sorry about that," she mumbled once she was on her feet.

"No need to apologize. I'm only glad I was here to catch you."

"So am I. If you hadn't been, I would've plowed headfirst into that wall."

The large man exited the treasurer's office and slowed down long enough to give them a disparagingly look for blocking the hallway. Christy and Jarrod watched him go and burst out laughing.

"I am really sorry, Jarrod," she said. "I need to learn to watch where I'm going, especially when I'm in a hurry."

"At least you didn't yell at me this time."

Christy winced. She had hoped he forgot the time she collided with him on the sidewalk in front of Wyatt's Drugstore. Close contact with a man so soon after being robbed in a hotel room in Kentucky had caused her to overreact. She had screamed like a crazy woman and cried her eyes out as soon as she got in the car.

Amazingly enough, Jarrod hadn't avoided her after that. He even asked her out. She declined, still gun shy around men. She hadn't seen him or heard from him since.

"I wish you didn't have such a good memory," she said.

"Things like that tend to stand out in a man's mind."

She couldn't tell if he was serious until she saw the playful gleam in his eyes. "So what brings you out in this weather?" he asked.

"I had to pay my mother's taxes." She motioned over her shoulder to the treasurer's office.

"That explains the long lines."

"With the blizzard and all…"

"Government offices are backed up," he finished.

Christy searched her mind for something else to say. Blast her pale skin. It was always a dead giveaway for her feelings. It flushed at the slightest provocation, letting the world know when she was angry, anxious, or just plain embarrassed for trying to knock down an incredibly handsome man—for the second time.

"You're not paying taxes, are you?"

He shook his head and lifted his briefcase. "I have a case upstairs..." He pulled back his sleeve to look at his watch. His eyes widened. "...in five minutes."

"I just keep causing you problems, don't I? I need to get back to work myself."

"Are you still at the library?"

She was flattered he remembered where she worked until she realized she had no reason to be. How could he forget the woman who nearly put him on disability every time they met?

"I'm on my lunch break. I just came over to..." Her voice trailed off as she realized what she was doing.

"Pay your mother's taxes?" He pursed his lips together to contain a grin.

"Yes," she admitted as heat once again crept into her face. Why was she so pathetic? He was just a guy. She talked to men every day. She used to work in an office full of the most self-important group of them on the planet, and she had handled herself just fine. But around this one she reverted to her tongue-tied, seventh grade days.

Jarrod paused as if deciding to say something more. Could he possibly be as nervous as she was? Finally he took a deep breath. "Okay, then, I'll let you get back to work." He started toward the stairwell but immediately turned back. "It was nice bumping into you again, Christy."

"Nice bumping into you, too, Jarrod," she quipped with a grin. Immediately, she wished she hadn't. She needed to turn around and leave if she hoped to maintain the façade that male companionship was something she could easily live without.

"Listen, Christy, do you think..." He looked at his watch and back at the stairwell.

"You should go. I don't want to get you in trouble. Judges generally don't have a sense of humor when someone keeps them waiting."

His eyebrows slid together.

"At least they don't seem to," she added quickly. She needed to stop talking before she put her foot completely in her mouth. No one in Jenna's Creek needed to know she had once worked for one of Ohio's most prestigious law firms, least of all a young attorney who would wonder why she wasn't still climbing the corporate ladder.

He reached inside his suit coat pocket and pulled out a business card. "Could I give you a call sometime? For dinner or something."

Christy stared transfixed at the business card while he fumbled in another pocket for a pen. He smiled at her hesitation. "You can reserve the right to say no. Or give me a phony number if you're worried about offending me."

She smiled in spite of herself, amazed that his infectious smile had such an effect on her. She barely knew him. Where was her customary reticence with men? He represented half the human race she had sworn off. But something about him made her lower her guard. That couldn't be good. She was the last person whose judgment she could trust.

She took the offered pen and card and scrawled Mom's number on the back. "Don't worry, I'm not afraid of offending you."

"That's good. I think." He gave the card a quick glance before shoving it, along with the pen, back in his breast pocket. "I'll be in touch."

"I look forward to it," she said easily, surprised that she actually meant it.

"Great." He gave his watch one last look. "I really have to go. Talk to you later." He spun around and hurried down the hallway.

Christy turned and headed in the opposite direction toward the side entrance. It took all the self-control inside her not to look over her shoulder to see if he was looking back to see if she was looking back at him.

She thought again of Sean, the man who had broken her heart and stolen her dignity and her trust—not to mention her career, future, and all her money. Sean's smile had been as genuine as Jarrod's. She had fallen for every velvet word out of his mouth. Was she doing the same thing again? She didn't want to get hurt. She didn't want to fall prey to another man's games designed to use her and discard her once he finished. Nor did she want to spend the remaining ten thousand Saturday nights of her life alone in her mother's house. Not all successful good-looking men were like Sean, she told herself. Surely there were at least one or two trustworthy ones left. Maybe Jarrod Bruckner was one of them.

She'd never know if she didn't say yes when he called to ask her out. If he called.

She zipped her coat against the arctic temperatures outside and stuffed her hands into her gloves. What was she thinking? She didn't need a man in her life. She was a modern woman—independent, self-sufficient, totally content to breeze through life without someone opening doors and holding umbrellas for her. She'd been telling herself that the last year and a half. But looking into Jarrod Bruckner's eyes made it easy to forget the feminist ideals on which she based her life.

She really hoped he'd call. As long as he didn't ask what she'd been doing during the five years between college and moving home to Jenna's Creek.

CHAPTER SEVEN

Melody dropped a freshly peeled potato into the colander and looked over her shoulder at her mother. "Why am I peeling so many potatoes? I know the Sheltons are farm people, but you have enough here to feed an army."

Judy gave the ham a satisfied pat with a potholder before backing away from the oven and closing the door. "I thought since we invited the Sheltons to dinner to thank Tim for his help last week, we'd make it a party. I invited your uncle Lowell, and Carson too."

Melody didn't try to suppress the groan on her lips. "Mom, you didn't."

Judy shot her a scathing look. "Why wouldn't I? This blizzard is wearing on everyone's nerves. We've been cooped up on this hill for eight days. It'll do all of us good to see some new faces. You know how Lowell loves to eat."

Melody gritted her teeth. "Especially when someone else is doing the work."

"Melody Knauff. Where's your compassion?"

"I have plenty of compassion, when someone deserves it."

"I don't think that's how compassion works."

From the look on Judy's face, Melody could see she was going too far again. She needed to pull back on the sarcasm, regardless of her personal opinions. She'd never been turned over her mother's knee, but after eight days trapped in close quarters without so much as a phone call to the outside, it wouldn't take much to snap what remained of Mom's maternal restraint. She palmed another potato and went after it with the knife. "I was looking forward to a peaceful evening with the Sheltons," she said as diplomatically as she could manage. "Now I'll have to watch every word I say."

Judy snorted. "That'll be a first."

Melody chose to change the subject rather than respond to the slight. "Are Grandma and Uncle Jay coming?"

"Your grandma doesn't feel like getting out in the weather so Jay's staying home with her." Judy carried a pan to the sink and drained the boiling water off a dozen eggs into the empty side. "I thought about hosting the dinner at the farm so Mom could participate, but that would be inconvenient for the Sheltons. Our house is already a big enough hike through six-foot snowdrifts for them without adding another quarter mile."

Melody diced the potato and dropped the pieces into the colander.

Judy set the pan of eggs in the sink and looked at Melody. "You could show your uncles and cousin a little appreciation, you know. If it weren't for them, Mom would be all alone in the house thinking about Pop."

"She wouldn't be alone. She would come here and stay with us."

Judy turned on the water over the eggs. "And do what? Mom loves having her boys with her. It gives her a purpose."

Melody's frustration bubbled over. "Don't you see they're using her? They're freeloaders."

Judy didn't answer right away. Melody knew she should shut up, but sometimes people needed a dose of the truth.

Judy began peeling shells off the eggs. "You can be so much like Pop."

"I take that as a compliment."

"It wasn't meant as one. Pop was very opinionated. So much so he alienated the people he loved. He expected everyone to see the world his way. You're just like him in that regard. You see your uncles and Carson as taking advantage of Mom while she sees them as lifesavers. If they weren't there she'd be fretting over Pop in the summer kitchen, worried to death animals would get to him or the ambulance will never get up the hill. With them there, she can stay in her own home where she's comfortable. They're keeping her mind off what she isn't ready to think about. She's in poor health, Melody. She shouldn't have to handle this alone. I have to admit I'd worry more if it were only Carson or Lowell with her. They're not exactly caregivers. But Jay's there to make sure she takes her medicine and eats enough."

She had a point, though just barely. Melody thought of all the other things Jay couldn't be depended upon to do, like obeying the law.

Judy turned from her eggs and pierced Melody with a stern gaze. "I've given your less-than-generous attitude toward your uncles and Carson a pass during this blizzard. It's been a stressful week for all of us. I know the county offices opened back up today, and you're upset because you can't get there."

Melody ground her teeth as she sent a glaring glance out the window. "If someone doesn't get up here soon with a snowplow, I might strap tennis rackets to my feet and try snowshoeing."

"While we're waiting..." Judy said, enunciating the last word. "...I expect you to put on your most gracious smile tonight and treat Lowell and Carson as well as you would any other guest in our home."

Melody exhaled, partly in defeat and partly because her mother was right. Whatever had happened the night Grandpa died, she needed to stop working out conspiracy theories in her mind. Though the county offices were now open, it looked like it would be at least another week before she was behind her desk again. Experience had proven families stranded together for extended periods of time dealt with increased stress and the volatile situations it caused. If she had to worry, she should worry about some of her clients who had real problems.

She thought about the Thompson girls stuck in a house with an abusive father and a mother who looked the other way. She remembered the black eye Betty Carmichael wore the last time she came into the office, insisting yet again, she had stumbled into a cabinet door. She remembered how little Jimmy Stephenson had flinched when his mother reached across the desk to take a file folder from Melody.

There were plenty of people in the county with real issues who were counting on her to do her job. She headed to the back porch to throw the onion and potato peelings into the bucket Dad would take out to the pigs after dinner. She would keep her dislike and distrust toward Lowell and Carson to herself. Knowing those two, they would give the Sheltons plenty of material to form their own opinions without her saying a word.

<hr>

"I'm sorry we have to eat in the kitchen," Judy apologized for the tenth time since her guests arrived. "Even with the power back on, the furnace isn't working to capacity. We have to call someone as soon as the roads are clear. Melody and I agreed the dining room was too cold to be comfortable."

"Please don't think a thing of it," Harriet Shelton said from her side of the table. "It's quite cozy in here. There's nothing I like more than a full table. Reminds me of when the children were at home." She gazed affectionately at Tim.

Melody smiled to herself. Tim Shelton was at least in his fifties. Enduring a nasty divorce and committing career suicide over an old girlfriend had driven him back to his family's table.

She was amazed Mrs. Shelton could remember when he had been an innocent young boy.

"I thought about having Pete move the dining room table into the living room next to the fireplace," Judy continued. "But it was so much trouble. He didn't think it would fit anyway. The kitchen is quite warm with the oven on all morning."

"Yes, dear, it's fine," Pete said with a slight edge in his voice. He gave Judy a measured look to tell her she'd apologized enough for something outside her control. "No one cares if the chairs don't match as long as the food's good. And everything's delicious."

Murmurs of assent echoed around the table. Judy ducked her head as if to apologize for excessive apologies.

"You did an excellent job with the ham, Sis," Lowell said around a forkful of food. "I was getting mighty tired of Jay's stews."

Melody wanted to ask why he didn't get off his backside and cook something himself if he was so tired of Jay's cooking. One look at Mom's warning glance reminded her of her vow to keep her mouth shut. She turned her attention back to her plate.

Judy turned to Harriet. "Melody and I have been reminiscing about past snowstorms. We've never seen anything like this though. I remember one winter when she didn't have school for a solid week. I finally couldn't take it anymore and sent her up the hill to drive Pop crazy." She bit her lip and glanced at Melody as the realization of her words hit her.

Tears stung Melody's eyes. She wondered if she'd ever get it through her head Grandpa was gone and not coming back.

Pete was the first to break the somber silence. "It looks like it'll be a lot longer this time around before school's back in session. This is probably new to you, Carson. I bet you never had a snow day when you were growing up in Texas."

Carson shook his head. "I remember missing school a few times in late summer because of the heat. Most of the buildings had air conditioning, but occasionally the cooling systems couldn't keep up with demand."

"The only air conditioning we had in school were the paper fans we used to make," Tim said.

Everyone except Carson smiled and nodded, remembering.

Melody chuckled. "All that rustling drove the teacher crazy. She tried to tell us we'd be cooler if we sat still, but we didn't believe her enough to try it."

Lowell sat forward in his chair. "Pass me more of those potatoes, Pete. I could eat cooking like this all day."

Pete laughed as he handed the bowl across Melody's plate. "You sure have a healthy appetite for somebody so skinny."

Lowell scooped several spoonfuls onto his plate. "If I ate like this every meal, I'd fatten up quick enough. You should invite us to dinner more often, Judy. Or maybe Carson and me will move down here for the duration of the winter."

Melody reached for her mother's ankle under the table. Her foot connected harder than she intended with what she hoped was a table leg. Tim's knee banged the bottom of the table. Silverware clanked and water sloshed out of his glass.

"Are you all right, son?" Dale asked him.

Tim grimaced and leaned forward to rub his ankle. "Yeah, sure."

Heat rushed into Melody's face. She shot Tim an apologetic glance before focusing on her plate. She could feel Carson and Mom's eyes on her from their positions around the table. Lowell barely glanced up from his potatoes.

"I'm afraid we don't have room for houseguests with most of the upstairs closed off to conserve heat," Pete told him.

Melody shot Dad an appreciative glance.

"You're welcome to come down for dinner anytime you like," Judy added pointedly. "That goes for all our neighbors. We have plenty."

Melody knew if Lowell pushed the issue Mom would find a way to squeeze a bed for him into the living room in front of the fireplace. Dinner a few times a week was bad enough. Fortunately, he was too lazy to walk down the hill very often, regardless of the quality of the food.

"Anything at all our family can do for yours, you just ask," Harriet returned.

"You've already done enough," Judy said as she refilled Lowell's coffee cup. "I don't know what we'd have done without Tim's help those first few days."

Tim swabbed at his gravy with a crust of bread. "Don't even mention it. I bet you miss the warm weather, Carson. I don't imagine they have blizzards like this in Texas."

Melody exhaled in relief that the conversation had steered away from Lowell's sleeping arrangements.

Carson shook his head. "I've seen a few blue northers, but nothing like this."

Dale put down his fork and folded his hands in front of his plate. "Where are you from in Texas?"

"Houston."

"Harriet and I went to San Antonio a few years ago when our nephew graduated from the Air Force. It's a beautiful city."

"I've never been."

"Really?"

"I never had a reason to go. It's a couple hundred miles from home."

Dale picked up his fork and speared a cooked carrot. "Oh. I'm afraid most of us keep forgetting how big Texas is."

Carson rewarded him with a faint smile.

"So what do you do?" Dale probed. "In Houston, I mean."

Melody stopped eating. She had wondered the same thing, but so far no one had been able to pin Carson down with a straight answer.

"I worked for my stepdad."

Dale rested an elbow on the table. "What business is he in?"

"Sanitation."

Lowell jerked his head up from where he'd been grazing. "Amy married a garbage man." He hooted in laughter at the joke toward his ex-wife only he got.

The rest of the table waited politely until his guffaws died away. "Perfectly respectable trade," Dale said to Carson. "I assume there's money in it."

Carson gave a slight nod. "Milt wouldn't be in it if there wasn't. His company owns eighty trucks and has corporate contracts all over the city."

Lowell gloomily turned his attention back to his plate.

"Do you mind if I ask what brought you to Ohio?" Dale asked.

Melody waited. She was heartened to see everyone else at the table, except for Lowell, was following the conversation as closely as she was.

Carson lifted one shoulder. "Mom thought it would be a good idea for me to get to know Dad's side of the family."

Dale considered the vague answer. He seemed ready to ask for more but thought better of it.

"Have you heard when the milk trucks might make it up the hill?" Pete asked Dale when it became clear Carson wasn't going to expound on his answer.

"According to the radio, the trucks are making progress in reaching some of the minor highways. Rationing of milk and eggs and other perishables is happening all over the state. If conditions last much longer, it'll be hard for a small operation like ours to recover."

"This morning they reported this part of the state got thirty-two inches of snow in January. We're on pace to break the record for the snowiest winter on record."

Everyone except Melody shook their heads in wonder at Pete's news. She wasn't interested in snowfall amounts or the effects of the blizzard on business. Pete listened to enough of the doomsday declarations on the radio every day. She wanted to know what was going on with Carson.

She opened her mouth to speak, but Tim was faster. "I'd say we got more than thirty-two inches here on the hill. There has to be at least three feet on the ground right now."

Dale nodded in agreement. "It's impossible to get an accurate measurement with all the drifting. I've tried."

"I've taken plenty of pictures," Judy said from her end of the table. "I just hope I can get off this hill to get them developed before spring."

Harriet Shelton faked a shudder and laughed. "Don't even suggest it. We've only been stranded for eight days but it feels like eight months."

Judy smiled back. "It won't hurt my feelings if it doesn't snow another flake the rest of the year."

Pete wagged a finger at her. "Snow's in the forecast for the weekend."

She gave him a mocking glare. "I'm going to throw your radio into a snow bank."

Everyone laughed again. Melody waited a moment for manners' sake before turning her attention to Carson. "Your stepdad's business sounds like quite a successful operation." She ignored the glares from Mom and Uncle Lowell. "You've been here for seven months. I'm surprised he doesn't have a position down there waiting for you."

"Nothing I'm interested in."

Melody ignored the scowl her mother directed at her. "He must have management opportunities available. You won't find anything better in Jenna's Creek."

"I'm not really looking for anything right now."

"Why? What are you? Thirty? What're you waiting for?"

A muscle twitched in Carson's jaw. "I'm twenty-eight as I'm sure you already know."

"Melody," Judy jumped in, her voice a little higher than usual. "Could you get some rolls off the stove?"

Melody motioned to the breadbasket. "There's plenty left." She turned back to Carson.

"I'd really like some fresh ones, honey."

Mother and daughter exchanged a long glance before Melody grabbed the basket and stomped to the stove where a hot towel covered another batch of rolls.

Judy set her coffee cup into the saucer with a clink and turned to the senior Sheltons. "I'm sure you remember the Blizzard of '53. We never thought we'd see another one like it."

Melody set the basket on the table next to her mother's plate with a thud before returning to her chair.

Harriet nodded. "We were stuck on the hill for weeks then, too. Weren't as many families up here in those days."

"It sure was lonely," Judy agreed. "Melody was two-months-old. She had the worst case of colic. Remember that, Pete?"

"I don't see how I could forget it. You never saw a more nervous mother," he told the rest of the table while he smiled affectionately at Judy. "Anything possible that could go wrong she was sure would happen to our little girl. Melody got really sick that week. Wouldn't eat. Kept us up all night. As soon as Warner caught wind of what was happening, he set off on foot over the hill to that little market Dean Schapp used to run at the Old State Route 150-Elmville intersection. Remember that store? Warner insisted some Karo syrup in warm water would settle whatever ailed our little girl and get her eating again."

Judy gaze lingered on Melody for a long moment before she looked back at the others. Tears sparkled in her eyes. "Pop would do anything for his Nugget. That's what he called Melody. She was born with a cap of red gold hair. He took one look at her and said she looked like a golden nugget. His little treasure, he called her."

She dabbed the end of her nose with her napkin. Melody reached for her water glass with shaking hands and took a sip.

"Dean Schapp hadn't opened the store that day," Pete continued. "He said nobody had been by in days so there was no point in him lighting the coal oil furnace. Warner walked the quarter-mile past the store to Schapp's house and wouldn't give the man a minute's peace until he agreed to walk back through the snow to open the store and sell him a bottle of syrup."

Judy reached across the table and squeezed Melody's hand. "Pop sure loved his Nugget."

Under normal circumstances, Melody would've been embarrassed by the story she'd heard a thousand times, especially with people from outside the family watching from the other side of the table. This time, she enjoyed the bittersweet memory of Grandpa.

"I never knew why he called you Nugget," Carson said.

Lowell glowered from his seat next to Carson. "Well, now you know. The sun rose and set on Melody." He spat out her name, along with a few specks of ham. "Pop didn't give a rat's behind about you other kids, but he bent over backwards where his little Nugget was concerned."

"Lowell," Judy hissed in the sudden silence.

Lowell's chair scraped against the linoleum as he scooted out his chair. "Pop had his favorites and didn't give a flip about the rest of us. Worked out pretty good if you were one of the chosen few. Huh, Judy?"

"Now isn't the time for this." Pete's voice was quiet but firm.

"Maybe not, but it'll work out the same when we see who ends up with what." He cuffed Carson on the shoulder. "It's a good thing for you, boy, that Pop went first. Since Mom's in charge of the estate your grandpa schemed his way into, you might end up with a few crumbs from the master's table after all."

"Lowell," Judy cried.

Melody bristled. "What are you talking about? Grandpa never schemed his way into anything."

Lowell gave her a wide-eyed look, then barked out a laugh. "You honestly don't know, do you? Ask your daddy someday why your great-aunts live in that shabby old house in town instead of on the farm. It was as much their birthright as it was Mom's."

Dale and Harriet exchanged glances and became fascinated with the pattern of the table linens. Tim sawed at a miniscule spot of gristle on his ham. Carson's eyes flitted around the table, his expression mirroring Melody's interest. Judy avoided eye contact with everyone.

Melody's cheeks burned. She wanted to demand someone tell her what Lowell was talking about. At the same time, she didn't want him to think she was giving his accusation any credence.

Pete set his hands on either side of his plate as if to rise. "Lowell, you can't talk to Melody that way, especially in light of what's happened in the last week. She and Judy went to a lot of trouble preparing this meal for you and our neighbors. Show them a little respect. Not to mention the respect due your father."

"Respect? You mean by covering up the truth the way this family's always done?" Lowell jabbed his finger in Melody's direction. "That girl should know what her granddaddy really was. A liar and a cheat and a thief."

Melody and Judy gasped simultaneously.

"My grandpa never lied or cheated or stole a thing in his life," Melody said between clenched teeth as soon as she found her voice.

Lowell rocked back on his heels. A smile exposed tobacco-stained teeth. His pale eyes glistened. "You've certainly led a sheltered life, girl. You really need to bring her up to speed, Pete. Tell her why Pop left Springfield. Tell her about the fire that burned away all the evidence." He looked back at Melody. "The whole thing was mighty convenient if you ask me."

Pete lunged to his feet and towered over the smaller man. "Nobody did ask you, Lowell. One more word and I'll throw you out of here myself."

Judy jumped up. The front of her legs smacked the table. Coffee sloshed over the rim of her cup and seeped into the tablecloth. "Pete. Lowell. We're having such a lovely dinner. Don't spoil it."

Lowell straightened his shoulders and puffed out his bony chest. "It wasn't me that spoiled anything, Judy. I just thought your girl deserved to hear the truth. Get your coat, Carson. We're leaving."

Judy looked desperately at her husband. "Pete, tell them to stay. We haven't had dessert yet."

Lowell glanced toward the countertop where two Dutch apple pies awaited slicing. His mouth practically watered at the sight of the golden brown crumb topping. His inner struggle visible to everyone, he dragged his gaze back to the table.

"I've been a second-class citizen in this family my whole life. I don't know why since I ain't done half the things Pop did. I stopped trying to please him when I realized it was never going to happen. I'm sure none of you good people know what it's like, but it feels lousy. Carson, if Pop had lasted a little longer, you would've seen you couldn't please him either. The rest of you might be all tore up he's gone, but you won't see me shedding any tears."

"It's time for you to go, Lowell," Pete said.

"Don't worry, I'm going. Come on, Carson."

Judy grabbed hold of Carson's sleeve. "You go if you want, Lowell. Carson can stay and have pie."

Lowell went to the counter and picked up the better looking of the two pies. "We'll take this one with us. I'll return your plate tomorrow or you can send Melody up to get it."

Carson sighed and pushed his chair away from the table. "Thanks for dinner, Judy. Pete." He nodded at the others and followed Lowell into the mudroom to begin the process of bundling up against the cold.

CHAPTER EIGHT

Melody didn't know what to think. Nine days trapped on the hill were making her stir crazy, especially with Lowell's words rattling around in her head. She had always thought of him as a lazy little man. Someone barely worth her notice. She had wondered over the years how he could have come from someone strong like Warner Beckwith, and how he could have a compassionate, giving sister like her mother. But after what he said last night at dinner she wondered if she had known Grandpa as well as she thought she had.

After the Sheltons left, her parents didn't say a word about Lowell's accusations. Typical. Pretend an uncomfortable situation never happened. Only because Mom had been through so much already and Lowell's words had definitely rattled her, Melody didn't push the matter. She was almost afraid of what they might say.

Still, she couldn't get the accusations out of her head. Her first impulse this morning was to march up the hill and demand Lowell finish what he started. He couldn't open his mouth like that and not explain himself. How dare he say Grandpa deserved what he got? Even if he didn't care about his own father, he should have enough respect for Mom not to say such a thing in her house at her table with company sitting right there.

If Mom wouldn't defend herself, Melody would.

At the same time she couldn't stop thinking of a few things that gave credence to Lowell's words. Grandpa never talked about his life before getting hired as a field hand and falling in love with the farmer's youngest daughter. He didn't share early childhood memories or family history. For all Melody knew, Warner Beckwith had dropped out of the sky and landed on Earl Salinski's doorstep.

Though he was never specific about how he ended up in Auburn County, he was never bashful about telling her how he fell in love with Grandma the moment he saw her. His eyes shone when he talked about those early years as a married man. The things that gave him the most pride were the soil and the farm and an exceptional crop of cattle. He wasn't shy about sharing his love for the Lord. According to Mom and Grandma, his faith hadn't always been a part of his life. Melody only knew the born again version

She couldn't, and would never believe, he had burned down a store. The idea was insane. The rest of Lowell's accusations weren't as easy to dismiss.

Melody had always known Grandpa had some sort of falling out with his oldest daughter Linda. She never thought to ask for details. She knew instinctively no one would give complete answers if she did. Linda and Hart's children came to visit the farm on the occasional summer. Melody was always happy to have company her own age, especially a girl cousin. Ellen was two years older, but still close enough in age they found things to do together during those visits. One year Melody asked Ellen why she didn't come every summer. Ellen looked at her like she had sprouted another head and didn't answer.

At the end of the visit, Uncle Allen and Aunt Bonnie loaded Ellen and her two brothers into the car for the drive back to Indianapolis. Melody asked Mom why Linda and Hart never came with the kids and why Allen and Bonnie were the ones to drive them home every year. Mom put an arm around her shoulders and told her some things weren't worth worrying over, especially things that couldn't be changed.

It wasn't only the strange situation between Grandpa and Linda that bothered Melody. She couldn't understand why the rest of the family didn't think he was the most fascinating person alive and didn't want to spend every waking minute with him like she did. Sometimes she wished she could make them see the Grandpa who cried at the sight of a new calf jostling its mother for its first meal. Or the way his gravelly tenor voice rang out in church as if he were singing right outside heaven's gate. Or the way he would slap her shoulder and laugh at his own jokes, especially the ones that weren't very funny.

It was a shame they never met the grandfather she knew and loved. Now that she thought about it, shouldn't the responsibility rest on his shoulders? Why hadn't he tried harder to show that side of himself to anyone but her?

Then there was the matter of the aunts. Another family anomaly Melody never took the time to ponder. She always assumed Grandma's sisters wanted to live in town. Naomi and Alma were older than Grandma, who had been the spoiled one of the family. They seldom came around. When they did on the occasional Christmas or Thanksgiving, they pretty much kept to themselves. Melody attributed their behavior to temperament, though they were both schoolteachers, a profession that typically required an outgoing personality. Both were retired now. Neither had ever married. Another thing Melody never thought about before now. All their adult lives, they had lived together in a two-story Colonial in the middle of Jenna's Creek, a block down from the elementary school. Alma was a leader in their local teachers' union and had become the first female member of the school board. Naomi wrote poems and songs. Her articles often appeared in educational publications. Other than that, Melody barely knew them.

It never occurred to her until the moment Lowell brought it up to question why Grandma inherited the house and not her sisters. She had assumed Grandma bought their shares, and the situation pleased all three sisters. Maybe it hadn't happened that way at all.

Judy came into the kitchen with a basket of dirty laundry. Because of the power outage, the family was behind on laundry, and she had been washing and drying all day. She smiled distractedly on her way through to the utility room.

Melody followed her to the doorway. "Why don't the aunts come out here to visit?"

Judy plunked the basket onto the floor. Without turning around, she began sorting whites into the machine. "We're in the middle of a blizzard in case you forgot."

She straightened and twisted the dial on the back of the machine. Melody raised her voice to be heard over the sudden rush of water. "I don't mean now. I mean all the time. They don't come here and we never go there."

Judy shook her head as she pushed through the doorway, forcing Melody to backpedal into the kitchen. "Everybody's busy."

Melody leaned against the counter within her mother's field of vision. She wasn't going to settle for half answers today. "That's not true, Mom. We make time for family. You say so all the time."

Judy took a pan from the cabinet and set it on the counter. "Why are we talking about the aunts? Is this about what Lowell said last night?"

Melody thought about playing it cool in hopes of getting uncensored information, but she knew it wouldn't work. If she wanted Mom to be honest with her, she needed to be transparent. "What did he mean about Grandpa scheming his way into the farm? I thought Grandpa Salinski left it to him and Grandma in the will."

She saw her mother take a deep breath as if deciding how much she wanted to get into this conversation. Apparently not a lot.

"You know Lowell," Judy said dismissively. "He shoots off his mouth every time he gets mad. Go into the pantry and get me two jars of green beans, will you?"

Melody straightened but remained where she was. "But why was he mad? Maybe I was Grandpa's favorite, but how does that mean he cheated the aunts out of their inheritance? I don't understand any of it."

Judy headed to the refrigerator as if she hadn't heard. "I need those green beans. Your father will be in shortly, and he'll be expecting his dinner."

Melody gritted her teeth for a moment before turning to fulfill her mother's request. It wouldn't do any good to make her mad. If she wanted answers, she needed to keep Mom talking. Within moments she returned with two jars of green beans they had canned last summer. Every year they put up green beans, corn, squash, and other vegetables for their own house and the farm. The two families shared the garden work and produce, though Melody and Judy did most of the work. Clarice spent most of those days in a kitchen chair with a glass of tea, regaling them with stories of growing up with the aunts. Melody always suspected, even back then, Clarice did more of the talking while Naomi and Alma did more of the working.

"What did Uncle Lowell mean about the aunts losing their share of the inheritance?" she asked as she reached for the can opener to pry the lids off the canning jars.

Judy peeled three slices of bacon off the pound and dropped them into the pan. She adjusted the heat to Low and turned to Melody. "The aunts didn't want to live on the farm. They never did. A lot of people don't, you know. They didn't want it. Mom and Dad did, and Grandma and Grandpa Salinski knew it."

Melody studied her face for a few moments. "And…"

"And that's all there was to it. Lowell has spent his whole life looking for the easy way into anything. You know that. Anytime it looks like someone got a better deal than him, he cries foul. He always brings up the farm when he doesn't get his way. Pop was closer to you than any of the other grandkids. I'm sure it's because we lived close and he knew you better than the others. It doesn't mean he loved the other children less."

Melody stared at the green beans for a moment. Grandpa may have favored her more because he had been around to watch every moment of her development. That didn't explain why Aunt Linda wasn't welcome in the house or why the aunts never came to visit. Lowell may cry foul when he didn't get his way, but in this instance, he might have a reason. Still, it wasn't likely she'd get more information out of her mother.

She set the opened jars of beans on the counter where they could be dumped in when Mom had enough bacon grease to her liking. Melody turned to the onion bin and pulled out one to chop and add to the beans and the bacon. Her mind turned to the aunts and their large Colonial in town. She wondered if they ended up there because they preferred it. As far as she knew, they were satisfied with their jobs and the life they had. Or maybe they made the best of an unjust situation. Regardless, she planned to get some answers somewhere.

❧❧❧

Christy Blackwood shuffled through the stack of mail with one hand as she unbuttoned her coat with the other and slid out of it. A despondent sigh escaped her lips. The only mail that came into the house was junk mail and utility bills—utility bills that kept climbing while hers and Abby's paychecks remained the same.

At least they had no debt to speak of. Her parents didn't believe in credit cards, and the house and car were paid off. Her job at the library paid sufficiently for a young woman living in her mother's house in Jenna's Creek, Ohio, but it wasn't enough to get ahead of the bills that kept slipping through the mail slot in the front door.

Moving back to Jenna's Creek was meant to be a temporary solution to a huge problem. Now a year and a half later, she was no closer to moving on than the first morning she woke up in her childhood bed. Sometimes she wondered why she didn't pack up and leave. There was nothing really tying her to this two-bit town. It wasn't as if she couldn't get another low paying, menial job anywhere in the country. She certainly wasn't sticking around for any emotional ties. It would suit her just fine if she never saw this town—this house—again.

Her conscience pricked at her for a moment. What would Mom do if she left? The bills would keep coming. Without Christy in the house, the water bill would go down a few dollars. She'd save some on groceries, but the fuel bill, the electric bill, the phone bill—they would keep coming with relentless regularity.

Christy slapped the pile of mail down on the kitchen table and headed for the refrigerator. None of this was her problem. Her mother wouldn't expect her to put her own life on hold in order to help pay the household bills. Christy certainly couldn't live here forever, even if she wanted to.

Every time she found a stack of bills on the floor inside the front door she thought about getting a part-time job. It would make her escape from the constraints of small town America that much quicker and easier. With her schedule at the library, she could easily wrangle sixteen to twenty additional hours out of the week in which to work. It wasn't like she had a personal life. Her family was too busy with their own lives to entertain her.

A few months ago while helping plan her brother's wedding to Jamie Steele, she had reconnected with Melody Knauff, a friend from high school. Obviously Melody was busy or not interested in pursuing a friendship since Christy hadn't heard from her in weeks. Of course the blizzard might have a lot to do with that.

It wasn't all Melody's responsibility to keep the friendship moving forward. Christy hadn't called her either. It wasn't that she didn't want a friend. She just wondered how much she'd have in common with someone who willingly chose to stay in Jenna's Creek. Any progressively minded woman Christy could relate to had already moved to *Somewhere Else*, the place she desperately wanted to be.

Abby had left a package of hamburger thawing in the refrigerator. Christy set it in the sink. She opened the cabinet door and retrieved the charred skillet that had been in the kitchen longer than she had. Mom needed new pots and pans. Maybe Christy would put a bug in her sisters' and brother's ears before Mother's Day. No fun loving, modern woman wanted pots and pans for Mother's Day, which made them the perfect gift for Abigail Blackwood.

Mother's Day? Christy couldn't look that far down the road. She'd be long gone by then.

She wrinkled her nose at the square of hamburger. She didn't remember any particular instructions about dinner. Not that it mattered. The only thing that sounded good was a nice porterhouse steak, and it didn't look like she'd be enjoying one of those anytime soon. Unless Jarrod Bruckner called and asked her out.

It had been a week since she ran into him at the courthouse, and he still hadn't called. He either lost her number or was hesitant to risk bodily injury in a restaurant with her. She might trip over a chair leg and stab him with a steak knife.

She turned the heat on under the skillet and headed for the pantry. Goulash sounded good. Hot and extra spicy. That's what she needed after stepping into a pothole in the parking lot behind the library and filling her boot with slush. The city streets were downright dismal after the blizzard. If she wasn't scaling drifts as high as one-story buildings, she was losing her car in potholes created by the plows.

Spring seemed like an eternity away.

She heard the front door open. "Honey, I'm home," Abby called out, followed by laughter. She never failed to find humor in the line she said every night Christy beat her home from work.

Christy backed out of the pantry, which was little more than an alcove next to the sink, her arms laden with cans of tomato juice and kidney beans and a box of dry pasta. "In the kitchen, Ma."

Abby entered the room and peered over Christy's shoulder. "I thought we were doing beef stroganoff."

"Oh, I forgot. Besides, it's so nasty outside, goulash sounded better."

Except of course for the porterhouse and Jarrod Bruckner across the table from her.

Abby went to the table and began sifting through the mail as Christy had done a few minutes ago. "Makes no never mind to me what we have. One's as good as the other."

Christy regarded Abby as she filled a pot with water to boil for the pasta.

Abby sank into a kitchen chair and stared at the mail.

"Mom, is everything okay?" Christy couldn't remember anything in the mail that could've been bad news, except there were more bills than money, which shouldn't have surprised anyone.

Without a word, Abby removed an envelope from her purse. Christy recognized it as the kind her paychecks came in. Abby stared thoughtfully at it for a moment before her eyes found Christy's.

She smiled weakly and held up the envelope. "I got a pink slip today."

Christy's heart sank. "Oh, Mom."

Though she knew she should sympathize, all she could think about was how this job loss would delay her move from the house even further.

"I didn't know what a pink slip was," Abby said with a little laugh. "I've heard of them, but it didn't hit me until Mr. Sanders handed me my paycheck. I knew as soon as I saw the look on his face."

Talk of layoffs was making the rounds at nearly every factory in town. Some places laid off while the talk quieted down at others and work started coming in again.

"You didn't suspect it was coming?"

Abby stared again at the envelope. "It's always a possibility with this recession. I try not to worry about things that haven't happened yet. Mr. Sanders called me into his office. He's never done that before. The whole time I was following him in, I kept trying to remember if I'd done anything wrong lately. I felt like a kid in school. My heart was in my throat. Isn't that funny? An old woman like me. I've been a mother for so long I didn't remember what it was like to be the one in trouble."

Christy lowered the heat under the skillet and went to Abby's side. She laid a hand on her shoulder. "You're not old. And, no, there's nothing funny about it."

"After he told me, I almost bawled my eyes out. It's a good thing the office was crowded the rest of the day and I barely had a chance to think. What good would crying do anyway? Mr. Sanders felt terrible. He said it had nothing to do with me. The factory lost over a week of production with the shutdown from the blizzard. We were barely getting by before then. Now with the lost revenue and a few accounts that probably won't come back, he says we have to cut back somewhere. I guess I was the somewhere. The last one hired, as they say. But I'm thankful. If he hadn't got rid of me, he might've laid off a few of the younger women. I'd feel terrible about that, them with families and all."

"You have a family."

Abby shrugged. "Not like them." She managed an encouraging smile. "We'll make do. Your father and I always did. This isn't the first time we had struggles. Mr. Sanders said if things don't change soon, they might have to close the doors forever. Can you imagine what that'll do to Jenna's Creek?"

"I'm having a harder time imagining what it'll do inside this house. You keep talking like you and Dad are still part of a team. You're not. Dad's gone. We're on our own here. It was a miracle you got that accounting job in the first place. Your work experience was practically nonexistent. Who do you think will hire you now?"

"Honey, don't get worked up. You said it yourself. Finding the job at the factory was a miracle. God will provide."

Christy resisted the urge to scream. "I don't think you appreciate how dire the situation is. This recession could go on for years. You're too young to depend on social security and too old to be considered for most of the jobs you're qualified for."

"Thanks a lot."

"I'm just telling you the way it is."

"I told you we mustn't worry about things that haven't happened yet. We'll be fine."

"There won't always be a *we*, Mom. I don't plan on living here forever. Even if I did, my salary at the library is barely enough to keep the lights turned on and food in our stomachs. Forget about clothes or property taxes. You can't have much life insurance money left. What are you going to do when it's gone? How will you survive?"

"Christy, we're not that desperate."

"How desperate are we? You never talk about money except to say we need to be careful with it. You and Dad didn't have much savings. What if someone slipped on the ice out front and sued us? You could develop a health condition that would wipe out whatever savings you have left. Are we going to starve? Is someone at the bank waiting to foreclose and throw us out in the streets like in those sad Christmas movies?"

Abby laughed. "Not quite." She sobered at the look on Christy's face. "We're fine, baby. I'll find something else."

"Where, Mom?"

Abby shrugged. "I don't know. God's never deserted me before. I know he goes before me and his hand is over me."

Christy swallowed a groan of frustration, knowing her mother wouldn't appreciate it. She went back to the stove to see if the water for the pasta was boiling yet. "I don't know how you can be so trusting. God left you without a husband when you were barely in your fifties. What makes you think he'll take care of you now?"

She took an onion out of the bin and began chopping with gusto. She stole a look over her shoulder, expecting Mom to be angry. Instead, her face remained unchanged. "God didn't take Jack from us, Christy. His death was an accident."

"God allowed it to happen. You and Dad lived for him your whole life...well, most of it anyway," she added pointedly.

Abby didn't flinch at the reminder she'd had an affair— an affair Christy had no intention of letting her forget. "God couldn't force the man in the other car to stay home that night. If God took the free will of someone who was about to sin, he would have to do the same to all of us. Would you prefer that?"

"I don't know if I believe what you're saying. You use your faith when it suits you. When something good happens, you say God blessed you. When something bad happens, you fall back on free will. You can't have it both ways, Mom. Either God loves you and measures your steps, or you're on your own. Which is it?"

Abby let out a small sigh, clearly wondering how she'd managed to raise such an irreverent daughter. "God isn't double minded, Christy. I'm sorry if I ever made it sound that way. He is absolute truth. There are no shades of gray. His word hasn't changed and it never will. Neither will my belief that he cares for me and is in charge of the universe and everything in it. Regardless of what happens to me or this family, I will go to my grave having given him complete control of my life."

Christy scraped the onion off the cutting board into the skillet with the hamburger. "I admire your faith, even if I don't know where it comes from. You might want to exercise a little of that faith over the hamburger. It looks like most of it has cooked away."

"God once multiplied two loaves and a few fish to feed a multitude. I suppose that hamburger will stretch as far as we need it."

Christy exhaled through clenched teeth as she began opening cans of juice and beans. "Let's suppose you're right about the hamburger. What about the electric bill or fuel oil for the furnace? Do you think it will last until the snow melts?"

"It might."

Christy turned away from the stove and crossed her arms over her chest. "Okay, have it your way. Let's imagine you have a hundred thousand dollars sitting in the bank and you never have to pay another utility bill. What are you going to do with the rest of your life? You can't sit around this house and wait for the Rapture."

"Why not?"

"Mom, be serious. You're not that old. You have a lot of years ahead of you."

"A minute ago I had one foot in the grave."

"That's not exactly what I said. You might have thirty years left. You don't have a pot of gold lying around and you sure can't wait on Jenna's Creek's job market to improve. What are you going to do? You must have thought a little bit about your future."

For the first time since coming through the door, Abby looked uncertain. "I try not to think about it at all."

Christy set the lid back on the skillet to cover the hamburger and keep it hot until she needed it. She studied the potholder under her hand for a moment. It was shaped like the profile of a Gingham girl with her face covered by a blue and white checked bonnet. She picked it up and turned to face her mother.

"You know…" She glanced at her mother and then back at the potholder.

"What?" Abby's eyes widened in confusion and concern.

A bubble of excitement worked its way into Christy's belly. "You could start your own business."

Abby's jaw dropped. "A business. What are you talking about?"

"This." Christy clenched the potholder and lunged across the kitchen. She dropped into the chair next to Mom. "These."

"Potholders?"

"Yes, Mom. Potholders. All of this. You could start your own sewing business. Or design business. Or something."

Abby looked at the potholder as if she'd never seen it before. "Christy, I honestly don't know what you're talking about."

Christy took a deep breath as she tried to rein in her mounting excitement. "I'm talking about your sewing. Remember when you made these potholders for everyone for Christmas with the matching dishtowels and kitchen curtains?

They were beautiful. Everyone loved them. Even Grandma Blackwood, and she hates everything."

Abby sat back in her chair. "Oh, Christy. That was just for fun. No one in Jenna's Creek would be interested in things like that when you can buy store bought much cheaper."

"You're right. Not everyone would be interested. But there are enough women in this town who want design originals."

"I would have to sell a million to break even."

Christy slapped the potholder onto the table. "Then forget potholders. You've always talked about running your own dress shop. Maybe this is the time to do it. This is the sign you've been waiting for."

Abby patted Christy's hand. "I don't know anything about starting a business and running one. Especially in this economy. Companies are going under in case you haven't noticed, not expanding."

"On the contrary, all the industry moguls started during the worst financial times in history. You have amazing talent when it comes to sewing and tailoring. Look at all the clothes you made us kids."

"Everyone in town makes their own kids' clothes."

Christy went on as if she hadn't spoken. "You've been dreaming about it since I was little. I know you have. You could use Dad's insurance money for capital. It wouldn't have to be much to start with," she added quickly when Abby's upper lip curled in protest. The more she thought about it, the more excited she became. "You would run the place out of the house so there'd be no overhead. I could help you. I know all the legal aspects. My library salary could keep us ahead of the bills as long as we tightened our belts."

Abby was shaking her head before Christy stopped to catch her breath. "I appreciate your faith in me, dear, but I wouldn't know where to begin."

"You begin with what you've been doing most of your life. Only make money at it instead of doing it for free."

"Two minutes ago you were afraid we'd get sued or thrown out on the streets. Now you're talking about opening a business. That's crazy. I don't know what's come over you. I'll find a cashier's job at a grocery store or something."

"Minimum wage to stand on your feet all day? You don't want to do that."

"I will if I have to."

"But you might not have to. You could do something you enjoy here at the house, at least in the beginning. You've got to think about your future. Invest in yourself."

A small smile played across Abby's lips. "It would be better than having a twenty-year-old telling me what to do."

Christy snorted. "You'd put up with that for about five minutes."

"Okay, okay. I'm going upstairs to change into something more comfortable and meditate on my future entrepreneurship. Keep coming up with those ingenious ideas and figure out where the money will come from. And put a little more pasta in the goulash. It might have to go a long way."

Christy went to the drawer to dig out a measuring cup. What was she thinking, encouraging her mother to start a business? The idea was ludicrous. Abby had no experience, and Jenna's Creek wasn't exactly a boomtown.

Worse than that, Christy had offered her own services in the process. She was leaving Jenna's Creek as soon as…well, as soon as she figured out where to go and she had enough money saved to fill up her gas tank.

She needed to get back to living her own life. She had dreams. Dreams of a law career that couldn't be lived in Jenna's Creek. She wanted independence. She couldn't do that if she spent her life worrying about what would happen to her mother after she was gone.

Noel Wyatt flashed through her mind. She wondered if Mom ever thought of him. They had loved each other once. With Noel in her life, she would never worry again about paying bills or if any business she started bombed or succeeded. Of course, Mom would never turn to Noel or any other man to solve her problems. She was on her own. She could believe whatever she wanted, but neither God nor Noel Wyatt could get her out of this fix.

The ringing telephone startled Christy out of her thoughts. "I've got it, Mom," she called as she crossed the room. She wondered if Mom had told anyone else about losing her job. Probably not. Christy doubted she was ready to talk to Karen or anyone else until she had time to figure out what she thought of being unemployed again after working less than a year. She certainly wouldn't want to discuss starting her own business until she had plenty of time to think and pray about it.

Christy expected her sister's voice when she answered the phone.

"Is this Christy?"

Her heart froze in recognition of the man's voice. "Jarrod?" She almost blurted out she'd just been thinking of him but stopped just in time.

"I'm sorry I didn't call sooner," he said. "My schedule's been full, and with the weather so unpredictable, I didn't want to make plans with you only to have to change them."

"It's the same with me," she lied. The unpredictability of the weather seldom affected her schedule, which hadn't changed in over a year.

"I don't mean to make excuses." Did he sound as nervous as she felt? "I just…I'm sorry. Is this a good time?"

"Sure. I was just…" She looked at the Gingham Girl potholder on the table. What had she been doing? "Fixing dinner for Mom and me."

"I guess I was trying to work my nerve up."

What was he talking about? Had she missed something? "Your nerve?"

"Yeah, I've been wanting to call." A pause. And then, "Are you free this weekend? Or anytime really. I thought we could have dinner."

His words trailed off as if he expected a refusal. Could he be as out of practice making dates as she was at receiving them?

"Sure," she cried before she could pretend to check her calendar. "I mean, what night were you thinking of?"

"Um, any night works for me. How about Friday?"

Friday. Three nights away. Christy didn't want to wait that long, but she certainly couldn't suggest they get together tonight. Could she?

"Sure. That sounds great."

"Okay. Around seven?"

Seven o'clock. The butterflies in Christy's stomach went into overdrive. This was definitely a dinner date. "That would be perfect."

"Good. I mean…"

Christy smiled at the phone. She couldn't imagine why he was so nervous, but she loved that he was.

"I'm glad you're not annoyed I hadn't called in so long."

Christy heard her mother coming downstairs. "I'm glad you called now, and I'm looking forward to Friday night."

"Me too. Have a good night, Christy. See you Friday."

Christy hung up and hurried back to the stove to add the pasta to the boiling water. Suddenly her concerns over how much help or encouragement to offer her mother when the odds of building a successful business were stacked against her didn't seem so overwhelming.

She had a date.

CHAPTER NINE

Eleven days after the Great Blizzard of '78 crippled much of the country, Melody was anxiously counting toilet paper rolls when the distinctive sound of a snowplow rumbled up the hill. She looked out the upstairs window in time to see a large plow hoisting a rooster tail of snow twenty-feet into the air. As thrilled as she was to be rescued from the hill, all she could think of was Grandpa. The family could finally plan a funeral. Grief and relief fought for dominance in her heart.

The next morning, against Mom's advice, she drove into town to see the devastation for herself. She couldn't believe how bad the situation still was. Downtown stores had reopened and offices were trying to make up for lost time, but Jenna's Creek looked liked a grimy, snowy war zone. Parking spots were obscured and meters were buried under eight feet of snow. Instead of the pristine beauty covering the hillsides at home, the snow inside the corporation limits was black with salt and fuel exhaust. Potholes expanded with every freezing and passing of snowplows. Snow had been plowed up to the very front of porches. Cars were still hopelessly buried. Trash trucks had been rerouted since many streets were impassable so mountains of garbage bags continued to grow atop the plowed snow.

An enterprising group of artists had found a way to bring some levity to the situation. Snowmen, dressed in colorful hats and scarves, stick arms, and mittened fingers, smiled down on passing motorists from atop the continuous wall of snow as high as a two-story building blocking the center lane on Main Street. Melody laughed in spite of herself. At least some residents were finding ways to find fun in the situation.

She had told her parents she needed to go to Jenna's Creek to check on her job. That was part of her motivation, but the bigger reason was to visit Grandma's sisters.

The aunts had off-street parking and a nice-sized front yard so Melody had no trouble pulling her Torina into the hand-shoveled driveway behind an oversized Buick that looked like it hadn't been moved in nearly two weeks. Mom had called them the day the phones came back on to tell them about Grandpa. She didn't tell Melody how they took the news. Melody doubted there had been much love lost, even if Lowell's version of events regarding the Salinski estate was overblown.

She walked gingerly along the narrow path, the snow piled three feet high on either side of her, to the swept porch. She stomped the loose snow off her boots and knocked on the glass exterior door.

Naomi's face appeared between two lace curtains. She broke into a broad smile and jerked open the door. She looked like a taller, thinner, more wrinkled version of Grandma. Grandma always said her skin was so smooth because fat didn't wrinkle. Melody never had the heart to tell her even fat wrinkled if it hung around on a face long enough.

"Melody, sweetheart, is it really you?" Naomi asked even as she ushered Melody inside. "What brings you out on a day like today? I sure am happy to see you. Alma, guess who's here. It's our Melody. Come see. I tell you, girl, you get prettier every time I see you. How's your grandma holding up? And your poor mother? Alma, where are you? Melody's here."

"I'm coming. I'm coming." Alma hustled into the room as quickly as her short legs would allow. All three Salinski sisters were petite, but Alma was the smallest of the lot. She was rounder and plumper than Naomi, but nearly everyone was. For most of their lives, Clarice had been the heaviest, but since the onset of cancer she was significantly smaller than Alma. There was virtually no brown remaining in Alma and Naomi's hair, and their once deep blue eyes had faded to a dull gray just as Grandma's had.

"Melody, how are you, sweetheart?" Alma pushed up to her and took hold of her elbows to study her as if she might be a figment of her imagination. "I wasn't sure I was hearing Naomi correctly when she said it was you. You look beautiful. Take off your coat. Are you hungry? We were just getting lunch on the table. You'll stay, won't you? We don't get much company these days, especially in this weather."

A pang of regret for not taking time to visit struck Melody as Alma took her coat and Naomi pulled her by the arm into the front room. She worked in town practically every day. Would it kill her to drop by now and then? She never considered herself a selfish person, but she sure felt like it at the moment.

Naomi ushered her to a seat on the sofa, and the aunts plopped down on either side of her and surveyed her expectantly.

"Today was my first chance to get off the hill," she said.

Their faces wrinkled with concern. Melody wished she hadn't opened with what sounded like an excuse. "It looks like you got just as much snow here as we did," she added conversationally.

"We got fifteen inches of new snow the night of the blizzard," Naomi said as though it had been her personal accomplishment. "It was raining when we went to bed so the back patio was clear. I made sure to measure the snowfall where the house prevented drifts. Fifteen inches. And that wind. My, how dreadful. I can't remember a blizzard this bad."

"Even growing up on the hill I don't remember a snow like this one," Alma finished.

They both studied Melody, as if worried their talk of the blizzard might upset her in light of what happened to Warner.

"Our power was out for four days," she told them. "The phones came on Sunday."

"Remember, Naomi, when they first brought phone lines up the hill?" Alma said. "Daddy thought we'd be fine without it, but Mother put her foot down. 'I've lived up here long enough', she told him. 'You put in a phone or I'm moving to town.' Remember that?"

Naomi pursed her lips. She was the most stringent with a dollar. "Daddy always gave Mother her way. He couldn't tell her no."

Melody had no opinion either way. Both Salinski grandparents were gone before she was born, and she'd heard few stories of them over the years.

Alma's expression sobered at her sister's inability to share in the joke. She reached over and clasped one of Melody's hands between hers. "We were so sorry to hear about your grandpa. We know how close the two of you were."

Melody's throat closed. Every time she thought she was getting used to the idea of losing Grandpa, someone said something or something happened to remind her all over again she would never share another moment of her life with him. She had always imagined her wedding day—if she ever found a man who interested her—with Grandpa helping the preacher perform the ceremony.

"Thanks."

She wanted to say more. She wanted someone to know how much Grandpa meant to her; that he wasn't as mean and close-minded as most of the world apparently saw him. Nothing sounded right or appropriate in her head so she said nothing.

Alma squeezed her hands, and Naomi patted her shoulder in the way people did when they wanted to make you feel better but didn't know you that well.

"We spoke to Clarice this morning," Naomi said. "We plan to get up the hill to see her as soon as possible, but we're a little nervous about driving that far with all the snow."

Melody sniffed away the tickle of tears. "I wouldn't try it yet. The roads are still pretty treacherous. Every time the wind blows, it drifts again and you have to wait for another plow. The funeral director said it might be a few more days before he can get up there to…" She stopped talking. "You can see her at the funeral."

The aunts slowly shook their heads and clicked their tongues.

"I just hate it we can't be there for Clarice," Alma said.

"It doesn't seem right with all this snow keeping family apart at a time like this," Naomi added.

Alma stood up as quickly as her girth and short legs would allow. "I didn't get you anything to drink. I'll brew a fresh pot of coffee."

"That's not necessary," Melody began.

"Nonsense. I need to finish warming up the stew."

Naomi stood, too, so Melody followed suit. "Come into the kitchen. It's the warmest room in the house."

Melody followed the aunts through the house with its high doorways and heavy crown molding and dark stained floors covered with inexpensive area rugs. Not a stick of furniture or piece of bric-a-brac had been altered since she was a kid and used to come visit with her parents and the aunts would offer her hard candy out of a glass bowl. Even the candy looked the same. Maybe it was.

Naomi ushered her to the table while Alma went to the stove to turn the heat on under the pot of stew. It was barely eleven-thirty. Too early for lunch after the country breakfast of eggs, biscuits, and sausage Melody had enjoyed with Dad after helping with the morning chores. Obediently, though, she dropped into a vinyl-padded kitchen chair. "Do either of you know anything about Grandpa's childhood?" she said before she lost her nerve. "I want to write something to read at the memorial service."

She had thought up the excuse on her way into town, but the more she thought about it, the more she liked the idea. If she couldn't write something appropriate to read at the funeral, no one could.

Naomi exchanged glances with her sister as she set a loaf of bread and a butter dish on the table. She turned back to the cabinet, leaving Alma to answer.

"I don't believe we ever heard much. You probably know more than we do." She looked to Naomi for confirmation. Naomi was busy looking for matching cups in the cabinet. Finally she gave up and set three mismatched ones next to the coffeepot.

"I don't know much either," Melody said. "He never told me stories about growing up, which is odd since he always had plenty to say about everything else."

"Well, we wouldn't know anything," Naomi said quickly. "We never met Warner until he came to work for Daddy."

"When was that?"

She pursed her lips. "When would you say, Alma? I believe I was in college at the time. Does that sound right?"

Alma shook her head as she stirred the stew. "I don't remember a thing. Your memory was always better than mine."

"It must've been a couple years before I graduated. Were you in college yet, Alma, when Warner showed up or were you still in high school?"

Alma studied the stew as if she couldn't identify the vegetables floating in it. "It was close to my last year of high school I think. Clarice was a year behind me. You should really ask her about all this, Melody. I'm sure she remembers the particulars."

Naomi set a steaming cup of coffee in front of Melody and turned back to the coffeepot. "Clarice was crazy about Warner from the start."

"So were you," Alma quipped.

The remaining two coffee cups rattled in their saucers. Melody pivoted her head to look at Naomi. The older woman's face had gone white. Her lips were pressed into a straight line. "He was quite taken with you too," Alma continued, unaware of the effect her words were having on Naomi. "But I guess Clarice was more his type. Their courtship was rather sudden, I always thought."

She turned off the heat under the stewpot. Her smile vanished at the expression on Naomi's face. The sisters stared at each other for a split second, their silent communication saying what didn't need to be spoken. Melody watched in awe, trying to figure out what was happening.

As if someone flipped a switch, Alma's smile was back. "Nice and hot. Nothing better on a frigid day."

Naomi headed to the stove to help Alma with the bowls. "We were all crazy about Warner," she said as if to take the insinuation out of Alma's words. "Daddy usually hired grizzly old codgers to work on the farm. Warner was the first one of our generation. He was quite handsome back then."

Melody could tell from the way Naomi was trying to downplay the situation Alma had spoken out of turn. She also knew she wasn't going to get anything more out of either of them on the subject. Warner was several years older than Clarice, which put him closer to Naomi's age. She wondered for the first time why he had fallen for Clarice who was obviously still a girl while Naomi had been available. Did a broken heart have anything to do with why the aunts lived in town and seldom visited the family?

She went to the counter and pulled open the drawer for spoons. As expected, they were right where they had been the last time she visited a decade ago. "How long did Grandpa work on the farm before he and Grandma became an item?"

Naomi looked relieved Melody wasn't pursuing her alleged interest in him. "Not long. A few months maybe. Alma and I went away to school. When we came home for Thanksgiving that year…" Her eyes clouded.

Alma set a basket on the table and began to fill it with slices of white Wonder bread.

Melody looked from one sister to the other. A secret communication passed between them again. She supposed after spending their entire lives together, they barely needed to speak at all. "What?"

Naomi set down the last bowl and clasped her hands, waiting for Melody to take her seat. Melody obediently sat down and forced herself to stay quiet.

"As our guest, would you care to say grace," Naomi asked her after she and Alma were seated.

Melody blessed the food while secretly asking the Lord to help her be patient and gentle while hopefully getting answers to her questions.

He must've been listening to her prayer because Alma went back to the topic almost immediately. "Clarice and Warner were in love," she said. "Mother wasn't happy. Clarice was still in high school. Mother wanted all of us girls to go to college. She hadn't been able to herself so it was very important to her that we get an education. Very few young women were so fortunate in our day."

Naomi took a tentative sip of the steaming stew. "Daddy was happy. He thought the world of Warner. He had great respect for a hard worker. I suppose he knew he would need a strong, capable man to take the reins someday. Warner knew it too," she added almost as an afterthought.

The sisters exchanged glances again. Melody held her breath and waited.

"Everything worked out for the best," Alma said at length. "Naomi and I got degrees and Clarice got all you grandchildren." She patted Melody's hand.

Naomi stared into her bowl, her cheeks tinged pink, whether from the heat off the stew or the conversation Melody couldn't tell. She wanted to ask if Naomi thought everything worked out for the best. Had she been in love with Warner? Even if she hadn't been, it must've been a bitter pill to swallow when she came home on Thanksgiving to learn her baby sister was marrying the man she liked.

"Is that how you two ended up here in town?" she asked carefully.

Naomi looked up from her stew. "I lived at the farm until I got my first fulltime position. I got me an apartment over one of the stores in town. When Alma graduated we started looking for a house together."

Melody wondered if either sister ever made time for romance. Or had those hopes been dashed for Naomi when Warner fell in love with her sister? She didn't dare ask.

"You didn't come here to hear about us," Alma said. "You wanted to know something about your grandpa."

Melody took a bite of the stew. Even though she wasn't hungry, the pungent aroma made it hard to resist. "Did you ever hear what he did for a living before he came here? I always heard he was from Springfield. Someone said he worked at a store there."

"If anyone ever said, I've forgotten. What about you, Naomi?"

Naomi shook her head. "I'm afraid you'll have to ask Clarice. I'm sure she'll appreciate an opportunity to reminisce."

"I hate to ask too many questions. Grandma's so fragile right now."

Alma and Naomi exchanged sympathetic looks. "Poor Clarice. She always leaned so much on Warner."

"I'm sure she'll tell you everything she can remember," Alma assured her. "Warner hung the moon as far as she was concerned. She didn't put any stock in those rumors going around town. She insisted he couldn't have done what some people said he did."

Melody kept her expression as neutral as possible. She didn't want Alma to know she didn't know what she was talking about. "Do you mean about the fire?"

Alma looked up from her bowl. "No, the—"

The spoon slipped out of Naomi's hand and splashed stew onto the tabletop. "Oh, dear. Look what I've done," she said a little too loudly as she jumped out of her chair. Alma jumped up too. As they sopped up the mess, Naomi silently warned her not to say too much while Alma's expression apologized.

"I'm sorry we couldn't be more helpful remembering Warner. You'll have to ask your grandmother," Naomi said as she took her seat, effectively closing the subject.

⁂

As Melody pushed her way out of her office building a gust of wind caught the door and dragged her the rest of the way onto the sidewalk. She had only intended to check in at the office and see if there was anything she could work on at home before beginning her usual schedule tomorrow. Instead, she ended up staying two hours. Her supervisor was out of the office all day, so she was able to sort through backlogged cases and touch base with caseworkers who hadn't missed two weeks of work the way she had.

She let go of the door and combed a strand of tangled hair away from her face. She turned into the wind and started the perilous trek toward her car at the end of the street. Business owners shoveled snow and put down salt in front of their buildings every morning, but it was impossible to stay ahead of the thawing and refreezing. Walking across the icy, uneven surface was treacherous at best.

"Beautiful day for a stroll," a woman called from the corner. Christy Blackwood stood between Melody's car and a blue compact parked crookedly against a snow bank.

Melody had parked between a light pole and a mound of snow. Under normal circumstances she would've gotten a ticket. Now, as long as motorists could maneuver around parked cars, authorities looked the other way. They had enough real accidents to report on without citing double-parked cars. Not to mention, the local economy had taken a hard enough hit from the blizzard. It wouldn't benefit anyone if city officials discouraged residents from coming to town.

Christy high-stepped through the snow and met Melody on the sidewalk. "You made it off the hill." They embraced.

"Finally," Melody said with fervor. "I had a severe case of cabin fever."

Christy buried her gloved hands in her pockets as a gust of wind showered a cloud of dirty snow on them from a nearby awning. "I was only stuck at home a few days, but it felt like forever."

"At least you could walk outside and see different people once in a while."

"It was an adventure all right." Christy looked around the busy streets. "Life seems to be returning to normal slowly but surely."

Melody thoughts jumped to Grandpa. He would've been fascinated with the most interesting and amazing natural phenomenon of Melody's lifetime and would want to share every moment of nature's majesty with her. He would've turned this tragedy and major inconvenience into a science lesson and pointed out God's awesome and diverse power. It broke her heart she couldn't share it with him. On the other hand, if the Great Blizzard of '78 hadn't occurred, he might still be alive.

She forced those thoughts from her mind. "Are you working today?" she asked Christy.

"This was one of my early shifts so I'm done for the day. Are you back to work?"

"Not officially. I'm back on the clock tomorrow. I had a few things to take care of in town, so I thought I'd see how backlogged I am."

Christy eyed the bulging satchel against Melody's side. "Apparently very. Do you have time to find some place a little warmer to catch up? Have you eaten? I missed lunch and I'm starved."

Melody thought of her early lunch with the aunts. Even though the stew was delicious, she hadn't been able to eat more than a few bites with her mind on what they *weren't* telling her about Grandpa.

"I could manage something."

"If I go home, I'll have to heat up leftovers," Christy said with a feigned grimace. "How about the diner? It's a little early for the dinner crowd so we'll have the place to ourselves."

"And it's close enough we won't have to move our cars."

A few minutes later they were seated in the warm diner. Melody didn't bother to consult a menu. "I think I'll get a bowl of chili."

"The clam chowder sounds good," Christy said. "I can't eat a full meal. Mom worries if I don't have a hearty appetite at dinnertime. I've gained ten pounds since I moved home."

Melody lifted an eyebrow. "From the way I remember, you needed it."

Christy didn't comment. When Melody ran into her a few months ago, she had barely recognized her old school friend. Christy had always been petite and slender, but she had looked downright waifish. Now she had color in her cheeks, and her eyes glowed with vitality. The ten pounds was a good start.

The waitress approached the table and took their orders. After she moved away, Melody clasped her hands and put them on the table. She had pushed most of her worries aside as she focused on her caseload at work. Now that she had a sympathetic ear, she could think of little else. "The real reason I came into town was to talk to my aunts, Grandma Clarice's sisters."

"Did they survive the blizzard okay?"

"Oh, they're fine. You won't meet two more independent ladies. Very resilient. They probably did better than most of us. What I meant was I wanted to talk to them about Grandpa."

"Sharing memories?"

Melody wasn't sure where to begin. She opened her mouth to reply but stopped when she saw the waitress approaching the table. The woman topped off their coffee cups and moved back to the counter.

"They say they barely knew Grandpa at all," she said when she was sure the waitress was out of earshot. "Maybe it's true. They were mostly away at school when Grandpa came to the farm, and he supposedly fell madly in love with Grandma at first sight."

Christy's eyes narrowed. "You sound like you don't believe it."

Melody inhaled deeply of her coffee cup and took a sip. "That's the story I heard my whole life. Grandpa always said he fell for Grandma the instant he saw her. But after talking to the aunts I'm beginning to think Grandpa liked Aunt Naomi first. She's the oldest sister. She went away to school. Grandma wanted to stay on the farm while her sisters didn't, and all the sudden, Grandpa was in love with her."

Christy's brow furrowed again. "I don't follow. You said the older sister was gone. Your grandpa couldn't fall in love with someone who wasn't around."

Melody shook her head to clear the cobwebs. "I know. I'm not making sense. But all this lines up with what Uncle Lowell told me the other night. He said Grandpa cheated the aunts out of their inheritance by marrying Grandma. He called him a liar and a thief."

"What did he lie about?"

"Well, for one, burning down a store, and that's why he moved to Jenna's Creek."

Christy leaned forward over her own cup. "Your grandpa burned down a store? Was it an accident?"

"Not from the way Lowell talked. I really don't have any details. My mother says it's just Lowell being Lowell. Wanting to stir up trouble to take the focus off his own miserable life. That's a good possibility. That's why I wanted to talk to the aunts. After spending the morning with them, I'm sort of thinking Lowell was right, at least about a few things, and Grandpa married my grandma just to get the farm. Aunt Alma said something about rumors circulating when Grandpa first came to the farm, but she wouldn't say what the rumors were."

The waitress set two steaming bowls in front of them. "Just the right thing for a cold afternoon," she said cheerily.

Christy smiled up at her. Melody felt like her lips were stuck to her teeth.

"We've sold our soups by the gallon the last few weeks." She folded her arms over her stomach and clasped her elbows with her hands. Melody and Christy were the only customers in the restaurant, and the waitress was obviously happy to have someone to talk to. "Nobody's buying ice cream, I can tell you that." She laughed.

"I wouldn't imagine so," Christy said.

"Well," the waitress said with a sigh. She looked around the empty restaurant, then back at them as if hoping they would strike up a conversation. "If you need anything else, just holler."

"We will." Melody managed. The waitress moved back behind the counter.

Christy bowed her head politely while Melody blessed the food and then broke a packet of crackers over her clam chowder. Melody began to stir her chili without crackers. The spicy aroma lifted her spirits. She took a tentative bite. It was completely different than the variety Dad made at home but equally delicious.

"What exactly did your uncle say about a fire?" Christy asked after both of them ate a little of their soup.

"Not much. We were having dinner the other night and he got upset about something. I don't remember what it was now. Anyway, he said Grandpa had to leave Springfield because he had set a fire to destroy some kind of evidence."

Christy took another bite as she considered Melody's words. "Evidence to what?"

"I asked Mom and Dad about it later, and they downplayed the whole thing. Maybe Lowell was pouting or wanted to be the center of attention, but why pull something like that out of thin air if there wasn't some truth to it?"

Her question didn't require a response, and Christy didn't offer one.

"You know what's strange about the whole thing, I seriously don't know anything about Grandpa's life before I was born. My first memories are of following him to the barn to do chores. I remember taking huge steps to try to step into his boot prints. I remember him setting me on his shoulders when I couldn't keep up. I remember riding the tractor with him, herding cattle, mending fencerows."

Her voice broke, and she sniffed back tears. Christy handed her a paper napkin, and she held it to the end of her nose. "He was always there. Always a huge force in my life. It was almost like he was plopped down on the farm to take care of me. Like my own personal Mary Poppins."

Christy set her spoon in her bowl. "Maybe he was adopted. There was much more of a stigma attached to it back then."

Melody nodded thoughtfully. "Anything's possible. I just wish he was here to ask. If he were here, I probably wouldn't be wondering why he never told me anything about his past. He never told me a single thing about his parents or friends he had in school or learning to ride a bike. Nothing. I was too stupid or too self-absorbed to ask." She pushed away her half-empty bowl.

Christy reached across the table and patted her arm. "I think you're really missing him. Like you said, this is the first time in your life you've not had him to talk to, and you're allowing everything everyone else says to cloud your memories of him."

Melody studied the bowl in front of her.

"I know it's hard," Christy continued. "After you lose someone you wish you'd made better use of your time together. You think of all the things you never said and the things they never said. Conversations and situations that can never happen because they're gone and you're alone."

Christy's voice cracked. Melody looked up. Christy had lost her own father a few years ago in a car accident. Melody needed to be more sympathetic. She wasn't the first person to suffer loss.

The front door opened, and a man and woman stepped in from the cold. A swirl of snow came in with them. They laughed as the man fought against the wind to make sure the door closed securely behind them. The waitress stopped scraping grease off the grill to pour two glasses of water and join them at a table overlooking the street.

Melody waited until they were involved in conversation before turning back to Christy. She lowered her voice and leaned closer across the table. "I haven't only been worrying about a fire that may or may not have happened, or why Grandpa married Grandma. There's always been strife between Uncle Lowell and Grandpa. Uncle Jay too. I guess you could say Grandpa was hard to please. He expected a lot from people. He had no respect for a man who didn't work hard and earn his own way. It bothered him that Jay and Lowell weren't very…industrious."

Christy smirked. "I have men like that in my family."

"Jay and Lowell are everything Grandpa couldn't respect, and they knew it." She leaned closer. "They were also in the house the night Grandpa fell down the stairs."

Christy tilted her head. "What are you saying?"

Melody had never voiced the thoughts that kept her awake at night since learning of Grandpa's death. She knew they were irrational and maybe a little hysterical, but she couldn't keep them to herself any longer. Despite what Christy might think, she needed to get the words out.

"Jay and Lowell knew, and probably Carson, too, that Grandma wouldn't be around much longer. She's already outlived her doctors' prognosis. They also knew they wouldn't get much from Grandpa if Grandma passed away first."

"I'm sure your grandparents drew up a will years ago to take care of those matters, regardless of which one went first."

"They did, but Grandpa would be in charge of everything after Grandma was gone. He could add any stipulation he wanted, and he could cut anyone out if he thought they didn't deserve to be included. He wouldn't bring up the matter as long as Grandma was alive, knowing she would throw a fit if he wanted to disinherit someone. But he wouldn't have a problem doing it if she wasn't around to stop him."

Christy glanced at the waitress and the couple across the restaurant to make sure they weren't paying attention. "So you think someone had a motive for helping Warner down the stairs that morning?"

"Lowell, for one, if he wanted Carson to inherit anything."

Christy's spoon froze halfway to her mouth.

"I know how it sounds. The farm belonged to Grandma's family. Her parents passed it down to her, not Grandpa. If someone wanted money, they would've needed to act before Grandma died. Carson, Lowell, and Jay knew there would be no free ride with Grandpa at the helm."

Christy sat back in her seat. "I don't know, Melody. You're talking about killing somebody. I don't mean to make light of your concerns, but is a family farm really worth that much? Who would risk life imprisonment for an inheritance that's going to be chopped up a dozen or so ways? Not only that, they may not have liked Warner, but I doubt the animosity ran deep enough to push him down a flight of stairs. What if it hadn't killed him? Then what? He would know who did it. They were taking a might big risk for a crime that might not pay off."

Melody nodded. "Everything you say makes perfect sense, but I can't forget the feeling I had the morning the blizzard hit. It was the strangest thing. I woke up with the strongest sense of dread I've ever experienced. I got out of bed and went to the window. All I could see was swirling snow, but I knew something was wrong. I knew Grandpa needed me."

"You always said you two had a strong connection."

"If something happened to Grandpa that morning besides just slipping and falling down the stairs, I owe it to him to bring it to light."

"What if you find out something you wish you didn't know?"

"I'll worry about that when it happens. I just keep thinking about what Uncle Lowell said about the fire in Springfield. If I can find out what happened there, it might answer some of my questions."

"How? Even if Warner burned down a hundred buildings, it happened sixty years ago. What could it have to do with him falling down the stairs two weeks ago?"

"Probably nothing, but I have to know what Uncle Lowell was talking about. If he was right about a fire being the reason Grandpa left Springfield, maybe he's right about other things too." She looked at Christy through fresh tears. "I always believed my grandfather was the smartest, strongest man who ever lived. He taught me about God and life and doing the right thing, even when it was hard. But since the accident, well, I'm beginning to wonder if I knew him at all."

CHAPTER TEN

A reverberating crash brought a hush to the already muted conversation. All eyes snapped toward the ceiling. The family had gathered at the farmhouse after the funeral, but Warner Beckwith was still not in the ground. Drifts as high as fifteen feet covered every cemetery in the county. Warner was once again relegated to the mortuary's basement with the rest of Jenna's Creek's dearly departed who were stacking up like cordwood to await the spring thaw. March was a mere two days away, but it didn't look like a proper burial for anyone would happen soon.

Melody was numb. Numb and exhausted. At the funeral the preacher had eulogized Grandpa just the way Grandma wanted, but Melody barely heard a word. She couldn't stop thinking he was not the man she thought she knew. If Lowell and the rest of the family hated him for what they saw as judgmental, and possibly criminal ways, that meant Melody was wrong. Grandpa had deceived her about who he was.

The worst thing was, since talking to Christy, she hadn't had a moment to herself with relatives descending from far and wide to bid farewell to the family patriarch. She wondered if their grief had driven them here as much as a need to get together and throw a party. After all, this winter so far had been a grueling disappointment.

Melody and Judy had cooked and cleaned and prepared both farmhouses for the onslaught of guests. Pete, Jay, and Carson kept the road and driveways plowed, cleared paths to the front doors, and chopped enough firewood to see them through another winter. Lowell helped out by brewing pots of coffee and pitchers of tea, and leaning against the fireplace in the living room and catching up with the out-of-towners. Allen Beckwith, the oldest son of the Beckwith clan, arrived from Jenna's Creek with his wife Bonnie. Their children came and went over the four days leading up to the funeral, running errands and helping liven Clarice's spirits who loved being the center of attention. Linda Bowden, Warner's ostracized daughter, arrived from Indianapolis with her husband.

Now that the funeral was over, Linda and Hart's children and grandchildren had returned to Indiana. The rest of the relatives had cleared out as well. The ladies from church, who had been so kind to replenish casseroles, pies, soup beans, toilet paper, and laundry detergent, returned to their homes and families. Peace finally settled over the groaning farmhouse. That is until Wayne, Allen's oldest and his associate at the insurance agency, stepped outside with Pete, Carson, and Jay to enjoy after-dinner cigars. Everyone liked Wayne. He was funny and gregarious, much like his father. Unfortunately, neither he nor Uncle Allen possessed Warner's constitution when it came to controlling youngsters.

The youngest two of Wayne and Marla's brood had thundered up the stairs upon arrival and hadn't been seen since. Melody didn't think it smart to allow a five and six-year-old alone upstairs, but she wasn't about to offer her services as babysitter. She spent enough time around the two little hooligans to know she didn't want the job.

Marla appeared in the doorway wiping her hands on the dishtowel tucked into the belt on the waistband of her polyester pantsuit. "Those two," she said, smiling apologetically at Clarice.

Clarice looked over at the settee under the window where Wayne's two daughters from his first marriage had spent the last two hours looking as if they would succumb to boredom or annoyance any minute. "Girls, go upstairs and see what your little brother and sister are up to."

She smiled at the room at large completely unaware of the daggers both girls shot Marla.

"No, no, no," Marla said quickly, her eyes wide at the prospect of what might become of her little darlings if their half-sisters got hold of them. "I'll take care of it. I'll be right back, everyone," she called out brightly as she trotted up the stairs.

Melody resisted the urge to put a pillow over her ears. She wished they would all go home. During the two weeks following the blizzard she thought she would go mad without anyone around to answer her questions about Grandpa and his past. Now that the house was full of people who surely possessed more reliable information than Lowell, she felt even more alone with her doubts.

Allen lowered his round body onto the small sofa beside her and squeezed her hand. He didn't get out to the farm very often. He was too busy overseeing his insurance company, which had four offices throughout the county. When he did show up, he spent most of his time doting on Clarice. Allen was the only son Warner and Clarice didn't have to worry about. He never asked for money or gave them sleepless nights. He was jovial and outgoing, which reminded Melody of Jay, only without the shifty demeanor and oily expression that made her wonder what he was up to.

Allen's eyes shone with compassion. He pressed a monogrammed handkerchief into her hand. She shook her head and indicated the crumpled tissue in her lap. Allen leaned to the side to stuff the handkerchief into the back pocket of his slacks. He put his arm around her. "I know this is doubly hard on you, Nugget."

Melody gulped at Grandpa's nickname for her on Allen's lips. She opened her mouth to speak but had to clear her throat first. "Thanks. It's been a tough month."

"You know Pop's in a better place."

She nodded. She'd heard the sentiment a thousand times and truly believed it. Believing it didn't make the reality of losing Grandpa any easier to accept. "I wasn't prepared for him to go the way he did."

Allen nodded in solemn agreement though she could tell from the look on his face he figured the death of someone Grandpa's age shouldn't have taken anyone completely by surprise. Melody studied her uncle out of the corner of her eye. Allen was the polar opposite of his younger brothers. While Jay and Lowell were thin and wiry and angular of face and frame, Allen was short and stout and carried a good thirty extra pounds. His hair was steely gray, and he sported a trim mustache and beard that had gone to salt and pepper. His jowls had begun to droop and his neck waddled like a turkey as he edged toward sixty, but his round face was nearly baby smooth. Good living, he claimed. Melody figured it didn't hurt that he never spent time in the sun if he could help it.

Not only was he different in appearance from Jay and Lowell, the brothers were as different in temperament as night and day. Jay was quiet and sullen, while Lowell could barely bring his hand to his mouth to eat. Allen, on the other hand, was ambitious and astute, the one most like Warner. Every business venture he touched seemingly turned to gold in his hands. He and Bonnie were happily married and had raised three sons who were successful in their own right, while Lowell's son was still freeloading off his grandparents and had given no indication he planned to move on.

Melody bit her bottom lip and considered her options on how to broach the subject that had been tormenting her for over a month. Better to take Allen by surprise and hope for an honest answer before he had a chance to measure how much to tell her.

"What did Grandpa tell you about growing up in Springfield?"

He snorted. "Probably about as much as he told you. Pop didn't talk about his past."

"Why?"

"Guess he didn't think it was important and I never thought to ask."

Melody wasn't going to let him off that easily. "He told stories all the time. He talked about when all of you were little. He talked about falling in love with Grandma. He talked about the Bible and he talked about when I was little. Why wouldn't he talk about his childhood?"

Allen exhaled and turned thoughtful. Melody held her breath, anxious to hear something real for a change. Finally he said, "From what I gather, those weren't fond memories. His family was very poor. He quit school to go to work. His dad took off and he needed to help support his mother and kid brother."

"Sounds like you know quite a bit."

"Not really. That's just what I got from Mom. Pop wasn't big on details."

Melody knew he was shutting down the way Mom always did when she didn't want to talk about something. She needed to get as much information as she could before he got off the couch.

"Did you ever hear about a fire at a store in Springfield where Grandpa worked?"

Allen furrowed his brow. "What store?"

He looked completely in the dark. Melody couldn't tell if it was an act to keep from talking about something he didn't want to discuss or if he had no idea.

"He worked in a store before he moved here from Springfield," she said to jog his memory, though the only one who could corroborate the story was Lowell. Perhaps he had made up the store as well as the fire. "It burned down, and some people believe Grandpa did it."

Allen's eyes narrowed. "That doesn't sound like something Pop would do. Where'd you hear this?"

If he knew more than he was saying, he sure was doing a good job of hiding it.

"I don't remember," she hedged, feeling only slightly guilty about the lie. "I thought it sounded out of character, too, but I wanted to know if there's any truth to it or how the rumors got started."

He squared his round shoulders. "I may not know much about Pop's past, but you'll never convince me he was a pyromaniac or a vandal. If a store burned down in his vicinity, I can guarantee it was a coincidence."

His explanation made sense. Still, it wasn't likely Lowell possessed the imagination to make anything up. He must've heard something from somewhere. One way or the other, Melody was going to find out what.

Allen relaxed into the sofa cushions, apparently satisfied the rumor was laid to rest. "Have you looked through any of Pop's papers? If anything happened when he was young, you know he wrote it down somewhere. I bet the old hoarder has every report card he ever got from grade school."

Melody struggled to keep her face impassive. Grandpa's compulsion to hold onto every scrap of paper that applied to him surely hadn't started in the last twenty years. If there had been a fire, it was highly probable she would find a newspaper clipping or even an old W-2 from the store. She might find an address or a date. It wasn't likely the information would benefit her after all this time except to satisfy her curiosity. For now, that was enough.

"I wouldn't know where to begin," she told Allen. "Grandpa was great at recording every moment of his life, but he was a terrible organizer."

Allen laughed. "Don't I know it." He patted her arm. "I doubt you'll find much to answer any questions. Like I said, Pop grew up as poor as a church mouse. As for a fire, if he was implicated in starting one, it was probably because people are always looking for someone to blame in those things, and who better than a poor young man without the means to defend himself."

"Did anyone else in his family move to Jenna's Creek with him? I don't even know his parents' names."

Allen cocked his head and studied her. "What are you after, Melody?"

"Nothing. Just curious is all. Doesn't everybody wonder about this stuff at funerals?"

He didn't look satisfied with her answer. "Pop didn't dwell on the past. He wouldn't want you to either."

She wanted to remind him no one dwelt on the past more than Warner Beckwith. He could recall any overcharge for feed from the mill or remember the name of the clerk at the grocery store who charged him twice for a gallon of ice cream in 1958.

"But his own parents? That has nothing to do with living in the past. What about brothers and sisters?"

Allen shrugged as if he had never thought of aunts and uncles and grandparents he never met. "I guess he was too busy raising us kids. And building this farm to support our family."

Melody pursed her lips. He knew more than he was telling. Even busy people who didn't live in the past would mention brothers or sisters. She hated to think Lowell of all people was the only member of the family who might give her a straight answer.

Allen misread her silence. He pulled her against him with a beefy arm. "We'll find out soon enough if Pop's wishes were carried out."

Melody shifted on the loveseat to face him head on. "What wishes?"

"You must know he wanted you to have the farm."

She frowned. "The farm? He never said anything to me about it." She thought of Aunt Linda and Uncle Hart's kids who barely knew Grandpa. They already believed they were held in less regard than the cousins who grew up in Auburn County. How would they feel if Melody inherited the entire property? While she was closer to her grandparents than the other grandchildren, it wasn't fair they not get part of the estate.

"I'm sorry, Nugget. I thought you knew. I thought Pop told everybody. He only did it because he knew if you got the farm, it would stay in the family. He and Mom talked to me about it a few years ago. They decided if Mom passed away first Pop would rewrite the will. You would inherit everything."

A chill washed over Melody like an icy river, sinking into her bones and joints. She wasn't sure Allen realized it, but he had just given everyone in the family a motive for pushing Grandpa down the basement stairs.

❧❧❧

"What are you doing in here by yourself?"

Melody froze at the sound of Carson's voice. She slammed the desk drawer shut with her thigh and turned to face the door. She should've known better than to start looking through Grandpa's things with people still in the house, but she couldn't resist once Allen reminded her if she wanted to know something about Grandpa, all she had to do was look through his writings. She didn't need an excuse for being in the front room. Grandpa had used it as his office for years. Everyone came in here whenever they needed paper or pens or insurance claims or bank deposit slips since Grandpa grabbed a handful every time he was at the bank, even though he had hundreds at home.

She hadn't been looking for paper clips or a small screwdriver to tighten the leg on a chair. She had been looking for proof Allen was right, and Grandpa planned to leave her the farm. Proof that someone had wanted to make sure he beat Grandma through the pearly gates.

Carson wasn't in the doorway. Or anyone else, though Melody clearly heard men's voices. Gingerly, so no creaky floorboards would alert them to her presence, she crept to the doorway.

Most of the relatives had gone, and the house was finally quiet. Wayne and Marla had left with their noisy offspring as soon as the dishes were washed and put away. Linda and Hart left for Indiana right after Wayne and Marla. They turned down Clarice's plea to spend another night. Hart couldn't miss more work, not to mention getting an early start since they had such a long drive. Dad had chores to do, so he and Mom went home a few minutes ago. Melody told them she wanted to hang around a little longer in case Grandma started to feel worse again. She'd have Allen and Bonnie give her a ride home if she needed one since her parents still worried about her walking alone in the snow.

She missed the next few words until she heard Allen's voice. "I never trust a man who always looks guilty of something."

She hurried the rest of the way to the door. So she wasn't the only one who thought Carson looked guilty of something.

She stopped two steps from the front room door to insure she stayed in the shadows. It was barely six o'clock but already as black as night outside. No one had turned on lights on this side of the house. Unless the men entered the front room or

Melody tripped over something, she could eavesdrop without detection.

"I'm not guilty of anything," Carson answered.

Allen chuckled. "Be that as it may, you needn't be so anxious."

Melody's brow furrowed as she edged closer to the crack between the door and the wall and strained to hear.

"With Dad and Jay hanging around, I have every right to be anxious," Carson said. "Those two leeches will bleed her dry before she has a chance to make a decision about anything else."

"There's nothing I can do, Carson. My hands are tied." Allen sounded tired.

"Don't give me that. You call the shots."

"Don't be like your father. You can't always take the easy road. There are some things you have to work for."

Carson barked out a laugh. "You mean the way you did?"

Melody held her breath as she waited for an answer, growing more and more confused with each syllable. What were they talking about?

"I worked for everything I have," Allen said. "No one gave me anything."

Carson grunted. "I know better than that. But don't worry. I respect you for it. That doesn't mean I don't want a piece of the action. I won't end up like those two."

"With that attitude, it's exactly where you'll end up, whether I help you or not."

Melody heard movement. From the shadow on the door, she could tell Allen was putting on his coat, apparently ready to head back to town.

"I'm not asking you to pay me for something I don't deserve. Look at all the work I'm doing around here. With Dad and Jay tied up in their business enterprise," Carson said, his voice thick with sarcasm, "I'm Grandma's primary caregiver.

Imagine what you'd pay for a full time quality nursing facility if I wasn't here. The way I look at it, you're getting a bargain."

"You're no bargain."

Carson laughed again. "Be that as it may, I'll earn my money as long as she's alive. After that, you can come up with some other excuse to give me what I want. I'll be more than happy to work with you at the insurance company. I'm a quick study."

"You're woefully under qualified."

An icy blast wrapped around Melody's legs as someone— she assumed Allen—opened the front door.

"Listen, Allen." Carson's voice had lost its humor. "I don't want to spill the beans on you. I stand to lose as much as you. But this is the only chance I have to get off this hill. If you don't help me, what happens next will be out of my control."

His words must've gotten Allen's attention. Allen pushed the door shut. "You've got some of the old man's grit. I'll give you that."

"I'm nothing like him."

"Open your eyes, boy. You're exactly the same. Always looking to scheme your way into something better."

Melody nearly gasped aloud. Allen's words mirrored what Lowell had said about Grandpa scheming his way into the farm. Had Allen lied when he told her he didn't know anything about the fire or was he talking about something else now?

A shadow fell across the doorway as Carson stepped into the light. Melody pressed against the wall. Carson's words were filled with derision. "Like you've got room to talk. Worked out pretty well that Warner fell headfirst down the basement stairs when he did."

Melody stiffened. What did Carson know, and what did Allen need to cover up?

"I hope you're not suggesting I had anything to do with it," Allen said.

"I guess the blizzard gives you a rock solid alibi. At least it bought you some time."

"Watch your mouth."

"Or what?"

The air crackled with tension. Melody wanted to peek around the corner to see what the men were doing but couldn't risk being seen. She held her breath and waited.

"I'll see what I can do," Allen finally said. Melody heard the doorknob turn again but no one pulled it open.

"I expect you to do more than that. I want something solid by the end of next week or I might forget and say something I shouldn't."

"I hope you're not threatening me."

"And I hope you're taking me seriously."

"You don't want to mess around and become a liability, boy."

Carson laughed. "You know all about that, don't you?"

After a painful moment of silence the door opened. "Goodbye, Carson. If you know what's good for you, you'll exercise a little patience."

As Allen walked out the front door, Melody hurried back to the desk in case Carson came in. She didn't want him to know she'd overheard anything. She wasn't sure what she'd heard. None of it made sense. Was Carson suggesting Allen had pushed Warner down the stairs? Or that he was the one who would benefit most in the end because of it? Whatever it meant, Allen hadn't worked very hard to defend himself.

CHAPTER ELEVEN

Clarice Beckwith carefully lowered herself into the chair Carson held out for her. She looked at the two place settings. "I guess this means it's just you and me for dinner again?"

Carson smiled apologetically as he spooned a helping of last night's stew onto her plate. "Looks like you're my date for another snowy Friday evening. Dad's asleep and Uncle Jay went to town."

"Again? He's never home now that they cleared the roads."

Carson didn't bother with excuses. There was no point. He sat down across from her and filled his own plate.

Clarice unfolded her napkin and spread it in her lap. "How can Lowell be asleep so early? It's barely five o'clock. I should go upstairs right this minute and drag him out of bed. He sleeps more than a man a hundred and two years old. He should be eating dinner with his son and his mother. And what about Jay? When your grandpa was here, we used to sit down and have dinner together nearly every night. His friends visited him here. I don't understand what's happening."

Carson didn't think Clarice really wanted answers to her questions. It was a bad situation all the way around. Her sons meant the world to her while they couldn't give her the time of day. Their behavior had gotten progressively worse in the weeks following Warner's death. While he was alive, they at least made a show of caring about her. Now the only attention they paid her was when they wanted money, which she freely doled out any time they asked.

Apparently that well was running dry.

Last night Carson caught Lowell with an old Army pistol from a trunk in the attic. He didn't even bother to hide his cache when Carson saw him. "Your granddaddy always was a packrat," he said. "There's plenty of junk up there nobody will miss as long as we keep our mouths shut."

Carson couldn't very well argue since he had used the same logic to assuage his conscience after snitching a few pieces from Clarice's jewelry armoire. She would be gone soon. Why leave a houseful of valuables for Judy and Linda and the other grandchildren to fight over?

"Jay will probably be home later tonight," he said, though he didn't see it happening. His uncle's visits away from the house were increasing in frequency and lasting longer. "At least with Dad in bed so early, you and I won't have to share the TV."

Clarice didn't look mollified. "He'll wake up as you and I are going to bed. Then he'll be down here all night with the TV up so loud I won't be able to sleep."

He gritted his teeth. If he thought it would do a bit of good, he'd talk to Dad about how his behavior was upsetting Grandma. But he knew Lowell wouldn't change, nor would Clarice confront him about it.

She patted his hand. "I'm so thankful I have you, Carson. I don't know what I'd do if you were still in Texas. Have I told you how much it meant to your grandpa and me that you came here?"

Carson arched his eyebrows. "It might've meant something to *you*."

"I know Warner was hard on you, dear. He only wanted you to apply yourself." She glanced toward the ceiling and lowered her voice. "He wanted you to amount to something."

Carson tipped the saltshaker over his plate. Clarice couldn't have much sodium so he and Jay used it sparingly in their cooking. "He had a funny way of showing it."

She sighed. "He thought by being hard on you, he would make you strong. He knew you had a rough time of it after Lowell left you in Houston with your mother and stepfather."

"That's probably the only good thing Dad did for me."

Clarice winced at his statement, and he regretted it as soon as it was out of his mouth. He should apologize but doing so would be hypocritical. Whether she wanted to hear it or not, it was the truth.

"Warner blamed himself for the way Jay and Lowell turned out," she said. "He lamented to me many times that if he had been a better father maybe Lowell would've been a better one to you."

Carson leveled a doubtful look at her.

"Warner wasn't good at expressing himself," she continued. "Men of his generation never learned how. He showed his love by trying to get the best out of people. I know you find this hard to believe, but he wanted a good life for all his children."

"Even Linda?"

Clarice glanced away. Carson inwardly kicked himself again. Why did he insist on taking his anger at Warner out on her?

"Linda hurt your grandfather very deeply by leaving the farm when she did," Clarice explained. "I've never been in good health and Judy was too little at the time to be any help around the house. Warner saw Linda's leaving as an affront to me. He couldn't forgive her for that."

"Didn't she have the right to fall in love and live her own life?"

"Of course, but Warner didn't see it that way. He didn't for years. I think he started changing his way of thinking, especially after I got sick. He began to talk about Linda for the first time since she went away. He often wondered what she was doing and how her children were. He even let me read her letters to him."

"Did he write to her?"

"Oh, no. He was too proud for that. I could tell he was building up to it though. If he hadn't died when he did… Well, now that he's gone, it's my duty to let her know he loved her and forgave her for what she did."

"I don't mean any disrespect, Grandma, but he had nothing to forgive her for. Shouldn't she be the one to forgive him?"

Clarice sighed and separated a canned mushroom from the stew. "That wasn't quite the way Warner saw it. Even though he was beginning to soften, he still thought she was wrong for leaving. He believed her place was here helping the family. No matter what you think you know about your grandfather, always remember he loved his family more than anything, except the Lord, of course."

Carson nodded for her benefit, though he still believed Warner was a hypocrite. "I'll remember."

She sat back in her chair. "I wish your daddy and Jay were as easy to talk to as you are. They wouldn't be here if they didn't think there was a financial reward waiting." She smiled at the surprise on Carson's face. "I'm old, dear, not naïve. I'm more to blame about the way they turned out than Warner. I always gave in to them. I couldn't help myself. I still can't. I want them to be happy. I want them to love me."

Carson's heart ached at the desperation in her voice. "You shouldn't have to buy love."

"Now who's naïve?"

"I'm serious, Grandma. If that's why you give in to them, you need to stop. They'll only keep taking advantage of you." Even as he said the words, he blanched, knowing he had been doing the same thing since his arrival. "That includes me. I'm sorry if you thought I only came here—"

She shook her head, cutting off his words. "It's too late for me to change now, dear. All I can do is try to leave a legacy for each of you. I'm not talking about a physical inheritance but a spiritual one. That's what Warner wanted in the end. I fear he didn't have time to do it. I know how most of you feel about him. It's a shame you couldn't see what a strong man of faith he was."

Carson tasted the stew. He reached for the saltshaker again but changed his mind. He didn't need the salt any more than Clarice. "I figure all a man needs is faith in himself. It's the only thing you can depend on in this world."

"Oh, Carson, you couldn't be more wrong. Your own abilities and powers are the last thing you can depend on. A man needs faith in his creator. Look at what happened to your grandpa. He was the strong one. I always thought he'd be here to take care of me as long as I needed him. Now he's gone and all I have left is this old body, broken down and eaten up with cancer. But God's still with me. He never changes and never fails."

"No offense, Grandma, but if God cares so much for you, why did he take Grandpa when you still needed him?"

"Because of what I just said. Bodies aren't meant to last forever. The Bible reminds us our eyesight will grow dim and our teeth will fall out. What happened to Warner is what happens to anything that's been walking around this earth for longer than it was designed to. He got old. It had nothing to do with God punishing him or leaving me to fend for myself."

"You're amazing, Grandma. I almost envy your simplistic attitude. I wasn't brought up that way. Mom and Milt didn't believe in filling my head with religious dogma. They thought I should make up my own mind once I got old enough to look into those kinds of things."

"Are you calling me simple-minded?"

"Of course not. That's not what I meant."

"I think you did a little."

She speared another mushroom and popped it in her mouth. Her once hearty appetite had fallen dramatically over the last few weeks. Carson wasn't sure if it was from losing Warner or if the progression of her disease had accelerated. He would tag along the next time Jay took her to the doctor to voice his concerns. He doubted Jay had even noticed. If he did, he probably wouldn't care enough to ask the doctor what it meant.

"Grandma, I'm sorry if I insulted you."

"Did you mother ever warn you about talking to strangers?" Clarice asked as if he hadn't spoken.

"Excuse me?"

"Did she teach you to wash behind your ears?"

Sometimes her medication made it hard to have a conversation with her. "Grandma, I—"

"Did she ever yell at you to get up and go to school when all you wanted to do was stay in bed?"

"Sure. I guess."

"What about college? I'll bet your stepdad encouraged you to pursue higher education?"

"Of course. Milt always said to work smart, not hard. He said if I wanted to get anywhere, I needed to depend on my brain."

"That's very good advice." She stared thoughtfully at her plate for a long time. Carson was about to ask if she wanted him to clear the table when she spoke again. "It seems to me they were good at giving advice but only when it suited them."

"Pardon?"

"You said they didn't believe in filling your head with dogma and traditions. As good parents, they believed they should let you make up your own mind about spiritual matters. If they truly believed that, why waste all those years making you floss your teeth and look both ways before crossing the street? Why not hand you a spool of dental floss and let you make up your own mind about using it or not."

"They were looking out for me. They wanted to keep me safe and healthy—" He smiled and held up his hands in surrender. "Okay. You got me. I gotta hand it to you, nobody'll ever get the best of you in an argument."

Clarice ignored his attempt at humor. Her expression remained earnest. "Spiritual training is as important a part of parenting as anything else. We all want our children to be happy and healthy and look both ways before crossing the street. Christian parents aren't trying to raise little zombies who can't formulate an individual thought. We love our children, too. Just like Milt thought it was important for you to go to college, I think it's important for children to go to church. When parents deny their children religious training, they may think they are liberating the child. On the contrary, they are committing them to a life of bondage."

"Now, wait a minute. I don't think—"

"No, you wait a minute. I said bondage. You may *think*, but I know. I've been around this world a lot longer than you, young man. I'm certainly not the smartest person you'll ever meet, but I've learned a thing or two about how this world works. If a young person is going to make any type of educated decision about his life, he needs to know his Bible. Even if he decides not to follow the holy precepts laid out within its pages, he'll have a strong foundation on which to build a life. A much broader and stronger foundation than someone who only received a limited education from a college. You don't have anything against opening your mind to another point of view, do you?"

Carson was beginning to feel like he'd been backed into a corner. "No," he said cautiously.

"Good." She set her fork next to her plate and leaned forward on her elbows. "After you tidy up the kitchen, you and I are going to begin a Bible study."

"Now, Grandma, I never said I'd—"

"Are you afraid your simple country granny might make you think about something you never considered before?"

"It's not that—"

"Wonderful. Consider it the next phase in your education. Who knows, you might find something to prove me wrong."

"Why do I get the feeling I've been duped?"

"Now, Carson, I'm just a helpless old lady. How could I possibly fool a man of the world such as yourself?"

Carson laughed in spite of himself. He wasn't particularly looking forward to spending the evening reading an ancient text that had no relevance to his life, but how could he turn her down? Regardless of the innocent act she put on, he was right; she was a clever old dame, even if no one else in the family realized it.

CHAPTER TWELVE

With mild amusement, Christy allowed Jarrod Bruckner to push her chair into the table before seating himself across from her. So far she was having a wonderful time. It wasn't until she was dressing for the evening that she realized she hadn't been on a real date in over two years. Sean hadn't been much for going out. He claimed to prefer quiet evenings in her apartment so he wouldn't have to share her with the rest of the world. That's what he said anyway. What a dummy she was for buying it. Not only was he a thief and a liar, he was a cheapskate.

Earlier, when Jarrod took the time to come to the door and introduce himself to Mom, Christy almost believed chivalry wasn't dead and buried in a cornfield near Louisville, Kentucky with the remains of her stolen car. She could tell by the look on Mom's face she agreed Jarrod was outrageously handsome in his black wool coat with a crimson turtleneck visible behind a Burberry scarf. His brown eyes had twinkled at Abby as he took Christy's hand and helped her down the icy steps to the sidewalk. Christy was thankful for the leather gloves they wore. Otherwise, she might've pulled away at the touch of a man's skin against hers. No man other than her brother had touched her since she moved back to Jenna's Creek. It happened on Christmas Day when Eric knocked her down during a snowball fight in the front yard. He pretended to help her up only to shove a handful of snow down her collar. Christy had jerked away, gritted her teeth, and barely suppressed a scream. As her heart rate returned to normal, she was thankful the red in her face and near panic in her eyes could be attributed to the cold and the indignation of her little brother getting the better of her. In reality, she had relived the moment when a thug in a remote motel had wrapped his hand around her throat and lifted her off the bed. At the time she hadn't known if he planned to rob her, murder her, or worse.

Those memories often came back to haunt her when she least expected them. She was determined not to spend the rest of her life jumping at every masculine voice. Unfortunately, thinking it and putting it into practice were two different things. When Jarrod slammed the car door behind her, her heart had leaped into her throat. It took every ounce of resolve not to race back inside the house and bolt the door. She took a deep breath and smoothed out the gouges her fingernails left on her purse strap and ordered herself to calm down. By the time he circled the car and climbed behind the wheel, her pulse had returned to normal. The robbery and battery had been a year and a half ago. She wouldn't let the experience dictate who she was.

"I haven't eaten here in years," she confessed as they cast their gaze around the restaurant's dimly lit interior. "I was with my date for the senior prom. I ordered the prime rib and he got fresh."

Jarrod laughed. "Young men can behave quite stupidly when they think a woman owes them something. I hope he outgrew his poor manners."

"I wouldn't know. I think he went to an out-of-state school. I haven't seen him since graduation."

A waiter in a black vest and tie appeared and handed each of them a menu.

"Feel free to order whatever you like," Jarrod said. "I won't get fresh."

"That's a relief," she said, though part of her wished he would.

The smile he gave her before burying his nose in the menu was downright delicious. She wondered if he spent his teenage years practicing that smile in front of a mirror. She reminded herself to go slowly. He was a man after all, and a lawyer to boot. He had won her mother over; she wouldn't be so easily swayed.

The smile appeared over the top of the menu. Okay, maybe she would.

"You made a good case for the prime rib. I think I'll try it."

She smiled in spite of her efforts to make it through the evening without falling for him. "Good choice, Counselor. If memory serves me correctly, it was worth the trouble it caused. I'll have the same." She closed her menu and laid it on the table.

The waiter returned, and Christy let Jarrod order for both of them. It was something she doubted Gloria Steinem would advise, but she didn't care. If old Gloria were sitting across from the handsome attorney, she'd probably lower her guard a little too.

After the waiter collected the menus and moved away, she said; "You never told me where you're from. It can't be Jenna's Creek or you would've eaten here before."

"Portsmouth. I only come here when I'm working a case."

"You're here now," she pointed out.

"Man cannot live by the law alone."

"That's good to hear. I mean..." Her cheeks warmed all the way up to her chestnut roots. *Stop flirting, Christy,* she scolded. *You're out of practice and it shows.*

"I was born and raised here," she said. "I never liked living in a small town, though. I couldn't wait for college so I could move away."

Something that looked like disappointment flashed across his face. "Where'd you go to school?" he asked after a brief hesitation.

"Ohio State. I know," she said at his raised eyebrows. "I didn't get far. What about you?"

"I went to UC. Cincinnati. Law school was at Northwestern."

"And you came home to work?"

He lifted a shoulder. "I never wanted to practice anywhere else."

It was her turn to be disappointed. It was unlikely a stick of dynamite could blast him out of southern Ohio. She reminded herself it didn't matter to her what he did with his life or where he did it.

"What did you do before you moved back to Jenna's Creek?" he asked.

The question she most wanted to avoid. How much honesty did one reveal on their first real date? In her case, not much if she hoped for a second. She thought of the flippant response she used whenever she ran into an old friend at the library. No one ever pressed for details, and she didn't offer. She doubted it would be as easy to sidestep Jarrod's questions or keep the conversation focused on him all night. Besides, she was beginning to like him.

"I was a paralegal for a firm in Columbus."

His eyes lit up. "Which one?"

She swallowed. "Bennis, Banociac, and Weiss."

He gave a low whistle. "Impressive. Even more impressive you gave up your position to come home and take care of your mother."

She bit the inside of her cheek. She should set the record straight. She couldn't let him think she left Columbus for her mother's sake when nothing could be further from the truth. A stupid lapse in judgment had cost her the best job she ever had. A noble gesture had nothing to do with it.

The waiter approached the table with a tray on his shoulder. Christy exhaled with relief. Hopefully the arrival of their entrees would distract him enough to forget her illustrious career.

It wasn't until she turned down the dessert menu and agreed to a final cup of coffee that he brought it up again. She had managed to steer the conversation in his direction throughout dinner. She listened, amused and totally enthralled, as he described the small practice his father ran in Portsmouth. Jarrod was the low man in the office, and apparently his father didn't give him any breaks. It was the main reason he kept showing up in Jenna's Creek, working the firm's more insignificant cases. Unless he requested those cases in hopes of running into a certain little redhead.

Good grief, Christy, get over yourself, she scolded again.

"How did you like working for Bennis, Banociac, and Weiss?" he asked. "I applied to a few similar firms after I passed the bar. It wasn't long, though, before I realized I wasn't cut out to be part of a big firm."

"I don't guess I am either," she replied, intentionally vague.

"I've thought of opening my own practice. Maybe even somewhere like Jenna's Creek."

"You're kidding."

He shrugged. "I like it here. What I'd really like is a chance to stand on my own two feet. At home I'll always be Harry Bruckner's son and Jeff Bruckner's kid brother. Jeff will probably run for governor someday. I'm afraid my aspirations don't run that high."

"But why Jenna's Creek? Nothing happens here. Wouldn't you go out of your mind from the monotony?"

"On the contrary, I'd have a lot more fun than in a big firm. Here I'd practice all sorts of cases. One morning I might defend an assault and close an estate case in the afternoon. In the larger firms you don't practice law, you shuffle papers. But you already know that."

"I guess I never thought of it that way."

"I hope you haven't lost respect for me because I don't want to be governor." He grinned, and his cheeks crinkled handsomely. Christy couldn't imagine ever losing respect for him. "I wouldn't mind being elected county prosecutor," he went on. "I like the idea of living where people know my name and I know theirs."

Christy liked the exact opposite. "I sort of like the anonymity of the city. No one knows your name, so they don't care a whole lot about what you do."

"That's true, but they don't care about you either. I had an apartment off campus while I was in law school. The week I was moving out I started talking to the couple across the hall. It turned out their son had died the winter before. I believe it was an aneurysm or something horrible like that. He was nine years old. They were really nice people. I could see they were still devastated by their loss. The whole time they were talking, I kept trying to remember the kid. I was so ashamed because a few weeks earlier I'd been thinking about how much quieter the building was than when I first moved in. All those weekends I was sleeping in, enjoying the peace and quiet, that couple was across the hall grieving the loss of their son. That never would've happened at home. Mom would've baked casseroles and sent flowers and offered to walk their dog." He shook his head in regret. "I couldn't even remember the kid. That's when I realized I wasn't cut out for city living."

Christy nodded thoughtfully. She could empathize with his helplessness, but at the same time, suspected no amount of casseroles or flowers would've eased their suffering. "I understand what you're saying, and I totally agree. It's just that, well, don't you have enough problems of your own without taking on everyone else's?"

Jarrod looked completely confused by her apparent lack of compassion. "I suppose. I'm sure sending flowers wouldn't have made much difference to that kid's parents. I just know if I went through a similar tragedy, it would mean a lot to know it mattered to someone else, too, even a little bit."

"I always thought the best part about living in the city was no one was interested in your business. I guess it's the worst part too."

Jarrod lowered his head and took a sip of his coffee. Christy wished she could explain herself better. If she tried, she would come off sounding even more heartless than she already did.

She took the easy way out and changed the subject.

"Besides small town living and maybe becoming prosecutor, what are you looking for, Jarrod Bruckner?"

"Same as everyone else I guess," he said without hesitation. "Success, happiness."

"You look like you've already achieved both."

"You think so?"

"Sure, don't you?"

He shrugged. "My brother's been married for years and has three kids. Every time my grandmother sees me, she asks if I've met a nice Christian girl yet. Mom and Dad got married in college. I can see the worry in their eyes sometimes, wondering where they went wrong with me."

"If you marry too early, people figure you had to. If you don't marry at all, they think something's wrong with you and nobody wants you."

He laughed. Christy liked the sound of it. "My uncle Dennis never married," he said. "I asked him once how he got the family to leave him alone about it. He said they never did. Around the time he hit sixty, he stopped caring what they thought."

They laughed together.

"Sixty, huh? That means I only have to weather it another thirty-odd years."

Jarrod reached across the table and snagged her hand with his. "Hang in there. You can make it."

At the touch of his hand, the smile died on Christy's lips. He stared at his hand covering hers and sobered, too, but didn't pull away. Christy fought the urge to pull her hand out from under his. She liked the contact, though she was fighting down the trapped sensation she always experienced when she remembered the two men who broke into her motel room.

As if by mutual consent, they withdrew their hands.

"It's getting late," she said. "You have a long drive ahead of you."

He glanced at his watch. Was it regret she saw on his face? "I suppose we should call it a night? I have to take a deposition in West Virginia in the morning."

"I have to work tomorrow, too."

"I'd like to see you again, Christy."

"That would be nice," she replied, meaning it.

"Good." He studied her for a moment until something over her shoulder caught his eye. "I just noticed a friend I haven't seen in a long time. Do you mind if I go over and say hello?"

"Of course not."

He scooted out his chair and placed the linen napkin on the table. "I'll just be a minute."

Christy watched as he maneuvered around tables to reach an older couple seated at a secluded table along the wall. Across the dining room, she heard the woman squeal at the sight of him and saw her take hold of his hands. Several patrons at nearby tables stopped eating to watch the exchange. Jarrod motioned to the table where Christy sat. The couple turned their heads to follow the direction of his pointing finger. Christy recognized Noreen Trimble, who worked at Wyatt's Drugstore. Her picture had been in the paper last year when she was released from prison after her murder sentence was overturned. Even if Christy hadn't been interested in the law, the case would have intrigued her. Though not reported in the paper, Mom told her the testimony of an old boyfriend had been integral to her release. Tim Shelton's picture hadn't made the paper, but Christy couldn't help wondering if he was the man at the table with Noreen. They looked to be enjoying an intimate dinner together.

Christy wasn't usually imaginative or romantic, but she couldn't help wondering if Tim and Noreen had been in love all these years, and Tim's role in her acquittal had been enough to rekindle an old flame. She might ask Jarrod when he got back to the table, if for no other reason than to prolong the evening.

Their date had gone well as far as she was concerned. They might not be two peas in a pod, but she had spent evenings in worse company. Jarrod said he wanted to see her again. She hoped he meant it. She really liked him. Too bad he would probably disappear without a trace the instant he met the real Christy Blackwood.

CHAPTER THIRTEEN

"What was Grandpa like when you first met him?"

Melody had been waiting for a week to get up to the farm to talk to Grandma. On Tuesday, her caseload was lighter than usual so she was able to leave her office in the early afternoon and come directly to the farm. She was thankful for the chance to get there when Jay and Carson were outside doing chores so they could talk alone. She didn't figure Lowell would get in her way. He was usually upstairs napping in the afternoons. Lying around the house watching TV, reading magazines, or listening to the radio could apparently zap the energy of a fifty-year-old man.

Clarice's face softened in memory. "Oh, sweetheart, you've heard all my stories a thousand times."

Melody reached over and squeezed Clarice's hand. Last week Carson and Jay had moved Grandma's bedroom downstairs. Going up and down the stairs several times a day had become too much for her. She had been sickly the last two years, but every time Melody saw her, it looked like she still managed to age another year or two. She figured it wasn't only the going up and down the stairs that had convinced Grandma to move downstairs. She missed Grandpa in the bed beside her.

Clarice was reclining on the pillows in her bed, and Melody sat in a chair she had scooted up to the bed. Clarice had just awoken from her afternoon nap when Melody arrived, so Melody couldn't have chosen a better time to visit.

"I want to hear them again. I miss Grandpa so much," she admitted with tears in her voice. "The only time I feel like I haven't lost him is when I talk to you."

Clarice smiled appreciatively, and her eyes grew misty. "I feel the same way about you, dear. You and I loved Warner so much. Sometimes I think we're the only two who really knew him. Your mother came pretty close, but even she didn't understand him the way we did."

Melody swallowed another round of tears. She wanted to ask why that was. Out of such a big family, why did only two people truly know the patriarch? Why had Grandpa believed he needed to shut himself off from the people who should've meant the most to him? Was it nature or nurture? Or something else completely?

She didn't ask any of it.

"Tell me, what was he like? Did he just show up on the farm one day looking for work?" Her conscience pricked at her for misleading Grandma with her questions. She quickly rationalized her behavior since she didn't know the whole story, and Grandma was probably the only one who did.

Clarice sat back in her chair and let her gaze drift toward the window as if looking back on that day sixty years ago. "That's pretty much how it happened. I was the only one living at home when Warner showed up and asked Daddy for work." Her nose wrinkled as she concentrated on the long ago memory. "Well, now, wait a minute. Alma may have been here. Yes, I think she was. I think it was the summer before she went away to school. Or maybe the year after. I guess none of it matters, now, does it? Either way, she and Naomi were busy getting ready to launch their careers. They were always so studious. Not like me. I didn't want anything more than to get married and have children."

"What did Grandpa want?"

Clarice looked startled. "Why, the same thing, of course. At least that's the only thing I ever heard him talk about. A family and the farm. He was naturally suited for taking over after Daddy." She leaned forward and lowered her voice as if her belated father might overhear. "Daddy was never the businessman Warner was. That's how the Storers and the Sheltons came to own part of the hill. A few years ago the Storers sold a couple acres to Mike and Erlene Kennedy. My family owned this whole hill at one time, don't you know? Then hard times hit. Daddy would've lost everything to the taxes if he hadn't sold off a few parcels when he had the chance." She leaned back into the pillows. "He was due to lose a lot more before Warner came along. Warner saved the farm," she added with earnest.

"Did he know the family was in dire straits when he showed up?"

Clarice shook her head. "I didn't say 'dire straits'. Times were hard for everybody."

"But the family would've lost the farm if not for Grandpa.".

Clarice frowned and backtracked. "It might never have come to that. We'll never know really. He and I fell in love, and it never became an issue. Daddy died knowing the farm was safe and I would be taken care of."

"What about the aunts? Did they want the farm?"

Clarice's face softened as if happy to be off that maudlin topic. "Not really. They were happy in their house in town. They wouldn't have liked farming for a living. They weren't suited for it."

"Didn't they move to town because there was no room for them here after you and Grandpa set up housekeeping?"

"Who told you that? We didn't kick them out if that's what you're wondering."

"No, I didn't mean that," Melody said quickly. "I meant they probably didn't feel like they belonged here after you and Grandpa got married. I'm sure they knew there would be babies eventually, and Grandpa was here to run things after Grandma and Grandpa Salinski died."

Clarice nodded. "I'm sure they did. To be honest, I never really thought about it."

Melody figured that was part of the problem. "Did the aunts tell you they weren't suited for the farm?"

Clarice regarded her with a frown. "I don't know what you're asking, Melody. They both went to college. Why would they have done that if they wanted to stay here?"

"Maybe they went looking for husbands. Didn't a lot of young women go to college in those days to find husbands?"

"I told you, they were studious. They wanted careers, not husbands. Back then, you couldn't have both."

Melody swallowed her frustration. Why was it so hard to get a simple answer? "Wasn't Aunt Naomi closer to Grandpa's age than you? Maybe she set her cap for him before he noticed you."

Clarice's lips pursed as she studied her granddaughter. "I don't know what you're talking about, Melody. Your grandpa and I fell in love practically the first moment we saw each other. Naomi was away at school. She didn't even know Warner."

Melody knew that wasn't true, but it was possible her grandmother didn't. Grandma had been a young girl when Warner Beckwith walked into her life. She probably didn't realize her older sister had also been interested in him. Naomi was four years older, and her time was spent going back and forth to school. They might never have had conversations about beaus and marriage and dreams of a future. To Naomi, Clarice was a little girl with whom she would have no reason to share her dreams. To Clarice, Naomi was a grown woman on her way to a career, who wouldn't understand life on the farm.

"What did Grandma and Grandpa Salinski think about you not going to college? They must've been disappointed you didn't have the same opportunities as Naomi and Alma."

"I couldn't leave. I had to take care of the farm. As soon as Warner showed up, all Daddy's problems were solved. I got the farm, and Naomi and Alma were free to pursue their careers."

"But it wasn't fair," Melody exclaimed, even while realizing if the farm had been split evenly her own life would've gone much differently. "The farm belonged to the aunts as much as it did to you."

Clarice shrugged as if to say it wasn't any of her concern. It probably wasn't. She had always been a bit narcissistic, if one could be a *bit* narcissistic. "Warner and Daddy talked it over. Naomi and Alma were making their livings teaching school by then. They didn't need the farm."

"You didn't either. You had a husband for financial support. That put all three of you on a level playing field. For the era, I mean. They deserved as much of the farm as you did. It was their inheritance too."

Clarice's gaze sharpened. "What are you getting at, Melody?"

"Nothing. I just never understood why the aunts stayed in town away from the rest of us. Was there bad blood between them and Grandpa after he talked Grandpa Salinski into giving you the farm instead of them?"

Clarice sighed in frustration. "He didn't talk Daddy into anything. I already told you they weren't interested in the farm. Daddy knew how much it meant to Warner and me. I think Daddy and Mama used the farm to keep me close, the way Warner and I did with your mother." She smiled and winked.

Melody had known most of her life her grandparents built the house where she now lived so Dad and Mom would be less likely to leave the hill like Linda had done, but she had never heard anyone actually admit it.

"Naomi and Alma weren't forgotten in the wills," Clarice clarified. "Mama and Daddy both had small insurance policies. After their debts were cleared, the remainder was split between the three of us. Naomi got Mama's wedding ring. Alma got the armoire Great-grandpa Salinski built for his wife for their wedding."

Melody doubted the aunts felt equally compensated with a third of two small insurance policies, a gold band, and a worm eaten chest of drawers compared to a prosperous hundred-acre farm.

She would've become the sole beneficiary of the farm if Grandma had gone first. She could understand why Grandpa might want to give it to her. For one, it would be his to give to whomever he wanted. He had been closer to Melody than the other children, and it made sense he leave it to her instead of someone who lived far away. But how would the cousins have felt? It wasn't their fault they weren't close to Grandpa. They barely knew him, which was no one's fault but his. He had never tried to get to know Linda and Hart's children. Allen and Bonnie's children had grown up a few miles away in Jenna's Creek, but Grandpa never fostered a close relationship with them as far as Melody could tell.

If there was bad blood between him and the aunts because Grandpa Salinski had given him the farm, how would the others feel toward her for the same thing?

"I just think it's sad none of us know the aunts better," she said. "After all these years of living so close to Grandpa, I feel the same way about him."

"For goodness sake, Melody. You know more about him than anyone. Maybe even more than me."

Melody grunted in frustration. "I sure don't feel like it. I don't even know his parents' names. Did he have brothers and sisters?"

"Warner never talked about his family." Clarice parroted everything Melody had heard so far. "He had a brother. He was several years younger than Warner."

"What was his name?"

"Ivan. I never met him. Warner didn't visit and he didn't come here. I suppose it's a little odd now that I think about it, him not visiting his only living relative." Clarice gave a little laugh. "I was too busy raising your mom and the other children to worry about it at the time."

Melody blinked away tears. "I'm sorry, but I don't understand why Grandpa wouldn't tell me he had family beyond us on this hill."

Clarice reached for the glass of water on the bedside table. Melody jumped up to make sure it made it safely to her grandmother's mouth and back again. "Warner was very private with his feelings," Clarice said after the drink.

Melody swallowed her irritation. "I don't buy that. Everyone who ever met him knew how he felt about everything. About people who wouldn't work. About the government. Doctors who kept their patients waiting. The highway department when they didn't fill potholes quickly enough. Grandpa never kept an opinion to himself in his life. Forgive me if I can't understand why he didn't tell me he had a brother. What was he hiding?"

"He knew you wouldn't understand."

"Wouldn't understand what?"

"Oh, Melody, why do you have to dredge up the past? Nothing can be gained by it."

"I want to understand. I want to know him better." She stopped short of saying she wanted to know who had a reason to push him down the basement stairs.

"There was nothing left for him in Springfield. His life was here."

Melody didn't argue farther. She sat back in the chair while Grandma began to talk about other things. As her grandmother talked, she mulled over all she had learned. With each passing day it seemed she knew Grandpa less and less.

⁂

Except for want of a good dusting, the outside of Grandpa's desk looked the same as it always had. The perpetual clutter was sheer chaos to a casual observer, but he could find anything within moments of beginning a search. It wasn't only money spent and earned he recorded in countless notebooks and tablets. Since the late 40's when electricity was brought up the hill, he read the meter at the back of the house every month and checked it against the readings sent out by the electric company. If the company's numbers were different from his more than two months in a row, he was on the phone, accusing them of trying to take advantage of a helpless old man.

As if.

He made meticulous grocery lists and kept them long after the trip to the store. "Keeps me from wasting good money on things we won't eat once we bring them home," he explained when Melody asked why he went to the trouble.

Grandpa was eighty-two when he died. According to Grandma, Ivan had been several years younger. There was a chance he was still alive, and at least a small chance he was still living in or around Springfield, Ohio.

The good thing about a grandfather with a compulsion to record everything meant Melody would probably find an address or phone number for the great-uncle she never knew existed. The bad thing about the same compulsion was Grandpa wrote down *everything*. Melody faced a long battle in finding what she was looking for. Any address could be long outdated.

Her only hope was Grandpa had stayed in touch with Ivan and hadn't bothered to keep his wife apprised of the relationship.

She cocked her head toward the back of the house where Grandma was taking a nap, and listened for a moment before easing open the narrow, center desk drawer.

She stared in dismay at the jumble and disorder. Apparently she wasn't the first person to look through the desk. She took a slow breath as she processed all the reasons someone might have for being here. Many reasons could be legitimized, like looking for insurance papers or the title to Grandpa's truck so someone could renew the tags. More than likely whoever had been snooping in the desk had less than honorable intentions.

She picked up an empty envelope sent by a utility company months ago. It was covered with Grandpa's small, neat script. Row after row of figures squeezed together in the tiny space had obviously been a recording of gas mileage for his truck. He never wasted a scrap of paper. Melody had seen him jot notes on gum wrappers or matchbook covers that he would neatly fold and file away in his desk.

She smiled in spite of herself as she thought of Grandpa's favorite phrase she'd heard at least a thousand times. "Use it up. Wear it out. Make it do or do without."

She returned the envelope to the crowded drawer and picked up a yellowed pocketsize tablet bearing the name of a hopeful politician who had probably died of old age several election cycles ago. She flipped it open to find more rows of figures and dates. A thorough log of when and in which fields he had planted crops in 1967. Not only did Grandpa's compulsion make him write everything down, it kept him from throwing any of it away.

Melody dropped the tablet and stirred the contents looking for something more recent. Her fingers closed around a thin palm-size tablet that looked and felt like it had only been in the drawer a short time. Sure enough, it was only half filled.

At the top of a page were the letters, *JB*.

Jay Beckwith?

She scanned down the page with her eyes. The more she read, the surer she became the notations were indeed about Jay. Times and dates had been recorded along with a time span, apparently recording when he left the house and when he returned. Many trips lasted less than ten minutes. To be gone and back in such a short amount of time meant Jay was probably conducting a business transaction with a customer in the cornfields down the road. There was a pull-off halfway down the hill along the creek bank where deer hunters or lovers often parked their cars before entering the woods. He could've easily made it there and back in ten minutes.

Dollar amounts followed several of the entries. A few notations had been scrawled in the margins. *$ comes in, $ goes out,* followed by question marks in dark ink.

Melody stared at the figures on the page and twisted her mouth in concentration. As far as she could tell there was only one explanation for Jay's behavior. Grandpa had obviously reached the same conclusion. Had he threatened to turn Jay in for selling drugs? She was sure he would go to the police if Jay was breaking the law rather than save his son's skin.

She flipped back to the front page. More columns were squeezed together in the narrow space. She slid her finger down the first column of numbers to keep them from blurring together. She had no idea what she was looking at or looking for. She turned a few pages to more figures and letters. At first glance, everything looked like gibberish. She should have paid more attention to his need to chronicle every moment of his life instead of considering it another of the harmless quirks that made him Warner Beckwith.

Had his compulsion been the cause of his death?

She scanned a few more rows of numbers, hoping to spot a common denominator that would tell her what she was reading. The dates on this page appeared out of order, if they were indeed dates she was looking at. Grandpa was meticulous about recording events chronologically. Perhaps as he got older, he became forgetful and recorded events he had written down before, though she didn't think it likely.

There had to be a pattern, even if she wasn't seeing it. Were the notations still about Jay?

She flipped another page and saw more notations above two columns labeled *LB* and *IN*.

LB could've stood for Lowell Beckwith. But who was *IN*? She didn't know anyone with those initials. Maybe it stood for Indiana. Linda lived in Indianapolis, and her initials had also been *LB* before she married Hart. Why would Grandpa record numbers about her? As far as anyone in the family knew, he had been completely out of touch with his daughter for the last forty years. Of course, it turned out there were plenty of things the rest of the family seemed to know while Melody had been kept intentionally in the dark. Maybe he had been sending her money all these years to assuage his conscience for the way he treated her.

Melody didn't think that was likely. Grandpa never felt guilty about anything.

She made an effort to get off the path her thoughts were taking. The initials most likely stood for something as benign as *LB* for pounds and *IN* for inches. Grandpa could've been measuring the size of a litter of piglets for all she could tell by the scribbling.

She shoved the notebook into her hip pocket and closed the drawer. She would puzzle over the figures and what they implied later. She needed to stop chasing rabbit trails and focus on finding something about Ivan. Her parents would call soon to ask if she was coming home for the night, and Jay and Carson would wonder what she was doing in here for so long.

She left the desk and moved to the built-in cabinets on either side of the fireplace. At one time, the farmhouse had been equipped with four fireplaces. They had all been bricked in when Warner installed the wood-burning furnace in the basement except for the one in the living room. The fireplaces had never been overly efficient, so he installed ductwork from the basement to heat the large house. Still, the fireplace in this room was a lovely accent, and the built-in cabinets made ample storage for his letters, journals, and quality control. Well, not ample, she reasoned, since he had purchased several army issue filing cabinets over the years for the overflow and stored them in the basement.

Melody groaned aloud and hoped she wouldn't have to continue her search down there.

She bypassed the top three drawers and knelt to open the bottom drawer nearly on the floor. The old wood had swollen and curled, and she had to jerk mightily to open the drawer.

She had spent enough hours in this room while Grandpa balanced his checkbook down to the penny, or recorded addresses of doctors or operators at billing companies he might need to file a complaint against in the future if they overcharged him for services. An address he didn't use often might be here.

She sat down in front of the drawer and began rifling through the contents for a large notebook that would contain addresses. Unfortunately, the drawer contained at least fifty wire bound notebooks, as well as hundreds of sheets of loose paper, all covered with Warner's small script.

She flipped through a few notebooks but found nothing that looked like what she needed. She quickly gave up on the notebooks and began looking for pictures instead. If she found one, maybe Grandpa would've written a clue on the back of how she could find Ivan. Every time her fingers closed around a picture, her heart leapt in her throat until she turned it over and saw someone she recognized. She nearly jumped up and down over a picture of a severe-looking man in a dark suit standing next to an equally gloomy woman who looked about the right age. She turned the picture over and read the notation: *Reverend and Mrs. Eugene Levy, 1935.*

This was going to take all night. In defeat, she started to push the drawer closed—which turned out to be as hard as opening it—when she spotted the white edge of a photograph standing against the side of the drawer. She stopped manhandling the drawer into place to snag the photograph. A young man stood with a long hand on the shoulder of a boy about eight years old. Even without looking for an inscription, Melody recognized the young man as her grandfather. She could see her mother's smile and Lowell and Jay's lean jaw line on his face. Tears sprang to her eyes. She smoothed her thumb over the picture and held it up to the light. Was the little boy her uncle Ivan? She turned the picture over. The only inscription was a date: *1913.*

Warner was born in July, 1895. According to the long sleeves in the picture and the small leaves on the trees behind them, the photograph had been taken in late spring. That meant Warner was seventeen. The boy was anywhere from eight to ten years old so that made him nearly a decade younger than Warner. If the boy was Ivan, there was a good chance he was still alive. If only she could find him.

Light flooded the room. Melody gasped aloud and dropped the picture back into the drawer. She jammed the drawer the rest of the way shut and jumped to her feet. Carson stood in the doorway, a sly smile on his face

"What are you doing in here in the dark?" he asked in a mocking tone.

Twilight had etched the corners of the room. "It wasn't dark when I came in." Guilt burned her cheeks, though she had nothing to feel guilty about. If anyone had a right to be in Grandpa's office going through his papers, it was she.

Carson crossed his arms over his chest and leaned against the doorjamb. "Can I help you find something?"

Melody crossed her arms over her chest, mimicking his posture. "I was looking for some old pictures. You scared me half to death."

He didn't move.

She took a few steps toward him and lowered her voice. "It doesn't look like Grandma's going to tell us anything about what's in the will, so I thought I'd look around for myself. If someone stood to inherit a lot of money, it might explain how Grandpa ended up at the bottom of the basement stairs."

She studied his face for a reaction. All she saw was confusion.

"What are you talking about?"

"I'm talking about someone pushing Grandpa down the basement stairs."

He straightened away from the doorjamb and came into the room. His expression was one of disbelief and a little concern for her mental stability. "I think this long winter has given you too much time to read mysteries in front of the fire. Nobody needed to push him, Mel. He was old."

Melody continued to study his face. He looked completely mystified by her suggestion. At least he was no longer interested in her snooping. "You could be right, unless he knew something someone wanted to keep quiet."

Carson's eyes darted past her to the desk. Was there something in there to implicate him, or like her, was he wondering what secrets the desk and the rest of the room held?

"You're wasting your time looking for a will or anything else in that mess," he finally said. "The only thing the old man hung onto was forty years worth of utility bills and checking account statements. Thought the whole world was trying to rob him of a nickel."

"Maybe he had good reason to be suspicious," she said, though she was wondering how Carson knew so much about what Grandpa had saved. Obviously, he had been snooping too.

"Maybe he was paranoid, the same as you."

"At least I have nothing to hide."

"We're all hiding something, Melody."

"Well, I plan to find out what."

Carson stared at her for a moment. Finally he shrugged. "Snoop through all the old junk you want. As it is, it's going to take an army to clear out the house of everything that packrat saved. Just don't expect to find proof of whatever conspiracy your mind's cooked up."

"I want to find out really happened that night."

He sniffed. "That's probably the last thing you want."

What did that mean? What did he know? They stared at each other a few moments before Melody stepped around him and out of the room, leaving him standing there wearing his indiscernible look.

Across the hall, Jay was scooping up a dustpan worth of wood shavings from in front of the fireplace. "Melody, I didn't know you were still here." He tossed the shavings into the fire.

"I was just leaving."

"You're welcome to stay for dinner. Carson made chicken manicotti. He's going to make somebody a great wife someday."

Melody ignored the insult wrapped in a thin layer of humor. She remembered the notebook in her back pocket filled with Jay's initials and Grandpa's suspicions. Not turning around in case he saw it, she edged toward the doorway. "Thanks anyway. I need to get home before it gets any darker. Mom worries." When she was out of his line of sight, she hurried into the kitchen to get her coat.

⋘

Carson waited until he heard the back door close behind Melody before he went to the built-in cabinets and pulled open the bottom drawer. He picked up the picture staring up at him and regarded it for a moment and then looked toward the back of the house where Melody had gone. He tucked the picture into his shirt pocket and stepped into the hall. Jay was no longer in the living room. Carson listened for a moment, but the old house was quiet. He headed to the kitchen and took the phone off the wall.

He dialed the familiar number and glanced back into the hallway to make sure he was alone as he waited until it was picked up on the other end.

"I thought you'd like to know Melody was just here," he said. "She's been going through Warner's desk and snooping in the cabinets. I'm pretty sure she took something, but who could tell in that mess? I don't know what she's looking for, but she's onto something. You know how close those two were."

He listened for a few moments, enjoying the impatience on the other end. After the tirade ended, he spoke again. "She's been suspicious from the beginning. If anyone's going to be a threat, it'll be her."

He smiled as he replaced the handset to the receiver. His call had accomplished exactly what he hoped it would.

CHAPTER FOURTEEN

Christy Blackwood turned off the heat under the pot and poured the noodles into a colander in the sink. She mixed the ingredients in a baking dish for yet another tuna casserole and added the noodles. She hadn't eaten this many casseroles since she learned to drive a car. With only her and Mom to eat them, neither had to worry about cooking the following night. The blessing was a double-headed coin. By the time they finished the casserole on the third day, they were both sick of it. Regardless of how dry and tasteless it became after several re-heatings, Mom couldn't bring herself to throw out a morsel of food.

The front door crashed open just as she slid the casserole into the oven.

"Christy, help," Abby called out breathlessly.

Christy slammed the oven door—extinguishing the pilot light of the old stove in the process—dropped the potholder on the counter, and ran toward the front of the house. She rounded the corner to find Abby under a pile of packages she was trying to keep from sliding to the floor in a puddle of melting snow.

"Hurry, I can't let these get wet."

Christy lunged forward to gather an armload of oversized envelopes before they slid out of Abby's grasp. "What's all this?"

Abby set the rest of the packages on the table and unwound her scarf from around her neck. "My new business."

"Your what?"

"You heard me." She motioned to the envelopes in Christy's hands as she took off her coat and hung it on the hall tree. She shook snow from her hair. "Whew. I'll be glad when this winter is over."

"What's this got to do with your business?"

"You're the one who lit the fire under me. Now, try to keep up." Abby scooped the packages off the table and headed into the room that once served as Jack's den. "Bring everything in here. Have you started dinner? I'm starved."

"Oh, no." Christy dropped the envelopes onto the small sofa in the center of the room. "I slammed the oven door so quickly the pilot light went out again. We need to figure out why that thing's so touchy."

"It's touchy because it's old," Abby said absently. "Like me." She was already sorting through the packages she brought in, oblivious for once to what her wet shoes were doing to the rug.

Christy relit the pilot light and double-checked the oven temperature before hurrying back to the den, her stomach aflutter with excitement. With all her research and brainstorming the last few weeks, she never really expected Mom to get on board with something as uncertain as a home-based business. Abigail Blackwood didn't possess the out-on-a-limb personality necessary for such a venture. Still, it had been Christy's idea. Mom needed her support and enthusiasm.

The bags were empty by the time she entered the room. Pattern envelopes and bits of fabric and notions were stacked neatly on the desk and the table at the end of the sofa. She picked up a pattern and examined it. "This is a doll pattern."

"A pattern for a doll dress," Abby clarified.

"You're going to make doll clothes."

Abby beamed. "Your dad always said the stores didn't sell as high quality doll clothes as I made. I've been talking to Georgia Harper at work. Her daughter-in-law owns a specialty store in Cincinnati. Georgia thinks she can talk her into selling my doll clothes. I'm going to whip up a few outfits. As soon as the snow melts a little, Georgia's taking me to the city to see if she'd be interested in carrying a line of my things."

Christy's mouth dropped open, unable to believe the thought and effort Mom had put into the idea. She wasn't sure sewing doll clothes on a kitchen table was a feasible business venture in the present economy, but she wouldn't be a naysayer at this stage in the game. She threw her arms around her mother. As soon as her arms locked, she realized it was the first contact she had initiated since moving home. She cleared her throat and stepped back. "Um, that's great, Mom. I'm happy for you."

"I had to do something. Friday's my last day at work. The scuttlebutt going around is there will be more layoffs by spring. It's not looking good for the plant."

"I heard a similar rumor the other day. This is the last thing Jenna's Creek needs."

"My heart breaks for all those people who'll be out of work. At least I have a little left from your dad's insurance to tide me over until something comes along. Or until my dress making business takes off," she added enthusiastically. "And of course, I have you."

Christy didn't want to measure the implications in that comment. She plopped onto the sofa with a handful of patterns. "You're going to have to sell a lot of dresses to make a living."

Abby sat down beside her. "Yes, lots. At least I won't have to put out a bunch of money to get started. I already have hundreds of patterns and material and notions from when you girls were little. I won't have any problem updating styles. The marketing details are what worry me. I don't know where to begin with that sort of thing. When I was at the dry goods store buying all this stuff, Eileen said she'd carry some on consignment. She has some antique dolls at home she's willing to bring in to make a window display." She sighed. "But business isn't great for her either. It's just her and her sister-in-law, and they can barely afford to keep the doors open. With everyone in town getting laid off, it will only get worse."

Christy fanned out the patterns like a deck of cards. "You shouldn't limit yourself to doll clothes. Have you thought about children's specialty clothes? That's where the money is."

"I don't think anyone around here would be interested in specialty clothes."

"Maybe the friend with the shop in Cincinnati would. Spring is coming. You could put an ad in the paper to make prom dresses. Every girl wants an original dress for prom. Or bridesmaids' dresses. Or graduation. You made all of our special event clothes." Christy nudged her with her shoulder. "You haven't even mentioned wedding gowns. The brides can come here with their mothers for fittings like Jamie did at Christmas."

"Hold it, hold it, hold it," Abby said, near panic. "I'm talking about cute little doll dresses, and you've got me outfitting a wedding party."

"You've made gowns before."

"I altered Jamie's to suit a winter wedding. Your sisters had garden weddings with simple A-line dresses. I didn't have to worry about one of them suing me if they lost a button. This is quickly becoming more than I can handle. I'd have to stay up on the latest fashions even before styles change. It would take a lot more capital than I'm anticipating."

Christy waved away her concerns. "Mom, you've dreamed about doing this since we girls were little."

"That's all it was, a dream."

"Dreams should be acted upon. You kept us fashionably dressed on a shoestring budget. As far as capital, it takes money to make money."

Abby looked forlornly at the stacks of supplies. "This is getting complicated."

"Everything about opening a small business is complicated. It'll be worth the effort."

What other choice do you have? she thought wryly. It wasn't like Jenna's Creek was teeming with career opportunities for an under-qualified, displaced homemaker.

"Have faith," she said, as much to herself as to Abby.

"That's about the only thing I have left."

Christy studied her mother's face. She wanted to say something encouraging and inspiring. Instead, she couldn't keep from wondering what would happen to them, now that Mom was about to receive her last paycheck from the plant. She probably had less than a few years of income squirreled away, regardless of how diligent a saver she had been. What if it took longer than she had saved for before she was able to support herself? What if financial independence never came?

Before the blizzard, Christy had sent out feelers to a few Midwest law firms. She was ready to get back to her life, but she couldn't up and leave with her mother struggling to sell enough doll dresses to keep the lights on. Nor could she live here forever. She didn't want to grow old in her mother's house. She wanted a life. She wanted a future. She wanted…

A man.

An image of Jarrod Bruckner's face reflecting candlelight at the restaurant rushed to mind. He was funny and honest and interesting, and he stirred feelings and hopes in her she thought were long dead. They worked in the same field—sort of—and she couldn't imagine ever getting tired of talking to him. But he didn't really know her. He only knew the funny, witty Christy she let him see. He didn't know the petty, insecure Christy who still broke out in a cold sweat every time she heard a strange man's voice at the library. He didn't know how much she hated Noel Wyatt. He didn't know she hated anything.

She didn't know him that well either, but she was pretty sure he wouldn't understand the weight of unforgiveness she carried in her heart toward her own mother.

She suddenly needed to leave the room or she might burst into tears. "I need to check the casserole. You can't start a business on an empty stomach." She started toward the door and then stopped. "I'm proud of you, Mom. It took a lot of nerve just to come up with the idea."

Abby jumped off the couch and caught hold of Christy's hand. "Sweetie, that means the world to me. This whole idea has got me more excited than I've been since…well, since your dad died. It's all because of your support." Her voice caught, and tears welled in the corners of her eyes. She kissed Christy on the cheek.

For an instant both women stared at each other. Abby pulled Christy into her arms. Christy tensed before allowing herself to relax. It had been a long time since she'd been in her mother's arms, right after Dad's funeral to be exact. It wasn't until a few months later she discovered her brother wasn't her full brother. The worst part about the whole thing was Dad had known all along that the son he loved didn't belong to him.

She pulled away and left the room without another word. The sofa springs groaned as Abby sat back down. Christy *was* proud of her, and she wished her all the best, but she didn't know how much help she could be. She wanted her mother to succeed, but she needed to think of her own future. A future that took her far away from Jenna's Creek.

❦❦❦

Melody didn't feel like eating. She had gone straight upstairs after she got home and started reading the notebook from cover to cover. Her vision blurred from the strain of going over Warner's tiny script, yet she was no closer to discovering the secrets the rows of columns held. Maybe *JB* didn't stand for Jay Beckwith. Maybe Uncle Jay wasn't a drug dealer. She had no proof beyond his habit of leaving the house for a few minutes at a time or having friends stop by at all hours and stay just long enough to meet with him in the driveway. The main proof was that he always had money. Instead of a drug dealer, maybe he was a bank robber. That would require thought and planning. She didn't see Jay putting that much effort into anything.

She turned another page and began sliding her finger along the page to keep from losing her place. She still couldn't figure out what the numbers meant? The bigger question was why Grandpa needed to record everything. Had he been crazy? Melody shook the thought out of her head. Set in his ways, definitely. Compulsive, sure. Even different. But not crazy. Crazy people didn't build up a farming operation the way he had. Crazy people couldn't make her feel loved and special and important and cherished.

He had truly loved her. But why? Why her and not everyone else in his life?

She sat back in the chair and stared unseeing at the row of numbers.

"You should've called Aunt Linda," she said aloud to the ledger under her finger. "She thought you didn't love her."

Her voice broke. She sat back in the chair and looked up at the ceiling. "You didn't call her for forty years. She was your daughter. How could you stay so mad for so long just because she wanted to have her own life?"

Melody shook her head at the futility of the conversation. If Grandpa were here, she wouldn't have the nerve to ask her questions. He wouldn't answer, even if she did. He would grunt and shake his head and tell her some things weren't for her to understand. In his day, a young person knew better than to question their elders. They respected them or earned a swat across their backside. Insolence wasn't tolerated.

"I'm not insolent," she mumbled. "I want to know. Did you love her? Did you love any of them? They don't think you did. Why did you have to be so hard?"

She exhaled and rubbed tears from her eyes. All her life people had told her she was like Grandpa. Mom said it the day after the blizzard when Melody was making judgments about Lowell, Jay, and Carson. At the time she was flattered. To be like Grandpa meant she was strong, confident, and committed to her beliefs. Now she realized it also meant she was stubborn, opinionated, and unforgiving.

She didn't want to be those things. She didn't want to be remembered as rigid and judgmental. Was that all Grandpa had been?

He always said the greatest legacy he could leave his family was his faith. But he hadn't. His faith and belief that God held the whole world in his hands were the last things people thought of when they remembered him. His testimony had been selfishness and unforgiveness, which was worse than no testimony at all in Melody's opinion.

Was that what was in store for her? The testimony of a bitter, self-righteous hag who snooped through drawers when no one was looking because she wanted to see the worst in everyone?

She steepled her fingers and rested her chin on them. She tried to formulate the thoughts she wanted to pray. "Grandpa wanted to serve you, Lord. He wanted people to see you in his life. At least that's what he said. It seems like all he really wanted was to be right, no matter who he hurt in the process."

As soon as she spoke the prayer, she knew it wasn't fair. Grandpa *had* left a legacy of faith, if only to her. She knew he loved the Lord. She knew he wanted his sons to be strong, even if he had gone about achieving his goal all wrong. Maybe he hadn't been taught to show love. He had never been shown grace or compassion so he didn't know how to extend it to others.

All the flip flopping back and forth was giving her a headache. She should go downstairs and get something to eat. Only she couldn't think about food right now. All she wanted to do was understand her grandfather. She thought of the parents he never talked about. She thought of his little brother. Was Ivan like him? Had a bad childhood created two men who loved their families but were totally ineffective at expressing it? Maybe there had been abuse. Normal people didn't burn down stores—if it had really happened. Normal people didn't live their entire lives without ever mentioning where and whom they had come from.

There must've been a reason.

Melody reached for the phone next to her bed. After two rings, it was picked up on the other end. "Hey, it's Melody," she said as soon as Christy spoke. "Are you free on Saturday?"

"I think so."

"Good. How about a road trip?"

"Where are we going?"

"Springfield, Ohio."

"Okay," Christy said cautiously. "What are we doing in Springfield?"

"We're going to find my uncle Ivan."

CHAPTER FIFTEEN

"Can one of you move my bureau for me after dinner?" Clarice asked the three men seated around the kitchen table. "I can't find my mother's sapphire broach. I want to wear it to church on Sunday. It must've gotten lost when you were setting up my room downstairs. I can't get down on my hands and knees to look."

Carson studied his plate. Out of the corner of his eye, he saw Jay shoot Lowell a scathing look. Lowell didn't stop eating his manicotti.

"You're not going to feel like going out in this weather, Mom," Jay said.

"I might. I want to lay out an outfit, just in case."

He exhaled and went back to his dinner. "That broach could've fallen out anywhere when we were moving the bureau downstairs. We'll have to search along every baseboard in this house."

"Well, at least you'll have somewhere to start looking."

Jay exhaled again, visibly fighting down his irritation. "I'll do it tomorrow. I'm going out tonight."

"Again? You haven't spent three consecutive nights in this house since your father died."

Carson tensed. He wished his grandmother would let the matter drop. Jay wasn't going to do anything he didn't want to do.

Jay shoveled another bite into his mouth without acknowledging her comment.

"Where are you going this time?"

"Out."

"Will you be with that Lenny Brown character again? I don't like you spending so much time with him."

"I'm not going to argue about this, Mom. I didn't let you pick my friends when I was in school and I'm not going to let you do it now."

"Jay, please. I've heard some very bad things about that man. He's had assault charges filed against him, and that's probably the least trouble he's been in. I don't know why you associate with someone like that."

"Maybe his mother says the same thing about me."

"That isn't funny." Clarice painted a petulant look on her face and tried another tactic. "Please, Jay. Stay home. I miss you."

Jay continued to eat, giving no indication he was listening.

"Well, if you can't stay home once in a while, the least you can do is go to church with me. In fact, we'll all go. It would've meant so much to your dad."

Jay snorted. "I have plans."

"Me too," Lowell echoed.

"It's only Friday. That gives you two days to clear your schedules," she said with uncharacteristic fervor. "I don't ask much from you boys. You can do this one thing for me."

Jay took one last bite and scooted out his chair.

"Jay," Clarice snapped. "We're not finished."

"I am."

"You can stay at the table until the rest of us are done."

"Mom, it's too late to try to turn us into some TV version of the perfect family."

Tears sparkled in Clarice's eyes, but she squared her shoulders. "You would never talk to me like that if your father were here. At least take your plate to the sink."

"I've got people waiting." He stalked out of the room.

"Who? Who's waiting?" Clarice asked no one in particular since Jay was already gone.

Carson reached for Jay's plate. "I've got it, Grandma."

"Brown nose," Lowell muttered.

"Thank you, dear," Clarice told Carson. She watched the doorway as if expecting Jay to reconsider and come back. "I don't understand that boy. He's either on his way out or his friends are dropping by at all hours. What's going on with him?"

Lowell kept eating while Carson rinsed Jay's plate in the sink.

Clarice slammed her hand down on the table, though in her weakened state, she barely rattled her own silverware. "I'm asking a question. Someone better tell me what's going on around here. What's Jay doing hanging around with Lenny Brown all the time? I thought Lenny was your friend, Lowell."

Lowell finally looked up from his plate. "Nobody's friends with Lenny."

Carson wanted to tell her a blind man could figure out what Jay was up to every time his roughneck friends showed up in the middle of the night. Instead, he turned off the water. "Nothing's going on, Grandma. Jay's just restless because he can't find work."

"Well, he better find something soon or he can move out."

Carson and Lowell exchanged glances. Clarice never made ultimatums, and neither was too worried she'd enforce this one. She would grumble and complain, but when it came down to it, she'd look the other way, and Jay would continue doing whatever it was he was doing, just like always.

"I miss Warner." Her voice quaked. "Things were so much easier when he was here. He would make Jay stay home."

"Pop didn't have as much control around here as you think," Lowell said.

"What's that supposed to mean?"

"Only that Jay's not doing anything he hasn't always done."

"I don't understand. What are you talking about? I have a right to know what's going on in my own house."

Lowell let out a belabored sigh and got up. He cut a large chunk out of the pineapple upside down cake Carson had baked earlier and put it on a plate. "Don't get yourself worked up, Mom. The less you know, the better. Take care of the dishes, Carson. I'm going upstairs. I have a headache."

Lowell hadn't washed a dish, swept a floor, or cooked a meal since he moved in. Tonight would be no exception. Carson watched Clarice out of the corner of his eye while he cleared the table. Did she truly have no idea what Jay was doing? Lowell was right; it wasn't anything new. Warner had complained, too, about cars pulling into the driveway at all hours of the day and night. His demands to know where Jay went for two or three days at a stretch were ignored as well. With Warner gone and the snow melting from the highway, Jay's trips out of town had increased while unsavory visitors showed up more and more often. If Grandma thought about it for a minute, she wouldn't have to wonder why Jay always had money even though he hadn't worked in two years.

"Where did I go wrong with those two?" she asked suddenly.

Carson was pretty sure she didn't expect an answer. He tucked a sheet of aluminum foil around the cake pan and put it in the breadbox.

"You can do that later, dear," Clarice said. "Sit down and talk to me."

He dropped into his chair and waited. He hoped she wouldn't ask about Jay. Every day it got harder and harder to lie to her.

"They don't respect me. They never have, but I thought at least they loved me." Tears simmered in her voice.

"They do love you, Grandma."

She stared at the wall as if he hadn't spoke. "Warner was the one who kept order. I was the one they came to when they needed something. Now I have to do both. Well, I'm not strong enough. I've never been able to tell them no and they know it."

"They're grown men. You shouldn't have to make them behave."

"I gave them whatever they wanted. I wanted them to love me, but it hasn't worked. They don't love me. They use me. Now they're hanging around waiting for me to die. As soon as I'm gone, they'll take what they can and never look back. I bet neither one of them will bother to visit my grave."

"Come on, Grandma, you know that's not true," Carson said in a lackluster tone. He was tired of defending his worthless father and uncle.

"You'll visit me, won't you, Carson? I couldn't bear it if my grave got overgrown with weeds. You know how people talk. They'll know nobody loved me while I was alive."

"Grandma, stop talking like that," he said sharply.

She looked up, startled.

"I mean it," he reiterated. "You're talking nonsense. You have plenty of people who love you." He swallowed and forced out the words that had never came easy. "I love you."

She tilted her head. "Do you really?" she asked hopefully.

Carson couldn't remember the last time he'd said those words to a living soul and actually meant them. He'd said it plenty of times to women when he knew it was what they wanted to hear before they gave him what he wanted. He used to say it to his mother when he was young and could earn her approval just by being her son. Those days were long gone.

"Of course I do. I'm sorry if you didn't know before."

Clarice placed her gnarled hands on top of his. Tears glistened in her eyes. Carson couldn't remember seeing her look so happy. Heaviness settled in his stomach, and a lump the size of a boulder rose in his throat. Good grief. What was the matter with him?

"You're a good boy, Carson," she said. "I know you had some trouble before you came here, but I've seen the changes in you. I hope you've seen them too."

He resisted the urge to pull his hands away. He didn't deserve her praise. He sure didn't deserve the look of adoration in her faded gray eyes. If she knew one thing about his past, one thing about what he was doing right now, she wouldn't offer her love so freely either.

"When's the last time you spoke to your mother?"

He swallowed the lump in his throat. He needed to get up and finish the dishes. Allen was compensating him handsomely. The least he could do was earn his keep by taking care of Grandma and the house. "Not since I got here."

She slapped his hands. "That's not acceptable. I want you to call her tonight. She's probably wondering how you fared during the blizzard."

"I doubt she's given me a second thought since I left Texas."

"Of course she has, even if she doesn't show it. You need to let her know you're all right and you miss her. You do miss her, don't you?"

"Sometimes," he lied.

"Then tell her, and tell her you love her. Mothers need to hear it."

He didn't answer.

She studied him in silence for a moment. "Carson, why did you come here?"

He thought about lying again. He had been doing it for so long, the words nearly slipped off his tongue. But Grandma looked so vulnerable, and she had been so good to him, she deserved the truth.

"They told me to leave."

"They?"

"Mom and Milt. I'd been working for Milt since I got out of school. I got in trouble with a couple of guys who play the horses. I skimmed a little money from the company to pay them back. It was pretty easy. I didn't think anyone noticed so I did it again."

It didn't look like Clarice was following. He went on anyway, liberated by how good the confession felt. "I kept helping myself to company funds. Not a lot. Just a couple hundred bucks here and there. Mom finally confronted me. I swore to her I'd stop. Then I bet against Seattle Slew to win the Triple Crown. I know it was a sucker bet, but who would'a thought there'd be three Triple Crown winners in the same decade. The odds were too good for a gambler like me to pass up."

Her answer was a blank stare.

"That race cost me a lot of money. I had to come up with it fast or I was going to pay the hard way. I guess Milt wasn't willing to look the other way anymore. He told me to get out of town. He was through covering for me. He and Mom didn't care where I went, as long as I went and didn't come back. If I didn't leave, or if I asked Mom to bail me out again, Milt was going to sic the cops on me. He had all the proof he needed to make sure I did a lot of time."

Clarice put her fingers against her lips. "Your poor mother doesn't know where you are?"

"She knows. I hid out with some friends for a few weeks before I left. I really didn't want to leave Houston. Not for my mom but for my friends. But it became apparent Milt wasn't the only one who wanted a pound of my flesh."

Clarice furrowed her brow. Carson didn't offer further explanation. She'd either figure it out or not. It was up to her. "I had to get the heck out of Dodge and go somewhere I knew I wouldn't be found. That's why I picked here. I gave Mom the same story I gave you. I told her I was coming because of your health and I wanted to spend time with Dad. Believe me, she took the news like a trooper. She was more relieved than anything."

"You're her only son."

He blew out a puff of air. "I've always been more trouble than I'm worth. She's glad I'm out of her hair."

Clarice nodded as only a mother who understood the disappointment in one's sons could. "That may have been true in the beginning, but I'm sure she wants to hear from you. If she was hard on you, it was because she wanted the best for you. It's a parent's way, Carson. That's how Warner was. I was the soft one. Look where it got me. No one comes around unless they want something."

"I'm here."

She reached over and touched his cheek. "Yes, my dear Carson. I'm sorry you got into trouble at home, but I believe you're here for a reason. Warner died before me for a reason. We can't usually see the big picture in the beginning, but it always works out for the best."

The moment had grown too uncomfortable. Carson pushed his chair away from the table and went back to the sink. "I'll go upstairs and look for your broach as soon as I finish these."

Clarice scooted out her chair and leaned against the table to heave herself to her feet. "Don't bother. The broach is gone. I knew before I asked."

"I'm sorry, Grandma."

She started the slow shuffle back to the living room. "So am I."

CHAPTER SIXTEEN

"I only found one listing for Beckwith in the Springfield phone book I got from the library," Melody said as she turned up the defroster inside the car. They were two weeks into March and it felt colder than ever. A gust of wind buffeted the car as she drove along the flat landscape. The hills of Auburn County had helped prevent major drifting in recent weeks. Now as she drove west toward Springfield she could see the hill wasn't the only place that suffered destruction from the snowdrifts.

"There was no Ivan Beckwith in the whole county. The only listing was for a Paul Beckwith. I called information to confirm the address."

"I'm not sure how this is going to work with us showing up out of the blue," Christy said. "Maybe we should've called first."

"I don't want to give anyone time to think up ways to sugarcoat the truth. I want real answers, even if I end up embarrassing myself."

"There's a possibility this Paul Beckwith isn't related to your grandpa. Warner moved away sixty years ago. There's also a possibility Ivan is dead. Didn't you figure he's about seventy-four? Men don't generally live much longer than that."

Melody tightened her grip on the steering wheel in agitation as much as in response to the gust of wind that threatened to push her into oncoming traffic. "I thought of all that, but I have to find out what I can. I can't keep sitting at home thinking about how I didn't know Grandpa the way I thought. I loved him more than anything. He was my best friend. He always told me he wanted to leave a legacy of faith for his children. It turns out the only legacy he left was jealousy, bitterness, and greed."

"I'm sure that isn't true."

Melody lifted her shoulders inside her coat. "It is as far as everyone else in the family is concerned. I only knew the side Grandpa allowed me to see. I sort of liked our close relationship that shut everyone else out. I knew I was special to him and I liked it that way. I was blind." She exhaled tears of frustration. "Or dumb. Maybe I didn't want to see how judgmental he was to the rest of the family. Maybe it's because I'm the same way."

"Sometimes the people we love disappoint us most." Christy turned from the window to look at her. "Sometimes we disappoint them. But it doesn't change our love for them. Nobody's perfect."

"That's strange coming from you, Christy."

Christy nodded. "I know. I never thought I could forgive Mom for what she did to Dad. But it takes so much energy holding the past against her. I want her to be happy. Whatever that means."

"Do you mean it?" Melody asked sharply.

"She got laid off last week."

"Oh, no. I hate to hear that."

Christy nodded. "More layoffs are coming. It's bad news for the whole area."

"It's happening everywhere. I'm so sorry for both of you."

Christy lifted one shoulder. "Me too, but maybe it's a blessing in disguise. She wasn't happy at that factory. It was just something to pay the bills while she got used to being without Dad."

"What's she going to do now?"

Christy turned halfway in her seat to face Melody. "She's thinking about starting her own business."

"Wow. How exciting."

Christy twisted her mouth in doubt and turned back to face the road. "I don't know. It's scary in this economy. It's a dress making business. I sort of pushed her into it. Now I feel guilty. She's always wanted to do something like this, but I don't know how feasible it'll be in Jenna's Creek, especially with so many factories shutting down and people losing their jobs."

"She'll never know if she can be successful unless she goes for it."

"I guess. Still scary."

"It's a good thing she has you." Melody watched Christy for a moment. "She does have you, right?"

"I don't know. A few months ago I was all ready to leave Jenna's Creek. I never would've come home at all if those idiots hadn't robbed me and left me stranded in Kentucky. I always wanted to have a career in law. I sure didn't imagine I'd be stuck living with my mother at this point in my life."

"And now you're not feeling so stuck?"

Christy laughed. "You're really good at reading people." She fiddled with the radio for a moment and turned down the volume on a commercial. "Mom and I have been getting along pretty well the last few months. I guess getting snowbound with someone will do that. You've been talking about how you didn't know your grandpa as well as you thought you did. I'm starting to feel the same way about Mom. Growing up, I always thought of her as some kind of drill sergeant. She was always so, I don't know...in charge."

It was Melody's turn to laugh. "You mean like you?"

"I'm not a drill sergeant." Christy twisted the dial on the car heater. "I can't believe how cold it is. It looks like they got more snow up here than we did."

"I think we got about the same amount. There's just not as many hills to slow down the drifting. Remember the wind speeds the first day of the blizzard?"

"One hundred miles an hour," they said in unison.

"I kept thinking I heard someone talking," Christy said. "It was weird with just Mom and me in the house. It was like we were in a bubble. Except for that infernal wind."

"On the hill, it made the hair stand up on the back of my neck." Melody rubbed her neck with one hand, remembering. "Don't change the subject. We were talking about you staying in Jenna's Creek."

"I thought we were talking about me being bossy like my mother."

"They're the same thing, aren't they?"

Christy gave her a wry smile.

"So, how do you feel about your mom now that you don't see her as a drill sergeant?"

"I don't know. I know she misses Dad. She's never been on her own. She would be terrified if I wasn't there. With me around, she's more courageous. She feels more confident about stepping out on her own and taking risks. I don't know if she'd do it if I left."

"I don't know if you'd be happy if you left."

Christy snagged her bottom lip with her teeth.

"What about Jarrod?"

Christy lowered her eyes, and a flush moved up her neck into her cheeks. "What about him?"

Melody exhaled. "Don't give me that? You know what I'm talking about."

"I'm not going to base my life around a man." She tried to look nonchalant, but Melody saw through the façade.

"I'm not suggesting you do. I just don't see why you can't have what you want in life, whatever that is, and a man too."

Christy cocked her head. "I could tell you the same thing."

"I haven't met the right one yet."

"Are you saying I have?"

Melody watched the telltale flush color Christy's cheeks. "I wouldn't know."

"Okay, I guess I do like him." She smiled. "A lot. But I don't know. I haven't told him about what happened at Bennis, Banociac, and Weiss."

Melody's eyes widened. "What are you waiting for?"

"I'm not ready for him to know how stupid I was. Once he meets the real me, he'll run in the other direction. If he's smart, he would."

"Christy, you weren't stupid."

Christy waved away her words. "Even if there wasn't that, there are so many other things that make me wonder if we're compatible. He's close to his family. He reveres his mother. If he knew how hard it's been for me to forgive Mom for what happened between her and Noel Wyatt, he would think I was a selfish brat."

"How hard is it?"

Christy shook her head and took a few moments to formulate a response. "It doesn't seem fair to keep punishing her for something that happened twenty-four years ago."

"Have you forgiven her?"

"Most of the time."

Christy continued looking out the window. Finally she looked back at Melody. "So here we are. Back to Mom, and me leaving or staying in Jenna's Creek. Every time I think of my brother giving up an exciting career somewhere for his small town wife, I think he's making a huge mistake. I mean, who would want to stay in Jenna's Creek when they could make a nice living in any city in the world?"

"Gee, thanks."

Christy shook her head again. "I didn't mean you. I just meant…well, when I think of everything I'd miss if I left, like you, I don't know if I want to go anymore."

Melody patted her shoulder. "That makes me feel better."

Both women watched the road and listened to the radio a few minutes. Melody broke the silence. "You know you don't have to go anywhere if you don't want. And you don't have to make a decision today."

"I know. It's just hard."

Melody pursed her lips and nodded thoughtfully as she thought about Christy's words. "Not for me. I've never wanted to leave home. I'd be perfectly content living on the farm and working at social services the rest of my life, even though it's so different now…" Her voice caught. It would never be the same without Grandpa. She wished she could talk to him one more time and ask him all the questions whirling in her head.

"Promise me you'll pray about leaving…or staying. I mean it, Christy. Pray. If you don't, you'll end up making a mistake."

Christy gave a quick nod before turning back to the highway. Melody glanced at her profile. She prayed Christy truly would pray, that she'd give her life to the Savior. Melody could understand why she still held onto unforgiveness for what Abby had done with Noel Wyatt. She also knew it would destroy her friend if she didn't find a way to banish it from her heart.

❧❧❧

Melody brought the car to a stop in front of a small house on a street in a rundown neighborhood. The houses looked like pre-World War Two when textile mills were going up all over Ohio. The house was painted a pale yellow that had probably been cheery in its day. Now the faded, flaking paint made the house look even more dismal against the grimy snow that had been shoveled into piles nearly as high as the low-pitched roof. A tan sedan sat under the carport and didn't look like it had been moved in weeks. The driveway had been shoveled out by hand though it had drifted over again in spots.

"This is the address from the phonebook," she said as she and Christy stared at the little house. They couldn't tell if there were lights on inside, but with the car under the carport and outside temperatures too low for most people to walk anywhere, it was a safe bet they'd find Paul Beckwith at home.

"What's the plan?" Christy asked without looking away from the house.

"We'll go up and knock." Melody realized she sounded more confident than she felt. She was already second-guessing the wisdom in this trip. She wasn't sure what she hoped to find. "I'm looking for family. People do it every day."

As if she thought Melody would talk herself out of it, Christy opened her door and swung her legs out. Melody had no choice but to turn off the car and follow suit. She zipped up her coat, threw her purse over her shoulder, and climbed out of the car. Christy was standing on the other side of the car waiting, her hands deep in her pockets and her shoulders hunched against the cold. The sky was clear, and a watery sun glistened off the snow blanketing the neighborhood. For once, there was no wind, though it couldn't have been more than twenty degrees. Too cold for dawdling or second-guessing. Melody hurried around the car and led the way up the short walk. She hoped Paul Beckwith had seen them pull up and wouldn't leave them waiting outside for long.

At the door, she and Christy exchanged looks. Melody barely completed her knock before a thin woman pulled it open. She was somewhere in her sixties with steel gray streaking her faded brown hair. Her lined face looked tired, but a cautious smile softened her features.

"Good morning," Melody said before the woman had a chance to speak. "I'm Melody Knauff. This is Christy Blackwood. We're looking for Paul Beckwith."

The woman studied them as her expression turned suspicious. "There is no Paul Beckwith."

Melody's heart sank. She was sure it showed on her face. "Oh, I…"

Christy stepped closer to the door. "Do you know if any Beckwiths ever lived here?"

The woman looked from one of them to the other, sizing them up. Finally she pushed open the storm door. "You might as well come in. It's much too cold to do this through the screen."

Melody and Christy stepped into the warmth of the house. The door opened directly into a small, cramped living room. Nearly every paneled wall was lined with pictures and shelves that reached to the ceiling, crammed full of framed photographs, books, bric-a-brac, and mementoes chronicling the woman's life and interests. Just like at the farmhouse, doilies topped the backs of every chair and sat under vases of silk flowers and picture arrangements.

The woman reached around them to close the door. "What's this all about? Why are you looking for Paul Beckwith?"

Melody took a deep breath. She glanced at Christy, almost hoping she would take over. Christy offered a nod of encouragement and nothing else.

"My grandfather is…" Melody began, "…*was* Warner Beckwith. He grew up around here. Well, he grew up in Springfield. Or as far as I can tell, he did. I don't know much about his family, and that's what I was hoping to find—"

Christy jumped in to end Melody's rambling and save them all a lot of time. "He had a brother Ivan. Since Paul was the only Beckwith in the phone book, we thought he, or you I guess, might know something about the family."

The woman visibly relaxed. "There's never been a Paul Beckwith, at least not to my knowledge. Ivan died years ago. Let me have your coats." She held out her hands expectantly. Melody and Christy complied, though Melody wasn't sure there was a point if this woman didn't know Paul, and Ivan had passed away.

After she and Christy handed over their coats, the woman motioned them toward the sofa as she hung the coats on a metal coat tree by the door. "You might as well make yourselves comfortable. Now, who did you girls say you were?"

"I'm—"

The woman clapped her hands together, startling Melody into silence. She hurried across the small room and opened a drawer in a credenza. Melody and Christy exchanged glances while she rooted around in the drawer. Finally she found what she was looking for and turned to face them with a triumphant look on her face. She held up a photograph. "Nugget."

"Excuse me," Christy said.

The woman hurried back to them and held the picture out to Melody. "I'm so sorry. I should've realized right away who you were when you said you were Warner's granddaughter. How could I have missed it with that beautiful hair?" Her voice caught. "Did you say Warner *was* your grandpa?"

Melody nodded as she took the picture from the woman. She gasped at the sight of it. She had never seen it before. It was her all right, perched on Grandpa's forearm. She must've been about two or three. It was summertime, and the bright sun glinted off the reddish blond hair she'd been born with. One arm was clasped around Warner's neck. With the other hand, she was pointing at the camera. She was grinning broadly, her eyes squinting against the summer sun. Warner was smiling, too, something he seldom did in photographs. He looked young and strong, the way Melody would always remember him.

Christy leaned toward her to peer at the picture. "Oh, Melody." She sounded choked up, too, but Melody didn't look at her to see.

She looked from the picture to the woman standing on the other side of the scarred coffee table. She started to speak but had to clear her throat first. "Where did you get this?"

"Warner sent it twenty-some years ago." The woman moved to a chair where she obviously spent a lot of time and sat down.

Tears pooled in Melody's eyes, making it hard to see the picture in her hand. She wouldn't want to give it back when it was time to leave, but she certainly didn't have the nerve to ask to keep it.

"Ivan was my husband," the woman said. "He died in 1970. When did Warner pass away? I wish I'd known."

Melody set the picture on the coffee table in front of her. "January. The morning the blizzard hit, actually. The phones were out and we didn't have a way to get in touch with anyone for a few weeks. We wouldn't have known how to reach you…" She took a deep breath. "I'm sorry."

"Oh, sweetheart, don't worry about me. It wasn't your fault. It was a decision Ivan and Warner made a long time ago." She sat back in the chair, and her eyes took on a distant expression. "Those men went through a lot growing up."

Melody sat forward on the couch. "That's why we came. I thought you might be able to answer some questions about Grandpa. I don't know anything about his life here. I don't even know your name."

"Oh, of course. I'm so sorry. When I figured out who you were, I guess my good sense flew right out of my head. I'm Paulette Beckwith. My son thought it best I not broadcast in the phonebook that I live alone. I shortened Paulette to Paul for the listing."

"You have a son?" Melody asked. She had a cousin. Or step-cousin.

"I have two." Paulette put her hands on the arms of the chair and stood with a slight groan. "Would you like some coffee?" She headed into the tiny kitchen. "I'll be so happy when this snow melts. I hate to complain about the weather, but it seems like we'll never see green grass again."

"We were talking about that on the way here," Christy said conversationally as she and Melody stood and followed.

Paulette motioned them to the table while she went to a coffeemaker on the counter. "I used to love snow. After this winter I won't mind if I never see it again. I can make some hot chocolate if you'd prefer."

Both women shook their heads and sat at the table facing the counter where Paulette worked. While the old coffeemaker hissed and gurgled, she took a plate of homemade bread out of the refrigerator. "I'm so glad I baked zucchini bread yesterday. It's from my last mess of the summer. She peeled back the cellophane wrap and cut off thick slices. "I don't get much company. Those first few weeks after the blizzard I thought I would go out of my mind. The young couple in the next house is very sweet. They came over that first day to check on me. It was sort of an adventure then. But they had their own family and things to tend to so I was here most of the time by myself. I couldn't get to church or run errands. I don't work anymore." She sighed. "Yes, it's been a long, lonely winter for me."

She put the zucchini bread slices on little plates and carried them to the table, then went back to the coffeemaker, which had stopped bubbling and hissing.

Christy slid one of the plates to Melody. "I live in a neighborhood much like this one. Even though there were people nearby, we felt so isolated."

Paulette's smile widened. "That's how it was for me. It's getting better all the time, but still lonely. I've had too much time on my hands since I stopped working, but I didn't notice it much before the blizzard."

"Is there anything I can do to help?" Christy asked.

Melody chastened herself for not thinking to offer. Her mind was going in too many directions to think of courtesy.

"No, no," Paulette said over her shoulder. "I'm sure you girls didn't drive all this way for zucchini bread." She looked at Melody. "I don't know how much I can tell you about your grandpa. Ivan didn't talk about him very often. I just know he loved his brother. And Warner loved him." Her voice grew clogged. "It broke his heart when Ivan died. He had all of you, of course, but Ivan was the last member of his family."

Melody wanted to tell her no, it hadn't broken Grandpa's heart. By all appearances, Ivan's passing hadn't even caused a ripple. Melody remembered 1970 well. It was her last full year in high school. She saw Grandpa every day, the same as she had every other year of her life. She never saw him cry. She didn't remember him acting morose or going off by himself. She never even saw him bow his head as if remembering something painful. Paulette might as well have been talking about a stranger. Not Warner Beckwith. Not the man in whose shadow Melody grew up.

She swallowed hard, not trusting her voice. "Grandpa never told me anything about Ivan. I didn't even know he had a brother until his funeral." She didn't add that she wouldn't have known then if she hadn't tricked Grandma into telling her.

Paulette nodded as if it came as no surprise. "Warner and Ivan were very private people. They grew up hard. Their dad wasn't around and their poor mommy had to work her fingers to the bone just to put food on the table."

Melody sat forward on the couch. "What happened to their dad?"

Paulette sighed as she poured coffee into three cups. "He took off. I thought you knew."

Melody wanted to scream. She thought she had already made it abundantly clear she didn't know anything. "Grandpa never intimated he wasn't raised by both his parents."

"I'm not surprised. Warner wouldn't want you to feel sorry for him."

Now that was the Grandpa Melody knew.

Paulette placed the cups on the table and sat in the chair across from Melody. "I must say it's nice making coffee for someone again. It sure is lonely without Ivan, even though he's been gone for so long." She sprinkled powdered creamer into her coffee and then slid the container to the center of the table in case the others wanted some.

"I wasn't Ivan's first wife," she said. "I'm his third. He wasn't the first man in my life either. Maybe that's how we both learned to keep some things in the past where they belonged."

Melody wasn't sure she agreed with that logic between people in such an intimate relationship, but she was the last person who knew what it took to make a successful relationship.

Paulette took a sip of coffee. "Maybe Ivan told his other wives more than he did me. I seriously doubt it, though. He did talk about how it was growing up without a daddy. I suppose that's why he looked up to Warner so much. Warner was nine years older than him. He idolized that man." She wrapped her hands around her coffee cup and stared into the creamy liquid for a moment. "I had some health problems before Ivan passed away and we were flat broke. Just as my health started improving, Ivan died. I didn't know what to do. My boys couldn't afford to help. They had families of their own. But as soon as Warner found out, he drove up here and offered to do whatever he could."

She broke off a piece of zucchini bread. "Warner took care of the whole thing. I didn't even have to ask. He even gave me a little money to tide me over." She smiled gently at Melody. "That was the kind of man your grandpa was."

Blood rushed to Melody's face. She fought back the urge to burst into tears. She had always known Grandpa as kind and generous, but apparently he was also selfish. How could he have kept back such an important part of himself from her and the rest of the family?

"Ivan was proud of how successful your grandpa became. When he did talk about the past, he said he always knew Warner would make something of himself. Not like Ivan. I love the man, but he didn't have Warner's gumption. Even he knew it. He said when they were kids, Warner was always scratching around, figuring out a way to bring home a few dollars. Nothing went to waste around him."

Melody's heart softened a little. "I used to wonder if Grandpa was always like that. He said it was a curse from growing up poor."

"That's one thing Ivan and Warner knew plenty about. Ivan used to say, 'Use it up, wear it out. Make it do...'"

"Or do without," Melody finished with her.

They looked at each other, and then all three women laughed.

"Grandpa said that all the time," she told Christy.

"I never heard that saying before, but it's a mentality my parents must've known well."

Paulette brushed zucchini crumbs off her blouse. "Most of us did in those days. I'm a bit of a packrat as you can see. I can't bear to throw anything out."

"Grandpa was the same way," Melody said.

"William, that was Ivan's daddy, he left the family when Ivan was just a little fella. Warner was more of a father to him than a brother, which is pretty amazing considering Warner didn't have a father of his own to teach him how to be one."

Melody nearly choked on her zucchini bread. "What? Grandpa didn't have a father? What about William?"

"Oh, honey, William wasn't Warner's father. I don't believe Rose ever married that man, though I can't say for sure. It was certainly taboo in those days. Good people didn't talk about it. I've heard tell of women who made up husbands who went away to war or off to work and died in a tragic mining accident or some such thing. It was better than admitting she wasn't married to her baby's daddy."

Melody sank against the chair back. "You mean Grandpa wasn't a Beckwith? My mother isn't a Beckwith?"

Christy put her hand on Melody's arm.

Paulette's gaze darkened with concern. "Maybe not legally, but it doesn't make no never mind now, does it? A last name doesn't mean anything."

"It does to me," Melody practically shrieked. "It would matter to my mother." Even as she said it, she wasn't so sure. Mom had been pushing aside her questions since Grandpa's death. Maybe she knew more than she had been telling and was hoping Melody would get tired of asking.

Christy's grip tightened on her arm. Melody took a deep breath and scrubbed a shaky hand over her face. "I'm sorry. You're right. A last name doesn't change the man he was."

Only he wasn't the same man. He was a total stranger.

CHAPTER SEVENTEEN

Paulette and Christy went back into the living room where Paulette showed Christy pictures of her grandchildren, and Christy told her about how much she enjoyed her job at the library when she hadn't expected to like it in the beginning. In the meantime, Melody went into the bathroom and had a good cry. Afterward, she washed her face and touched up her makeup. She hated making a scene in front of Christy and a woman she hadn't known was her great-aunt. It took about twenty minutes to pull herself together enough to go back into the living room. Christy and Paulette warily watched her take her place on the couch and tried to pretend they didn't know what had gone on in the bathroom.

"I'm sorry," she told both of them.

Paulette tilted her head in sympathy. "It's all right, sweetheart. We've all lost someone we love."

At least the person you loved didn't turn out to be a complete stranger, she wanted to say.

Instead she nodded. She wanted to learn as much as she could from Paulette, and she couldn't do so if she kept crying or getting defensive at every new development.

"I didn't give you the chance to tell me what happened to William."

Paulette sat back in her chair apparently relieved Melody wasn't about to have another meltdown. "The way Ivan talked, it sounded like he had itchy feet. Like I said before, Ivan didn't remember him that well. One day he was there, and then he wasn't. Neither Rose nor Warner talked about it. Warner left school to find work and become the man of the house."

"That must've been hard," Christy said.

Melody realized she had been selfish the whole day. Christy had lost her own father a few years ago and was still rebuilding a tenuous relationship with her mother. To have a father just disappear, and then for no one to mention him again, would add insult to injury.

Paulette nodded. "It was. It was around the time of the First World War. Warner couldn't go because he was responsible for his mother and little brother. That always tortured him. Ivan said he would get all quiet and brooding when he heard about young men in their town dying." She exhaled and looked out the window. "Ivan said Warner never complained about their lot in life. It wouldn't have done any good. At least not until that business with the store, that is. Ivan never knew the details, but he figured out enough. He overheard the arguments."

Melody's heart leapt into her throat. The store. Had it burned down like Lowell said? Did Paulette know if Grandpa was responsible?

"Arguments with the storeowner?" Christy asked.

Paulette turned her gaze to Christy. "No. Arguments between Warner and Rose. From what I understood, Rose got into some kind of trouble with Ab Keim. My, my, my. Ivan said he never saw Warner so mad. He wanted to kill Ab. Ivan was afraid he would."

Melody shook her head. "Wait a minute. Can we go back to the beginning? Is Ab Keim the man who owned the store where Grandpa worked?"

Paulette nodded. "He owned several other businesses in the neighborhood as well. He was very successful. He had taken Warner under his wing, so to speak, for a long time. Then all the sudden, something went sour and Warner hated the man. Ivan never knew what it was about though."

Melody's mind raced. If Rose had gotten into trouble with the storeowner, it would definitely give Grandpa motive to burn down the store. She could imagine he would do anything to protect his mother. Perhaps his intention had been more sinister. What if he meant to kill Ab Keim? That would explain him showing up on the farm and his reluctance to talk about the past. Had authorities questioned him, or tried to, and that's when he ran? And how would Lowell have found out any of it? If Ivan barely knew anything, it didn't make sense that Lowell, of all people, knew anything at all.

"What made Ivan think Warner would kill the man?" Christy asked. "What did he do that made him so mad?"

Paulette lifted one narrow shoulder. "I'm sorry, honey. I really don't know. It had something to do with Rose, though. That's all I know. Neither of them ever said and Ivan was too young to understand. To be honest, he never thought much about it, even after he got older."

Paulette leaned forward and slowly got to her feet. "I have something for you, Melody."

She left the room. Christy and Melody exchanged glances. Melody's heart rose. Maybe it was an old notebook of Grandpa's. Dare she hope he left something in writing that would answer her questions?

After several minutes Paulette returned clutching a hardback Bible to her chest. She stopped in front of the women, still holding it like a prized possession. "This belonged to your grandmother. Rose was a devout woman of faith. Ivan remembers her reading him stories from this Bible. It doesn't seem right that I keep it. My boys were from my first husband. Rose was your grandma."

She held out the Bible, and Melody took it. "I know you're hurt Warner wasn't a Beckwith. But maybe having the Bible that meant so much to your great-grandmother will bring you comfort."

Melody gazed up at Paulette through tear-filled eyes. "Thank you," she mumbled. She struggled to stand with the heavy bible in her hands and circled the coffee table to hug her. "This means a lot to me." She realized it was true. Even though it wasn't a journal from Grandpa explaining everything, a Bible from the grandmother she never knew was a precious gift.

⸙⸙⸙

Melody backed out of Paulette's driveway and headed to the downtown district they had come through on their way into town.

After a few blocks Christy broke the silence. "It was very nice of Paulette to give you the Bible."

"It's nice imagining Rose reading it to Grandpa and Ivan."

Christy nodded thoughtfully but didn't speak.

"He wasn't always a Christian." Melody gave Christy a wry smile. "I guess none of us were. Grandpa said when he was a young man he didn't see a need for God in his life. Working the land was what made him aware of a Creator. He couldn't figure out how a person could look at creation and doubt the presence of a holy God."

Her voice broke. "Of course it turns out he lied to me about a lot of things."

"Don't say that," Christy said quickly. "I know you feel like you don't know him right now. But the man he was, the man you knew and loved, he's still the same."

Melody shook her head as she blinked away tears. "I don't know if he is. What if he killed that man? Maybe that's why he burned down the store. To hide the evidence. Or maybe he set the fire in hopes of killing him."

"Melody, you're making a big leap here. For one, we don't even know if the guy's dead. Well, I'm sure he's dead now. It's been sixty years. But we don't know if there was a fire. You're basing everything on what your uncle told you. You said from the beginning he can't be trusted."

"He isn't the kind of person to make up something with absolutely no basis in fact. He's not that imaginative."

"He may have heard a story when he was a kid, a rumor or a half-truth, and he filled in the blanks."

Melody focused on the headlight beams illuminating an arc of blacktop in front of her. The blacktop glinted silver. Salt and scraping from snowplows over the last two months had done a lot of damage to local roadways. No one could know the extent of the damage until well into the spring.

"I wonder who my grandpa really was," she said at length.

Christy didn't have to ask what she meant. "He was the man you knew and loved. The man who helped raise you."

"Was he?" Melody demanded sharply. She took a deep breath. She couldn't take her frustration out on Christy. "I hoped coming here would help me know him better. I wonder if Mom knows she's not a Beckwith. And Grandma. She's been Clarice Beckwith for sixty years. I don't know how to tell them."

"William may have adopted your grandpa. That makes him a Beckwith as much as if he'd been born one."

"William and Rose might not have worried about making it legal. For all I know my mom's name is really Judy Smith. Or Judy Hitler."

Christy barked out a laugh but quickly reined it in. Melody smiled in spite of herself.

"Does it really matter?" Christy asked. "It's just a last name."

Melody didn't answer right away. She wasn't sure how to make Christy understand what she was thinking. She wasn't sure herself.

"It's like Grandpa played two roles his whole life. With me, he was honest and hardworking and full of faith. With everyone else, he was judgmental and suspicious. Now I wonder which one he really was. He didn't tell me the most basic things. Why? It doesn't make sense. If he didn't have anything to hide about coming to Jenna's Creek, why didn't I know about his mother and brother? I don't know what's true anymore. I feel like I was duped by this master manipulator. It makes me question my own judgment. Maybe everything I ever believed is wrong."

"You weren't duped. He told you the biggest truth. You always knew he loved you."

"I'm so tired of all the secrets. It seems everyone in the family has some, and no one will tell me anything because they think I can't handle it. I don't understand why it has to be this way."

Christy stared out the side window at the passing farmland. Even though it was dark and only a sliver of moon shone between the clouds, the light reflecting off the snow-covered landscape made it semi-light outside. "Like it or not, every family has secrets."

"Maybe so, but I'll never know what happened to Grandpa the morning the blizzard hit until I know what he was hiding."

"How are you going to do that?"

Melody's jaw clenched as her gaze slid back to the roadway. "I guess I'll have to ask."

CHAPTER EIGHTEEN

Christy barely noticed the black Cadillac at the stop sign until she pulled into her own driveway and saw fresh, wide tire tracks outlined in the snow. She climbed out of the car. In the glow from the streetlamps, she saw distinct tracks leading from her driveway to the intersection. She looked that way. The Cadillac was gone.

Surely it wasn't...

Everyone in town knew Noel Wyatt bought a new black Caddy every other year or so, and this one sure looked like his. But he would never visit her house. Not in a million years.

Inside the house, she let the front door slam behind her. "Christy, is that you?" Mom asked benignly from the direction of the kitchen.

"Did you have company?" Christy called out as she headed that way without bothering to remove her coat or boots. Perhaps it was her imagination, but she thought she detected lingering traces of a man's aftershave in the air.

Abby came down the hallway toward her, drying her hands on a dishtowel. "Hello, dear. Did you have a nice time with Melody?"

Her expression looked innocent enough, but Christy suspected she was stalling. "Who was here, Mom? I saw tracks in the driveway."

Abby finished drying her hands and flipped the dishtowel onto her shoulder. She turned and headed back to the kitchen. "Are you hungry? I made a cake earlier."

Christy clenched her teeth to keep from shouting. She had been extremely charitable the last few months. She hadn't even mentioned Noel. She'd gone out of her way to be supportive of Mom's business venture. Now this.

"Mom," she said in warning.

When Abby reached the kitchen she turned to face Christy. Her own jaw was clenched. "It was Noel Wyatt, but I expect you already know that."

"I could see it on your face. Why was he here?"

Abby exhaled, clearly struggling to hold her own temper in check. "He was here to drop off some insurance papers for your brother for school. Eric is still covered under Noel's policy, not that it's any of your business."

"It's my business if you're trying to keep it from me."

"This is ridiculous. I'll keep anything from anyone if I want." She tossed the dishtowel onto the counter. "Do you want a piece of cake of not?"

"No, I don't want cake." Christy followed her across the kitchen. Two cups and two dessert plates sat incriminatingly on the draining rack on the counter. "It looks to me like a lot more than dropping off insurance forms."

Abby spun around and set her clenched fists on her hips. "I'm a grown woman, Christy. I'm allowed to have company after dark. I'll serve cake in my kitchen every day of the week if I want to. If I was keeping anything from you it's because I knew you would make a big thing out of it."

"It is a big thing, Mom. Noel Wyatt of all people. Are you that lonely?

Abby looked like she'd been kicked in the stomach. "Yes, Christy, I'm lonely. I miss your father. I miss the life we had. I miss the sound of a man's voice. I miss talking to one. I'm very lonely. I'm lonely for your dad."

"So, what are we doing here? Replacing him?"

Abby pursed her lips and took a deep breath. "I should slap your face," she said as a vein throbbed at her temple.

For once, Christy was shocked into silence.

"You need to grow up. I'm not replacing anyone, but if I ever decide to, I sure won't ask your permission. You asked if I was lonely and I gave you an honest answer. I thought we were to the point where we could be honest and truthful with one another, even if it was ugly. I thought a few things had changed in the last year. But I guess you only want honesty and transparency when things are going your way."

"Mom, this isn't about me. You had an affair with that man and now you're inviting him into the house for coffee when you knew I'd be out all day."

"We were friends. Years ago, before your father and I got engaged, Noel was one of the only friends I had. It's been a lifetime since I've even spoken to him. I don't see anything wrong with catching up with an old friend." She raised her hand to cut off Christy's protestations. "Yes, we became more than friends. We have a child together. Whether you like it or not, that man will always be in our lives because of Eric. I won't pretend to hate him or be disgusted by him simply because you can't handle the two of us sharing coffee."

Christy gripped the back of a kitchen chair. "It seems to me, if all this is so innocent, you wouldn't have him bring the papers over when you knew I was out of the house. Why couldn't he mail the papers to Eric and Jamie?"

"The mail wouldn't have got the forms there before Eric needed them. He and Jamie are coming for dinner tomorrow and they'll pick them up then. This wasn't a conspiracy to hide a tryst from you. Like I said, I didn't think it was a big deal. I knew you wouldn't want me to go to Noel's house to pick up the papers. So, yes, I called him and he graciously brought the papers here to save you the scandal of me going there. I served him coffee and cake while he was here and we talked for about twenty minutes. Is that okay, warden? In case you're wondering, he drinks decaf this time of night and he said he shouldn't eat the cake because he wants to lose a few pounds. Anything else you want to know?"

"For crying out loud, Mom. You don't have to give me the play-by-play?"

"Don't I? It sure sounds like I do."

"Eric should know better than to wait until the last minute to take care of insurance forms. He's a grown man. You need to start treating him like one."

Abby's face grew a few shades darker. "Are we finished because I'm growing weary of defending myself?"

"Yes, Mom, we're finished. I'm tired of this whole thing too."

Abby's fists were still planted on her hips when Christy stomped out of the room and upstairs. She hadn't lied; she was tired. Tired of the whole situation. Tired of living paycheck to paycheck and never accumulating enough money to move forward with her Great Escape. Tired of holding Mom's past sins over her head. Tired of avoiding Noel Wyatt in a very small town. Tired of not knowing if she wanted to leave Jenna's Creek.

By the time she reached the top of the stairs her anger had dissipated. So why were tears of frustration pressing at the backs of her eyes?

She liked her life in Jenna's Creek. She liked working at the library. She liked her coworkers and the patrons she once thought of as yokels who didn't have the good sense to leave town the minute they had the chance to escape the oppression.

She went into the bedroom she had shared with her sister Elaine about a hundred years ago. She had been so happy when her oldest sister moved out and Elaine took the bigger bedroom, leaving Christy alone for the first time. The third daughter, she never owned anything that hadn't already passed through the hands of her sisters. The only thing she could claim as her own was her dreams of leaving Jenna's Creek. Even when she was little and her friends talked of growing up and getting married and having babies, she thought it sounded like prison. While they played house, she wanted to play Office or Airplane, a game where she had an exciting career, not a bunch of baby dolls pretend-crying for her attention.

She didn't have a husband and babies controlling her every thought and action, but she was still shackled to this house, this life.

She went to the window and stared out, though all she could see was her own reflection thrown back at her. Why was she still here? What was she waiting for?

She raked her hands through her shoulder-length, copper-colored curls. "This isn't my life," she said aloud to her reflection. "I have dreams. I was supposed to go to law school. I want my own place. I don't want to be sleeping in this room every night until I die."

She thought of Mom enjoying coffee and cake with Noel Wyatt before she came home to spoil the party. Mom was a grown woman. She didn't need to clear her decisions with anyone. Christy was always the one spouting off about a woman's right to do what she wanted. Who was Christy to tell Mom what to do with her life when she was so out of control of her own?

What if Mom started dating Noel? They were both ancient. No one else wanted either one of them. They could even get married. Christy shuddered at the thought. They would move to Noel's big, brick Federalist on Bryton Avenue. Where would that leave her? Probably living in Noel's guest quarters.

"Uck." She threw herself across the bed and stared at the ceiling. "This isn't my life," she said again. "This isn't what I want."

She thought of Melody and the trip to Springfield. It had felt good. It felt right being there for Melody and supporting her through a very emotional day. She had been through so much in the last few months, and Christy was genuinely glad she had been able to help in a small way. If she left Jenna's Creek, she would lose the only real friend she'd had in years, if not ever.

Would she find another friend like Melody? Friendship had always been difficult for her. It took so much work. There was always more compromise involved than she wanted to invest. It had been easy with Melody. She wasn't sure if it was because they were at the same stage in their lives—stuck between home and growing up—a little late in the game compared to most of their counterparts, but understanding of the other's concerns.

This was why she didn't pursue friendship. She didn't like things holding her back, making it hard to walk away. It was easier to focus on her own life and concerns than to make room for someone else.

She thought of the little boy who had died in Jarrod's apartment building. It bothered him that he couldn't remember the kid, let alone comfort the parents. Christy doubted she would've given the kid or his grief-stricken parents a second thought. To her, the anonymity of the city was its best feature. Maybe Jarrod was right, and anonymity was an excuse for not doing anything for anyone else.

Jarrod.

Another person who had come to mean more to her than she wanted. If she left town, she would never see him again. She wasn't sure why the thought of it made her heartsick. She didn't need anyone in her life, certainly not a man who would end up trying to control her. Jarrod had never given her a reason to think that was his end goal, but wasn't it what all men ultimately wanted?

She sighed. Maybe she wasn't being fair, or she was worrying about something that would never happen. Dad never tried to control Mom. Karen's husband Roger was supportive. Christy had never seen him try to control Karen. If he did, Karen would probably sock him in the nose.

Christy wasn't sure she wanted to take the chance. Jarrod seemed perfect. That alone was a red flag. History had proven what a bad judge of character she was. If she thought he was wonderful, he probably drowned kittens in his bathtub

She sat up in the bed and swung her legs off the side. She couldn't put her life on hold one more day. Not for her mother. Not for Jarrod. Not even for Melody. As frugal as she'd been, she would never save enough money working at the library to leave Jenna's Creek. The time would never be right. She was going to have to leave work one Friday with her last paycheck, get in the car, and start driving. Where, she wasn't sure yet, but she couldn't put it off any longer.

She went back to the window. She didn't have a clear picture of what the next day would bring, but she knew she couldn't keep living this lie. She would get on with her life and let Mom get on with hers. She would no longer stand in the way of her mother's happiness. If that meant Noel Wyatt, more power to both of them. But Christy would not sit here and watch it happen.

CHAPTER NINETEEN

Since coming back from Springfield three days ago, Melody hadn't been able to think of anything but what she'd learned there. And what she hadn't learned. All the way home, she imagined running into the house and telling her mother she had never been Judy Beckwith. Grandpa was a liar who hadn't bothered to tell his family where he was from or his father's real name, if he even knew.

By the time Melody dropped Christy off and got back to the farm, she had decided against it. For one, there was still too much she didn't know. Maybe she'd say something after she had all the facts, after she knew what else Grandpa was hiding, after she knew his real last name.

She hadn't even told Mom she had gone to Springfield. She would never understand why Melody needed to go or what she hoped to learn, so why upset everyone? What difference did any of it make now anyway? She shouldn't have let Lowell's words get to her. Christy was right. Grandpa's real last name didn't matter. There was no shame in adoption, if that's what happened. He might not have known. If he had, he would've been ashamed his father never married his mother. It was a different time then. A different generation. Whatever the result of his birth, it had no bearing on him or the man he became.

Still, Melody knew she wouldn't be satisfied until she filled in the blanks. Whether a pyromaniac, a thief, or a grifter, she needed to know who Warner Beckwith had been, not only who he allowed her to see.

Lowell was the only person who might have answers and a willingness to divulge them. She doubted he knew much more than innuendo and rumors, but she needed to find out. He had been proven right about the store fire. Maybe he was right about Grandpa cheating the aunts out of their share of the property. No matter what Christy and Paulette said about remembering her grandfather for the man she knew, she needed more.

The way to her skinny uncle's heart was through his stomach. Mom was working the second shift at the grocery store all week and wouldn't be home until after the store closed. Melody bought fresh bakery rolls on her way home to go with the two cheesy sausage casseroles she had prepared that morning. She wrapped aluminum foil around the bigger casserole and drove the short distance up the hill.

She parked at the side of the house and went in through the kitchen door. As expected, the kitchen was in disarray. Carson spent most of his days outside with Dad. Jay did, too, when he was home. Very little was done by way of housework. Breakfast dishes waited in the sink. Someone had made sandwiches for lunch. Crumbs and condiment bottles still littered the table and countertops. Coffee grounds hadn't been emptied from the filter basket. When Melody slid the sugar canister back to its position along the wall, it stuck a little.

While the casserole baked she ran a sink of sudsy water and returned everything to the refrigerator that belonged there. The interior of the fridge hadn't seen much attention lately either. If she had time, she'd clean it out. If not, she'd come back tomorrow evening.

By the time the aroma of melting cheese and garlic filled the air, the worst of the kitchen was returned to the condition it had been before Grandpa passed away. Melody let the dishwater out of the sink and was just about to open the oven door and fan the escaping steam toward the heating vents in the ceiling when she heard Lowell's tread on the stairs. For once, she was thankful he was predictable. She took out the casserole and popped a pan of rolls into the oven to warm.

Lowell stopped short in the kitchen doorway. "I thought I smelled Judy's cooking."

"It's Mom's recipe but my cooking."

Her first instinct was to chastise him for the state of the kitchen. If he was too lazy to go outside and help Dad and Carson with the animals, the least he could do was keep the dishes done up. Instead, she waved him toward the table where several place settings awaited. She wanted information, not an argument she was destined to lose.

"Have a seat. I'll dish you up a plate."

His face tightened with suspicion. "You will?"

Melody smiled generously. "Of course. You're hungry, aren't you?"

He slid into the chair without reply. "You didn't bring dessert by any chance, did you? Carson over bakes everything, and Jay doesn't do anything anymore but open cans."

She wanted to remind him Carson was probably too busy to watch the oven, what with the housework and keeping the farm running and taking care of Grandma and all. If Lowell wanted a pie or cake, surely he could figure out something to do in the kitchen besides complain about how he was going hungry. Instead, she frowned. "I didn't. I'm sorry. Mom's working late all week, and I just got home myself. I'll see if I can put something together for you later in the week."

He brightened the instant she set the plate in front of him. Melody moved back to the oven and pulled out the rolls, then took the butter dish out of the refrigerator. Carson would be in soon, hungry and appreciative he wouldn't have to cook or clean the kitchen. Whatever she hoped to get out of Lowell, she needed to make quick work of it.

She set two rolls on his plate. She took the remaining rolls off the pan so they wouldn't dry out and placed a clean towel over the basket to keep them warm. "Would you like something to drink?"

He barely looked up from his plate. "Milk's fine. There's always plenty of that around here."

Melody poured him a tall glass. She pulled out a chair on the other side of the table, facing him. *Lord, give me an opening so I can ask my questions without offending him*, she prayed.

"You gonna eat?" he asked around a mouthful of cheesy noodles and bits of broccoli and cauliflower.

She shook her head. "I made the same thing for us at home. I'm waiting on Dad."

After another huge bite, the edge must've assuaged from Lowell's hunger. He glanced around the kitchen and looked at her, suspicion back on his face. "What you doing here anyway, Melody? We hardly see you anymore."

Her stomach tightened. God had answered her prayer already. She put her elbow on the table and propped her chin in her hand. "I've been thinking a lot about Grandpa, I guess. I was hoping you and I could talk."

Lowell stopped chewing. "What d'you want to talk to me about?"

Melody figured the best way to get her information in the shortest time was to be brutally honest. "I spent nearly every day of my life with Grandpa. I thought I knew him better than anyone. Lately I've begun to think I didn't know him at all. Not like you and Mom and Uncle Jay."

The more she talked, the more she realized she didn't need to use subtly to get her information. There was no need to trick Lowell into thinking she was sincere when all she wanted was honest answers. "Until last month, I didn't even know where he was from."

Lowell turned his attention back to his plate, clearly wondering why anyone would care to know something like that.

"I can't talk to Mom and I don't want to upset Grandma."

He sniffed in agreement. "You can't talk to nobody in this family. Nobody ever tells you nothing."

Her pulse quickened. "I've noticed that. I think you're the only person who's been honest with me since Grandpa died."

She waited for him to ask what she was talking about, but he kept digging away at the casserole. "Do you remember the night we had dinner with the Sheltons? You said something about a fire in Springfield. Do you know the story behind it?"

He peered at her from under graying eyebrows in need of a trim. "Of course I know the story," he said around his food. He swallowed a large bite and raised his head. "Not like anybody around here gives me credit for knowing anything. But I know plenty, don't think I don't."

Melody bit her tongue and waited as he smeared a generous blob of butter on a roll. He might close down if she appeared too anxious. She waited until he filled his mouth again before she spoke. "I don't know anything. The whole family acts like I'm still a kid and can't handle the truth. Or maybe they're trying to protect me from something."

Lowell snorted. "Try growing up in this house with ever'body thinking you don't got a lick of sense in your head."

Melody resisted the urge to remind him he mustn't lay all the blame on the family for the way they treated him. If he wanted to change their perception, he could start by taking initiative in something.

Her conscience pricked at her. There she went again. Painting Lowell with Grandpa's brush. Not willing to see things from another person's point of view. She wasn't here to figure out what had turned Lowell into the man he was, nor did she have the time. It would take a team of psychologists years to adequately analyze the tragedy that was her uncle's life.

"That night, you said Grandpa moved to Jenna's Creek because he set a store on fire. All my life I heard Grandpa came here looking for work. He was dead broke and down on his luck. He fell in love with Grandma and the rest was history."

Lowell smirked. "I reckon that sounds like a good enough story to satisfy a little girl. Let me give you the more accurate version." He set down his fork, leaned back in the chair, and folded his hands on his stomach swollen with casserole. "He was dead broke. That much was true. Pop got caught stealing from the store where he worked and burned the place down to cover his tracks. He took off, leaving his mom and little brother high and dry. He came here and ended up falling headfirst into a pretty sweet deal. Got the farmer's daughter and the farm in one fell swoop."

Melody gripped the edge of her chair and tried to keep her emotions under control. She didn't want him to see how much his words had shocked her, but she figured it was evident on her face. Was any of it true? Or was Lowell being a petty windbag again, simply trying to hurt her?

"How do you know any of this?" she asked in as level a voice as she could manage.

He shook his head. "It's a wonder you grew up at all, Melody, standing in Pop's shadow all the time the way you did. He told you his pasteurized version of whatever story he wanted you to hear, and you bought it, no questions asked. I'm telling you what really happened. He burned that store down and came here, barely two steps ahead of the law."

Melody wanted to jump up and run from the room. She wanted to scream for him to stop lying and stop acting like she was a dumb kid who couldn't distinguish fact from fantasy instead of a twenty-five-year-old woman.

In the meantime, Lowell tore off the top of a roll and used it to sop up the sauce from his casserole.

She took a deep breath. "Anything that happened was years before you were born. How do you know you aren't the one who heard a version of someone else's truth?"

He stuffed the roll in his mouth. "I heard it straight from the horse's mouth. More'n once. I heard all about how Pop stayed cause the farm was better than anything else he figured he'd find. How he had Grandpa Salinski hornswaggled just like he did everybody else."

Melody swallowed her revulsion at his insinuation as much as from the sight of half-chewed food in his mouth. "What do your mean by hornswoggled?"

She had never talked to Lowell this much before, but he seemed to enjoy being the center of her attention. His gaze moved toward the baking dish on the stove. She didn't want to distract him with more food, but if she didn't keep feeding him he would probably head upstairs to sleep off the meal. She took his plate back to the stove and dished up another generous helping.

When she set the plate in front of him, he started talking again as he ate. "Pop was a hard worker, I'll give him that. But he knew what he wanted. The farm. He made himself indispensable to Grandpa Salinski. Then he moved in for the kill."

She stiffened at his choice of words. "Grandpa always told me he loved Grandma from the instant he saw her standing on that little ridge above the property. He said he had been here for about three days. Grandpa Salinski was working him like a borrowed mule and he barely had a chance to look up from his work. One day he was walking through the field toward the barns when he saw Grandma on the ridge. She was watching the sun go down. The sun had turned her hair to spun gold. He said it looked like she was standing in a cloud. He told me he knew right then she was the woman he was going to marry." Her voice went soft as she remembered the way Grandpa used to tell the story.

Lowell laughed. "Grow up, Melody. Do you really believe that's what happened? If Pop fell in love with anything that day, it was the farm. It just took him three days to figure out Mom was the key to getting it."

"That isn't fair. Nobody can know what goes on inside another person's heart or head."

Even as she said it, she thought of the look on Naomi's face the day she talked to the aunts in town. It was obvious Naomi had feelings for Grandpa at one time, and Alma had spoken out of turn when she told Melody. The aunts were busy with their schoolwork back then. If Grandpa was more interested in the farm than a wife, it wouldn't have taken long to figure out the youngest sister was his key to it instead of an older one who would probably move away as soon as she finished her education.

She brought her thoughts back to the present. "Even if he did fall in love with the farm before Grandma, I know he loved her. They were happy together."

Lowell nodded begrudgingly. "They seemed to be. I just got tired of hearing the story like it was some kind of fairy tale, especially after everything else I knew about what happened in Springfield."

Melody dropped into the chair across from him. "What exactly happened?" she asked with a knot in her stomach. "And how are you the only one who knows anything? I never heard a hint of a fire until you brought it up."

His pace had slowed, but he still savored every bite of the meal. "I've been around a long time, little girl. I'm not as dumb as I look, neither. Who do you think rode to Springfield with Pop all the time?"

"Grandpa took you to Springfield to visit his family?"

Lowell cast a longing glance toward the stove before pushing the empty plate away. He probably wanted a third helping but knew the rest of the family still needed to eat. "I was the youngest boy. Allen and Jay always had ball practice or summer jobs or some such that got them out of going. Mom kept the girls busy with chores, so Pop would throw me in the truck with him and the two of us would drive to Springfield. It didn't happen often. Just a few times that I remember. Still, those were the only times I remember Pop being halfway nice to me."

His expression turned distant, and he seemed to forget the casserole. "The drive there and back took most of the day so I had Pop to myself. He didn't talk a lot. Not like he always did with you. It's sad I guess, but I didn't know him very well. He dang sure didn't know me. The only thing I knew was he was always disappointed in me."

Melody never dreamed Lowell was capable of making such a determination about someone. She knew Grandpa was disappointed in his two younger sons. He had been disappointed in Linda. Everyone disappointed him sooner or later in one way or another. Everyone but her. Now she was the one disappointed. Disappointed Grandpa couldn't tell her he had a brother or the real reason he left Springfield. Disappointed he was so judgmental with everyone he claimed to love. Disappointed his young son never felt loved or accepted by him.

Lowell hadn't always been a lazy man who never thought beyond his next meal. Long ago, he'd been a little boy longing for his pop's approval. He must've learned pretty quickly he wasn't going to get it. Maybe that was part of why he decided there was no point in trying to earn it. Melody wanted to lean across the table and hug him. She wanted to tell him she was sorry for how Grandpa treated him, for every moment he felt like he didn't matter to his own dad.

She cleared her throat. "I've begun to think I don't know Grandpa the way I thought I did, either. We talked all the time. We spent so much time walking this farm. Since he died I realized there was a whole other part of him I never knew. It makes me wonder if anything I knew was real."

Lowell leveled a look at her as if seeing her as a real person for the first time in her life. She wondered briefly if he ever liked her or if he saw her as a rival for his father's attention.

"It's just the way things were, Nugget. We all knew where we stood with Pop. That's how I knew those trips to Springfield were special, how I knew they were supposed to stay between us. I never mattered a whole lot to him, but during those trips I felt like he trusted me more than anyone else. That's not why he took me." He gave a wry laugh. "He took me on account'a he didn't have anything else to do with me. Whatever the reason, I never said a word to anybody about where we went or who we went to see. Those trips to Springfield were our secret."

Again, Melody felt a kinship with her uncle she never imagined. "What did you do when you went there?" She no longer cared if Lowell was in charge of the conversation. She wanted to know everything he knew.

"Not a whole lot. We only went a handful of times. I guess it was from the time I was ten or eleven until I was around fourteen. The only thing we did was visit his brother Ivan. He was the only family Pop had left as far as I could tell. He was quite a bit younger than Pop. Ten years, I expect, even though he looked like an old man to me. He had a lot of health problems. He never lived in very nice places. It seemed like every time we went, he lived in a different house with a different old lady."

He laughed. "I guess that's where Jay gets it. The Beckwith men sure like the ladies."

Melody smiled politely at the insinuation. She hoped he wouldn't lose track of what he was saying.

"The visits never lasted long. Pop and Ivan would sit at the kitchen table or out on the porch if the weather was nice and sort of look at each other. I would'a went out of my mind from boredom if I didn't know we were going to stop for dinner at the Dairy Queen on the way home. Ivan was just like Pop. Neither of them had much to say, and they sure didn't have nothing to say to me. Ivan would ask about the farm and Pop would ask Ivan how work was going or if he thought it would be a wet spring or if he thought the Reds would have a good season.

"Ivan always had a ballgame on, so I'd go in the living room and watch while they talked. One time I remember they got into a little bit of an argument. I was watching the game. A woman was sitting on the front porch smoking. She went outside as soon as we got there like she didn't want to be around us. I don't blame her. I don't know if she was a wife or a girlfriend or what. I just knew she was different from the one the time before. Anyway, she was on the porch smoking or whatever she was doing, and I was watching the game when I heard Pop and Ivan's voices getting loud in the kitchen."

Melody leaned forward in her chair, afraid to miss a word.

"I don't know what the conversation was about. When I stopped watching the game and started listening, they were talking about the time right before Pop took off from Springfield. Ivan said something about how Pop never should've left him and their mother alone. Pop told him he didn't have a choice. Ivan got really mad. He said if Pop had minded his own business and let their ma take care of things the way she wanted, Pop wouldn't have had to leave. Ivan was still a kid when Pop left. Without him there it got really tough on them. Ivan said Pop never cared about anyone but himself."

Melody wondered if that was why Grandpa had helped Paulette pay for Ivan's funeral. "What was Ivan talking about?"

He scraped the last of the cheese sauce off his plate with his fork. "I couldn't piece it all together. They were leaving a lot of stuff out. Pop kept defending himself, saying he handled the situation the only way he knew how. That's when he mentioned the fire at the store."

He no longer seemed to enjoy telling the tale for the sake of telling it, but as though he was relieved to finally unburden himself.

"I kept as quiet as I could. I turned down the volume on the ballgame so I could hear better but they wouldn't know I was listening. I kept watching the woman through the front window, hoping she wouldn't hear and come in and tell them to knock it off. That's when Pop said he didn't have no choice but to burn that store down. If he hadn't done it, their ma would've gone to jail."

"Jail?" Melody shrieked. She and Lowell snapped their gazes toward the kitchen door, thinking of Grandma asleep in the living room. Melody leaned closer to Lowell, making sure to keep her voice down. "Why would she have gone to jail?"

He shrugged. "I don't know. All I know is Pop said if the store hadn't burned Rose would've been in big trouble."

Melody sat back in her chair. "I wonder what kind of trouble he was talking about."

Lowell looked back at the casserole dish on the counter. All his talking must've worked up an appetite. "No way of knowing now. It just looks awful suspicious to me that the store where he worked burned down and he showed up on the farm a week later."

"A minute ago you said Grandpa left because he got caught stealing from the store," she reminded him.

"Yeah, that's what Ivan said. Pop told him he only took what the storeowner owed him. Makes no never mind to me what you call it. Stealing's stealing."

He got up and carried his plate to the counter. Melody thought he was going to get another serving of casserole. Instead he set his plate in the sink and ran water over it.

"Is that what you meant when you said Grandpa got what he deserved?"

He looked at her over his shoulder. "I regret telling you that, Nugget. It wasn't right. I was mad. It seems like Pop got everything he ever wanted by taking advantage of somebody or something. Then he degraded us for doing something that wasn't half as bad. Still, he didn't deserve to die alone on a basement floor. I'm sorry I said it."

"That isn't how you said it, Lowell. You made it sound like he was pushed him down those stairs because of something he did."

Lowell came back to the table and sat down. "Naw. That's not what I meant. I just meant you shouldn't treat people bad your whole life and not expect it to come back to bite you."

"Grandpa Warner helped Grandpa Salinski run the farm, just like Dad did all these years. He didn't exactly get something for nothing. They needed each other."

"I guess they did at that. But Pop knew what he wanted." He looked at Melody as if making sure she was keeping up. "Nobody could ever say Warner Beckwith didn't know how to get exactly what he wanted, no matter what he had to do to get it."

CHAPTER TWENTY

Ancient lore went up in smoke when March of 1978 came in like a lion and went out just as fiercely. Fortunately, the first week of April saw a warming in temperatures and a rise in the general mood of Auburn County. Parking meters along Main Street reappeared from beneath mountains of salt and grime. The yellow line down the middle of Main Street was visible for the first time in three months. Melting snow filled reservoirs and overflowed creek banks throughout the county. School children once again played outside during recess as merry-go-rounds and jungle gyms emerged on playgrounds like skeletal serpents rising out of the sea of white. Much to the delight of harried parents, public schools announced they would remain in session until June twenty-sixth to make up for a record thirty-one snow days accumulated from December to March.

The appearance of green grass was documented on the evening news. Motorists killed deer in record numbers as herds moved out of the forests to lap up salt left at the edge of the roads by countless snowplows. Chains were taken off tires, and boots were stashed in closets in the hope neither would be seen again for a very long time.

Christy hadn't slept much Saturday night after she and Melody got home from Springfield and she saw Noel's Cadillac pulling away from the intersection on her street. She had been full of sage wisdom when it came to Melody's problems. Every family had secrets, she'd intoned. Nobody was perfect. All that mattered was knowing one was loved and belonged.

The only problem was she wasn't sure she believed any of it. She didn't know how she fit into her family. The rest of them had readily forgiven Mom for her indiscretion with Noel Wyatt. It was a pretty safe bet they would accept him as their mother's second husband, should it come to that.

Christy was willing to accept it too. Just not in Jenna's Creek. It would be much easier to live with her mother's decisions if she was far removed from the situation. Like Denver. Or San Francisco. Or Miami. Anywhere but Auburn County where she might have to watch Mom set up housekeeping on Bryton Avenue.

Her shift ended at four o'clock Thursday. At home she had successfully avoided any real conversations all week, which was hard to do with Mom at the house all the time, working on patterns and marketing ideas. In the beginning, Christy had been just as excited. Now all she could envision was Noel sitting on the couch when she got home, sipping a martini—or whatever old, wealthy men drank after work—with his slippered feet on her coffee table.

She had returned to her desk after shelving a heavy reference volume on South America a patron left on a table, and was reaching for her purse when the phone rang.

"Christy?" said a delightfully familiar voice.

She couldn't suppress a smile. "Jarrod, you have perfect timing. I was on my way out the door."

"You're right. It is perfect. Can you come downtown? I have something I want to show you."

"Downtown? You mean Jenna's Creek?" She wasn't sure if he was referring to here or his hometown of Portsmouth.

"Of course." He rattled off an address two blocks from the courthouse.

Christy didn't recognize the address, but it didn't matter. She would've driven to Portsmouth to see him if he asked. It gave her an excuse not to go straight home, but more importantly, she would see *him*. They hadn't been able to connect for almost two weeks. She told herself it didn't matter. She was leaving this town. He was just a nice diversion until she did.

Five minutes later, she pulled up to a gray brick, two-story house with black trim and a narrow front porch. She couldn't see through the first story windows, but the ones upstairs suggested it was vacant. Jarrod's car was parked in the short driveway. Street parking was still at a minimum though much of the plowed snow had melted. Christy squeezed her car in behind his. By the time she got out of the car, he was on the front porch, wearing a huge, cheesy grin. She couldn't keep from smiling herself. Wow, she really liked this guy.

He stepped to the edge of the porch and opened his arms wide. "What do you think?"

"About what?" though she had a pretty good idea.

He practically bounced down the two steps and met her on the sidewalk. "About my new house."

She resisted the urge to wipe a smudge of dirt off his cheek. She had never seen him dressed in jeans and a flannel shirt. Who would've guessed flannel could look so good? She gave herself a mental shake and turned her attention to the stately house. It must've been impressive in its day. It could be again with a fresh paint job and some trim work.

"You're buying a house? In Jenna's Creek?" She knew he liked the town, but was he really crazy enough to move here? People left Auburn County, they didn't move in. Unless he had an ulterior motive.

Rein it in, Christy. This isn't about you. Though she sort of hoped it was.

"I told you I've always loved Jenna's Creek. It's close enough to home without my parents knowing my every move. I can be my own man, but still be close enough to have my mother cook for me."

"Very funny."

"I thought so." He grabbed her arm and turned her toward the house. Keeping her arm locked in his, he escorted her onto the porch to the front door he had left open.

"This is what you wanted to show me?"

"What do you think?"

"I don't know." They stepped across the threshold into a large front room. Through the door she could see another room and part of a kitchen. To her left was a smaller room that looked like it led into a utility room or mudroom. She assumed it connected to the kitchen in the rear and probably led to a small backyard.

Heavy, walnut trim accented every door and baseboard. The crown molding looked ancient and could use a good scrubbing, but it was beautiful. Dark hardwood floors sloped toward the center of the room. It was an old house showing its age but still full of character and charm.

"It's beautiful, Jarrod. I can imagine the stories it could tell."

He laughed. "That's exactly what I thought the first time I walked in." He sobered and looked at her.

Christy looked into his eyes, suddenly uncomfortable at the intensity there. Why was she here? She wanted to ask why he called her to show her this house when she wasn't anything to him. They'd only been out a handful of times. They had fun together. He was smart and funny and handsome, and she liked him. What she couldn't figure out was why he seemed to like her. Why he wanted to include her in this huge advance in his life.

"I think I'm falling in love with you," she thought.

She wondered how he would react if she said it out loud right this minute. He'd probably run back to the hills of Scioto County. She'd be rid of him once and for all. Wasn't that what she wanted?

Uncertainty the size of a ball of lead settled in her stomach. Why did she always fall for a guy who couldn't offer her a future? The one least suited to give her forever? She needed to get out of this town before she did something stupid like tell him how she felt. She needed to go where nobody knew her. She could finally start law school. Work a few jobs, apply for some grants and scholarships, and work on making real dreams come true. Not settle for what she might find here.

Two minutes ago she had been ready to give the library director her two-week notice. Now Jarrod was showing her this house, and she couldn't help wanting to be part of it. Whatever this was, whatever it meant, she wanted to be included. She had already talked herself into leaving. She didn't belong in this town. In this house next to Jarrod. This was his Utopia, not hers.

She looked at the tall windows that nearly reached the nine-foot ceiling. "It's really lovely. It looks like a..." She looked back at him, wide-eyed. "...law office."

"That's what I told him," he said.

"Him who?" she said as she heard what sounded like a cabinet door closing in the kitchen.

"You're right about the cabinets," a man said as he headed their way. "The water damage under the sink isn't too bad, but that base cabinet will have to be replaced." He stopped talking when he noticed Christy at Jarrod's elbow.

It never ceased to amaze Christy how Noel Wyatt could fill a space, no matter where he was or what he was doing.

She nearly pulled free of Jarrod's hand and headed for the door. She should've known this fine old house belonged to Noel. Nearly half the town did.

He stopped short at the sight of her. Christy stared back. He recovered first. "Hello, Christy. How are you?"

"I'm good."

Jarrod looked back and forth between them. "Oh, that's right. You two know each other."

Christy's throat threatened to close. "We've met."

Noel rocked back on his heels. "Yup. We sure have." He set his hands on his hips and looked around the room. "Well, Jarrod. I have to go. Gotta get back to the store. Place can't run without me." He laughed at his joke. "Yeah, right. Noreen's there. I could disappear for a month and nobody'd notice. Anyway, I'll get Ernie on that cabinet first thing in the morning and we'll go from there. Talk to you tomorrow."

He started toward the door without giving either of them a chance to speak. Christy and Jarrod parted to let him through. He turned sideways as he moved between them. Christy couldn't help but notice the guy still cut a commanding figure even though he must've been in his mid-sixties. He was trim and straight-backed and handsome. Little wonder he had turned her mother's head thirty years ago. She watched him stride down the sidewalk and across the street to the Cadillac she hadn't noticed when she arrived.

After he drove away, she turned to find Jarrod staring at her. "What's the matter?"

"Nothing. Nothing." She fixed her gaze on his chin. Five o'clock shadow darkened his jaw, and his rich cocoa brown hair was disheveled.

He looked thoughtfully out the door to the empty parking space where Noel's Caddy had been. "I forgot about you and Noel knowing each other. In fact, the first time I saw you was at his house. Well, not the first time. Earlier that day you screamed at me on the street. Then I ran into you at Noel's."

Christy laughed nervously. "I'm glad I left such an impression."

"It was hard not to."

There it was again, that earnest look on his face that made her want to fall into his arms and run away from the intensity all at the same time.

She stepped away from him and turned in a slow circle, surveying the room. "It's a nice house. Good bones. Great location. I suppose it will serve your purposes."

"I'm glad you approve."

She looked back at him, mindful to keep a few feet of space between them. "I get you want to start your own practice. What I don't get is why Jenna's Creek? Ohio is filled with little towns where you can start a practice and get out from under your brother's shadow."

He smiled in that delicious way that made her want to kiss him for as long as he would allow. "You don't think I'm here because of you, do you?"

That's exactly what she'd been thinking.

"That's not what I mean," she insisted. "You already told me you'd like to become a small town prosecutor. I just wondered why here."

"That's good, because it has nothing to do with you, if that's what you're thinking."

"I wasn't thinking it. You know, it's a wonder you, me, and your gigantic ego can even fit in this room together."

"And the effort you put into cutting me down to size is a wonder to me."

"I'm just trying to keep you grounded in reality, Counselor."

He laughed. "What would I do without you?" As soon as the words were out of his mouth, they stared at each other.

Christy's mind whirled. She needed to leave. She needed to turn around and walk out the door. This house, his choices, had nothing to do with her. Jarrod was a great guy. He deserved a lot better than her. He just didn't seem to realize it yet.

"Are you going to show me the rest of the house or not?" she said to get him to stop looking at her like that. "What are your plans? Will you live upstairs and operate your practice down here?"

She wanted to ask if he planned to hire a staff. He couldn't run the whole practice by himself. Even in the beginning, he would need someone to help with phones and filing and research and a myriad of other chores she loved to do. If she asked, he'd think she was applying for a job. That was the last thing either of them needed.

Jarrod didn't answer right away. He looked like he was trying to process the change of subject. "These front three rooms will be my office. I might install a studier door to the kitchen so whatever happens in there won't disturb clients."

"Like when you burn your dinner?"

He looked offended. "I happen to be a good cook."

"I thought your mother cooked for you."

"Not every night. Sometimes she plays bridge."

She laughed, enjoying the playfulness. She couldn't remember the last time a man had put her so at ease without even trying. She could get used to Jarrod's sense of humor and honesty and intensity. And the way the corner of his mouth tilted on the left side when he was teasing her.

"Come on," she said, a little too loud. "Let's get this tour started. We're burning daylight. I can't be here all night."

Jarrod cocked an eyebrow, which she chose to ignore. He really needed to stop looking at her like that if he knew what was good for both of them.

She made all the appropriate sounds of approval as they walked around the house and he pointed out the features. It was a beautiful house. It almost made her second guess her decision to leave town. She would love to see the place when he was finished. She didn't tell him that either.

In the kitchen he opened a narrow door and stuck his head inside. "What do you think of this?"

Christy leaned her shoulders into the tiny space. "A closet?" Inside, they were shoulder to shoulder.

"It's a pantry."

"Isn't that just a word for a glorified closet?"

"I thought women always went ga ga over a pantry."

She sniffed. "I'll save my enthusiasm for the end of the tour."

They backed out together. Their shoulders were still touching and they were nearly nose to nose. "What do I have to do to impress you?"

She could think of a few things. The overhead light was on, but they were still in the shadow of the darkened pantry. She hoped he couldn't see the pink in her cheeks. "You impress me every day."

"Really? It's hard to tell."

"I don't want you to get big-headed."

"No chance of that happening with you around."

"What's that supposed to mean?"

Jarrod lifted a shoulder. "You don't make things easy for a guy."

She humphed. "Life is always easier for guys."

"So you're trying to level the playing field?"

Christy looked up at him. He wasn't overly tall. Probably about five-ten, but he practically towered over her five-feet, one-inch frame.

He smiled and stepped a little closer. "You're cute when you're nervous."

"I'm not nervous."

"Are you sure?" He wrapped his finger and thumb around a lock of hair and pulled. "Spider web," he explained. He let go of the piece of fluff and let it drift to the floor.

Christy was barely aware of the tightening of his fingers on her chin until he tilted her face upward and lowered his mouth to hers. The kiss was feather light for a moment before he moved closer. As if it had a mind of its own, her body melded against his. A groan of pleasure escaped her lips, and her arms curled around his neck. After a long moment, he pulled back.

She dropped her chin and put a few inches of space between them. She couldn't let him kiss her again. She needed to focus. She had made up her mind to leave Jenna's Creek. She had to get out of her mother's house.

The more immediate threat was getting out of Jarrod's arms. If she didn't, she couldn't be responsible for her actions.

"It's late. I have to go."

"Where?" His whisper was soft on her face.

Her gaze remained fixed on his mouth. That beautiful, quirky, luscious mouth. "I don't know."

Jarrod put a hand behind her head and combed his fingers through the short curls at the nape of her neck. He kissed her jaw and moved to the corner of her mouth before finally pressing his lips against hers again, longer this time and more than enough to make her want to hurl her body into his arms and forget about leaving Jenna's Creek forever.

He drew back enough so he could look into her eyes but still close enough that his breath was warm on her face. His fingers tangled in her hair. "I want to know everything about you, Christy Blackwood." His voice was husky with emotion.

She swallowed hard before she dared speak. "There's nothing to tell."

"Yes, there is, and you know it." He straightened, leaving her staring at the hollow of his throat. "I want to know all your secrets."

She blinked and forced her gaze to his face. "What makes you think I have secrets? I'm an open book."

"That's the last thing you are. I probably know everything you'd rather a man never pick up on, but I don't know the basics. Like why you're living at home with your mother when you obviously don't think much of Jenna's Creek. And why you left Bennis, Banociac, and Weiss when you still miss it."

The dreaminess was gone from his voice, the spell broken. Christy backed away. "I wasn't as suited for that line of work as I thought."

"Then why do you miss it?"

"I never said I do."

"You don't have to."

"Would you stop playing amateur mind reader?"

"I wouldn't have to read your mind if we could have an honest conversation for once."

"I've always been honest with you, Jarrod."

"Maybe with the little you've told me. You know what a lie of omission is, don't you? You leave a lot of things out. Like why you hate Noel Wyatt."

She blanched. Her emotions were too close to the surface. She stepped away from him and went to the big window where a kitchen table would someday sit. It looked out over a narrow yard that separated the house from the neighbor's. "I don't hate anyone," she said, her gaze directed at the chipped siding of the next house.

"Then why is your jaw clenched so tight you can barely speak?"

She started to respond but stopped. He would see right through her. She made an effort to relax her face. "Noel Wyatt seldom crosses my mind."

Jarrod stepped up next to her. "But when he does, you aren't happy."

She wanted to lash out at him but saw only compassion and understanding on his face. "How could I hate the man? He'll probably be my stepfather someday."

His expression didn't change. So he knew. Everyone in town probably did. "Noel is my brother's real father."

"And you think he's going to marry your mother?"

"Yes. I don't know. Maybe not. They used to be in love. I don't know what they feel now."

"How do *you* feel about it?"

She moved to the center of the kitchen. How did they end up on this topic? "It doesn't make any never mind to me. They're adults. They can do whatever they want."

"You sure are worked up about something you don't care about."

"What has me worked up is you making us waste time on this conversation. None of this affects me. I don't know why we're talking about it. Is the tour over?"

"It's over when you want it to be. I want you to know you can talk to me about anything."

Christy ground her teeth. "People always say that, but they never mean it. As soon as you start talking about something real, something hard, they shut you down. It's like when someone asks you how you are. You're supposed to say, 'I'm fine' and be done with it. Nobody wants to hear anything else."

"I do."

"Well, I don't want to talk about it. Good grief, Jarrod. You are the most difficult person I've ever tried to talk to."

"I'll take that as a compliment."

"It wasn't meant as one."

"Only because you put on this bristly suit of armor and most people back away."

"You should take the hint."

He stepped even closer. "I'm not as skittish as most people. I told you, I want us to be honest with each other."

"I'm being honest. You are exhausting."

He laughed. "Finally. Something real. I love it when you don't hold back." He took hold of her hands. "Why did you leave your job in Columbus? Why are you in Jenna's Creek? I know it isn't where you want to be."

She wanted to tell him he didn't know anything about what she wanted. She wanted to tell him to mind his own business. She wanted to say she was through with this conversation. She wouldn't be bullied into talking about something she didn't want to talk about.

But she did want to talk about it. She wanted to tell him of the hurt and fear and betrayal that drove her back to Jenna's Creek. A few people knew the details of that night in Louisville. No one knew exactly what she experienced or how it still bothered her late at night when Mom was asleep and she heard a strange sound outside, and the thought of someone breaking in and hurting her was so intense she thought she would jump out of her skin.

She pulled her hands free. "I was robbed. I was in a motel in Louisville and two idiots stole my car and everything I owned in the world. I had no choice but to come home."

His face fell. He reached out to touch her arm, but she pulled out of reach. "Christy, I'm so sorry. How did it happen?"

"The usual way. They overpowered me and took my car."

"Why was everything you owned in your car?"

Naturally, he would pick up on that incriminating detail.

"I had just left my job in Columbus. I was fired, Jarrod. Fired from the best job I ever had. Fired for making the stupidest mistake in the history of the world. I couldn't get a job at any firm in Ohio so I left. I barely made it across the state line before I had to call my mommy to come get me."

He took hold of her hand. This time she didn't pull away.

"I let a smooth talking jackass get his hands on my office keys. He broke in and stole some very important files on a case the firm was pursuing." Usually just thinking about Sean

Hatcher and how he had tricked her into thinking he cared about her for more than her office keys made her feel stupid and terrible. This time all she felt was relief.

"I'm sorry I forced you to tell me that before you wanted to. You should've told me to shut up."

She cocked an eyebrow. "Easier said than done."

"I guess so." He pulled her against him. She sank into him, drawing from his strength. She hadn't lowered her guard in so long, she almost forgot how. She had definitely forgotten how good it felt. She took a few deep breaths and pulled herself together. She stepped back and ran her hand over her face.

Jarrod patted his pockets for a handkerchief and then held up his hands apologetically. "Sorry."

"It's okay." She found a crumpled tissue in her back pocket and blew her nose. He smoothed her curls away from her face. "Are you ready to finish the tour?"

"I can't. I should go. It's getting late. In fact," she took a deep breath, "I'm leaving in a few days."

His face fell. "Leaving? You mean for good?"

She couldn't meet his gaze. "I have to get on with my life."

"I thought that's what you were doing. I thought *we* were doing that."

Disappointment darkened his face. Christy almost caved. A huge part of her wanted to tell him he was part of her life, and she couldn't imagine it any other way. All her life she had dreamed of leaving Jenna's Creek, but now all she wanted was to stay and help him start his practice. She wanted to be part of whatever he was doing here. She wanted to be at his side when he ran for county prosecutor. She'd get her law degree and maybe run for mayor. Even the State Senate. Wouldn't that be something?

If she stayed, it would be for him or her mother or Melody. It wouldn't be because this is where she belonged. She couldn't do it. She couldn't give anyone so much control of her life. She was the only person equipped for the job, and she usually ended up falling on her face.

"I want to work as a paralegal. I might go to law school." The words didn't fill her with the excitement they once did. "That won't happen around here. I need to go where no one knows me. Where Bennis, Banociac, and Weiss's long arm doesn't reach."

"That's…crazy. What about your mother?" He stared at her for a moment. His face hardened. "What about us?"

Guilt stirred at the thought of Mom at home, fretting over paying the light bill without a paycheck coming in. She thought of Jarrod's kiss a few minutes ago. Her belly filled with warmth. She couldn't pretend she hadn't fallen for him. Was it love? She wasn't sure, but the thought of walking away made her sick to her stomach.

She looked away, unable to think about it right now. "It's better this way. I need to get out of everyone's way. Mom and Noel can do whatever they want without me raining on their parade. And you…" Her gaze landed on his for a split second before breaking contact. "You can open your practice and find a nice Christian girl who doesn't give you so much grief."

His jaw tightened. "Who says that's what I want?"

"I thought…" She looked helplessly around the kitchen. "I thought that's what all this is about."

"I told you buying this house has nothing to do with you. And I sure don't need your permission to find someone."

"I wasn't…I didn't mean to…" Her words trailed off.

He stepped away from her.

Christy couldn't understand the regret flooding through her. She wanted him to pull her into his arms and demand she stay. He didn't want a woman who wouldn't give him grief. He wanted annoying and irascible Christy Blackwood.

Instead he turned toward the window she had looked out a few moments ago. "I'm sorry you think you have to go," he said without turning around, "but you're right. It probably is better if you get out of everyone's way."

Tears clogged her throat. He was giving her exactly what she wanted. So why did her chest feel like a hundred-pound weight had settled on it? If only she could start this conversation over again. But what could she say differently? This was hard, but it was best for everyone. They just didn't realize it yet. She stared at his back for a moment and then headed back through the house to the front door. As far as she could tell, he never left the kitchen window.

CHAPTER TWENTY-ONE

Gone.

Tears stung Melody's eyes as she stood in the doorway and gaped. Every personal item of Grandpa's had been scrubbed from the room.

She had taken advantage of a Saturday afternoon with everyone out of the farmhouse to snoop through Grandma and Grandpa's room. Even her own parents were away, having taken advantage of the break in the weather to do some much needed shopping. Jay had left last night to parts unknown with a duffle under his arm and no explanation about where he'd be or when he'd be back. Melody didn't expect him back before Sunday night. Lowell had gone into Jenna's Creek to spend a few days at his little trailer. He said he needed to make sure the place hadn't washed away in the melting snow. Melody figured he hoped to unload a one of Grandpa's Swiss Army knives or his stamp collection.

This morning Carson had driven Grandma to visit her cousin Arleen in Hamden. She planned to spend a few days, but Carson would be back this afternoon. Vinton County was over an hour away. Melody could easily add an hour to his trip due to the weather, not to mention the hour or two for lunch that Grandma and Cousin Arleen would force on him.

Melody went to the dresser in the upstairs bedroom her grandparents had occupied since Grandpa Salinski passed away and laid her hand on the smooth varnished top where Warner's grooming kit always sat. She wondered what happened to it. Surely Carson or one of the uncles hadn't taken it too. It wouldn't bring any money, but it was priceless to her.

She didn't expect the family to keep this room as a shrine to Grandpa, but he hadn't yet been gone three full months. Jay had a perfectly good room across the hall. Was it too much to ask that he not eradicate every shred of proof his father ever walked the earth? Was no one mourning Grandpa's passing besides her and Grandma?

She wasn't surprised when she opened the closet door. Instead of Grandpa's military precision—every stitch of clothing pointed due west—the contents had been reduced to a tangle of hangers with Jay's faded shirts slipping off at the shoulders, belts still in the belt loops of pants that looked like he'd just stepped out of them, and shoes in a pile on the floor.

Pushed to the back behind Jay's rumpled clothes, she found a few shirts that had slipped his notice. She slid a familiar plaid summer shirt off the hanger and brought it to her nose. The scent was faint but there. She instantly saw Grandpa's face, heard his gravelly voice, smelled his winter coat as they walked the fields side by side, she hurrying to keep pace with his long strides. She was still upset over everything she'd learned since his death. Mad he'd died before he could answer the questions the last few months had brought up. Hurt he hadn't been completely honest with her the way she had been with him. Sorry he made Lowell feel like a disappointment, even when he was a little kid.

Regardless of those feelings, she loved Grandpa and missed him. Much of the time, it seemed like he was out of town. Then something like this would happen and she'd remember all over again he wasn't coming home.

It was permanent. He was gone.

She wasn't here today to dwell on Jay's callous behavior or compile a mental list of all the ways Grandpa had failed in his role as parent and spiritual leader of the family. She hadn't found anything in the front room about a fire or what kind of trouble his mother may have been in with the storeowner. The odds anything remained after all this time were slim, but she couldn't rest until she explored every possibility.

Grandpa would've kept any newspaper clipping about a fire, especially if it involved his mother. He would've followed an investigation. His compulsion would've made it impossible to walk away from Springfield without looking back.

She looked up at the stack of boxes on the shelf above the hanging rod in the closet. At least they hadn't been thrown out or moved to somewhere she'd never find them. The boxes had always been cataloged and stored neatly and chronologically. Now and then Grandma would complain enough, and Grandpa would get rid of a box or two. Melody figured he got better at storing things rather than throwing anything out to appease his wife.

The boxes weren't stacked neatly or chronologically now. Someone—or several someones—had been here before her.

She pulled a box off the shelf and tightened her grip at the heft of it. She set it heavily on the floor at her feet. It contained just what she expected to find in a box in Grandpa's room. Stacks of wire-bound notebooks, newspapers, and loose sheets and scraps of paper. She picked up a stack of newspapers and leafed through them. Nothing was dated as far back as the 1940's. She glanced at a few headlines but couldn't see any reason he may have kept the entire paper. She dug back into the box and stirred through other clippings. Nothing to explain why a person would keep them for thirty years. She gave up on the newspapers and turned her attention to the notebooks. Like the papers, they were old and faded and didn't seem to contain anything worth keeping. She replaced the lid and stood to return the box to its spot.

The next box was worrisomely light as it settled into her arms. She carried it to the bed and pulled off the lid. Her heart lurched. The bottom of the box was lined with little plastic bags, each containing pills of assorted colors. Melody wasn't completely naïve to the ways of the world. Among the rainbow of capsules she recognized what was called black beauties on the street. Through the plastic bags she saw a layer of twenty-dollar bills. She pushed aside the plastic bags to reach the money. Her hand landed on a hard object. An oddly familiar object. Even as she picked up the small canvas bag at the bottom of the box, she knew what it contained. She folded back the material to reveal the snub nose of a .38.

If Jay left this gun in the closet, he must've taken his preferred method of protection with him last night.

Melody folded the canvas bag back over the gun but kept her hand closed around it. Should she take it? If she didn't, Grandma could get hurt. If she took it, Grandma might not be the only one who got hurt.

Her first instinct was to tell someone. Who? Her parents weren't home. If they were, what could they do? She could leave the gun and take a few bogs of pills to use as evidence. Or blackmail. She could tell Jay if he didn't get his things and get out of her grandmother's house, she was calling the police.

Immediately she recognized that as a fool's errand. The contents of the box told her Jay's operation was serious enough that he would fight to keep it operational. Was that what happened the night before the blizzard struck? Had Grandpa confronted Jay with the evidence Melody now had? Had Jay decided he had no choice but to keep his father quiet?

Melody's blood ran cold. Jay was a criminal, a liar, a manipulator, and a little bit lazy. Could he also be a murderer? Every day in her office, she came across people who let addiction or desperation or criminal activity push them to do things they wouldn't normally do. Such people were only interested in protecting their investments, even when people they loved got in the way.

She had to do something, but what? She wasn't equipped for this. Anything she did could get someone hurt. Or killed. Even if Jay wasn't responsible for Grandpa ending up on the basement floor, she couldn't stand aside and let him continue his illegal activity. She smoothed the layer of pill bags back over the money and returned the box to the closet. She brushed her sweating hands on the seat of her pants and stared up at it.

Now what?

She definitely needed to tell someone. She needed to get out of this room. She needed to convince Jay to leave and never come back. But that wasn't fair. She couldn't send her family's problems down the road. Drug abuse had destroyed so many families in Jenna's Creek. All around the world. She should call the police. Let them handle the situation. They were trained for it. She wasn't.

Probable cause.

That was the first thing authorities needed to search someone's property. Melody had found the drugs and gun by an illegal search. Like it or not, this was Jay's space. She hadn't been invited to snoop. She might end up the one in trouble. If not with the authorities, her mother would be furious she put the rest of the family in danger by threatening Jay's enterprise.

Christy. She would call Christy. She wouldn't know anymore than Melody about how to handle the situation, but it would feel good to have someone in her corner. She closed her eyes and thanked God Grandma was safely away in Vinton County for a few days. At least she didn't have to worry about her for now.

Her gaze swept the room to make sure she hadn't left proof of her invasion. Even though she had every right to enter her grandparents' room, she doubted Jay would see it that way. Those involved in criminal activity were generally paranoid and always looking for things out of place to feed their suspicions. She made sure the drawers were perfectly straight, and the closet door was securely closed.

She started out the door when she remembered she had run her hand across the top of the bureau while thinking of Grandpa's missing shaving kit. Sure enough, she had left a feminine hand-sized smear in the dust. She took a dirty sock off the floor and slapped the top of the bureau from a few different angles. Thank goodness her uncle wasn't a neat housekeeper. Now the entire surface looked smudged and dirty.

The sound of tires crunching on the frozen driveway made Melody's heart skip a beat. She pulled back her sleeve with trembling fingers and looked at her watch. She had been in the house less than thirty minutes. Carson was probably still on his way to Hamden. Unless Grandma had forgotten something her life depended on, Carson shouldn't be back before the middle of the afternoon. The most logical explanation was Jay had returned early from wherever he'd gone.

She moved to the window and peered around the open curtains to the barnyard beneath. The window faced east, revealing a bird's eye view of her own house. She could see the top of the Sheltons' farmhouse and the copse of trees that concealed the former field hands' house Tim was renovating for himself.

She couldn't see the driveway from where she stood. She'd need to move across the hall in order to do that. Gingerly, so to avoid the spot where the floor creaked, she left the room. If it was Jay, she would tell him she had come upstairs to find something for Mom or to dust or change the sheets and tidy up while Grandma was out. Any excuse would suffice. She had as much right to the house as he did.

The bedroom Carson occupied at the end of the hallway offered the least obstructed view of the driveway. Before she could take a step in that direction, a loud pounding sounded at the front door.

She shrieked aloud in surprise and clapped her hand over her mouth. No one in the family bothered to knock. Even out of town relatives knew the door was always unlocked, and would stick their head inside and shout out a 'Yoo hoo' before barging in. They surely wouldn't pound on the door as if to knock it off its hinges. Neither would the pastor or one of the ladies from church who sometimes stopped by unannounced to check on Grandma.

The pounding came again, louder and more insistent. A man let out a harsh curse in a voice Melody did not recognize. It had to be one of Jay's frequent customers who didn't know he was away.

She hurried to the top of the landing and peered over the side. Through the front door's glass, she could make out the shape of a man. He looked over his shoulder toward the road and then back to the door. Melody backed into the shadows.

She would wait him out. She had walked here, and she was sure her boot prints in the snow were indistinguishable from those that had been there for weeks. No cars were parked out front. Whoever was at the door would believe the house was empty and go away.

The knob rattled and then turned.

Melody's breath caught in her throat. Did this joker actually plan to walk into her grandparents' home when it was obvious no one was there? If she were braver...if she hadn't found the gun and pills in the closet...if she wasn't the only one on the hill, she would march downstairs and demand to know what he thought he was doing. How dare he pound on the door. Did he have no respect for an old lady trying to live out her remaining days in peace? To actually turn the knob of a house where he didn't live. Of all the nerve.

She needed to say something. Do something.

Before she could build up enough righteous indignation to march downstairs and confront him, the door swung open, and the man stuck his head and shoulders inside. She recognized him instantly.

Lenny Brown.

She nearly squealed aloud again. Instead, she pressed her back against the wall out of sight.

"Jay?" Lenny called. Then louder, as if in warning. "Jay? You here?" In the ensuing quiet, the only sound was the ticking clock on the mantle in the living room and Melody's rapidly pounding heart.

She should call out. She should let him know the house was not empty. She was here and willing to protect her grandparents' property. Her tongue remained glued to the roof of her mouth. She couldn't have scared away a swallow from under the porch eaves. She looked side to side. Carson's door was the closest. She could hide there, but then she would be trapped if Lenny decided to search the house for whatever he came after. Not only that, the old house would probably give her away with creaks and groans if she tried to walk more than a few steps.

"Hello? Anybody home?" he called again.

Melody heard him step across the threshold and close the door behind him. Indignation at his intrusion battled against her fear. He would be shocked out of his socks if she went downstairs at this moment and told him to get out.

What if he refused? He was obviously here for a reason. He must've known no one was around. The perfect time to... To what? Get his share of the stash upstairs. Had Jay been shortchanging him, and he was here to get what he thought was owed him?

She would call the police. That's what she'd do. The closest phone was in Grandma and Grandpa's room—Jay's room now—but she would have to step into view to get there. Even if she was able to make the call without being heard, it could take an hour for authorities to show up. That gave Lenny plenty of time to choke the life out of her and pillage the house. Her only hope was he would go away. Or she could sneak out of the house without him knowing she was here.

Across from Carson's door was an old credenza. It had stood downstairs for years until new furniture replaced it and it was relegated to the upstairs landing. Now it stored overflow from the bedrooms and the bathroom closet. There was just enough space between the credenza and the wall to wedge her body in. She cocked her head and listened. Lenny hadn't left the entryway. She could imagine him craning his neck to see into as many rooms as possible from where he stood to make sure he was alone. Then she heard him start toward the stairwell.

She had to act. She could either stomp to the edge of the landing and demand to know what he wanted, or hide. Decision made, she dove to the end of the hall and squeezed between the credenza and the wall. She wasn't brave. Not that brave anyway.

Her shoulders and hips were a tight squeeze, but she made it just as Lenny started up the stairs below her. The credenza stood about an inch from the wall. A sliver of daylight between the credenza and the wall offered a narrow view of the landing. She was almost afraid to look. What if he sensed her presence when he reached the top step and looked in her direction like the villain always did in late-night movies? Still, she couldn't tear her gaze away as he lumbered up the stairs, making no effort to keep quiet. Why would he? He thought he was alone. Melody concentrated on making herself as small a target as possible. Lenny was tall, at least six feet, and thin and lanky, yet he sounded like a linebacker coming up the stairs. Or maybe it was Melody's ear pressed against the wall and the pounding of her heart that made it sound that way.

She checked to make sure her knees weren't sticking out past the edge of the credenza. For the first time in her life, she was glad she wasn't long-legged. Her leg muscles began to tighten. She couldn't maintain this position forever. She was almost directly across from Carson's doorway. If Lenny came this way, he would see her. He had no reason to unless he was after something in Carson's room. She still didn't know if Carson was involved in Jay's business. After all this time, she didn't know anything about him except he was a freeloader. Technically not a freeloader anymore since he had taken over much of the farm chores, but she still didn't trust him.

All she knew for sure was she was a sitting duck if Lenny came her way.

"Oh, Lord, make him change his mind about searching the house," she prayed silently. *"Make someone come home. Make him not come this way. Help me out of this spot."*

Lenny didn't pause at the top of the stairs but turned immediately toward Grandma and Grandpa's bedroom. Melody almost immediately lost sight of him. She leaned out past the credenza and watched him move down the hall. As expected, he turned into her grandparents' bedroom. She gritted her teeth. How did he know which room was theirs? She couldn't decide if she was madder at Lenny for practically breaking in, or at Jay for allowing him to become so familiar with the farmhouse.

The sound of sticky drawers grating against their guides reached her ears. When she was satisfied he was as far away from the door as the room allowed, she took a deep breath and thrust off the wall. Her legs trembled from squatting, but she ignored the needles and moved stealthily but quickly toward the stairway. She reached the stairs in six strides and started down, resisting the nearly overwhelming urge to break into a flat run. She didn't realize until she hit the bottom stair she couldn't go out the front door. Lenny would hear her. She rounded the bottom of the staircase and headed through the house. She grabbed her coat off the back of Grandma's chair on her way past and set it to rocking. She didn't take the time to stop the motion. All she could hope was it would stop on its own by the time Lenny came downstairs.

She stuffed her arms inside the coat as she moved toward the kitchen. Over her own heavy breathing she couldn't hear if Lenny was still searching the room or if he had stopped to wonder if he heard something. She reached the kitchen and glided around the heavy table in the center of the room. She had nearly cleared the space between the cook table and dining table when she hooked her toe on a kitchen chair. The chair grated against the old linoleum. Even a deaf man would've heard it. Melody gave up on staying quiet as she wrenched open the kitchen door and leaped onto the porch.

The sound of pounding feet on the stairs reverberated in her ears.

The fastest way home was a straight path off the porch, across the snow-covered yard, and down the hill to her house. It was also the easiest way for Lenny to catch up with her. Her only hope was a circuitous route she knew well, and hopefully he didn't, that allowed her to blend into the tree line.

Melody ran as fast as she could across the nearly frozen snow. She ducked behind one of the outbuildings and slowed to catch her breath. She looked down in dismay at the clear set of footprints she left in the snow. There was no hiding out here. Her only hope was to outrun him. The tree line dipped and curved behind her house to the back of the Shelton property. Hopefully, Lenny would convince himself she didn't know anything and go home. If he pursued, she would follow the tree line until she reached the Sheltons' barn. Surely someone would be there. If not, she would keep going until she got to the Storer house or the Kennedys'. Or Jenna's Creek if she had to.

She peered out from behind the outbuilding. She nearly collapsed in relief at the sight of Lenny on the back porch. He wasn't following her. Maybe he didn't realize she knew he had been upstairs. Perhaps she'd overreacted, and he had come to retrieve something left for him by Jay or Lowell.

Regardless of his guilt or innocence, she'd prefer to debate it at home.

She took a deep breath and stepped away from the shelter of the outbuilding, knowing she had made herself a vivid target against the white backdrop. The tree line was only twenty yards ahead. It was slow going. Drifts were still deep in the fields, and the ground was spongy from all the melting. With each step, she sank to her knees in the drifted snow, and the soft earth sucked at her boots. Despite trying to convince herself Lenny was on an innocent errand, she knew in her heart he wasn't. He had been looking for what she found in the closet, and he wasn't going to let her tell anyone else about it.

Nearly to the tree line, she glanced over her shoulder in time to see him jump off the porch onto the densely packed snow in the yard. Even from this distance, he was a menacing figure. He advanced a few steps and raised his arm.

Melody couldn't tell if he had something in his hand or if he was trying to get her attention. It didn't matter. He knew she was running from him, which meant she was hiding something. Ignoring the pain in her side and her boots full of snow, she charged toward the safety of the trees.

A gunshot split the quiet afternoon. A limb splintered above her head and a sprinkling of snow danced down around her in the sparkling sunlight. Melody cried out and dove behind the trees. This wasn't happening. Her mind wouldn't compute he fired at her. People like her didn't get chased through the woods and shot at like the insipid heroine in a bad movie.

There had to be another explanation. Jay was selfish and thoughtless and definitely involved in the trafficking of narcotics, but he was harmless. He took care of his sick mother. He cut firewood for the family. Last month he helped Dad clear snow from the paddock for the cows. He would never put his own niece in a situation like this.

As the thoughts tumbled over one another inside her head, Melody ran deeper into the cover of the trees. She wanted to keep going, far into the forest where Lenny would never find her. But she needed to stay close to the field and the route that would take her to the Shelton farm. Her ears tensed for the sound of another gunshot or feet crashing through the trees after her. All was quiet except for her own labored breathing and racing thoughts. When she reached a break in the trees, she glanced behind her. Lenny wasn't where he had been. Her gaze flitted around the farmyard. She didn't see him, but there were plenty of obstacles he could be hiding behind as he closed the gap between them. She looked back at the spot where she had entered the woods. All clear. Only her footprints marred the snow.

She ducked behind the biggest tree in her vicinity and clutched at her side, her breath coming in greedy gulps. Her legs shook with fatigue, and a line of perspiration trickled between her shoulder blades. She thought she heard a distant thump and hazarded a look around the tree. She was within sight of her own driveway. Dad's truck was still gone. He and Mom hadn't gotten home yet, not that she expected them to.

She crouched as low as she could and ran in the general direction of the Shelton farm. The snow wasn't as deep under the trees, and she was able to move faster. She could practically make the trip blindfolded. Even with snow on the ground, the trails fashioned by decades of deer moving through the trees were clearly visible. If Lenny gave chase, he would easily distinguish the trail she was leaving behind.

She slowed a little from fatigue and the sense the immediate danger was over. If Lenny had followed, she would've seen or heard him by now. He had either given up the hunt or he was much stealthier than she imagined. What if she had been wrong about a gunshot? Perhaps her ears and fear had been playing tricks on her.

She thought of the tree limb splintering over her head and the snow raining down on her, and knew she hadn't imagined anything.

Then she heard it. The distinct sound of someone in the trees behind her. Footfalls crunched the heavy snow, and cedar branches swished as they were pushed aside. Despite her fear of another gunshot, Melody leaped out from the cover of the trees and headed in a direct line toward the Shelton farm.

A deep voice sounded behind her. Her heart lurched, and she nearly dove for cover into a snow bank.

The voice came again over the sound of heavy footsteps. Louder and closer this time. "Melody."

She stopped in her tracks and turned around.

Tim Shelton stepped out of the trees, a plaid bill hat pulled low over his face. He wore a bright orange safety vest over his coveralls. He carried a chainsaw and was covered in sawdust. Melody cried out in relief and ran at him, nearly knocking the chainsaw out of his hands.

He set the chainsaw down and put both hands on her shoulders. "What's wrong?"

"Stay near the trees," she said, panting. "I think...someone..."

He squeezed her shoulders through her heavy coat. "Someone what?"

"I...he was..."

"Who? What happened?"

She started to tell him everything. Lenny Brown had shot at her. He had been inside the house, and Jay was a drug dealer like she and Grandpa suspected. She and Tim were sitting ducks. They needed to hide. They needed to get the police.

The sound of a car door slamming easily reached their ears across the wide open space. A car engine roared to life and backed out of the Beckwith driveway. The car came into view between the buildings and the rise and fall of the landscape. Even at this distance, she recognized Lenny's car.

"I thought…" She looked back at Tim. "Lenny was in Grandma's house. I heard him and I ran. I thought…someone was shooting."

Relief flooded Tim's face. "I heard some hunters in the woods earlier when I came out to cut firewood."

Melody shook her head. "It wasn't hunters. It was…"

Was she wrong? She hadn't actually seen Lenny raise a gun to shoot. She hadn't heard hunters, but that didn't mean they weren't in the woods. She encountered them all the time.

But it hadn't been hunters. It was…

"Someone fired at me. A bullet hit a tree right over my head. It missed me by inches." Her knees nearly buckled at the thought of it.

Tim's face went white. "Melody, you know better than to be out here without safety clothing. Some of those hunters are from the city and have no business carrying a rifle. They'll shoot at anything that moves."

Melody wanted to insist it wasn't hunters. Tim wouldn't believe her. He would react the same way her parents would if she told them what happened.

"How could you be so foolish?" Mom would demand. *"If you thought Lenny Brown was dangerous, you should've left before he came into the house. It's a miracle he didn't shoot you. What if he takes revenge on your grandma?"*

"I guess I wasn't thinking," she told Tim. "I need to stay out of the woods when I'm not properly dressed."

Tim seemed relieved her panic had subsided. He picked up the chainsaw, and they fell into step together as they headed toward her house, the closest one from where they stood.

"There are people in the woods all the time," he said. "Hunters that shoot first and ask questions later."

Melody knew she was being chastised. She didn't bother to respond. She was too busy trying to figure out what to do next. She couldn't go to the police. She had no proof Lenny followed her out of the house. He couldn't have pushed Grandpa down the stairs either. Until she figured out what happened the morning of the blizzard, she couldn't say a word to her parents or Jay about what she found. She couldn't put Grandma or other innocent people in danger.

CHAPTER TWENTY-TWO

Melody sat down on her bed and picked up the narrow tablet she had sneaked out of the house the day Carson caught her going through the built-in cabinets. She'd been through each one a dozen times. She was still shaky and skittish from her run through the woods. Tim had nearly convinced her no one had shot at her. But why had Lenny gone into the house unless he was after something he had no right to? Why had he chased her downstairs and through the kitchen if he didn't intend to keep her quiet?

Maybe he had only intended to scare her into minding her own business. If that was the case, he succeeded beyond his wildest dreams.

As soon as she got home after her flight across the field, she had taken a hot shower, all the while reliving those moments in Grandpa's room. After finding the box of drugs and money, she had forgotten her original purpose. She hadn't found anything about a fire or why Grandpa needed to protect his mother, but she believed she knew everything she needed to know about how he ended up at the bottom of the stairs. Everyone in the house seemed to have a reason to want him to beat Grandma to the grave. Jay was the only one whose motive could lead to violence.

Grandpa must've known what she figured out today. Nothing got past him. He wouldn't have stood by and allowed the business to continue, even at the risk of his own safety.

Lowell obviously hated his father and knew Melody would inherit most of the estate if Grandpa was left in charge of the new will. But he was barely ambitious enough to butter his own bread. Melody doubted he was much of a cog in any money making scheme. Maybe he was grooming Carson to become Jay's new right hand man. That would have made him Lenny's enemy rather than a business partner. Lowell wasn't likely to ever do anything but complain about what he saw as the injustices in his life. After her talk with him last week, she saw him as a broken man who never lived up to his family's expectations, not a criminal mastermind.

Lowell and Jay weren't the only ones in the house to raise questions in her mind. She wouldn't forget the day she caught Carson in the bedroom with his hand in Grandma's purse. Like Lowell, there had been no love lost when Grandpa died, though he was gracious enough not to voice his feelings. Did any of it have to do with Lenny chasing her through the woods? They must've known each other. Lenny made regular visits up the hill with Lowell and Jay. Maybe Carson decided the drug trade was more profitable than waiting for his grandparents to die and leave him a small portion of an inheritance. Christy was right, even a large farm wasn't worth much split a dozen ways.

Lowell may have written to him in Texas about all the money he and Jay were making and invited him to take part in the Ohio drug trade. Or was something else going on? Melody couldn't forget the talk she overheard between him and Allen the night of the funeral. Carson had nearly threatened Allen about something. But what? It couldn't have had anything to do with Jay's illegal activity. She was sure Allen had nothing to do with that. So what else was going on?

She resituated a stack of pillows against the headboard and leaned into them. She flipped through the tablet until she found the initials *LB* and *IN*. In the margins Grandpa had written *Money in* and *Money out* followed by several question marks.

Had *LB* stood for Lenny Brown instead of Lowell Beckwith?

She reread the figures and notations for what seemed like the thousandth time. She could almost hear Grandpa's voice in her head telling her to stop looking so hard. *"You can't see the forest for the trees,"* he would say if he were sitting beside her.

"Give me a discerning heart, Lord," Melody prayed aloud. "If something's here, help me to see it."

She started to flip the notebook closed when she noticed something. The initials *IN* were in a crinkle of the page. She looked closer. It looked like another letter had been made blurred by the fold. She ran her forefinger over the crease to smooth it out. She held the page closer to the lamp. There was definitely another letter after the N. It looked like an O. Or a C. She tilted the page into the lamplight and stared at it. She looked at the *Money In, Money Out* notation on the margin. A memory nagged at her. Something Allen had said after the funeral. Or had Carson said it?

She continued to study the tiny scrawl as she struggled to remember exactly what the men had said. Then it came to her. She looked back at the letters *LB*. It wasn't what she first thought. *LB* did not stand for Lenny Brown or Lowell Beckwith. Lenny was guilty all right, but he hadn't been on the farm during the blizzard to push Grandpa down the stairs. In fact, she was sure he was innocent of any involvement in Grandpa's death

She looked back at the figures, written in tiny, neat rows, the likes of which she'd watched Grandpa write all her life. She had been wrong all along. The amounts recorded were out of order and too large to be what she originally thought. She ran her thumb across a smear of ink at the bottom of the page. She squinted at the notations to make sure they read the way she thought they did.

She concentrated on what Carson had said that night. He had wanted something from Allen, and Allen accused him of threatening him. None of it had made sense at the time. Even now, she had no idea what was going on. But she remembered Allen's reply.

"You don't want to mess around and become a liability, boy."

Everything fell into place. Finally. Melody knew what happened. If not how, at least she knew why.

Her mind whirling, she leaped out of bed. She hurried across the room to her phone and dialed. The phone was picked up on the first ring.

"Christy," she said breathlessly

"Melody? What's going on? Are you all right?"

Melody thought of telling her about Lenny chasing her into the woods. She thought about the gun and the money in Grandpa's closet. Before she could form the words, tears spilled down her cheeks. "Oh, Christy. It's Grandpa. I know who killed him."

❧❧❧

The ringing phone roused Noel Wyatt from sleep. He squinted at the clock next to the bed. 12:40. No good news ever came at 12:40 in the morning. He was instantly awake as he lunged for the phone.

"Noel Wyatt," he said warily, expecting the professional voice of an emergency room doctor or other healthcare professional on the other end calling about his ninety-seven-year old mother.

"Hey, Noel, this is Vinnie Dalton at the firehouse. You need to get downtown. We just got the call. Your store's on fire. Looks like the whole blame town is on fire."

◄◄◄

Allen Beckwith was jerked awake a little after three by a hysterical occupant of one of the apartments over Manny Peterson's appliance store. After the phone call, Allen tried to ignore the dread in his stomach. Ordinarily he could drift back to sleep like a newborn baby, regardless of the situation. Not tonight. He lay awake and stared at the ceiling for over an hour. Things would look better in the light of day, he told himself over and over. Apartment renters seldom bothered with insurance, and if they did, they didn't have much of value to insure. The problem would iron itself out. He rolled away from Bonnie, sleeping peacefully beside him, and hoped they wouldn't need to have an uncomfortable conversation in the morning.

Four hours later he was in the bathroom shaving when Manny Peterson called. His appliance store had taken a big hit, not to mention the jeweler's on one side and Wyatt's Drugstore on the other. Thirty minutes later, after hanging up from a third call, Allen fastened his gold watch around his wrist and dried the beads of sweat from his top lip. Bonnie would come in any minute, telling him they needed to hurry if they didn't want to be late for church. She mustn't think anything was amiss.

So far, nothing was. His insurance office was closed today. Nothing could be done about the fire beyond the beginning of cleanup and an assessment of damages. He'd attend to that after church. He would smile and offer comfort the way he always did and worry about tomorrow when it came.

He straightened his tie and wiped his index finger across his upper lip again just as Bonnie swept into the bathroom. "Wayne called a few minutes ago. He said he'll meet you at the office after church to start going over policies."

In the mirror Allen studied the perfectly straight Windsor knot in his tie. "No need for that. We can't do anything beyond hand holding until tomorrow. Call him back for me, would you? Tell him we have a big enough week ahead of us. Let him enjoy the rest of the weekend and I'll handle today."

She stretched forward on her toes and kissed his cheek. "Nobody realizes what a kind heart you have, darling. Those poor people. It's only fortunate no one got hurt."

Allen stared at his reflection and shuddered as she left the room. She didn't realize how true her statement was. He didn't feel like worshipping this morning. He didn't feel like doing anything except digging a hole and climbing in it. Bonnie was so worried about the people who had lost their belongings in the fire. Within a few hours, if he didn't act quickly, she would have far graver matters to worry about.

CHAPTER TWENTY-THREE

A gentle rain began to fall Monday morning, causing a pallor of black smoke to hover over the downtown area. Noel Wyatt hoped it would wash away the remnants of snow and grime in the city's alleys and parking lots. He couldn't remember the last Monday he wasn't up with the dawn and ready to open the drugstore for another workweek. He didn't take vacations or personal days. He no longer drove his aging mother to Florida for the winter. He was at the store every morning of his life, save Sunday. Today it was closed and waiting for the all-clear from the fire department, thus he didn't know what to do with himself. Somehow he had turned into an old man living a very shallow existence.

His usual parking spot in the alley behind the store was blocked by debris left behind by firefighters. He parked in front of the store and hoped he could get in and out without anyone seeing him. It was still early; the downtown area wouldn't start bustling for another hour or so. He didn't want to talk to anyone. He didn't want to answer the questions he'd already answered at least a hundred times.

"Was anyone hurt?"

"How extensive are the damages?"

"Do they have any idea what caused it?"

In the wee hours Sunday morning he had stood at the intersection across the street from the drugstore with other downtown shop owners and renters thrust out of their apartments by the early morning blaze. Most everyone was crying. The renters were wrapped in blankets. Most had only been able to grab their shoes and coats before fleeing the fire. Those who couldn't do even that were sitting in the backs of ambulances or patrol cars parked along the street. Everyone's eyes were glued to the firefighters working to keep the fires from spreading. Some took pictures. Noel figured he should too. One day he might be interested in remembering this night. At the time, all he wanted to do was look away.

While many around him were suffering the loss of everything they owned, Noel had experienced a very selfish sense of freedom. The drugstore his father built was his life. It was all he'd ever known. It had allowed him a good life. The revenue had financed investment opportunities and built wealth beyond anything he could've imagined. Losing the business would break his mother's heart. She loved it because her husband loved it and died while turning it into the enterprise it was today. All Noel could think while standing on the street corner was, if it burned, he would no longer be tied to this town.

For a brief moment, Noel thought of Abby and how—without the store—the two of them could walk away. Last week when he went to her house to sign some insurance forms for Eric she told him she lost her job. He didn't know how she felt about anything, but the sight of her at the kitchen table serving cake and coffee had reminded him of the young woman he fell in love with thirty-plus years ago. He knew better than to think she was still that girl, but he wanted to spend the last years of his life getting to know who she was now.

From that short conversation, he knew he wasn't what Abby wanted. At least not now. She wanted her family restored. She still loved her husband and missed what they had lost. More than anything, she loved her daughter and mourned the relationship they might never have again.

While she talked about her uncertainty for the future and worried about Christy, Noel had wanted to tell her he was here for her. Whatever she needed, he was happy to provide. It wasn't the right time. It may never be. He had made peace with the mess of his life years ago. He had accepted he missed his opportunity with Abby before she ever married, and this was his penance to bear. He might never have her in his life, but he couldn't help imagining a life he dreamed of while the fire raged.

Then the wind died. As if God were sending a message, Noel realized his store would be spared. After a few days to repair the water damage, his life would go on as it always had.

Noel spotted Manny Peterson's car on the corner. The owner of the appliance store had been his downtown neighbor for almost thirty years. He dropped the key to the drugstore back into his front pocket and headed down the street to the appliance store.

The door was open. Manny was on a small ladder near the back examining water spots on the ceiling. Noel zigzagged around buckets and pails of water and drop cloth-covered floor lamps to get to him. He looked in dismay at a puddle of water atop a console television. The wooden top had already bubbled and cracked.

"Looks like they soaked you good."

Manny started at the sound of Noel's voice. He hadn't shaved this morning, and it looked like he hadn't slept since the fire. "Yeah, I got more water than fire damage down here. The upstairs is almost a total loss. What about you?"

"Not as bad. Water damage, mostly. Do you know when you'll be able to reopen for business?"

"Not soon enough. I don't know how long I can keep going if the clean-up process takes a while. It's hard enough for a man to make a living with those big chains moving into the county."

Noel had suffered similar losses. Some of the floors in the upstairs apartments would have to be replaced. At least they were vacant so losses were minimal. The east wall of the drugstore had major water damage, but his losses were nothing compared to Manny's. "The little man is a dying breed," he said in agreement. "Won't be long before they put us out to pasture."

Manny shook his head and started his slow descent down the ladder. He was a small man, just over five feet tall and well into his sixties. The top of a ladder was not where he belonged. "Noel, I was wondering," he began when he safely reached the floor, "have you talked to anybody from the insurance company? I'm hearing some crazy things."

"What do you mean?"

"You're insured with Beckwith, aren't you?"

He nodded. "Have been for years."

"That's what I thought. I was here last night when the claims adjustor came through. He said I might not have enough coverage for all the damage."

Noel sucked air between his teeth. "That's a shame, Manny."

Manny turned in a half circle and surveyed the damage around him. When he looked back at Noel, tears shone in his eyes. "At least I got a home to go to. I feel bad for my renters. One of them belongs to the Lutheran church and they're talking of organizing a benefit for everybody affected."

"I heard something about that. Their minister called mine. They hope to get all the churches involved."

"I was thinking about going to the Chamber of Commerce to see if area businesses would pitch in."

"Sounds like a plan, Manny. I'm on the board. I'll see what I can do."

"Great, Noel, thanks. None of my renters had insurance. When you're young and broke, the last thing you have room for in your budget is insurance. The thing is, I'll be in a world of hurt if the insurance won't pay to rebuild those apartments. I don't make enough selling appliances anymore with the big boys giving credit and selling below wholesale. I gotta have those apartments if I want to put food on the table."

Noel wanted to kick himself for the other night when he had envisioned the fire as freedom. Manny stood to lose everything. "I hear you."

"I can't understand that adjustor saying I don't have enough coverage. He can't be right, can he? I paid my premiums right on time for years. Beckwith always assured me I have enough coverage to withstand any kind of claim. I couldn't risk having a renter or somebody slip and fall down the stairs or set the place on fire with a mislaid cigarette. You know how some of them are, careless if their name isn't on the deed."

"Have you talked to Allen?"

Manny let out a belabored sigh. "Yesterday and then again this morning. He tells me not to worry. It's some kind of oversight. I don't know, Noel. Something isn't sitting well about the whole situation."

Noel pushed a shock of graying hair away from his forehead, a habit he developed back when his hair was thick enough to fall across his eyes. "I'm sure it's nothing. If you've paid your premiums, you should be good to go. Have you looked over your policy?"

"That's all I've done the last two days. It looks fine to me."

"Then don't worry about it. The adjustor doesn't have all the facts. I'm sure he's in his office right now going over your policy, and he sees he's mistaken."

Manny didn't look convinced. "Those fellows don't usually talk off the top of their heads."

For the first time Noel wondered about his own policy. He hadn't looked at it in two years, the last time he went over it in Allen's office. "I'm sure you're worrying over nothing," he said, though Manny wasn't the worrying kind. "You'll end up with a nice fat check and you can make some of those improvements you've been putting off."

"I sure hope so. You should look through your policy, too. You might be in for a surprise."

Noel brushed aside the comment. "I'm sure I have enough coverage."

"That's what I thought. Well, if you hear anything, let me know, would you? I'm anxious to see how this thing pans out."

"Sure thing, Manny. I'll probably talk to you tomorrow when you come downtown to open for business."

"I wouldn't count on it."

Noel put his hands in his pockets and headed out of the store. Was Manny right and neither man was adequately covered? Impossible. Noel always planned for the worst. It was how he stayed in business through the lean times. Manny Peterson was no slacker when it came to details either. If he thought he was adequately insured, he was. The adjustor had made a mistake. That was all. Noel trudged past the drugstore entrance and climbed into his Cadillac. He needed to go home and take a look at his policy.

❧❧❧

Peggy Winston was a pro at handling confused, frustrated, and even irate policyholders and fielding questions until Allen or one of the agents got to the office. She had worked at Beckwith Insurance for thirty-one years. She started when her youngest son went to kindergarten, and Mr. Winston decided he would rather spend his time on Knapp Street with his girlfriend instead of at home with Peggy and the children. Peggy's mother advised her to look the other way. Phil was, after all, a good provider, and he didn't slap her around. Peggy wanted more from a marriage, but regardless of what she wanted, she needed to protect her family. She needed a job.

She possessed absolutely no marketable job skills. Using a friend's typewriter, she created the most imaginative and optimistic resume ever penned and hit the streets of Jenna's Creek. Since she didn't drive, her job search was limited.

That particular year—that month actually, though Peggy had no way of knowing at the time—also happened to be when Bonnie Beckwith decided she'd enough of juggling babies on one hip and Allen's books on the other and left the insurance company to stay home with her three boys.

The morning Peggy walked through the door of Beckwith Insurance Allen was having a particularly bad day. He had a client in his office, one sitting in the reception area, as it were, and the phone was ringing incessantly. Peggy listened to the phone ring for the fourth time and watched Allen's face contort as he struggled to focus on his client's needs while risking losing another by not answering the phone. If there was one thing Peggy knew how to do, it was recognizing when things were falling apart around her. She took action.

She left the doorway where she'd been hovering, set her purse and the last copy of her resume on the desk, and picked up the phone. "Beckwith Insurance," she said as firmly as she could muster with every eye in the room on her. "How can I help you?"

Only after she wrote down the message on the back of an overdue light bill with a trembling hand and hung up the phone did she dare to look up. She either had a job or she lost her last chance in town of getting one.

Allen didn't acknowledge her until after he finished with the man at his desk. He stood up, shook hands with the new client, and told him his secretary would fill out the additional paperwork. He plopped the papers down on the front desk and motioned for Peggy to take a seat behind it. He turned his attention to the next customer while Peggy scrolled the first form into the typewriter.

After the second client left, Peggy asked why he gave her the job. Allen smiled his soon to be famous smile that could convince an old lady to part with her last dime, and said, "You know how to answer the phone and you can type. Two things I'm terrible at."

Allen and Peggy became close friends. He counseled her through her impending divorce, and she helped him choose Christmas gifts for Bonnie and even arranged a surprise cruise to Bermuda for their twenty-fifth wedding anniversary. She thought she knew Allen Beckwith better than she knew her own children. For the first part of the week after the fire, she reminded herself he wasn't the kind of man who could do what everyone in town was accusing him of having done. He would never betray his clients' trust. He would never betray *her*.

While she didn't have much trouble ignoring the talk around town or the other agents huddled in corners speculating when they didn't think she or Allen were paying attention, it wasn't as easy to ignore Allen himself. He waltzed into the office two minutes before nine on Monday morning as if he didn't have a care in the world. Underneath his dark suit and perfectly pomaded hair, though, it was obvious to Peggy he hadn't slept all weekend. As the week wore on, he looked more and more haggard and concerned, even as his voice became brighter and louder and more determinedly confident.

Peggy Winston wasn't the same naïve woman who picked up the phone one morning to hear a stranger demand child support from her husband for the child he'd fathered with a woman he met in a bar. The betrayal from what Allen may have done sat more solidly in her stomach than what she endured with that phone call so many years ago.

Between fielding complaints and answering the same questions over and over, Peggy studied files. She never would've seen the evidence if she hadn't known to look for it. She scolded herself for being blind for so long. She should've seen the signs. If she figured out what appeared to have been happening for twenty years, the authorities would too.

It came as no surprise when the police chief came in a little after eleven Friday morning, flanked by three men in dark suits, and told everyone to go home. The Ohio Bureau of Investigation was confiscating every file and scrap of paper in the office. Peggy's gaze sought out Allen as she gathered her purse and coat. When he picked up his briefcase, one of the state investigators stepped forward and took it out of his hand.

"I'll be needing that, too, Mr. Beckwith."

Peggy had never seen Allen when he wasn't exuding confidence and charm. This time, she feared he would burst into tears in front of all of them.

CHAPTER TWENTY-FOUR

The phone rang just as Melody was leaving her office. She almost didn't pick up. It had been a long week. She was tired of answering the same questions over and over, tired of her job, and tired of people so willing to judge her uncle without one shred of wrongdoing. Everyone in town was questioning the integrity of Beckwith Insurance and going over policies with a fine-tooth comb. She wanted nothing more than to go home, pull her covers over her head, and have a good cry. A few short months ago her biggest problems came at work where she was learning the fine art of leaving them in the office. Since the morning of the blizzard, it seemed everything she believed was nothing more than a house of cards rapidly falling down around her ears.

After she called Christy Saturday night, they made plans to meet Sunday after church and talk about what she had found in the closet and what she believed she knew. Then one of the apartments over Manny Peterson's appliance store caught fire and ignited what looked like half the uptown business district. Four separate buildings had been affected, with Manny's taking the worst hit. The devastation was bad enough. City streets were more clogged now than they had been at the height of the blizzard with everyone in three counties driving through to assess the damage for themselves. The three major networks ran stories every night, and each one had a more negative spin, chiefly the insufficiency of insurance policies covering the buildings.

She and her parents had gone to Allen and Bonnie's after church to try to find out where the rumors were coming from. Melody kept her suspicions to herself. It wouldn't do any good to tell Mom and Dad what she had found among Warner's papers.

Allen had been characteristically optimistic. "People always get up in arms over things like this. They've lost everything and they want someone to blame. It's a waiting game. This will all blow over."

The look on his face suggested it wasn't going to blow over.

Against her better judgment, Melody picked up her office phone and prayed it was something that could be taken care of in under a minute. She wanted to go home. "Melody Knauff," she said briskly.

"I'm glad I caught you. It's Christy."

The tension slid out of her shoulders. She sank into her office chair and let her purse drop to the floor. "Christy, hi. Sorry I haven't had a chance to get back with you, especially after my cryptic phone call the other night."

"Don't apologize. I know you've had other things to worry about this week, though I must admit I'm anxious to hear what you learned."

Melody didn't bother to repress a sigh. "It's been crazy. After Mom gets off work tonight, she and I are driving to Hamden to pick Grandma up from her cousin's. We'd rather spare her from dealing with everything going on around here, but she's worried sick about Uncle Allen and wants to come home."

"Do you have time for a cup of coffee or something before you go?"

Melody glanced at her watch. "Sure. Mom's always late getting out of the store on Fridays. Are you at the library?"

"No, I'm home, but I can meet you at the diner in ten minutes."

"Okay, good. I'll see you there." Melody hung up. Judy's shift at the grocery store ended in thirty minutes. It wasn't long, but she couldn't resist putting everything aside for a few minutes to share what she'd found with Christy.

❈❈❈

"I'm sure this whole thing is a huge misunderstanding," Christy said ten minutes later after the waitress filled their coffee cups and went back behind the counter.

Melody didn't add cream to her coffee like she usually did. Tonight she needed it as strong as she could stand it. "I'm not so sure. Uncle Allen has always been the most stable member of our family. I never thought he was capable of something like this."

"What exactly is he accused of?" Christy asked.

"People are saying he's been underselling policies and pocketing the premiums. Manny Peterson from the appliance store is telling everybody his policy is practically worthless. He claims he's been paying premiums for years, and now the company tells him he doesn't have coverage."

"Shouldn't people know if they had adequate coverage?"

"They should, but lots of people never read the fine print in their policies. They believe whatever their agent tells them. I doubt I've read every single line on every form I ever signed. You can bet I will from now on. You can't be too trusting. But Uncle Allen." Melody stared into her coffee cup for a moment. "I can't believe it. He's lived in this town his whole life. He wouldn't take advantage of his own neighbors."

"I can't believe a man would risk his livelihood and reputation for a few dollars."

"It's more than a few dollars. Mom and Dad were speculating about it last night when they didn't think I could hear. They figure it could be hundreds of thousands of dollars. That's why the state got involved."

Christy's eyes widened. "Oh, my. I had no idea."

"None of us did." Melody leaned forward over her coffee cup. Christy mirrored her. "It's part of why I called you the other night." Over Christy's head, she checked to make sure the waitress was well out of earshot. "I found some notations in one of Grandpa's notebooks that finally made sense to me. He had huge dollar amounts and dates in columns I now realize were marked *Income* and *Liabilities*. Everything that's happened this week confirmed it. Grandpa knew something was going on. I thought all along the notebook was about Jay, but now with the state investigating Allen, Grandpa must've had suspicions about him as well."

"And you believe whoever your grandpa was referring to in those notebooks was responsible for his fall?"

"I'm sure of it."

"Then it couldn't have been Allen. The blizzard had everyone stranded. I live in town, and I had to walk everywhere I went for eight days."

"That's what has me stumped. There were only a few people in the house that night. Grandma and Grandpa.,Carson, Jay, and Lowell." Melody ticked them off on her fingers. "There's a possibility someone else was there too. Lenny Brown. He's the one who drove Lowell to the farm the night before. I saw him drive by on his way to the farm, but I'm not positive I saw his car go back."

Christy's face was blank. "Who's Lenny Brown?"

"I believe he's in business with Uncle Jay. They…um…ply their trade together. Where you see one, the other is usually close at hand."

Christy leaned closer and whispered. "You mean he's a dealer?"

Melody nodded. "I think he shot at me Saturday."

"He what?" Christy shrieked. Conversation around them came to a halt. Christy bit down on her lip. "What do you mean he shot at you?" she hissed, her eyes wide.

"I mean what you think I mean. I was at the farmhouse alone. Everyone was gone so I went there to see if I could find any newspaper clippings about the fire in Springfield. I didn't find any clippings, but..." She stopped and looked around the restaurant. "I found some pills and a pile of cash and a gun."

Christy's eyes went wider, but she kept any outburst inside this time.

"They belong to Jay. He's moved into Grandma and Grandpa's room. I can't stay quiet about it any longer. I've had my suspicions for a while. So did Grandpa. Now I'm sure. I want to call the police, but I don't know what to do about Grandma. She's so fragile, even before this happened with Allen. It will break her heart. That's the only thing keeping me from marching into the police station right now."

Christy waved the words away with her hand. "What does this have to do with someone trying to shoot you?"

"Oh, right. I was in the bedroom. I had just found Jay's stash when Lenny showed up. He barged in like he owned the place. I hid and he went straight to the bedroom. Obviously he was looking for what I found. I was afraid he'd search the house so I ran, and well, he shot at me."

Christy looked sick. "Melody, this is crazy. What did you do? Did you call the police?"

Melody shook her head. "I couldn't. I came across my neighbor in the woods and he nearly convinced me it was probably hunters or some such. I thought I might be overreacting, but when I got home and went through Grandpa's writings, I was sure Lenny knew exactly what he was doing."

"But he still couldn't have pushed your grandpa down the stairs? You may not have seen him go home the night before the blizzard hit, but there's no way he could've gotten off the hill for weeks after. He certainly couldn't have hid out from everyone for that long. He couldn't have hid his car either."

"I know. I realized that the other night. I thought all along the one with the most reason to push Grandpa was Jay. But..." She looked around the restaurant again. "When the whole family got together after the funeral I heard Carson and Allen talking. It sounded like Carson was blackmailing him, but I couldn't imagine what he would have to blackmail him about. Now I wonder if Carson knew what Allen was doing. He said he wanted a piece of the action."

The color rushed out of Christy's face. "Do you think he may have hurt your grandpa to protect Allen?"

Melody grimaced. "I don't know. I still don't know what's going on. How could Carson figure out what Allen was doing? Mom and Dad say Allen may have gotten away with this for twenty years."

"What are you going to do?"

"I thought about telling Mom my suspicions on our way to Cousin Arleen's. I hate to get into it. She's already worried sick about Uncle Allen and Aunt Bonnie. She would never believe Carson did anything. Like everyone else, she thinks Grandpa slipped on those basement stairs, and she wants me to accept facts. That's another reason I didn't tell her about Lenny Brown chasing me out of the farmhouse. She'd be livid that all my snooping put me in a dangerous position."

"Do you think your grandma's safe in that house with everything that's happening?"

Melody shook her head. "None of them would hurt Grandma. Grandpa obviously figured out what they were doing and he became a threat. Grandma isn't a threat to anyone."

"What about you? I'm sure Lenny told Jay he saw you in the house that day."

Melody wrapped her hands around her coffee cup, more to still the shaking than to take a drink. "I thought about that. He'll probably think I was there cleaning or something and got spooked by seeing Lenny in the house. I tried not to leave any evidence I'd been in the closet."

"Regardless, I'd avoid the guy if I were you. Make sure you're not alone in the house with him."

"Don't worry, I don't plan to be." Melody pulled her sleeve back to look at her watch. She took a sip from the coffee that was no longer hot enough to taste good. "We should finish up. Mom'll be ready to go soon. I'm going to pick her up at the store and we'll leave her car parked there till we get back."

Christy put her hand on Melody's arm. "Wait. Um…I hate to tell you like this with everything going on. I'm afraid I might not have a chance to talk to you again before…"

"Before what?" Melody didn't like the look on Christy's face. "Is everything okay?"

Christy had a hard time meeting her gaze. "Yeah, sure, everything's fine. It's just with everything your family is going through, I know my timing's terrible."

Melody's impatience sparked. She didn't have time to guess what Christy was alluding to. "Terrible how?"

"I'm moving. I'm leaving Jenna's Creek."

Melody wondered if she'd heard correctly. "You're doing what?"

"I'm leaving. I can't stay here. Mom and I got into a huge fight the night you and I got back from Springfield. Well, actually, I got into a fight. I told her I didn't care what she did, and I was leaving town. I've been thinking about it for a long time anyway. I kept coming up with excuses to put it off, but there's no point now."

"If you've been thinking about it for so long, why haven't you said anything?"

"I don't know. It wasn't set in stone and…well, it's a long story. I never felt like I belonged in Jenna's Creek. Especially after I got older. I've told you that. It was just a holding pattern until I decided what I wanted to do. Now with Mom and Noel Wyatt…"

Melody sighed. "That again. For crying out loud, Christy, get over it. She's a grown woman."

"I know. That's why I'm no longer going to stand in her way. She can get on with her life and I can get on with mine. I hate that all this is happening the same time as what you're going through, but it can't be helped."

"Oh, it can't be helped, huh? What about Jarrod? Have you told him? What about me? I need a friend right now. I just spilled my guts about my family. I told you things no one else in the world knows, and you're leaving like none of it matters."

"This has nothing to do with you, Melody."

"Of course it doesn't. It never does. It's always about you."

Color crept into Christy's porcelain cheeks. "I can't do this anymore. I thought you would at least try to understand."

"What's there to understand?"

"I can't keep pretending to be someone I'm not. I have to think about what's best for me. This…" She swept her arms around the café. "…this town. This life. It isn't what I want. It isn't who I am. It never has been."

"We all know who you are, Christy. You're selfish. That's who you are. It's who you've always been. You're the most selfish person I ever met. You told me a few weeks ago your mom got fired. She's trying to start a business. How's she going to get it off the ground without you at home helping out? She was there for you when you put yourself in a stupid position and got attacked in that hotel room. You had nowhere to go. Not a nickel to your name. She came through with no questions asked. Unconditional love. That's what she gave you and this is how you throw it back in her face. How is she going to survive without someone bringing home a paycheck? Not only does she need you, she probably wants you to stay."

Christy opened her mouth, but Melody rushed on.

"Because you're not getting your way, because your mom isn't ignoring what she wants in order to keep her precious baby girl happy, you're walking away."

"That isn't what's happening," Christy said, through clenched teeth in a struggle to control her temper. "I wanted to tell you my plans instead of just disappearing like the old Christy would've done. I'm sorry this coincides with what's going on with your uncle and your grandma and everything, but I can't stay here and take care of everybody."

"Oh, the whole world knows that already, Christy. Nobody can depend on you for anything. You make that perfectly clear with every word out of your mouth. Don't depend on Christy because Christy is only looking out for herself."

Melody was so angry she could barely see as she grabbed her purse. She opened her wallet and pulled out a couple of bills to cover the cost of the coffee without looking to see what they were, and threw them on the table. She was probably leaving the best tip the waitress would receive all night. The bell over the door let out a peal of alarm as she slammed her way outside.

CHAPTER TWENTY-FIVE

Carson was worried about Grandma. She hadn't moved from in front of the television since Judy and Melody brought her home from Cousin Arleen's Friday night. He had barely gotten three words out of her in three days. She wasn't interested in continuing their Bible study. Warner's death had been a severe blow. He doubted she'd survive what was happening with Allen.

Authorities hadn't released the exact number of complaints filed against him, but the number was growing every day, and could continue to do so for months. People from all over the state—some representing family members long since deceased—were coming forward to claim they had been cheated by Beckwith Insurance. They accused Allen of selling them too much coverage or not enough, and then refusing to pay out on legitimate claims. Everyone wanted a piece of him, and it didn't look like they'd back down until they had their pound of flesh.

Carson figured most of the charges would be dropped in favor of pursuing a few larger, easier-to-prove ones. Either way, Allen was in a world of trouble. He had been stealing from his clients for years, cheating those who trusted him most. Even if he got off with a fine and a slap on the wrist, he'd never work in Auburn County again. The locals would never forgive him. One thing Carson had learned about the moral majority; they talked a big game about turning the other cheek, but when you hit them in the wallet, they wanted blood.

Allen had been 'invited' to the police station several times to answer questions. So far, it was too soon to make an arrest. Regardless, an arrest was coming. As much as Carson loved his grandmother and dreaded the day she would pass, he almost hoped she wouldn't live to see it happen.

His stomach let out a low rumble. He hadn't eaten since the handful of crackers he swallowed at lunch while trying to coerce Clarice into eating more then the weak beef broth he served her in the living room. He glanced at his watch. It was too late in the day to begin something as labor intensive as a roast or stew. Maybe he'd put something in the Crock Pot first thing in the morning so she could smell it cooking all day and work up an appetite. For tonight he'd settle for spaghetti. Not too spicy, but with enough garlic and seasoning to fill the house with an aroma she couldn't resist.

He pushed away from Warner's old desk where he'd been trying to figure out what Melody had taken out of the house the last time she was here and headed to the kitchen by way of the dining room. He didn't want to disturb Clarice who had fallen asleep in front of Name That Tune, the game show she watched this time every afternoon. While the pasta cooked, he'd put some garlic bread in the oven and let the smell wake her up. She usually couldn't say no to garlic bread.

The dining room was dark and cool. The room faced north and got little sun exposure. The settee in the corner was perfect for sneaking naps last summer when he should've been finishing a chore Warner found for him to do. With the long shadows and only one working vent, the room was best avoided in winter. He didn't bother to turn on a light as he maneuvered between the table and the heavy buffet. His boot kicked a chair leg that hadn't been completely pushed in, and he stopped to straighten it. When he stepped away from the table, his belt loop caught on something. He turned around carefully to disengage himself, assuming Judy or Melody had not closed a buffet drawer all the way the last time they were in here cleaning.

He saw right away it wasn't a drawer that grabbed him. The tiny silver lock on the buffet had been jimmied and hung askew. He yanked the drawer open, knowing already what he would find, or rather, not find. The silverware case wasn't in its usual spot. He pulled the drawer the rest of the way open, though he could tell from the weight it was empty. He slapped the top of the buffet with one hand and slammed the drawer shut with the other rattling Clarice's collection of good plates she kept standing upright in the plate rail.

He stormed into the kitchen where he found Lowell sitting at the table in front of a bowl of Corn Flakes. Jay was coming up from the basement with a dusty mason jar of last year's green beans in each hand.

"Don't you think you've done enough around here?" Carson said around a tightened jaw.

Jay toed the basement door shut and set the jars on the counter. "I was planning to rustle up some grub." He jerked his thumb at Lowell. "If we wait on your daddy to lift a finger, we'll starve to death."

Lowell slurped another spoonful of cereal without taking offense.

"I'm not talking about dinner." Carson looked toward the door to make sure Clarice hadn't overheard. "I'm talking about the silver." He looked squarely at Lowell. "Put it back."

Lowell smoothed his hand over the vinyl tablecloth. "I ain't touched it."

"Well, someone did." Carson stared at him a moment longer before turning his attention to Jay. "It'll break her heart to realize it's gone. Don't you think she's been through enough the last couple of weeks?"

Jay lifted an eyebrow. "I hope you're not accusing me of anything."

Carson flicked out his tongue and wet his upper lip. For the most part Jay was an easy-going fellow who would rather enjoy a few beers and kick back with his buddies than look for a fight. Carson had seen his type before. When crossed, it wouldn't take much provocation for mellow old Jay to pull a knife or something worse from his sock and shut the mouth of whoever was stupid enough to push him too far. At this point Carson was too mad to care. He was tired of keeping quiet while Lowell and Jay plundered their mother's house.

"All I know is the silver's gone and I want it put back where it belongs."

Jay came forward until his hips were against the table. Carson resisted the urge to step back. Like a junkyard dog, Jay would see the move as weakness, and attack.

"How do we know you're not the one who stole it?"

"Yeah," Lowell said, spooning more cereal into his mouth. "Coulda been anybody."

Carson swallowed the lump in his dry mouth. "It wasn't anybody. It was one of you or both. Doesn't matter either way. God knows she isn't going to last much longer. Could you at least wait until she's dead before you steal everything that's not nailed down?"

Jay lunged forward, shoving the table aside as he went. With surprising agility, Lowell scooped up the cereal bowl and jumped away from the table. His chair crashed against the stove, and his spoon clattered to the floor. Jay circled the table and grabbed Carson by the collar before Carson could react. Even though he'd been expecting it, he was still shocked by Jay's speed and strength. Jay's wiry frame slammed into Carson's chest and forced the younger man to backpedal until the doorjamb brought them to a stop.

"I ain't never took nothing that don't belong to me, boy."

Carson struggled to catch his breath. The wind was knocked out of him when he hit the wall, and his shirt collar dug into his throat. He looked over his shoulder at Lowell. For a moment he wondered if his father would step in and diffuse the situation. One look at the apathetic look on Dad's face, and Carson knew he was on his own. Lowell probably figured he had it coming.

Carson pressed his head against the wall to loosen Jay's grip on his collar. "Then take the rest of it and go," he rasped. "None of us need you here."

Jay barked out a humorless laugh. "You're starting to sound more like Pop every day. I'll tell you what I told him. I ain't in no hurry to go, and there ain't a thing you can do to get rid of me."

"This isn't your home."

Jay drew back to hit him. He laughed when Carson flinched. "I got more right to be here than you do, boy."

"At least I'm not breaking any laws."

Jay tightened his grip on Carson's shirt collar. "Is that right? You think I don't know what you've been up to?"

He dropped his hand and threw a punch into Carson's stomach. Carson doubled over, but Jay jerked him upright. He hissed into Carson's ear. "You think I don't know you've been in my closet?"

"I—"

"I suggest you keep your nose outta other folk's business, boy. It's a good way of getting yourself hurt real bad."

He loosened his grip, and Carson leaned into the pain in his stomach. He gulped a few breaths, thankful he'd skipped lunch and didn't have anything to throw up on the floor. He didn't have a chance to recover before he was jerked upright again.

Jay's thumb pressed into the hollow of his throat. His hazel eyes were pinpricks of anger. "Wasn't long ago you were helping yourself to whatever you could get your hands on, same as us."

"I'm going to pay her back," Carson hissed, barely able to speak.

"Sure you are."

"She's an old woman. She'll be dead in a matter of weeks, and everything will be yours anyway. Leave her a little dignity."

Jay drew back his fist. Carson tensed, preparing to dodge the blow. The physical work around the farm the last few months had turned most of his fat to muscle. He may live to regret it, but he wasn't going to stand still and take a beating when he was capable of defending himself. He'd worry about the damage to the kitchen later.

"What's going on in here?" Clarice screeched near his right ear. "Jay, let go of him this instant."

The pressure on Carson's throat fell away, and he stumbled forward and caught himself on the table. Jay smiled disarmingly at his mother. "Just a little misunderstanding, Mom." He slapped Carson on the back.

Carson let out a slow breath to still the pounding in his veins. "Yeah, a misunderstanding."

Clarice straightened to her full height and glared at Jay. "I opened my house to you. I took up for you with your father. This is how you repay me? Well, I won't have it. Things are going to change, starting now. I've looked the other way long enough, Jay, but I'm through watching you bully your way around this house. I want you out. Get your things and go. Tonight."

No one in the room could believe their ears, Jay most of all. "Mom, you don't mean that? I don't have anyplace to go." His voice became a helpless whine, not like a few minutes when he spewed venom in Carson's ear.

"I have faith in you, son. You'll figure something out."

Jay's jaw dropped. Then he flashed the smile that never failed to win over his mother. "Mom, you need me around here. Carson can't handle the farm by himself. Besides, you wouldn't turn out your own son over a little fight. You know how it is. We're all a little stir crazy after being cooped up all winter. Everything's under control now. Right, Carson?"

Carson looked toward the window and then back at Jay. Though he wanted the man gone, he wouldn't let his grandma fight his battles for him. He'd be the one to get rid of Jay, not her. "Just blowing off a little steam, Grandma."

Jay smiled.

Clarice studied Carson for a moment before turning her attention on Jay. "The lock on my old bedroom window is broken. It has been for years. Warner always said he would fix it, but…well, you know. Things have been disappearing out of this house all winter. I believe someone is climbing in and out of the window and robbing me blind."

"Mom, there's no way anyone is climbing in and out of that—"

"Then how else do you explain everything that's gone missing?"

When none of them replied, she went on, her voice louder and stronger than Carson had heard since she got home from Cousin Arleen's. "I'm calling the sheriff in the morning and having him send someone out to dust for fingerprints. I know you wouldn't do anything to stand in the way of an investigation."

Jay's jaw clenched. "I'd know if someone was coming into the house through that window. In the middle of a blizzard, no less," he added pointedly.

Clarice leaned against the table for support. The situation was taking what remained of her strength. "No matter how unlikely, I know you don't want me unprotected with a burglar running rampant. Years ago, Allen insisted I catalog all my valuables so I will have no trouble proving what's missing. The police will want to search your room, of course, since I'm positive that's the point of entry. They'll go over every inch."

Carson nearly fell over. He couldn't believe Grandma knew what had been going on in her old bedroom, and she was now challenging Jay.

Jay's jaw clenched. He glared at Carson over Clarice's head. "Don't worry about it, Mom. I'll leave tonight. Board up the window if it makes you feel better, though I doubt anything else will go missing as long as you have your little lapdog here to keep an eye on things."

He gave Carson one last scathing look before storming out of the room. Clarice's expression was unreadable as she shuffled back to the living room.

After she was gone, Lowell put his hand on Carson's shoulder. "I'd watch my back if I were you, Son. Your uncle Jay has a temper. He won't take kindly to you putting him out of business."

"He should be the one watching his back," Carson shot back.

Lowell snickered. "Keep telling yourself that, boy. Just be thankful you've got your old granny watching out for you."

Carson wasn't particularly worried at the moment about Jay's threats. All he was concerned with was if Grandma had heard him say she'd be dead in a few weeks. If there was a God in heaven the way shee insisted, Carson hoped he hadn't been listening and would punish Carson by acting on his careless words.

CHAPTER TWENTY-SIX

Christy had gone to work Monday morning with every intention of telling the director she was quitting at the end of the week. She would apologize for not giving the customary notice. She would express her appreciation toward the library for giving her a chance when she needed a job, but she was ready to move on.

She did feel a little guilty when she thought of leaving her mother without a paycheck while she worked to establish her business. Before Melody brought it up so brutally the other day, Christy hadn't given Mom's financial situation much thought. Now that she was thinking about it, she didn't know how Mom would survive without Christy in the house? Money had been tight since Dad died. They budgeted and pinched every penny within an inch of its life. Every stew and casserole she'd eaten in the last year contained three times as much vegetables and pasta than meat. Now she was planning to walk away without a backward glance.

Melody's words still rang in her ears after four days. Christy didn't generally care what people thought of her. She had never let the judgments or attitudes of small-minded people dictate the way she lived her life.

The only problem was she didn't think Melody was small-minded or judgmental. In fact, she had hit the nail squarely on the head. Christy had been thinking she was superior to everyone else in Jenna's Creek the last couple of years. She was a product of the Me generation. Looking out for number one and all that noise. The days of relying on a man to ride in on a white steed to rescue her were over. She was alone in this world, and she liked it that way.

Or at least, she put a lot of effort into believing it.

If she liked it so much, why hadn't she moved out a month ago? Or a year ago? Why did the thought of leaving Jenna's Creek and never seeing Jarrod Bruckner again bring tears to her eyes? It was almost as hard to think of leaving Melody. Melody was right. Christy always held part of herself back from everyone. Her mother. Her coworkers. Even her niece and nephews who idolized her and treated her like a rock star every time she went to visit.

She reached under her bed and drew out the packet of cash she had withdrawn from the bank yesterday during her lunch break. She had made two car payments—leaving eight more to go before the secondhand economy model belonged to her free and clear—and taken the rest in cash. The packet wasn't as thick as she would've liked. In fact it was pretty pathetic as far as running-off money went. But it was a start. She removed the money from the packet and fanned it across her unmade bed.

She recounted the money for the tenth time since bringing it home from the bank. Six hundred and sixty-two dollars. It wouldn't go far in setting her up in the city, or getting her there for that matter. But it would pay some bills around the house and give Mom a little breathing room while she got her dress making business off the ground if Christy stayed.

She swept the money into her hands and straightened it like a deck of cards. She wasn't staying. Mom's job loss and the empty refrigerator downstairs were not her problem. The problems here would be the same if she had never returned home after the robbery in Louisville. Mom would be in the same boat, whether Christy was in the house or now. She could start her business or build a life with Noel Wyatt, and Christy could move on like she should've done after the disaster with Sean Hatcher.

Sean.

Even after all this time, the thought of him filled her with anger. Only now the anger wasn't directed at Sean so much as at herself. For two years she blamed him for all her problems. He had made a fool of her and cost her the career she loved and everything she thought that mattered. Slowly she realized the blame belonged at her feet. The warning signs had been there. Sean was a snake when she met him. He was probably a snake now, wherever he was. Probably taking advantage of another gullible woman who would choose to look the other way when his lies were so apparent.

Christy was through letting Sean or any other man define her. She had already put her life on hold for two years for her mother. It was time she started looking out for herself again.

She hadn't really put her life on hold for Mom's sake. Melody's words rang in her head. Mom had saved her when she had nowhere else to go. She didn't know what she would've done if Mom had refused to help the night of the robbery in the motel room. If she hadn't driven five hours to pick Christy up from a remote sheriff's station. That's what family did for each other. After the crisis passed, things went back to normal.

Only Christy wasn't sure what normal was supposed to look like anymore.

She once believed her childhood had been nauseatingly normal with a bossy mom and a loving dad and too many kids in a crowded house. Then she learned Bossy Mom had cheated with another man and one of those kids belonged to someone else.

Maybe that was more normal than what she always thought.

How was Mom's affair with Noel Wyatt any different than Christy's relationship with Sean Hatcher? Mom had known going in, she was wrong. Christy had known the same. She knew Sean didn't love her. She hadn't loved him either. Not really. She sort of thought she might for about five minutes, but she was no dummy. He was fun and handsome and dangerous. Nothing more. His unsuitability was what she liked best. At least Mom loved the man who caused so much disruption in her life. He had loved her back. Unlike Christy, who had thrown her career away over barely more than a one-night stand.

She turned her face toward the ceiling. "Is that what I'm doing, Dad?" she asked aloud. "Am I consumed with Mom's mistakes because they're so much like mine?"

Before she even finished speaking, she knew what Jack Blackwood would say if he were here. He had loved Abby with every fiber of his being; enough to forgive her for the sin she committed against him. A man who could love that strongly wouldn't expect his wife to pay penance the rest of her life. He would want her to find happiness, regardless of where and with whom.

Christy sighed. "If you saw me now, you probably wouldn't recognize me."

Her voice cracked, dangerously close to tears. Dad had always understood her better than anyone. He supported her right to make her own decisions even when he couldn't disagree more. Except for his brief stint in the Army, he never lived outside Auburn County. To think his youngest, fiery daughter couldn't get away fast enough must have been a hard pill to swallow.

Knowing she wanted to leave home as soon as possible, Mom and Dad had cinched their belts even tighter to make sure she got into the college she wanted. Dad worked every hour of overtime he could at the factory during her last year of high school to cover what her scholarships and grants would not.

Christy never heard a word of complaint out of his mouth. Mom's either, for that matter. They were ready to do whatever was necessary to help her dreams come true. The night of her high school graduation when the house was full of relatives and friends, Dad toasted her with punch and 7-up.

"We tried tying lead weights to Christy's tricycle tires, but nothing slowed our little girl down," he said, his eyes glistening. "Now the day we dreaded most is here. She's going out into the world. I pray the world is ready because she's been looking forward to this moment since those tricycle days."

Everyone had laughed, including Christy, though she didn't realize the significance of the moment. She didn't cry the day Mom and Dad followed her to campus to help her settle in. She didn't cry as they drove away, Dad trying to smile and Mom crying into a handkerchief. She had tripped back up to her third floor dorm room with a song in her heart, relieved her life had finally begun. Jenna's Creek, Ohio was behind her, along with all the things that held her back thus far.

But she was crying now.

"Daddy, are you happy with the woman I've become?" she whispered through her tears.

She already knew the answer. He wouldn't be happy. He would be saddened and disappointed that she couldn't take her eyes off herself long enough to forgive Mom.

"He that is without sin among you, let him first cast a stone."

Christy couldn't remember where the quote was in the Bible or whom it had been spoken to, but she knew who said it.

Jesus.

Someone she hadn't thought of in a long time. He was disappointed in her, too, but like her father, he still loved her and was waiting for her to come to her senses.

She crumpled the money in her fist and threw it across the room. It scattered as soon as it left her hand and fluttered to the floor. She crawled onto the bed and wept into her pillow. When had she become this spiteful, hateful person? Was she so miserable in her own life, she couldn't bear the thought of seeing her mother happy?

She hated it when someone tried to tell her what to do, yet she had been doing the same thing to everyone she knew for as long as she could remember. She had looked down her nose at kids in school who chose to stay in Jenna's Creek. She figured they were too scared or too stupid to leave the comforts of home and step into the unknown.

She did it to Eric for not going after the life she thought he was born for. He had been fortunate to find a woman he loved to share his life. What right did Christy have to accuse him of settling for an ordinary life? He wasn't settling; he was living.

Worst of all, she did it to Mom, the person who knew her faults better than anyone and loved her anyway.

Mom still grieved for Dad, but more than that, she grieved for Christy. She wanted her daughter back. Christy was tired of depriving her of one. Yes, she had made mistakes in her marriage. She might not have loved Dad the way he needed her to. But it was too late for would've's and should've's. Dad was gone. Christy was still here. Here, but a million miles away.

She dried her face on her pillow and slid off the edge of the bed. She leaned against it and clasped her hands in front of her the way she did when she was little and Elaine knelt beside her as they said their bedtime prayers.

"Jesus…" She cleared her throat and began again. "Okay, here goes. You know already what I need to say, but I'm saying it anyway. I'm sorry for the lousy daughter and sister and friend and overall rotten person I've been the last few years. Oh, who are we kidding? The last lifetime. I'm a self-righteous pig and nobody likes me. I don't even like me. You probably don't think much of me either, but I'm asking you to forgive me anyway and give me a new heart. I don't want to be this person anymore. I want to start over."

Her tears flowed down her cheeks, but this time they were peaceful, cleansing tears. She cried into the bedspread until her legs began to cramp. She clambered to her feet. She remembered enough from her long ago Sunday school lessons that she needed to confess her salvation to someone. She didn't have to ponder long on who that person should be.

She took a deep breath and strode out of the room on shaky legs, treading six hundred dollars underfoot as she went. Mom's bedroom door was open, but the room was empty. From the bathroom came the sound of running water. The light was on and the door open. Abby turned off the water just as Christy reached the doorway.

Abby buried her face in a towel and opened the medicine cabinet without looking, and began rummaging for something, probably the Extra Strength Tylenol she took for her headaches. The walls still bore blank spots and dings in the plaster where the tiles had popped off during the blizzard. The women had cleaned up the mess but hadn't replaced the broken tiles. There never seemed to be enough time or money.

Christy knew where they could find six hundred dollars for repairs.

Abby sensed her presence and lowered the towel from her face. Her brows went together as she took in Christy's bleary eyes and disheveled appearance. Before she could open her mouth, Christy lunged forward.

"Mom. I love you. I don't want to leave."

She fell into her mother's open arms, unaware of a pill bottle falling and rolling across the floor where it came to rest against the tub. Abby stroked the back of her head and made shushing noises as they cried together. "Leave?" she asked. "Where are you going?"

Christy pulled back. "Nowhere. At least if you still want me around. I can't imagine why you would."

Abby smiled through her tears. "You're my daughter, Christy. I love you no matter what. Just like I pray you love me the same way."

Christy pulled completely out of her arms and unwound a length of toilet paper from the roll on the spool. "I do. I'm just sorry it took me so long to realize it."

CHAPTER TWENTY-SEVEN

At the top of the stairs, Melody leaned against the banister and took a shuddering breath. It had been a long couple of days. Today had been the longest. More than once, it looked like Grandma would take her last breath. Dad kept telling anyone who would listen they needed to call the ambulance. Grandma wouldn't hear of it. When they realized no amount of begging or bullying would get her to change her mind, they begged her to let them drive her to the hospital.

"I don't want to die in a hospital." She took hold of Judy's hand with an unexpected strength. "Please don't take me. If it's my time to go, I want to go at home the way Warner did."

Carson surprised everyone by stepping forward and demanding they stop bothering her about it. "It's what she wants. Who are we to tell her how to go?" Without another word, he headed to the phone to call Linda in Indianapolis.

Melody hated to think of more relatives descending on the farmhouse. She had been able to breath easier when she found out Jay was gone. Carson had been the one to tell her.

"He's gone and everything he brought with him."

No one else in the room asked what he meant. Melody and Carson had exchanged a knowing glance. She wondered what else he knew, but so far, she hadn't had the chance to ask. For now, she didn't want to know.

She wished she could call Christy. She wanted to talk to someone removed from the situation. She missed having a compassionate ear. But every time she thought of Christy, she wondered if there had ever been a compassionate ear. She didn't think Christy was completely selfish. She should call and apologize for saying it. While Melody believed everything she said as she was saying it, she hadn't been exactly tactful in delivering the criticism. Dad always said you could catch more flies with honey than with vinegar.

It was too late anyway. Surely Christy was gone by now. Melody wondered if she'd ever hear from her again. It wasn't likely. Once Christy left town and started a new life—wherever that was—she would have no reason to come back to Jenna's Creek. If she did, she surely wouldn't look up someone whose only purpose in life was to point out the flaws of others.

Melody sagged against the banister. She was just like Grandpa. Judgmental and quick to speak before considering what the hearer was ready to hear. She thought of the scripture admonition to be quick to hear, slow to anger.

Neither she nor Grandpa was good at heeding that advice. They believed when they were right it was their duty to point it out, regardless of the affects their words might have. They didn't know the meaning of patience or discretion.

She slid to a seated position on the stairs. Dad was outside in the barns, fiddling around, pretending to do chores. She knew he just wanted to get out of the sick house. His way to deal with uncomfortable situations was to stay busy. Mom was in the kitchen washing dishes and planning dinner for tomorrow. Lowell hadn't come back from his trailer in town. He probably hoped to avoid any work Mom or Dad might find for him.

Melody immediately corrected herself. Lowell had lost one parent a few months ago. He was now days away—perhaps moments—from losing the other. Who was she to tell him how to react to it? She thought of the kid who remembered the trips to Springfield as the only times in his life his pop wasn't disappointed in him. She couldn't imagine what it would be like to think your parent didn't really like you. No wonder Lowell never had much incentive to apply himself to anything.

Carson had also become a surprise to her. She still wasn't convinced he didn't have something to do with Grandpa ending up at the bottom of the stairs. He had obviously known about Allen's illegal dealings and knew that Grandpa knew. But he had become invaluable around the house the last few days. Caring for Grandma. Standing up for her. Pulling double duty on the farm with Dad now that Jay was gone.

He was certainly an enigma. She hadn't liked him since back when he was an annoying kid who showed up on the farm to upset her apple cart. Looking back, she realized the main reason she didn't like or trust him was because Grandpa didn't. She rested her chin on her fist and wondered if she ever had an independent thought outside her grandfather.

Lowell had told her once it was a wonder she grew up at all, always in Grandpa's larger-than-life shadow. Truer words had never been spoken.

She loved her grandfather more than anyone she ever met. Despite his faults, she still believed most of his influence on her had been good. But she wished she had been honest with him more often. She wished she'd told him he was wrong not to call Aunt Linda. He shouldn't judge Carson without knowing the young man's story. He should've kicked Jay out of the house the minute he suspected he was dealing drugs no matter how mad it would've made Grandma. Most importantly, if he truly wanted to leave a legacy of faith behind for his family, he should've shown them compassion and tenderness instead of harshness.

It was too late for Grandpa, but it wasn't too late for her.

Carson appeared at the foot of the stairs. Melody jumped to her feet. "What is it?"

"Grandma wants to talk to you."

Her heart leaped into her throat at the solemn look on his face. "Is she...all right?"

"Feeling better, actually. She had a bit of a nap." Carson's eyes were red-rimmed, and his hair was rumpled. A two-day growth darkened his jaw.

Melody put her hand on his shoulder as she passed him at the corner of the stairs. "Thank you."

He started up without answering. She hoped he was on his way to grab a nap himself.

At the back of the house she tapped on the door lintel of the room that had been converted to Grandma's bedroom.

"Melody, honey?" Clarice said softly. "Is that you?"

"It's me, Grandma."

She stepped up to the large bed and took Grandma's hand. She was instantly aware of the papery thin quality of her grandmother's skin. Even after the cancer diagnosis, Grandma maintained warm soft hands and a sturdy frame. To see what the disease and last few months had done to her body was a shock. She had lost even more weight since Grandpa's funeral. Allen's trouble had been the final straw. All week the family tried to trivialize his role in the insurance scandal, but Grandma understood more than they hoped she would.

"You've always been a good girl, Melody," she said.

Melody was heartened by the strength in Grandma's tone and the color that brightened her cheeks. Maybe all she needed was rest and for her family to stop pestering her about going to the hospital.

"You were always your grandpa's favorite."

"I know," she said without smugness.

"I'll never forget what he told me after seeing you in the hospital when you were born. He said, 'This one's special,

Clarey. I don't know what the Lord's got in store for her, but she's going to do something great.' Every day we watched you growing up, I saw his prophecy come true. Always know you're special, Nugget. Sometimes I wish you had a husband to take care of you. I used to worry about you being alone, but I guess times have changed. You don't need a man or babies to make you happy. Do what God's called you to do, honey, and we'll be proud of you. Your grandpa and me both."

Melody swallowed the lump in her throat. "I will."

"If your grandpa had his way you would've inherited everything. The entire farm."

Melody lowered her eyes. She wouldn't deny she already knew.

"I hope you understand, honey, but I can't do that. I can't leave the others out. I don't want them to think they aren't part of the family. Even Jay. He did wrong, but he's still our son. What Warner and I worked for belongs to him too. You understand that, don't you, Nugget?"

It didn't escape Melody's notice that Grandma didn't mention Allen and his problems. She supposed until a court convicted him, he was innocent in his mother's eyes. Probably even after. "Of course, Grandma."

Relief smoothed the wrinkles in Clarice's face. She tightened her grip on Melody's hand. "You were the apple of our eyes. We spoiled you, often at the expense of the other children. I suppose it wasn't fair."

"I've been thinking the same thing lately."

Clarice's eyes darkened with concern. "The others might hold it against you. Don't begrudge them their feelings, sweetheart. They don't understand. Some of them haven't had the advantages you had."

"Are you talking about Carson?"

Her expression softened. "He's a dear boy. I'm only sorry Warner never got to know him the way I have."

"I'm sure he would be too."

Clarice angled her head toward the window. Melody used the opportunity to pull a chair over to the bed and sit down.

"He was an old man," Clarice said. "Old men aren't steady on their feet."

Melody cocked her head and waited, wondering where the conversation was headed.

Clarice turned back to her. "He knew about Allen. We both did. I heard them arguing on the phone the weekend before the blizzard. I only heard Warner's side of the conversation, but I knew it was bad. I asked him about it after he hung up. He wouldn't say much. You know your grandfather, stubborn as the day is long."

Melody leaned forward in the chair. The allegations against Allen were true, and Grandma and Grandpa had known. What would happen to the family once it became public? It was inconceivable Allen might end up in jail. She wondered if he and Jay could share a cell.

Clarice didn't seem to notice her mind had drifted. "When he went outside to do his chores, I went through some of the notebooks in his desk. That man was always writing down figures that didn't make sense to anyone. Keeping track of every penny any of us made or spent. I couldn't deduce anything from his scribbling, but I finally got him to explain it."

She turned her face back to the window. She closed her eyes and folded her hands over her chest. Melody knew she wasn't finished, so she sat and waited for her to gather enough strength to continue. She couldn't help but think it wouldn't be long before this was the last image she had of her grandmother before they laid her to rest. She resolutely pushed the maudlin thought out of her head.

Slowly Clarice brought her eyes back to Melody. "After I told Warner I knew what was going on, he said he'd been trying to get Allen to stop cheating those people. He suggested Allen tell them they were entitled to a rebate or something. That way he could fix things without anyone knowing. Allen refused. He told Warner to mind his own business."

Dread rose up in Melody's chest. "Oh, Grandma, you don't think—"

"Allen would never hurt his daddy," Clarice cut in. "I think he was just trying to tell him everything was under control. He never dreamed he'd get caught, that's all. If not for that fire, he probably never would have."

Melody blinked at the regret in her voice. "Grandma, he was stealing from his clients."

Clarice nodded gravely. "That's what Warner couldn't abide. He could never tolerate a thief. But you knew that already." She smiled at Melody. "That's why he couldn't abide that awful Keim man taking advantage of his poor mother. He had to make it right. He wasn't the one who burned down that store, but he made sure Ab Kiem never cheated another widow."

"Ab Keim?" Melody interjected. "You mean the storeowner from Springfield?"

Clarice's eyes cleared as if coming back from a far trip. "Why, yes. I didn't realize you knew about him. Be that as it may, it's ancient history now. I meant to tell you about Allen."

Melody suddenly had a hundred questions about Ab Keim and how Grandpa made sure the man never cheated another widow, but she couldn't distract Grandma from the conversation now. She needed to hear what happened between Allen and Grandpa.

"Warner told both of us he was going to the police. He said big corporations were already taking advantage of the little man and getting away with it. He couldn't sit back and let his son be a part of it. That was Warner, always defending the underdog."

She brought her gaze up to Melody. "Do you remember the Cluxtons? They lived in Jenna's Creek on Munroe Street and used to go to our church."

Melody wanted to tell her to get back to the story, but it never did any good to try to derail one of Grandma's detours.

"Gloria Cluxton's paperboy tripped going down her porch steps last summer. He took a really nasty break to his knee. Allen told Gloria her homeowner's policy wouldn't cover the claim. He gave her some song and dance about the flowerpots on her porch and how they negated her coverage. Gloria couldn't follow his reasoning, but Allen kept talking and explaining. After a while she felt pretty silly for not understanding. George bought the policy years ago. Gloria never worried about those things, even after George passed away. She said she always let Allen do her worrying for her. She trusted him. When he wouldn't pay the claim, she took a loan on George's retirement and paid the boy's parents for their medical expenses.

"Well, Gloria's son told Warner about Gloria using George's retirement and Warner went to Allen. He was as mad as thunder. He said he wasn't going to let him cheat another old lady out of her life's savings. He said one of these days Allen's scam was going to cost a lot of people a world of hurt. Maybe he was prophesizing again." She clicked her tongue. "I'm sure thankful he isn't here to see what those people lost. And he isn't here to see what those state investigators are putting poor Allen through. It's a disgrace, I tell you."

Melody swallowed her indignation. "He wanted Allen to do the right thing."

"And he would have," Clarice said firmly. "Allen is a good boy. He's a pillar of the community, Melody. A good, God-fearing man. Not like Jay."

She gave Melody a sad look. "I don't know how to tell you this, honey, but your uncle Jay is selling drugs. As far as I can tell, he's been doing it as long as he's lived here. Probably long before that. I kicked him out of the house."

"I know. Carson told me."

"It was the hardest thing I ever had to do. But he was hurting people. Not like Allen. Jay was endangering people's health and wrecking marriages. He let daddies spend their paychecks on drugs while their children went hungry. I love my boy, but I can't keep letting him do that. It wasn't like what Allen did. Allen didn't hurt anybody."

"Grandma, how can you say that? The police say he's been stealing from half the people in this county for over twenty years."

Clarice frowned. "Oh, Melody, only a fraction of homeowners ever make a claim on their policies. Sometimes when a family filed a claim, Allen paid the client out of his own pocket."

"Only because he was stealing their money and didn't want to get caught." Melody took a deep breath and tried to bring her voice under control. It wouldn't do good to yell at her grandmother. Besides, she didn't want Mom or Dad to hear her and chase her out of the bedroom before she heard the whole story.

"He did it because he cared for them," Clarice insisted. "He never kept premiums of young families or high risk clients. He only did it to the ones who wouldn't use their policies anyway or could afford to pay a little if the need arose."

"Grandma, how long have you known about this?"

She looked back toward the window. "A while."

Melody resisted the urge to pound her fists on the bedside table. Grandma had probably known for years and looked the other way out of blind devotion, the same as she did with Jay and Lowell.

"His clients gave him money in good faith. You said yourself they trusted him. They were paying for something they weren't getting."

Clarice pulled her hand out from under Melody's. "You're just like Warner. Both of you always fighting for the downtrodden. Allen did what he did for his family. I thought you would understand that. He wanted to give Bonnie and the boys a good life the way Warner did for us. I tried with Warner, but he couldn't understand either.

"Allen was always there for Warner and me. Remember that winter I got pneumonia? Allen hired a nurse to come in and look after me. Your mother said I didn't need one. She said you and she could come over in the afternoons and take care of me."

"We gladly would've helped out, Grandma."

Clarice's nose tilted toward the ceiling. "Allen understood I needed someone around the clock. A professional. Not Warner. He said when his mother got pneumonia, she had dinner on the table every night and the family never had to deal with dirty laundry. Well, that woman must've been built like a plow horse. Allen is the only one who cared about what I needed. I could always count on him, so don't tell me he would intentionally hurt anyone."

Any further argument would not dissuade Grandma from defending her son, but Melody had to know how Allen got into the house the morning of the blizzard. "What did you mean earlier when you said old men were always unsteady on their feet?"

Clarice pursed her lips. "You wouldn't understand."

"I'll try," she said gently.

Clarice was quiet for a long time. Melody was beginning to think she had dozed off or was too tired to go on. "Warner was going to the state board," she said after a while. "He was going to tell them everything. He told Allen he would give him another week to turn himself in. I tried to convince him to keep quiet. I couldn't let him ruin Allen's career and everything he worked so hard to build. Warner was insistent. I told him his responsibility was with his family. He wouldn't listen."

"Grandma…"

"The thunder woke me up. I rolled over and saw Warner in front of the window watching the blizzard. After he went to light the furnace, I got up. When I heard how fierce the winds were, I knew it was my only chance. He'd never hear me over the storm. I'd been telling him for years he needed a hearing aid, but he brushed me off. Said they were for old men."

Her eyes grew misty. "Warner was always good to me. He never accused me of faking my ailments like some people." She paused and pinned Melody with a knowing look. "Other than comparing me to his mother now and then, he supported me and took care of me. He was a good husband. The best a woman could hope for."

Melody bit down on her bottom lip. She wanted to run out of the room. She already knew too much. She didn't want to hear another word.

"I followed him downstairs. The wind was whipping hard enough to shake the house. I thought the roof was going to tear off any minute. He didn't know I was behind him until he was almost to the bottom of the stairs. He must've heard me or sensed me or something. Before he could turn around or grab the rail, I pushed him. I didn't know if I had enough strength to make him fall, but the stairs were icy. I almost lost my balance myself."

Melody's jaw worked up and down several times before she could get any sound out. "Grandma…there must've been another way. You didn't have to push him."

Tears filled Clarice's eyes. "Don't you understand? He was going to tell the board about Allen. It would've caused nothing but heartache. I had to protect the family."

"You didn't protect anybody. Allen is still probably going to jail."

Clarice sighed, visibly irritated by Melody's lack of comprehension. "It wasn't only about Allen. My time is nearly up. If I went before Warner, he wouldn't leave the boys anything in the will. That wouldn't have been right. It isn't their fault they aren't strong. They shouldn't be punished for the way God made them. Warner couldn't understand weakness. He couldn't understand it in me and he never understood it in Lowell and Jay."

Melody pushed her hands through her hair. Her scalp prickled with tension. "Why are you telling me this? You have to know I wouldn't agree with you."

"I know you've been blaming Carson and Jay for the accident. I didn't want you worrying yourself sick about it the rest of your life. I knew you wouldn't let it go."

Melody dropped her head in her hands and then looked back at her grandmother. "What am I supposed to do now? You pushed him. What if someone finds out? What if they put you in jail?"

Clarice reached for her hand, but Melody saw her coming and pulled away. "I'm going home soon, Nugget. I won't live long enough for anyone to do anything. I'll regret what I did for as long as the Lord sees fit to leave me here. But I was thinking of the greater good."

"Greater good? If Grandpa had the chance to tell the board what Uncle Allen was doing, those people might've had insurance to replace what they lost in the fire. Manny Peterson could lose his store, Grandma. Or his home. Do you realize that? By going forward, Uncle Allen might've gotten a lighter sentence. It would've been a scandal, but at least Manny wouldn't be losing everything he has. Now no one will forget. This town will never forgive him."

"He didn't mean to hurt Manny or anyone else. He's a good person, Melody."

Melody stood up quickly, sending her chair scooting across the floor. "Grandma, how can you be so blind? He didn't care about anyone but himself."

"That's not true. What can I say to make you understand?"

"Nothing. You can't say one thing that will make me understand what either of you did. You made things worse by covering for him. You're as guilty as he is." She turned and left the room, unable to stand the sight of her grandmother for one more minute.

CHAPTER TWENTY-EIGHT

Two weeks ago Christy had been ready to leave Jenna's Creek. Ready enough to tell the only man she'd cared about in as long as she could remember, and ready enough to insult the only true friend she had. She missed Melody already, and she hadn't even left town yet. The last week had been lonely without her. Christy thought she knew loneliness during the blizzard when it had been her and Mom alone in the house. No phones. No visitors. No jobs to go to for eight days. Looking back, Christy realized it had been the highlight of her winter. The highlight of her nearly two years back in Jenna's Creek.

She had probably burned her bridges with Jarrod the same as she had with Melody. No matter how much she dreaded it, she couldn't let one more day go by without rectifying the situation with both of them. She was sorry for her selfishness and wanted them to know. She also wanted them to know she was a Christian now. It didn't seem right not to share the most important thing that had happened to her, though she didn't know if either wanted to see her again.

Saturday her brother Eric and his wife Jamie came from Athens where they lived on campus at Ohio University to spend the afternoon. They visited a couple times a month so Christy didn't feel too guilty for rushing through lunch and excusing herself to run an errand. Today was probably her best chance to find Jarrod at his house on Spruce Street. If he wasn't there, she guessed she'd be driving to Portsmouth to track him down. She nearly wept with relief at the sight of his car in the driveway. She blew out the breath she didn't realize she was holding as her grip tightened on the steering wheel. Even though she really needed to have this conversation, she wasn't looking forward to what he may say back.

She parked behind his car and hurried up the walk before she lost her nerve, all the while imagining the look on his face when he saw her. Would he ask what she was still doing in town? Would he slam the door in her face? What would she even say?

She knocked. For a heart pounding moment she listened for sound inside. The old floors creaked inside the house. He was coming. *Please, please, don't look out the window first.* If he saw who was knocking, there was a good chance he wouldn't open the door.

The door swung open, and Christy steeled herself against the earful he was about to give her. If he said anything at all. She wasn't sure which would be worse. For him to tell her what he thought of her, or to say nothing.

Jarrod's expression was completely unreadable when he looked down at her. The threshold was a few inches above the porch, and she was a good eight inches shorter than him already. She had to tip her head back like a naughty elementary student facing the principal. "I was hoping to catch you here," she said when he didn't speak.

"I was on my way out," he answered tonelessly. "I've been working on the house since yesterday. I spent the night."

She was encouraged he offered details. He wouldn't have bothered if she were an encyclopedia salesman like the way he was treating her.

"I'm sorry. I don't want to hold you up. I…I wanted to talk."

His expression remained stoic. "I figured you'd be gone already."

Her heart sank. Tears threatened. For a moment she wondered if they would make an impact. From the look on his face, it wasn't likely. Besides, she wasn't a crier. Never had been. What had she expected? For Jarrod to take her in his arms and tell her he'd been praying she'd come to her senses and come back to him? That if she didn't come back, he had decided he would never hold another woman the way he'd held her, never kiss another?

Christy hadn't been expecting it, but she couldn't stop wishing it would happen anyway.

"I wanted to say I shouldn't have said what I said last week. I'm sorry."

He didn't budge from the doorway. "What are you sorry for saying? That you're leaving? It's the truth, isn't it? A person should never be sorry for telling the truth."

"No, that's not what I meant. I meant I'm sorry for being a jerk. I hurt you. I hurt my mom. I hurt my best friend. I think I even hurt myself. I didn't consider how my actions would affect anyone else. I was playing the martyr again and figured if things didn't go my way, I'd leave. That's what I always do. If you don't play the way I want, I take my dolly and go home."

Jarrod glanced away, then let out a sigh. "You don't owe me anything, Christy. If you want to go, go. I'm not holding a gun to your head."

This was turning out a lot harder than she expected. She had been prepared for him to accept her apology or slam the door in her face. Either of which would've been easier than standing on the stoop gazing up at him, trying to figure out how to make him see how much he meant to her.

"I'm sorry, Jarrod. You mean a lot to me, and I treated you like you don't. I was wrong."

He looked out at the street over the top of her head. "If that's all you needed, I have a few more things to take care of before I head home."

"I'm not leaving Jenna's Creek," she blurted in desperation.

He looked back at her. "What's that got to do with me? You made it clear the other day you only do what matters to you."

Christy felt like she'd been punched in the stomach. Melody had said basically the same thing. It was true. She was a terrible friend, and any guy would be a fool to want to spend time with her. She couldn't bear the thought of losing him though. She squared her shoulders. Maybe she was an arrogant jerk, but she was no quitter. She wasn't leaving this porch until she told him what she needed to say, even if he didn't want to hear it and she never saw him again.

"Can I come in? Just for a few minutes."

April had been nearly as cold as March with rain and fierce winds that caused flooding over the eastern half of the United States as snow melted and swelled rivers and streams. The month was in its final week, and the weather was only marginally more hospitable than the first week.

Jarrod looked out over the neighborhood again. No one was outside considering the dreary day and bone chilling wet. When he looked back at Christy, the only thing in his eyes was impatience. After a nerve-rattling hesitation for her, he stepped back from the door. She nearly leaped across the threshold before he changed his mind. He closed the door behind her but didn't move or invite her to sit on the small faded sofa, the only piece of furniture in the room. She hoped he hadn't slept there last night. It was much too small for him and didn't look very comfortable.

Christy stood in front of him for a moment, waiting for him to say or do something. When he didn't, she figured she'd better talk before he lost what remained of his patience. "I thought if I left town, everything would be better for everyone. My mom could get on with her life with Noel Wyatt, if that's what she wants to do. I could go to law school and you could, well, do whatever it is you want to do."

He was watching her, but she couldn't tell if he was really hearing her. Time for brutal honesty. "I'm a selfish person, Jarrod. I wanted to get away from my problems, from the pain of Dad's death, even if it hurt everyone else in the process. I thought if I left, I would leave my problems and regret and unforgiveness here. Then I realized they were mine and would go wherever I went. No matter how far I go or how I try to put the past out of my head, it will be waiting for me when I get there."

He crossed his arms over his chest. "Well, I'm happy you reached this epiphany. But again, I'm not clear about what it has to do with me. If you want the truth, I've pretty much had enough."

Again, tears threatened. Christy had gone too far this time. She hurt Melody, and she hurt Jarrod and probably lost both of them forever. But this wasn't about her. It wasn't about what she lost or what she hoped to gain. It was about being a friend and letting the other person know how much they meant to her.

"I don't blame you, Jarrod. I've had enough of me too. I just wanted you to know I'm sorry. I was rude and insensitive and always thinking of myself. For that I apologize."

He stared at her a long moment. She nearly squirmed under his gaze. Finally he uncrossed his arms and unclenched his jaw. "I'm a nice guy, Christy. I can take a lot of garbage from someone before I lose my temper. It's a required skill in my line of work. When someone doesn't like me or doesn't understand me, it rolls right off my back. But with you, I cared. I cared a lot."

Hope rose inside Christy, though she cautioned herself to tamp it down. "You did?"

The impatience was back. "Didn't you know that?"

"Well, I hoped."

He stepped away from the door. For the first time, he didn't look like he was tempted to physically toss her out into the cold. "Listen, Christy, I don't fill my life with surface relationships. I'm busy. I only have time for people who matter to me. I certainly don't have time for someone who isn't as invested in me as I am in her." He pinned her with a stern gaze. "Why did you come here? What do you want?"

"I…uh…I wanted you to know I'm sorry."

"What were you hoping would happen?"

"I don't know."

One look at his face told her the answer wasn't enough. If she wasn't ready to be honest with him, she might as well leave now. "I hoped you would forgive me. I…" She steeled her nerve. "I hoped you would tell me it wasn't too late. I hadn't gone too far. I hadn't totally blown it, and you never wanted to see me again."

He cocked his head and continued to stare, daring her to say more.

"I care about you, too, Jarrod. A lot. A lot lot. The thought of not having you to care for…" A sob worked its way out of her throat. She shook her head in aggravation at herself. "I don't want to lose you, Jarrod. If it's too late for us, if I went too far, well, that's a mistake I'll have to live with the rest of my life."

Pinpricks of heat warmed her cheeks. She imagined the color of heat and shame against her stark white skin all the way up to her chestnut roots. She had never been able to hide her feelings. It was why she tried to never have any.

Jarrod slowly moved his head from side to side as he stared at her, sizing her up, making her feel like a bug under a microscope. She deserved it. She just wished he would say something, even if it was to tell her, yes, she had gone too far, and she'd have the rest of her life to regret it.

He raked his hand over his jaw, a roughened jaw that looked like he hadn't shaved this morning. He looked more handsome than Christy had ever seen him. Maybe it was the sparks of fire in his dark eyes.

He leaned away from her. "So now I guess I have to decide if I want to put up with being yanked around by you or kicked in the teeth every time you're in a bad mood or don't get your way about something."

"That's not what I meant to do," she cried. "I don't have to get my way about everything."

Jarrod barked out a laugh. Christy was heartened by the first chink in his armor. "You're kidding, right? You want your way in everything."

Indignation crowded out the threatening tears. "Okay, maybe I do, but who doesn't? Who chooses to compromise? Who would prefer to give in or lose an argument? Nobody, that's who. Nobody walks into an ice cream parlor and asks for two scoops of their least favorite flavor. Wanting my own way doesn't make me wrong or weird or crazy. It makes me ordinary, Counselor."

She crossed her arms over her chest and didn't try to squelch the smile tugging at the corners of her mouth. She lifted her chin. "I'm just like everybody else. I'm perfectly ordinary."

Jarrod put his hands on her shoulders and pulled her against him, knocking the air out of her. "You are anything but ordinary. God, help me, I love you, Christy Blackwood." He looked at the ceiling and growled deep in his throat. "I don't know what's wrong with me. That's probably the dumbest thing I ever admitted. But I do. I love you, and I can't imagine my life without you and all the aggravation you'll bring."

Christy didn't dare hope he had forgiven her. "I can't tell if I should be flattered or insulted."

He laughed. "I'll let you know as soon as I figure it out." He cupped her face with his hands, cool against her hot cheeks. "I told you, I'm not into casual. If you're in my life, you're all in."

Cautiously, in case she was misreading everything, she slid her arms around his neck and stretched onto her toes as high as she could go. "Oh, Jarrod."

He pulled her closer until her toes barely brushed the floor, and kissed her, erasing every doubt.

When they finally drew apart, she could barely catch her breath. "I love you, too, Jarrod," she whispered. "I'm sorry I'm so aggravating. I'll try to rein it in."

He shook his head, his nose brushing hers with each pass. He leaned forward until her feet were once again flat on the floor. "Don't do that. Don't ever change. Just be prepared to lose an argument now and then."

"I don't think I know how. I've never done it."

He laughed again. "I'll teach you, but you're probably not going to like it."

She pulled her mouth into a pout. "Then how about we do some more of that stuff I do like?"

Jarrod grinned. A smile Christy couldn't imagine getting tired of and lowered his mouth to hers, bristly jaw and all.

CHAPTER TWENTY-NINE

Melody closed the photo album and reached for the next one in the stack. After putting a meatloaf in the oven for supper, she had sat down in front of the fireplace and started going through albums, trying to reconcile the memories of the Warner Beckwith she knew and the Warner Beckwith everyone else in the family remembered. The photo albums were filled with pictures of her at various stages in her life. As an only child, she was the subject of more than the average number of candid shots taken by her parents. In at least half the pictures, Grandpa was right beside her.

She opened the next album to reveal a photograph of the two of them standing in the window of the hayloft, silhouetted by a low slanted sun. Both held pitchforks and looked down at the bearer of the camera on the ground. Melody had been around thirteen at the time and stood more than a head shorter than Grandpa. Unlike most thirteen-year-olds who would've begun pulling away from parental authority, she had loved spending time with him in the fields. Every day at school, her thoughts were on whatever was happening at the farm. Most days, she had the bus driver drop her off at the top of the hill when he drove the bus up to turn around, to save her the walk. It wasn't like her parents wouldn't know where she was.

Tears pricked the backs of her eyes as she gazed at the picture, but not for the reason it had in the last two months. Instead of the man she had always looked up to, she saw a hard-hearted man too proud or too stubborn to let his family know how much they meant to him. Maybe they meant nothing. He had successfully walked out on his own mother and brother and never looked back. Maybe he could've done it again if he thought it necessary.

Melody leaned forward and took the heavy Bible Paulette Beckwith had given her in Springfield. She had barely looked inside it. She had too much else on her mind at the time. Too many other discoveries to absorb.

Now she opened the Bible at the halfway point and found herself in the book of Isaiah. No scribblings marred the margins like the insides of every Bible Grandpa ever owned. Melody skipped through a few other pages. They were clean, though well worn. It brought her a measure of comfort. Paulette said Ivan remembered his mother reading to the boys from this Bible. Grandpa hadn't become a Christian until later in life, but his mother obviously planted a seed that needed watering to blossom.

Melody flipped the heavy volume back to the title page. In small tight script that reminded her of Grandpa's, she read the inscription: *To my darling Rose. March 5, 1895.*

Her expression tightened. Who had given Rose the Bible? A parent wouldn't have referred to her as darling.

She quickly did the calculations. Grandpa was born in June of 1895. According to Paulette, Rose had not been married to his father.

Was the giver of the Bible Grandpa's father? She gently turned the next few pages until she came to the page featuring the family tree. Only a few lines were filled in. No marriages or deaths were recorded. The only lines with anything on them were the ones recording the births of Warner and Ivan.

Above Grandpa's name were the names of his mother and father. Melody nearly dropped the Bible.

Rose Simmons and Absalom Keim.

It wasn't possible. Not Ab Keim, the man whose store Grandpa was suspected of burning down. It couldn't be anyone else. Even eighty-two years ago Absalom Keim couldn't have been a common name.

Had Grandpa known his father's identity? Had Mr. Keim?

Grandma said Grandpa stopped Ab Keim from taking advantage of other widows. Had he taken advantage of Rose years earlier, and it resulted in Grandpa's birth? Rose and Ab must've been in love, at least at one time. Ab wouldn't have given her such a beautiful Bible that must've cost a great deal of money—a gift she obviously treasured all her life—if he hadn't loved her. Rose wouldn't have recorded Ab's name in the Bible, knowing the scandal and condemnation it would bring since they weren't married, unless she truly loved him. Had they married after Rose recorded the names in the Bible, and Ivan just didn't know? Maybe they kept the marriage secret because of opposing families. Or, the most likely scenario, they never married at all, and the romance and resulting child were a disgrace neither could escape.

Melody's head hurt from all the possibilities and unanswered questions. She wished she could take the Bible to Grandma and ask what she knew about the situation, if anything.

She couldn't do that. She hadn't spoken to her grandmother in four days. Not since Grandma's confession. Melody couldn't wrap her mind around the fact that the grandmother she loved had killed Grandpa and rationalized her actions.

She needed to tell someone. Grandma was a killer. She had knowingly with malice and forethought pushed her husband down the stairs to his death.

How could she keep quiet? How could she allow the crime to go unpunished? It wasn't fair to Grandpa. It wasn't fair to the rest of the family. Justice was required.

But what good would it do? Grandma was right; she would be dead long before her case went to trial. No jail in the country, let alone Jenna's Creek, was equipped to adequately care for a terminal cancer patient in her late seventies. No matter how much Melody esteemed justice, she wasn't ready to send her beloved grandmother to prison for a crime she wasn't sure she completely understood she had committed.

The kitchen door opened and slammed shut, and Dad's heavy tread moved toward the refrigerator. Mom wasn't home, and Melody was supposed to cook dinner tonight. A meatloaf was in the oven, but she hadn't started anything else to go with it.

She set the Bible aside and went into the kitchen, her thoughts on Ab Keim and everything else she would never know about her grandfather.

Pete was peering into the oven at the meatloaf. The pungent aroma filled the kitchen. Melody's stomach growled.

"This all we're having?" he asked over his shoulder as he closed the door.

Melody hurried to the sink to wash her hands. "No. Sorry. Time got away from me."

Pete gave her a sympathetic smile. "Hard to keep our thoughts where they should be these days."

She nodded. She was happy he understood, but he worked hard all day and deserved a hearty dinner.

"You go ahead and peel some potatoes," he told her. "I'll fix a salad after I wash up."

Before he could leave the room, she burst out, "Did you know Grandpa planned to leave me the farm?"

Pete looks sheepish. "Yes, I knew."

"Am I the only person in the family who didn't? It seems like I've been in the dark my entire life."

"Don't beat yourself up, Nugget? It was your grandparents' property to do with what they wanted. If they want you to have it, nobody else can say anything to the contrary."

"Only it isn't just their property. It's Aunt Naomi's and Aunt Alma's too. Grandma and Grandpa were only entitled to a third, not the whole thing. He stole it from the aunts."

"He didn't steal it, Melody. Your great-grandpa Salinski knew what he was doing when he put Warner in charge."

"Not really. He was a male chauvinist. He didn't think his daughters could run a business because they were women. He gave the whole operation to somebody who wasn't even a blood relative."

"It may look like it from the outside, and it could very well be the case. But you have no right to assume you know what was going through that old man's head. It was a different generation. You can't blame the guy for thinking an ambitious young man who wanted nothing more than to learn the business was better equipped to run it than three young women who showed no interest. Earl wanted to keep the farm in the family. He wanted to see it prosper. I love your aunts. They are wonderful, hard working women, but Warner was by far the best candidate for turning the farm into what it is today. Look at what he's done over the last fifty years."

Melody couldn't argue with his logic or the proof staring her in the face. "Maybe everything worked out for the best, and maybe the aunts are happy with their careers, but I wonder if they got what they wanted out of life or just what was given them."

"Again, Melody, it was a different generation. Men had their roles and women had theirs. Here it is, 1978, and there are still occupations off limits to women. Or nearly off limits."

She sighed at the injustice of the situation. "It still isn't fair."

Pete went to her and folded his calloused hands over hers that still held a potato in one hand and a paring knife in the other. "I know you've been through a lot these last few months since we lost Warner. He was your best friend and losing him was harder than any of us anticipated." He chuckled. "To tell you the truth, I thought the old cuss would outlive us all. It hasn't helped that you've learned he wasn't exactly the man you believed him to be. I hate to tell you, sweetie, but none of us are. If he told you everything he ever did, pointed out every mistake and flaw, you would've overlooked them because he was Warner Beckwith. You thought he hung the moon. I know this is hard for you. It's always hard when we find out our heroes are fallible. They're regular people, just like the rest of us. Your grandpa loved you more than anyone. And you loved him. Don't let what you've seen and heard these last few months take that away from you."

"But he lied to me about so many things."

Pete's grip tightened around her hands. "He never lied to you. He may not have told you all the things he did earlier in his life. He didn't tell any of us much." He let go of her hands and tilted her chin up to look into his eyes.

"I remember one time years ago. You were a little thing. I don't think it was long after you started school. Warner and I were in the fields about twilight gathering up some calves to take to auction the next day. For whatever reason, he got to talking. You know for your granddaddy that wasn't often. He said how thankful he was the Lord had made him a new creation. He said since he gave his life to Jesus, he tried real hard not to look back on the man he had been. Thanks to the Lord, that man was dead, along with all the terrible things he might've done and the cruel thoughts he might've had."

Pete let go of her chin but kept one hand folded around hers. "That conversation bothered me for a while. It got me to wondering what sort of stuff he could've been talking about. After a while I realized it didn't matter. He was absolutely right. God doesn't want us looking back, reliving our sins and selfish deeds or thinking about every careless word we threw at someone. If God can forget the dirty, rotten, selfish people we were, we owe it to him to do the same."

Melody stared past her father for a moment and considered her grandpa. That sounded like the man she remembered. The man who lived in the present with his trust in God and his love for a family that often disappointed him.

She brought her gaze back to her dad. "Do you think he loved Grandma?"

Pete blinked. "What? Of course. I never saw a man so devoted…"

She shook her head. "No, I mean in the beginning, when he first came to the farm to work. He always said he loved her from the moment he laid eyes on her. Aunt Naomi was interested in him too. Did he fall in love with Grandma or the farm?"

"Melody, what a cruel thing to say. Do you really believe your grandpa would lie to Earl and your grandmother to get this farm?"

She leaned back over the sink. "I don't know what to believe."

Pete's gaze softened. "Listen, each and every one of us wax romantic when we think back to falling in love. Once we notice the one that captures our hearts, we forget every pretty face that might've turned our heads before. There were girls that got my attention before I met your mother, but after I fell for her, I honestly can't remember a one of them. They've all blurred together like faces in a picture I only glanced at. I'm sure I didn't fall in love with your mom the moment I laid eyes on her, but it sure feels that way now."

Melody tilted her head at the glassy expression is his eyes. Her insides warmed. She knew Mom and Dad loved each other, but she'd never seen it so clearly in Dad's eyes the way it shone now.

"It's impossible to know what falling in love was like for someone else," he said. "If Warner was here for you to ask, he would tell you the way he remembered it, as I'm sure he told you your entire life. As far as he was concerned, he loved Clarice from the moment he laid eyes on her. None of us knew much about Warner, but I know one thing. He was no liar. Everything he told you was the truth as he saw it at the time, the way he remembered it. Isn't that what we all do?"

Melody set the knife and potato in the sink and hugged him. "Thanks, Dad." She wiped a tear off her cheek with the back of her hand before turning back to the sink.

Pete leaned into her peripheral vision. "Could I ask you one more thing?" Before she could answer, he went on. "I don't know what happened up at the farm the other night when you talked to Clarice, but you've been quiet and sullen ever since. Your grandma is who she is. You love her. She loves you. We all know she isn't going to be around much longer. When that happens you will never forgive yourself if you don't come to terms with whatever was said or done up there."

Melody stared at the potato in her hand. "There's a lot I need to think about, Dad. A lot of things have happened, and I can't pretend they haven't."

Pete took the knife and potato from her and set them in the sink. He took her hands again and turned her to face him. He brushed a strand of hair away from her face. "When I see you standing there like that, you look just like Clarice. You are her baby. You always have been. I'll never forget the way she'd light up whenever we took you up there to visit. Did you know she didn't like me much when I married your mother? Even Warner liked me more than she did. She was sure I was going to take your mom away, and they'd never see her again, just like Hart did with Linda. Then you came along." He puffed out his chest. "I could do no wrong in their eyes after that. You know that's when they decided to build us the house, right? They would've built us twenty houses to keep you and your mother on this hill."

Tears blurred Melody's vision. "I always knew they built this house to keep Mom close, but I didn't know it was after I was born."

Pete chuckled. "Are you kidding? They would've moved you right into the farmhouse if they thought we'd go along with it. You mean the world to your grandma, Nugget. I'm sure a lot has changed between you. Maybe some things that can't be undone. But she doesn't have time for you to think about stuff. Before you decide you need hours or days or weeks to ponder all the wrong that's been committed, be aware she might not have those hours or days or weeks left."

⚜

Melody didn't wait to eat dinner with her parents. As soon as she finished mashing the potatoes and setting the table, she donned her coat and boots and headed up the hill to the farm.

"Is Grandma awake?" she asked Carson as she hung her coat on a hook by the back door.

He was at the sink cleaning up the dinner dishes. The rest of the house was quiet. Carson and Clarice were alone in the house most of the time these days. Lowell hadn't come back from town. Jay was staying with friends. Melody wasn't sure if that meant Lenny Brown or another low life. She didn't particularly want to see either one of them. Aunt Linda and her daughter Ellen were due in tomorrow. Everyone knew Clarice wouldn't be here much longer. If anyone wanted to see her, they needed to get here soon.

Carson looked at her over his shoulder. "I'm not sure. She dozed on and off all day."

Without another word she headed through the kitchen to Grandma's room. She tapped on the doorframe before going into the darkened room. The only light came from the kitchen. "Grandma, are you up?"

"Melody, is that you? I'm so glad you came. I prayed today you'd come see me."

As soon as Melody saw her grandmother's wilted form, she knew she had already forgiven her. Her crime was inexcusable, but Melody loved her and couldn't hate her for the evil deed she had done. She rushed to the bed and clasped Grandma's cool hands. They felt as fragile as a baby bird in hers.

"Ooh, you're cold," Clarice said with a weak laugh.

"I'm sorry. I should've warmed my hands at the stove before I came in."

"Oh, no, that's all right. I'll warm them up for you." Clarice smiled up at her.

"I love you, Grandma. I'm sorry I didn't come sooner. I wanted to spend a little time with you before you went to bed."

Clarice's smile widened. "I'm so glad you did. I prayed today you'd come see me."

A lump rose in Melody's throat as Grandma repeated the sentiment. Dad was right; it wouldn't be long before she was gone. "Would you like me to read to you?"

"I would love that. I think my Bible's in the kitchen. Carson and I have been having Bible study. Did he tell you that?"

Melody couldn't hide her surprise. "No, he didn't."

"He's such a smart boy. I've really enjoyed it. I'm not the only one doing the teaching. I'm learning a lot from him, too, you know. He's a very astute young man. He really keeps me on my toes with his questions. Anyway, go in there and get the Bible, would you, dear, and read a little to me."

Melody let go of Clarice's hands and started to rise. Clarice grabbed hold of her shirtsleeve. "Thanks for coming, Melody. You'll never know how much this means to me."

"Of course, Grandma." She leaned over and kissed her grandmother on the forehead. "You'll never know how much you mean to me."

CHAPTER THIRTY

Melody leaned forward to accept the kiss Christy placed on her cheek. "Thanks for coming."

"I'm so sorry, Melody. I know how difficult this is after…everything you've been through."

Melody stepped back from the doorway to let her in. The farmhouse was filled with visitors. They had been coming and going all day, ever since word got out that Clarice passed away during the night. Melody almost wished for another blizzard so she would have a little while to grieve alone the way she had with Grandpa. But she'd lived on the hill long enough to know this was how people dealt with loss.

"How's you family doing?" Christy asked.

"Like you'd expect," she replied for the fortieth time today. "We've known this was coming. She was in so much pain the last few days."

"Did you…" Christy looked uneasy. "…have a chance to say goodbye?"

Melody inhaled and let out a slow breath. Grandma lasted twenty-four hours after Pete made her realize she needed to go to the farmhouse and get over what had happened between them. She had stayed up all night reading the Bible, even though Grandma slept most of the time. A few times she stopped reading, and Carson took over while she catnapped in the easy chair in the corner of the room.

Linda and her family, Lowell, Allen and Bonnie, and their three sons and wives arrived in time to circle the bed with Melody, Carson, Judy, and Pete and sing *Amazing Grace* while Clarice slipped away. It was the ending Grandma would've wanted.

In her heart of hearts, Melody knew she had truly forgiven her grandmother, but she didn't know what to do about her actions. Grandma couldn't be punished in this life for what she'd done. Yet Melody couldn't sit idly by and listen to everyone talk about what a kind, gentle, compassionate soul Grandma had been when Melody knew she had purposefully taken a life to protect her son. Whether Grandma saw the harm in it was neither here nor there. She had caused her husband's death. Melody knew she should do or say something.

"I don't think we ever say goodbye," she told Christy.

"I guess not."

"She slipped in and out of consciousness a lot at the end. Just long enough to demand that we not to take her to the hospital."

"Full of fire until the end."

Melody smiled at Christy's attempt to comfort her. "That was Grandma. She wanted us to believe she was some delicate flower when she was anything but."

"Sort of like her granddaughter."

Melody's smile widened. Then she sobered. "Listen, Christy, about that day in the café…"

Christy held up her hand. "Please, no. Everything you said was absolutely right. I'm glad you had the nerve to tell me what I needed to hear."

"I could've been a little gentler with my execution. The Bible says a gentle answer turns away wrath."

"It also says sometimes a foolish woman needs to be knocked upside the head."

Melody laughed. "I don't believe I'm familiar with that verse."

"I'm sure I read it somewhere." Christy wrapped an arm around her and squeezed. "Is there somewhere we could talk? I mean if you're up to it."

"Sure." Melody led her past the front room where several cousins lounged on the new sofa that replaced the one Grandpa had been laid on before Jay and Carson moved his remains to the summer kitchen. Even though it was a different couch, Melody doubted she would ever sit on it.

They passed the kitchen where most of the female visitors were helping Judy, Bonnie, and Linda wash dishes and reheat casseroles for the cadre of mourners trooping in and out of the house. Melody took a lightweight jacket off the hook, and Christy zipped hers as they stepped onto the back porch.

The wall of firewood that had insulated the porch was gone, burned during the long winter. The porch was swept clean, and Carson had brought some of the lawn furniture out of the outbuildings to celebrate the emergence of spring.

Melody sat down and motioned Christy into the other chair. "I heard on the radio this morning the last of the blizzard's snow finally melted."

Christy wagged her head. "Who would've thought snow from a January blizzard would be around until the fifth of May?"

"It's been a long winter."

"Too long."

They lapsed into silence as they listened to a burst of laughter from the kitchen. "I'm glad to see you're still in town," Melody said after a few minutes. "I didn't know if I'd see you again."

"I think I'll hang around a while. Maybe forever."

"Are you serious?"

"A woman saw Mom's dresses in the dry goods store window and commissioned her to make a flower girl dress and matching ring bearer suit for her daughter's wedding next month. Last week she made a prom dress for a girl in Blanton. If she plays her cards right, her new business could actually turn into a moneymaker. But she has absolutely no business sense. I hate to see her lose a golden opportunity from mismanagement."

"That's very thoughtful of you."

"Yeah, well, a friend of mine pointed out a couple weeks ago I was pretty self absorbed. She suggested rather adamantly that I stop holding everyone's mistakes over their heads when I couldn't deal with my own."

"Your friend sounds very astute."

"Oh, she is. To a fault. I guess she was right."

Christy wrapped her arms around herself. Even though green grass rippled in the breeze, winter wasn't going away quietly.

"Mom and I talked...about a lot of things. Trying to keep the rest of the world in line is too much work. It's enough trouble keeping Christy Blackwood on the straight and narrow."

"That's wonderful. I'm so happy for both of you."

"Me, too. Mom isn't the only person I reconciled with. After I talked to you, I withdrew my money from the bank, gassed up the car, and was all ready to leave town. Something held me back. Maybe it was your screeching words echoing in my head," she added with a smile.

"Or maybe someone a little higher was trying to get my attention. Either way, I knew I'd never find the peace I was looking for no matter how far I went until I asked Jesus into my heart."

Melody lunged across the expanse of porch and wrapped her arms around the other woman's neck. "Oh, Christy."

Christy laughed and returned the hug. "Easy there. The pollen you're stirring up is hard on my allergies."

Melody sat back in her chair. "You're okay with your mom and everything that happened between her and Noel Wyatt?"

"I'm getting there. He came to the house last night for dinner. He still loves Mom. He didn't say anything, but it was written all over his face. I want them both to be happy, I truly do. What I want isn't important, though. Besides, I'll probably be too busy with my new career to worry about what they're doing."

"Your new career?"

Christy's face flushed. "Oh, didn't I mention who else was at dinner? Jarrod Bruckner. He's opening a law office in Jenna's Creek. I think I can convince him he'll need an associate. Especially after I get my law license."

Melody squealed. "Christy! You're going back to law school."

"My schedule will be very busy. I'll have to keep working at the library to pay for school, and what with planning the wedding at all…" She let her words trail off intentionally.

It's was Melody's turn to let out a war whoop.

Christy unwrapped her arms from around herself and held out her hand.

Melody leaped out of her chair, dragging Christy along with her. They grabbed each other's arms through their jacket sleeves and jumped around in a circle.

The back door burst open. "Melody, what's happening out here?"

They stopped jumping and looked at the worried faces of various aunts and women from church.

Melody grabbed Christy's hand and thrust it under her mother's nose. "Christy's getting married. And going to law school," she added as an afterthought.

There was a moment of stunned silence, then everyone was shrieking and laughing and crying and hugging everyone else.

Melody's happiness soon turned to tears for her grandmother. Grandma would've been so happy to hear of a wedding and hopeful it would spark the bug in Melody. But Melody couldn't reconcile how the woman she loved had killed her best friend.

She never would until there was some form of justice.

CHAPTER THIRTY-ONE

It was nearly ten o'clock before the last guest left. Judy and Linda had taken Grandma's favorite dress to the funeral home after dinner and gone straight to the Knauff house afterward. Linda and Hart were spending the night there, unable to sleep in the farmhouse. Lowell returned to his trailer in town. Now that his chance to earn brownie points was over, Melody figured he was anxious to get back to his usual routine, whatever that was. Jay was spending the night in the county jail. On his way to Lenny Brown's house from a local tavern, he had been pulled over and arrested for driving under the influence. The police impounded his car and found enough evidence to lock him up for quite some time. Sheriff Patterson was going to let him attend the funeral on Monday with a deputy escort.

Melody could only imagine Grandma's reaction to her son in handcuffs at her funeral.

She hadn't decided yet where she'd spend the night. She longed for her own bed after the last few sleepless nights, but part of her wanted to stay one last time at the farm while it still felt like Grandma and Grandpa's home.

The house would never seem the same now that her grandparents were gone. Grandma had shown her and Carson, Judy, Pete, and Linda a copy of the will the afternoon before she died. All property and monies were to be divided evenly between the five Beckwith children and Melody. Warner and Clarice hoped the four older siblings would sell out to Judy and Pete, who would stay on the property as long as they lived. Upon their deaths, it was assumed they would will the property completely to Melody.

However it worked out, Melody was glad the farm would stay in the family. She couldn't imagine what it would be like, someday moving into the farmhouse that had meant so much to her grandparents and their parents before them. Maybe she would invite Naomi and Alma to move in with her, though she figured they would turn down the offer.

She looked out the picture window to make sure the driveway was free of cars of those who didn't live on the hill before heading to the kitchen. Whether she went home or stayed the night, she couldn't go to bed as long as there was a chance one dirty dish remained in the sink.

Grandpa never went to bed with dirty dishes lingering in the kitchen.

"What if thieves broke in during the night and saw dishes in the sink?" he always asked. "They'd think we were a bunch of Philistines."

Carson was already at the sink, up to his elbows in suds.

"I was hoping those would be finished by now," Melody said.

He snickered without turning around. "Doesn't anyone in this county know there's an amazing innovation called the paper plate? You people should try it sometime."

"Hm. We'll discuss it at our next meeting."

He looked at her over his shoulder. "That would really help me out."

She took a serving bowl from the draining rack and waved it in the air to dry as she reached for a towel. "I thought the ladies from church took care of this before they left."

"They were working on it, but I told them I'd finish up. They looked dead on their feet." He winced. "Sorry."

Melody shook her head to let him know she wasn't offended.

"Anyway," Carson continued, "I needed a little quiet. You know…before tomorrow."

His voice faltered. Melody looked at him sharply. "Are you all right?"

Without looking up, he scrubbed the bottom of a pan that already sparkled. Melody put the serving bowl on the table and touched his elbow. "Carson?"

He stopped scrubbing and stared at the pan for a moment. When he brought his gaze around to hers, she was surprised to see tears in his eyes. "I knew I would miss her," he croaked. "I just didn't think it would hurt this bad."

Melody let out a little sob and threw her arms around his neck. He let go of the pan, and it disappeared under the suds. He turned into her and wrapped his wet arms around her. They cried together for a few moments before he made an effort to pull himself together.

"Sorry about that." He nodded at the watermarks on her shirt. He snatched a paper towel off the roll above the sink and handed it to her, then took one for himself.

Shocked by his display, Melody watched him while she blew her nose with the paper towel. "Don't apologize," she whispered hoarsely.

He wadded up his paper towel and tossed it into the trashcan at the end of the counter. "I'm not very good at…you know."

"Neither am I."

They stared into the sink for a moment. Carson reached for the pot. He rinsed it off and set it in the drainer. He pulled the stopper in the sink. "I think I'll go to bed. Tomorrow's going to be a long day." He grabbed another paper towel and began to dry his hands one finger at a time.

"Carson, wait a minute."

He stopped and looked at her.

Everything she planned to say flew out of her head. "I…um…I'm sorry about…everything."

He cocked an eyebrow.

"I never went out of my way to be nice to you. When we were kids…well, I was a girl and used to the world revolving around me. You were a boy who liked to grate on my nerves, so that made us natural enemies. But now…I don't have an excuse for treating you the way I have. I'm sorry."

"I always said you and Warner were cut from the same cloth."

She wrinkled her nose. "You meant it as an insult."

He nodded. "At the time, yes. Let's just say I understand the old man a lot better now than I did a few months ago."

"Because of Grandma?"

A faraway look crossed his face. "I spent the winter holed up in this house with that lady. You don't think we played Gin Rummy the whole time, do you?" He laughed out loud. "She used the cards to get me to sit still. Then she'd start preaching at me."

Melody laughed along with him. "That sounds like Grandma."

"I never intended to stay here as long as I did. Then Dad moved in and he and Jay started pillaging the house every chance they had. I wasn't totally innocent. I plan to pay somebody back for everything I took."

She waved away his words. "You were going to go to work for Uncle Allen, weren't you?"

"How'd you know?"

"I heard the two of you talking the day of Grandpa's funeral. I had no idea what it was about until after the fire."

Carson dropped the paper towel into the trashcan and pulled out a kitchen chair. "I overheard Grandpa tell Grandma he was turning Allen in. I didn't think he'd actually do anything. I figured he was just trying to scare Allen into doing the right thing. I figured I'd cash in and get off the farm at the same time. I told Allen if he didn't set me up at the agency I was turning him in."

"Why didn't he?"

"After Grandpa fell down the stairs, there was too much else going on. Jay was getting more brazen. After a while I started thinking you might be right and Jay pushed him. I didn't want Grandma to be here alone."

"You really love her, don't you?"

He fixed his gaze on a spot on the wall. "She's the first person who loved me for who I am, not for what she thought she could turn me into. Then she told me something that changed my life forever. She told me about someone who loves me even more than she does. She made me understand my need for a savior. She also talked me into going back to Houston to see my mom and make things right with her and my stepdad. I'm leaving after the funeral."

Melody was surprised at how his news saddened her. "But...what about..."

He chucked her on the chin with his knuckles. "Don't tell me you're going to miss me, Cousin."

"I guess I got used to having you around."

"I got used to being here."

"Are you coming back?"

Carson shrugged. "With Grandma gone, I really don't have anything to come back for."

"What about the farm?"

"The farm's yours. Yours and Dad's and the aunts' and uncles'. I need a job."

"It would break Grandma and Grandpa's hearts to think this place was sitting idle. Take care of whatever you need to with your mother and then come back and run it."

"You don't need me for that."

"No, but Dad will. He's always wanted to return the farm to its glory days, but it's a two-man operation. What do you say? It would solve everyone's problems."

His eyes took on a hopeful expression. "I don't know. I guess we could give it a shot. I never saw myself as a farmer. I was always taught to—"

"Work smart, not hard," Melody said for him.

"Exactly. One lesson I learned from Grandpa is farming is about the hardest work you can find."

She put her hand on his arm. "At least say you'll think about it."

"I can do that."

"I really am happy you found Jesus. Maybe that's why you came here. You're Grandma's legacy."

"I like the sound of that. I came here from Texas to see what I could get off these people. I felt like they owed me. They had so much, and I never had a thing. The more I got to know Grandma, the more I realized none of their stuff mattered. I don't care that I'm not getting a dime from the inheritance. Grandma already gave me more than I deserved. I want to spend the rest of my life paying back her memory. I don't want to focus on her failings."

Melody cocked her head. "Her failings?"

Carson leveled a grave look at her. Did he know?

As if reading her mind, he said, "Grandma was a wonderful woman. She had some odd ideas, but she loved her family. She was willing to sacrifice everything to protect them."

"Good intentions are no excuse for doing wrong."

He nodded thoughtfully. "The night Grandma and I prayed for my salvation, she told me everyone had sinned and fallen short of God's grace. She said everyone was evil in God's sight until they were washed clean by the blood of Jesus. She said even she needed to be washed clean. I thought she meant about being born with a sinful nature, but that wasn't it."

He set his hands on the tabletop and began picking at a ragged thumbnail. Just when Melody was ready to scream at him to stop, he looked up at her.

"She told me everything, Mel. She said it was the biggest mistake of her life and she'd give anything to take it back. We talked a long time. I told her she might go to prison for it, but it would be worse if she went to hell for it. We both cried. Then we prayed and she asked God to forgive her."

Melody swallowed back tears. She had been so consumed the last few days with the whole idea of justice for Grandpa, she hadn't even thought to ask Grandma to repent of her sins before it was eternally too late.

"But is that the end? Aren't we obligated to do something, to tell somebody?"

Carson stared at his clasped hands. "Why?"

"She committed a crime. What if someone finds out we knew? They'll want to know why we didn't tell. We'll be accessories after the fact."

"It won't change anything. What good will come of us destroying the family's memories of her over one ugly incident?"

"It was more than an ugly incident. It was…"

"I know what it was," he said gently. "Grandma knew too."

Tears stung Melody's nose. It couldn't end that easily. "What about…Grandpa? She should've made it right."

He unclasped his hands and looked back at her. "She did make it right. She told you."

Melody blinked. "What?"

"She told you, Mel. She didn't know what to do. She was beside herself with grief and guilt. After we prayed, I told her she needed to tell you. I told her you were convinced Jay or Dad or somebody hurt Warner so she needed to set the record straight. It was the only way she'd have peace. She couldn't let you go through life with all those unanswered questions. So that's what she did."

"You? You were the reason she told me?"

He reached across the table and covered her hands with one of his. "It's over, Melody. Grandpa was as ready to meet death as anybody ever was, and Grandma repented for her role in it. Her sins were washed clean. It's all in God's hands now."

She stared at the worn linoleum at her feet. Was he right? Since restitution was impossible, they should keep quiet and let God sort it out? Tears stung the end of her nose. Was God releasing her of the responsibility?

"Thank you, Carson. Thanks for being here for her."

He lifted one shoulder. "I didn't do anything you wouldn't have done."

"I don't know about that. I've been so mad the last few days, the last few months really. All I've been able to think about was the mistakes they both made. Grandpa always did what he thought was right, but I'm afraid he missed it by a mile."

She got up and went to the window over the sink and looked out at the green grass growing in the meadow again. "He always talked about the physical inheritance he wanted to leave the family. He should've taken five minutes and thought about the spiritual inheritance he was leaving behind. He could've sowed peace and contentment in his family instead of bitterness and jealousy. He could've called Aunt Linda and told her he loved her. He was the one who needed to apologize, not her."

"Men of his generation didn't say they were sorry, Mel."

She turned back to him. "I'm really tired of that excuse. He should've told her. He shouldn't have been so hard on everyone. He shouldn't have treated me better than he did the rest of you."

"Do you believe for one minute any of us didn't know what Warner Beckwith thought at any given moment?"

Her eyes widened. "I can't believe you're defending him."

"I can't either." He smiled and shook his head. "Since I was a kid I knew he thought I was a lump of wasted space. I think he saw Dad in me and it scared him to death. He knew Dad would never amount to a hill of beans, but he hoped I would. He wanted me to live up to my potential. That meant he had to push a little."

"I never thought about it like that."

"Whether we want to give him credit or not, he always had our best interests at heart. Jay or Dad or even Allen can blame their cold, aloof father for the rotten circumstances they're in now. If they honestly look at the situation, they'll see Grandpa was a pretty amazing man. He wanted to make them strong, not take the easy road the way I always did."

"How did you get to be so profound?"

"From playing cards all winter with Grandma, I guess. She never got enough credit. I'm glad I had the opportunity to absorb some of her wisdom for a few months. No, scratch that. I was blessed to know her."

"Thank you, Carson. Thanks for everything. Instead of looking for conspiracies and worrying about what couldn't be changed, I should've spent more time up here with you two playing cards."

He laughed. "You would've saved yourself a lot of frustration." He scooted out his chair and joined her at the window. "Stop worrying about the man Warner wasn't and remember the man he was—the man who loved you and you loved back."

She smiled as tension slid out of her shoulders for the first time in a week. If she was truly cut from the same cloth as Warner Beckwith, she had a lot of work to do. She didn't want to be remembered as opinionated and judgmental, even though she often was. She wanted to leave a legacy of faith behind for those who came after.

"I never thought I'd say this, Carson, but you're absolutely right. Grandpa was my best friend. I owe him my respect, not criticism. From this moment forward, I'll focus on the good things he taught me. That's his true legacy anyway. Now let's finish drying the dishes and put them away. If thieves break in during the night, we wouldn't want them to think a bunch of Philistines live here."

They laughed together and turned back to the sink. "You don't by any chance know anything about a store that burned down in Springfield, do you?"

Carson's brow went together. "What store?"

Melody shook her head. "Oh, never mind. I guess there are some things I'll never know."

"Are you talking about the store Dad brought up the night we had dinner at your house with the Sheltons?"

Melody gaped. "That's the one."

"Was it the one owned by Warner's dad?"

Melody nearly dropped the pan she was drying. "You knew about him."

Carson shrugged. "Doesn't everybody?"

"I just found out about him the other day, and not for lack of trying. Nobody tells me anything."

Carson snickered. "You spent your time around the wrong people. Grandma told me all about it. Several times, really. She loved a juicy story. She said Warner's parents weren't married. I guess Warner's dad was already married to someone else. But he loved Rose. That was Warner's mom's name. Anyway, after a while, Absalom, the married guy, went back to his wife. Over the years Rose found out he had a lot of women on the side. I guess he was real scum. He was letting these women run up tabs in his store and then he'd let them off the hook if they slept with him. Warner worked for the guy, if you can believe that, and he found out what was going on. I guess he told Rose, and she about blew a gasket. Warner said Rose went there one night after the store was closed and burned it to the ground. Then she ran Warner off because she knew everybody in town would blame him. Neither of them ever told anyone. Even Warner's little brother Ivan didn't know."

Carson turned to face her. "I can't believe you never heard that story before. It was one of Grandma's favorites."

It took a minute for Melody to pick her jaw up off the floor. She should've spent a little time in the house with the women all those summers when she was running the fields with Grandpa. Apparently, all the good stories were inside.

THE END

Before You Go

If you enjoyed Melody and Christy's stories or any of my other titles, please consider recommending them to a friend or posting a review on Amazon, Goodreads, your blog, or any other online site that allows reviews.

To stay up to date with new releases or special promos
sign up for my Mailing List
Thanks so much & happy reading.

The Jenna's Creek Series:
Streams of Mercy
Redemption's Song
Evidence of Grace
A Jenna's Creek Wedding (A Christmas Novella)

Joy Redefined
Runaway Heart
The Ultimate Guide to Darcy Carter

Tender Blessings Series:
Love Begins
A Little Goodbye

About the Author

Teresa Slack's down-to-earth writing style and endearing, true-to-life characters can be attributed to her upbringing in rural Ohio. Writing from her home near Hillsboro, Teresa is thankful for the opportunity to do what she loves while sharing her faith with readers.

"I write stories to entertain first. Reading should be fun—an escape. Secondly, I want my stories to inspire and edify the reader. If we're breathing, we're going to face conflict in our daily lives. I want to create characters my readers can identify with and learn from. Life isn't easy, but it's good to know we don't have to do it alone."

Learn more about Teresa and her books at her website www.teresaslack.com or on her Facebook author page. Like all writers, she loves hearing from readers. Contact her at teresa@teresaslack.com

www.ingramcontent.com/pod-product-compliance
Lightning Source LLC
Chambersburg PA
CBHW071510260626
47170CB00002B/333